MOLLY GREEN has travelled the world, unpacking her suitcase in a score of countries. On returning to England, Molly decided to pursue her life-long passion for writing. She now lives and writes in Kent. Following her debut novel, *An Orphan in the Snow*, this is the second book in a series set in Liverpool during the Second World War.

Also by Molly Green

An Orphan in the Snow

MOLLY
GREEN

Published by AVON
A Division of HarperCollins*Publishers* Ltd
1 London Bridge Street
London SE1 9GF

www.harpercollins.co.uk

First published in Great Britain by HarperCollins*Publishers* 2018

A catalogue record for this book is
available from the British Library

ISBN 978-0-00-836366-6

Set in Minion 11/14 pt by Palimpsest Book Production Limited,
Falkirk, Stirlingshire

Printed and bound in the United States of America
by LSC Communications

19 20 21 22 LSC 10 9 8 7 6 5 4 3 2 1

For more information visit: **www.harpercollins.co.uk/green**

For the five nurses who were killed on 10th September 1940 when a bomb completely destroyed the Nurses' Wing at St Thomas' Hospital (I have changed their names in the novel).

To all Dr Barnardo's children during the Second World War who were the inspiration for this series.

Lastly, to all those who served in the RAF's Coastal Command.

Chapter One

Liverpool, September 1939

Three days after war was declared, Maxine Grey walked slowly down the aisle, her fingers nervously gripping her father's rigid arm, towards the man she had promised to marry – her best friend, Johnny Taylor. In spite of the bad luck she'd warned him it would bring, Johnny had turned at her entrance, and now he gave her his wide smile and a cheeky wink. She knew it was meant to reassure her, but if anything it made her more conscious of the huge step she was taking. The strident notes of 'Here Comes the Bride' from the organist almost took her by surprise, making her pause, her ears hum. She pulled in a deep breath to slow down her heartbeat. Her father gave her a quick glance and patted her hand.

She could hear the swish of the satin-like material of her dress; feel it catch at the back of her legs with every stride. It had taken her a month of evenings and half-days off from the hospital to make the simple cream dress which swept the floor, and the little matching cropped jacket, from a McCall's pattern – the same amount of time Johnny had given her when he'd persuaded her they should get married. There was definitely going to be a war, he'd said,

1

and it would probably come sooner rather than later. She swallowed. How right he'd been.

Another step, then another, and another. She took a deep breath but the scent of the flowers left over from last Sunday's service was cloying and she pulled her stomach in tight to stop herself from feeling faint. A final step. She'd reached him. Her father nudged her forward and a little to the right where Johnny stood waiting for her, watching her every movement. His smile had faded now as if it had finally dawned on him too that this was a serious event. How different he looked in his grey suit. Older. Not like her Johnny.

Her fingers reluctantly left her father's arm and she was alone. But of course, she wasn't alone. Johnny was here. They were going to be married. Every bride was nervous on her wedding day, so her mother had said when they'd shared a pot of tea that morning. It was to be expected. She wasn't to worry. Johnny was a good boy. He'd always look after her, her mother had said.

'Johnny's who we always wanted for you, Maxine. Your dad's so happy. He can die in peace knowing he's left you in good hands.'

It was no secret that her dad had a dicky heart. Oh, he probably had another year or two left, Dr Turnbull had assured them – maybe more – but he'd encouraged the family to enjoy as much time together as possible. And now she was leaving him in the hands of her mother who constantly fussed over him, making him feel closer to death's door than he probably was.

She took her place next to Johnny, her shoulder only inches away from his, and tried to draw his easy confidence into her own body, now taut with the thought of the unknown.

As the vicar started to address the congregation, Johnny turned towards her and Maxine noticed the same concerned expression he'd had only a few weeks ago, when they were sitting on their favourite park bench feeding the pigeons.

'I've got something to tell you, Max,' he'd said then. 'I'm joining the army. I think I can be of use with my medical training.'

At his words her heart had turned over. Johnny. If anything should happen to him . . . She daren't think further.

'So what say you and I get hitched?' He'd coated the words with a mock-American accent. It had taken her completely by surprise. Yes, she loved him. More than anyone in the world. He was the one she'd run to since she was a little girl, right from when he and his parents had moved next door but one. Being a boy of eleven, he hadn't wanted to be bothered with an eight-year-old, and a girl at that, but she'd badgered him until he'd sometimes nodded and allowed her to accompany him when he went off bird-watching, or climbed trees in the nearby woods. Best of all she loved it when he'd take her down to the docks. She'd hand over her pocket money to Johnny and they'd go a couple of stations on the 'Dockers' Umbrella', the overhead railway which followed the seven miles of docklands. She could have watched the ships come and go for hours, her eyes stretching all the way across the Mersey. Luckily, he was every bit as fascinated and would tell her where the ships had come from and where they were going.

He'd always been her teacher and her 'bestest' friend, as she used to call him when she was a child – sometimes still did, to make him laugh – but her lover? She'd never once thought of him in that way, and had suddenly felt almost embarrassed when he'd made his proposal.

'You've been watching too many cowboy films,' she'd

answered, trying to make light of his clumsy proposal, not wanting to hurt him by saying she didn't think she loved him in the way a wife should love her husband. She saw his face drop.

'You do love me, don't you?' As if he'd read her mind, he'd grabbed both her hands and planted a firm kiss on her lips, then grinned at her. 'You always said you'd marry me when you grew up.'

'It's what children say to one another.' Maxine had bitten her lip. 'Why don't we wait and see what happens. If there really *is* going to be a war—'

'Not "if" but "when",' Johnny had said, his grin fading. 'And if the worst should happen—'

'Don't say it!' Maxine jumped up. 'Don't tempt fate.'

'We have to be realistic.' Johnny took hold of her hand and gently pulled her back onto the seat again. 'If it does, then at least you'll get a pension as a soldier's widow. And if we start a family – which I'd love more than anything in the world – you'll be glad of the extra money for the baby.'

She couldn't answer. Didn't want to think beyond Johnny becoming a soldier. He was closer to her than her own flesh and blood. Mickey had never taken any interest in her whatsoever, even though there was only thirteen months between them. That was the trouble. Johnny was the brother she'd never had.

For a moment neither had spoken. Then he'd taken her chin in his hand and turned her face towards him.

'I love you so much, Max,' Johnny said, his voice thick. 'Right from when you were a snotty-nosed kid. I'd do anything for you – you know that. And because I'm older you've usually left me to make the decisions – so I'm making *this* one for you. You'll make me the happiest man in town

4

and the envy of all the lads if you say yes.' He looked at her, his eyes the colour of the conkers they used to play with. 'Maybe this will help make up your mind.' He drew from his pocket a small navy blue velvet box.

And then she knew. Before he'd even flipped open the lid on its little spring with his thumb, she knew she couldn't turn him down. He was quite the dearest man on Earth. If there was a war and he died she'd never forgive herself for not making him happy by telling him she would be honoured to be his wife.

The emerald had shone back at her, as though to reinforce her thoughts.

She hadn't the heart to tell him that emeralds were considered to bring bad luck.

'Do you, Maxine Elizabeth, take John Laurence to be thy wedded husband?'

The words rang in Maxine's ears and she gave a start, pulling herself out of the past and back to the church where she was getting married. Forcing herself to be calm, she repeated the words of the vicar as though in a dream, her voice low and trembling. She felt the brush of Johnny's hand, and when he said his vows she realised he wasn't quite so assured as he made out. Twice he stumbled on the words and sent her a rueful smile, but when it was over he grasped her hand and they stepped to the back of the altar where they signed the register.

She looked down at her signature. Strange how it was still Maxine Grey. But it would be the last time. From now on she would be known as Mrs Maxine Taylor. And on letters even worse – she would be Mrs *John* Taylor.

Would Maxine Grey be gone forever?

* * *

'Now we're married you won't have to work anymore.'

Maxine regarded her new husband with astonishment. Breaking away from the small party the two sets of parents had given them had proved more difficult than she'd imagined, but now they were in a comfortable bedroom in The Royal Hotel, which Johnny had chosen for their first three nights together. He'd already had his call-up papers and would be leaving in four days. Maxine's mind whirled with events that were racing ahead. He'd never mentioned her giving up work before. She hadn't even thought to discuss it as she'd never imagined marrying him. During this past month she'd seen very little of her fiancé to talk about such matters, what with making the wedding dress in every spare moment she'd had from the hospital. Now that war had been officially declared she'd naturally assumed she'd carry on and finish her training.

Her mother had wanted her to become a nurse ever since she'd watched her bandaging her dolls one day and talking to them in a wise and encouraging seven-year-old voice.

'You're a born nurse,' her mother always said.

At sixteen Maxine knew she wanted to teach, not nurse, but her father had insisted she stay on at grammar school for at least another year to give her time to make up her mind. When she was eighteen and told her parents she had applied to the teachers' training college in Cambridge which specialised in teaching young children with no fathers, her mother put her foot down.

'It's a more important job to heal the sick,' her mother told her. 'Your father and I have set our hearts on you becoming a nurse . . . and one day, when you're higher up in the hospital, you'll catch the eye of a nice doctor – or even a surgeon,' she laughed. 'I can't wait to help you arrange the wedding.' She giggled like a young girl. 'You'll be set for life . . . and one day we'll be able to look forward to our first grandchild.'

Maxine couldn't answer. Her mother gave her a sharp look. 'I know you'll always make us proud, my dear, and always do the right thing.'

Maxine felt a shudder of despair. Her mother had already planned every important aspect of her life.

'We're going to do everything in our power to see that you're trained in the best hospital,' her mother went on. 'We've decided you're going to The Royal Infirmary, right here in Liverpool, so you can come and see us regularly. You'll make us so proud.'

Maxine's heart had plummeted. Her mother's dream wasn't *her* dream. But they'd been so good to her, sending her to grammar school when they could ill afford it. Yes, she'd won a scholarship but it hadn't paid for many of the books, nor the uniform, and the shoes that had to be Clarks. The trouble was that Mickey had turned out to be the biggest disappointment to her parents, although her mother would never admit it. She doggedly went to visit him in prison every month, her head rigid in front of the gossiping neighbours, who apparently knew before she did that her son was in for multiple burglaries. *Now she's pinning her hopes on me*, Maxine thought.

Her first year as a probationer had been a shock. She'd been sick so many times at the sight of blood and frightful injuries, shouted at by many of the senior staff, complained about by some of the patients, but she'd gradually learned how to handle it – well, most of the time, anyway. She'd cried often, wishing she'd stood up to her mother, but the worst was over now, so the other nurses had told her when she'd been tempted to pack it all in. Now she was about to start her second year she was looking forward to continuing her studies and

7

taking her finals, knowing she'd be needed, what with the war on. So why did Johnny think he could wave her nurse's training to one side? He, of all people, knew what a commitment she'd made.

'Give up my training, do you mean?' she demanded. 'When I've worked so hard.'

'Well, I suppose it wouldn't hurt to finish it,' Johnny said, his eyes fixed on hers. 'But there's no need to continue when you've got your certificate.'

'Johnny, why does being married have anything to do with my nursing?'

'Because you're my wife, and I don't want you working. What would the lads say? "Can't support your wife, Johnny-boy?" No, I'm not having that.'

'I'm not interested in "the lads" and what they think,' Maxine flashed. She tried to keep the bubble of irritation pressed down. 'We're talking about *me*. My parents nearly killed themselves to pay for my training. Think what a waste that would be. What am I supposed to do all day long? It'd be different if we'd been married longer and I had a child to look after.'

'We can easily remedy that right away.' Johnny gave an exaggerated wink, but if anything it made her even more cross. It wasn't a joking matter and she knew she must stand firm. 'You could help your mum . . . especially as your dad isn't well,' he continued. 'That's where your nursing will come in handy.'

'Mum wouldn't want that at all. She prides herself on looking after Dad. I'll be much more valuable in the hospital when the wounded start coming in.'

'We'll talk about it some other time.' Johnny took the last drags of his cigarette as though it was the end of the conversation as far as he was concerned. He was sitting on the edge of the bed and reached over to stub his cigarette into the ashtray on the bedside table. 'Come over here, Mrs Taylor.' He spread his arms.

'No, Johnny, it's too important. We'll talk about this right now.'

'Let's not spoil our first night, Max.' Johnny looked across at her, his brown eyes afire with anticipation. 'We haven't got much time together.'

Maxine hesitated. If she let this go, she'd be paving the way for him never taking her seriously – that his needs and wants were more important than hers. That his decisions didn't invite even discussion. A little voice reminded her that she had, only a few hours ago, promised to love, honour and obey him, but she shook it away. She took a deep breath and forced herself to speak calmly.

'Johnny, I know *most* women leave work when they get married, but this is different. The war's started. We don't know how long it will last, but I want to do everything I can to help – the same as you. Everyone who can will contribute something. Mum's even talking about organising knitting circles to make socks for the soldiers.'

Johnny opened his mouth to speak but she stopped him.

'What do you think would have happened in the last war if all the women had stayed at home – married or not? They set to immediately. Servants who'd never been out in the world learned to drive and do all sorts of things that were considered men's work. And spoilt rich girls who'd never lifted a finger equally rolled up their sleeves, and one of the things they did successfully was nursing – even going to the front.'

'Max—'

'I can't . . . *won't* give up my nursing,' she flung at him. 'It's not fair of you to ask me. If you felt that strongly, you

9

should have made it clear *before* the wedding – and I may have thought twice about marrying you.' She ignored his shocked expression. 'There's no point in any further discussion. I'm carrying on working and that's that.'

'Don't let's quarrel, Max, especially not tonight of all nights.'

She hesitated. It was their wedding night, after all. Slowly, she walked towards him, her smile only an echo of his sudden happy grin.

Jones at the hospital had warned her the wedding night would be painful, but it wasn't the physical pain that had hurt so much. Maxine had lain awake through the early hours, every muscle tense as she relived what should have been the culmination of their love. But Johnny had been silent throughout and she'd been too embarrassed to say anything. Afterwards, he'd simply kissed her on the forehead, rolled over and gone straight to sleep. Was this normal? Or was it because she'd stuck up for herself and it had clouded any words and gestures of love he might have given? She thought of all the happy times they'd spent together when they were children, but did she really know him now they were both grown up?

She closed her eyes and an unwelcome thought flashed across her mind. Had she made a terrible mistake? She sighed and turned over, hugging her pillow. Maybe things would look different in the morning.

Chapter Two

It was almost a guilty relief that Johnny was to leave so soon after they were married. Maxine was sure this was not a normal response to a new husband, but she couldn't get out of her mind what Johnny had said. Although he'd not referred to the conversation again, she was sure he was still smarting at her refusal to leave work, and this must be what was affecting their marital relationship. They'd only had three days together but their perfunctory love-making didn't quite match her dreams of romance.

Christmas came and went, and then it was 1940. Nothing seemed to happen. Sirens occasionally went off and Maxine, along with others at the hospital, practised making sure the patients were as safe as possible before the staff dived into the basement. And out on the streets, everyone, including babies, were given their gas masks, but it quickly became a bit of a joke. People started to leave their gas masks at home and she read that an American senator called it the Phoney War. Johnny came home on leave in April, telling her and her parents that the British were regularly flying over Germany, but instead of dropping bombs they were merely dropping propaganda leaflets, warning the people not to be taken in by Hitler and his empty promises. Johnny was so full of the chaps on the camp and how they passed their time together, he seemed hardly bothered that she was continuing her training. Or if he was, he didn't show it.

Actually he didn't show an awful lot, Maxine thought. He had a closed look about him these days. A tightening of the tiny muscles around his mouth. Eyes that didn't twinkle at her like they used to. The army's changing him, Maxine noticed. Taking him from her. He couldn't wait to get back with his mates – she was sure of it.

An idea had begun to form in her mind. If she stayed in Liverpool she would naturally continue to live with her parents until she and Johnny had some time to look for somewhere to rent. But if she transferred to, say, a London hospital, she would gain some independence and be involved in proper war work. Johnny had already told her he wouldn't be given much leave for the foreseeable future, so she couldn't see he'd be affected much, one way or the other. At the moment it was only an idea, and she needed to think about it.

'The sooner the real action starts, the sooner it will be over,' Johnny said, when they came out of the cinema one evening, the second of the two days' leave he'd been given. 'It's a pity we haven't had a chance to look for our own place, but I'm glad you're safe with your parents. It's one thing I don't have to worry about.' He stopped her on the pavement and smacked a kiss on her cheek, then looked at her closely. 'What's up, Max? You seem rather quiet? Those aren't tears, are they?'

'No, it's—'

'Not upset because I've got to go back to camp tomorrow, are you?' Johnny interrupted as though he was too impatient to listen to her. 'Because if you are, forget it. You don't have to worry about me.'

12

'I know I don't, Johnny. You can take care of yourself. You'll be busy and that's why *I* want to keep busy . . . and not just wait until you come home.'

His eyes were on her, as though he was trying to decipher her meaning. 'Even with me away you can be busy looking for a place to rent. Give you something to think about. And if you really like something, I'll be happy if you sign up. After all, you'll be the one in it all day – not me.'

A spurt of anger leapt in her chest.

'Johnny, you don't seem to understand. I *am* going to finish my training and take my finals. And what's more, I'm thinking of applying to one of the London hospitals to do just that.'

His face set in a hard expression she'd never seen before. 'Since when did you decide *this*?'

'I haven't made any decision yet, but I've been thinking about it a lot lately. Mum has the best intentions but she smothers me. Living at home I'm still her child. She forgets I'm a grown woman.'

'And a *married* one.' Johnny's voice had an edge to it. 'My *wife*, in case you've forgotten.'

'Please don't start that again, Johnny. I'm not a simpering female – you should know that by now.'

'Why do you want to leave Liverpool, for heaven's sake? Your father's not in the best health. Aren't you being selfish?'

'He's all right at the moment. If anything should happen – if he gets worse – I'd come home immediately.'

Johnny took his time to light a cigarette. He inhaled deeply and blew out a stream of smoke.

'If – and I say "*if*" – I allow you to carry on working, against all my better judgement, will you forget the idea of London?'

'I told you, Johnny, it's just a thought.'

* * *

Johnny had refused to discuss her idea of going to London anymore. She knew he wouldn't understand why she'd want to leave Liverpool as he'd always said he'd never want to live anywhere else in the world. But this was far more serious. His attitude seemed to be that she was a possession rather than a woman with her own brain, and the Johnny she'd known and adored was fading. It was as though being married had cost them their precious friendship. Somehow it made it even more imperative that she take decisions for her own career. And that might mean transferring to London.

'Take care of yourself, Max,' Johnny shouted from the open window of the train as it began to roll out of the station the next morning.

'You, too,' she called, swallowing the lump in her throat. In spite of their disagreement, she knew she'd worry herself sick about him until she heard from him.

She half ran to catch the tram to take her back to the hospital. Her shift would start in an hour so she needed to hurry.

As the tram trundled along, Maxine peered out of the window, which for once was reasonably clean. Liverpool looked exactly the same as it always did. People rushing to work, shopping, the familiar landmarks of the adjoining historic buildings – the Derby Museum, the Walker Art Gallery and the impressive Central Library – no signs at all that the country was at war.

Her attention was suddenly caught by a tall RAF officer with a couple of books under his arm, running from the library towards her tram. There was something about him. A sense of urgency and the determined expression on his face as he drew nearer. She couldn't help watching him, wondering if he'd manage to catch the tram before it pulled

14

away. Just as he was about to board, the doors shut in his face and Maxine noticed his expression turned to raw annoyance. Before she could look away he gazed directly up at her through the window, his dark eyes holding hers for several long seconds. Her stomach fluttered. She had the strangest feeling that he knew her.

She felt disappointed for him that he hadn't quite made it; she refused to acknowledge that she was a trifle disappointed for herself.

'Mum?'

'Is that you, dear?'

Her mother always asked the same question every evening, as if it was possible she was someone else calling her 'Mum'.

Maxine opened the kitchen door where her mother was making supper.

'Ah, there you are. I'm nearly ready.' She tipped her cheek for her daughter's kiss. 'Go and call your father . . . Oh, there's a letter for you.'

Maxine hung up her coat in the hall and picked up the envelope that was propped on the chiffonier behind an empty jug. She glanced at the large sprawling writing. Pearl. Hmm. Her cousin didn't usually write unless she wanted something. She'd look at it later. For now she'd decided to talk to her parents. Tell them her idea. They needed time to digest this kind of plan.

Supper was quiet, as usual. Her father liked to eat in peace and it was rare for the three of them to have a conversation, let alone a serious discussion, unless Mickey was home. Then he'd talk non-stop and her mother would smile indulgently. Thank goodness Mickey wouldn't be coming home yet. He'd have plenty to say about her announcement, throwing it in the worst possible light and alarming her mother. Maxine

15

sighed. She would have to wait until she'd helped her mother clear the table and wash up. By then her father would be settled in his favourite armchair, smoking his pipe and listening to the wireless.

'Are you quite well, Maxine?' Her mother's voice sounded anxious. 'You haven't finished your supper . . . it's your favourite.'

She sent her mother an apologetic smile.

'I think I'm a bit tired, that's all. It's been a long day.' She put another small forkful in her mouth but it stuck in her throat. She swallowed twice to dislodge it and laid her fork down. 'It's just that I want to tell you both something, though it's not *absolutely* definite yet.'

Her mother looked across the table, her face suddenly wreathed in smiles. 'Oh, my dear. How wonderful.' She turned to Maxine's father. 'Isn't it wonderful, Stan? Our little girl.'

Her father looked bemused. 'Let her finish, Edna. She's—'

'I'm sure it's definite,' Maxine's mother broke in. 'And I've been hoping you wouldn't keep us waiting too long.' She sent her daughter a tender look. 'That's why you've lost your appetite.'

Whatever was her mother on about? But then the penny dropped. She thought her daughter was going to have a baby.

'You'll be giving up work now, won't you?' her mother went on. 'I know what it's like. You'll need me to look after you.'

'Mum, I'm not expecting, if that's what you're thinking.'

Her mother's face visibly fell. 'Well, of course that's what I thought you meant. What else could it be?'

'Let her tell us herself, Edna. Try not to keep interrupting.' Her father's tone was calm.

'I've been thinking about going to St Thomas' hospital

16

me over? Maybe £25? I think that would do it. Of course I'd pay you back at the first opportunity. I'm not a star or anything, but I have got quite a good part, though it won't pay any more than Woolworth's to begin with, and we don't get paid until the show opens in six weeks' time.

I didn't really know anyone to ask in the family, but if you don't have the cash, or are unwilling, I quite understand. But if you can help I'd be very grateful.

Much love,

Your cousin Pearl

XX

She might have known. And she did have some money tucked away. It was difficult to save anything from her modest wages after giving her mother ten shillings a week for her board, but she made some extra cash by doing sewing for some of the nurses in the evenings and weekends. Twenty-five pounds though would wipe out most of it. She'd need a buffer to pay for her fare to London and a bit over to manage with until she got paid at the end of her first week. That is, if she got an offer.

No, it was impossible. She might be able to lend her cousin a fiver, but no more. And she wouldn't trust the post. She'd go and see Pearl tomorrow evening, straight from work.

Chapter Three

Maxine took the tram to Bold Street where Pearl lived, still in two minds how much to lend her. Her cousin's lodgings consisted of two rooms and a shared bathroom above a fish and chip shop. As she approached the building she noticed four lads huddled together on top of a pile of planks on the shop's windowsill, poring over a newspaper. She hid a smile. They couldn't have been more than eight or nine, she thought, but they were intently reading the headlines. They didn't even look up as she brushed past them and entered the shop. The stale smell of fried dripping immediately filled her nostrils.

'We haven't seen you for a time, young Maxine,' Mr Rowe glanced up from his deep-fat frying pan, his face red from the heat and his greying moustache bristling as he beamed at her.

'I've been very busy at the hospital and don't get a lot of time off.'

'How's that husband of yours?'

Maxine sighed. 'I haven't heard for the past two weeks so can only hope he's all right.' She needed to change the subject quickly. 'Do you know if Pearl's in?'

'Far as I know.' He deftly removed some sizzling pieces of fish and laid them out in the warming cabinet. 'She's already been in for her lunch.' He nodded. 'Go on through, love.'

Maxine stepped through the back of the shop and climbed a flight of stairs. She could still hear muffled sounds of the traffic inside the building, but even though Pearl's rooms were in the centre of a noisy commercial district she couldn't help feeling a twinge of envy. Pearl lived on her own – answerable to no one. She did exactly what she wanted and blow everyone else. She'd been expelled from school for smoking and her parents had had no control over her whatsoever. Maxine believed her aunt and uncle were secretly relieved when their daughter was off their hands. But Pearl hadn't until now been able to fulfil her dream of going on the stage. Her parents had done their best to persuade her to learn shorthand and typewriting but being in an office was the last thing Pearl was going to do. Instead she'd accepted a job in the haberdashery department of Woolworth's, much to their shame.

She and Pearl were different in every way, Maxine mused, but they'd always been friends, against both mothers' wishes. Her mother was forever warning Maxine that Pearl was a bad influence and not to spend too long in her company.

Guiltily, she realised she hadn't visited Pearl since her wedding, though the lapse was nothing to do with her mother's comments. Maxine had had several months of nights at the hospital and it had been difficult to fit in social visits with trying to sleep in the daytime – almost impossible in a small terraced house.

Bits of lino were missing on some of the treads of the second flight of stairs to Pearl's quarters, and once Maxine caught her heel, ripping it a little further. A baby cried and the smell of soiled babies' napkins from one of the first-floor flats wafted up, but she was used to worse when she walked through the babies' ward. She knocked and instantly the door opened. There stood Pearl looking lovely as always in a navy straight skirt that slimmed her eager curves and a bright pink top with scooped neckline and short sleeves. High heels raised her a little nearer Maxine's height. Her grin nearly split her face in two.

'Max! What a lovely surprise. I didn't expect you to come over this quickly. You're lucky I'm here. Come on in.'

She stood aside while Maxine brushed past her into the one large room with a kitchenette at one end. Pearl had a bedroom and use of a box room off the landing, and shared a bathroom with the family downstairs. Although Pearl kept it clean enough, the room was terribly untidy; so different from the way Maxine's house-proud mother kept her home. She mustn't compare. This was homely and friendly, which Maxine didn't always feel in her own house.

'Take your jacket off. I'll make some tea. Or would you like something stronger?' Her cousin sent her a mischievous smile. 'A gin and orange?'

'No, thanks. But tea would be lovely.'

Pearl filled the kettle and put it on to boil, all the while talking to Maxine.

'Nursing seems to suit you.' She turned to have a closer look at her cousin. 'Or is it married life you've taken to?' she asked, a chuckle escaping her full lips. 'Can't believe it's been nearly a year since the wedding when I last saw you.'

'I could count on two hands how many days Johnny and I have spent together,' Maxine said, ruefully.

'Yeah, but what about the nights? That's the bit I want to hear about.'

Maxine laughed. 'I don't think it's all people make out.'

'Hmm . . . maybe not, if it's not with the right person.' Pearl frowned as she measured out one-and-a-half level teaspoons

22

of tea in the pot and poured the boiling water over the leaves. She popped a tea cosy over the teapot and looked up. 'I always thought Johnny was more a brother than a boyfriend. No one was more surprised than me when I got the invitation to say you were marrying him. Sounded like a hurried decision to me. I even wondered if you'd got a pea in the pod.'

Maxine couldn't help laughing. Pearl always prided herself on calling a spade a spade.

'Not then or now,' she said. 'I've little time for that, though Johnny would love it if I did. But I want to continue my training and eventually do my finals before I even think about starting a family.'

She felt Pearl give her a sharp look. 'And how does Johnny feel about that?'

'He's not keen,' Maxine admitted. 'But I think I've talked him round.'

Pearl shook her head. 'It's impossible to talk any man round,' she said firmly as she set out the tea tray.

'Let me help,' Maxine offered.

'No, you sit there. I know what it's like to be on your feet all day.' Pearl brought the tray over and poured out the two cups. 'Biscuit?'

Maxine shook her head. 'I had an early supper in the canteen.' She paused. 'Anyway, enough of me. It's *you* I've come to talk about.'

'You got my letter?' Pearl sucked in her breath as though bracing herself for her cousin's answer.

'Yes, I did. And congratulations for getting through the audition. That was marvellous news. I know it's what you've always wanted, ever since you were a little girl and made us act out your stories with strange costumes and props.'

'Being an only child, I had to make do with you as my nearest playmate.' Pearl grinned. 'We had fun, didn't we?'

23

'We certainly did.' Maxine chuckled. 'Until you moved over the other side of town. I can't believe how the time's gone. All those years ago. And now you've become a real actress. What did your parents say when you told them?'

Pearl's face fell. 'They've washed their hands of me. My father said he's not going to come and see it. Mam didn't exactly say that, but you know how she always does what he says.'

'I'm sorry to hear that. But they're a bit old-fashioned. You have to see it from their point of view.'

'Well, I'm not letting them stop me. It's my dream and I'm going to grab it with both hands.'

'Have you started rehearsals yet?'

'Next week.' Pearl gulped her tea and set down her cup and saucer on a small table by her chair. 'I've met most of the cast. They seem a nice crowd.' She looked at Maxine. 'I've had to give my notice in at Woolworth's.'

'What did they say?'

'Oh, they were sorry to lose me . . . that sort of thing. They did give me an extra week's wages, which I didn't expect.' She withdrew a packet of cigarettes from her handbag and took two out, offering one to Maxine who shook her head. Pearl lit it and inhaled deeply. 'I hope you didn't mind me asking, Max . . . about the money.' She looked directly at Maxine.

'No, I didn't mind. The only problem is, I'll need some extra money myself because I'm thinking of transferring to St Thomas' hospital in London.'

Pearl raised her eyebrows. 'Oh? Any particular reason?'

'I want to specialise in heart diseases, and they're known for it.'

Pearl narrowed her eyes. 'The truth now.'

Maxine's face flooded with heat.

'You've been married less than a year and Johnny's away practically all the time so you can't feel stifled.' She stared at Maxine. 'Or is it Aunt Edna and Uncle Stan?'

'Well, it's time I broke from them,' Maxine said, a little pink that Pearl had grasped the main reason for going. 'After all, I *am* married, and if Johnny hadn't joined up we'd have our own place by now. It doesn't even feel as though I'm married when I'm still living at home.'

'I can't blame you there.' Pearl was thoughtful for once. 'No, of course you need your bit of cash. I'll manage all right – something will turn up – it always does.

'I've got nearly thirty pounds put by.' Pearl's mouth opened in amazement. Maxine looked at her cousin. She had to do a bit more to help her. 'So I'm willing to share it with you – fifteen pounds each. Will that help?'

Pearls's face broke into a beam. 'That would be marvellous, Max . . . but are you sure?'

'Yes, I'm sure. Far be it from me putting obstacles in the way of my cousin's forthcoming fame.' She smiled.

Pearl jumped from her chair and hugged Maxine. 'You're a real pal, besides being my favourite cousin.'

'I believe I'm your *only* cousin.' Maxine grinned, hugging her in return.

Pearl laughed. 'You know I'll pay you back.'

'You don't have to. Regard it as a present . . . my faith in your acting and singing abilities. Just make sure I get given a ticket to this first show. What's it about anyway?'

'It's a musical called *Better Days*. I do a bit of singing and dancing, mainly in the chorus. Thanks so much.' She kissed Maxine's cheek. 'I really mean it, Max. You're a darling. And if I can ever return the favour . . . you know you've only got to ask.'

Chapter Four

Maxine rushed upstairs to read Johnny's latest letter in the privacy of her bedroom. Sometimes they were censored and someone would black out words or even whole sentences. In the last letter, he mentioned he was going abroad but couldn't say any more, but in this one he sounded excited and told her not to worry if she didn't hear from him for some time. Something big was on. He finished off:

But if anything should happen to me, Max darling, be happy knowing I wanted to do the right thing and fight for my country. And don't waste a minute of your life.
   All my love, and can't wait to see you again.
   Always your Johnny xxx

She looked at the date – 8th May, but the postmark was blurred. It had taken nearly three weeks to arrive. This was the first time Johnny had hinted that he might not make it. Maxine chewed her bottom lip as she carefully folded his letter and put it back into the envelope. What if he was severely injured? Needing her. She'd never forgive herself if she wasn't there for him. Momentarily, she closed her eyes. London was out of the question.

*   *   *

The following day, she was in the nurses' common room when she picked up the *Daily Express* one of the other nurses had tossed aside. The headlines shouted triumphantly:

TENS OF THOUSANDS SAFELY HOME ALREADY
Many more coming by day and night
SHIPS OF ALL SIZES DARE THE GERMAN GUNS

Conscious she was due back on the ward in ten minutes, she skimmed the article. Every possible vessel which sailed had been sent out to rescue the men . . . the British, French and Allied troops trapped on the French coast. Her heart missed a beat. She knew without a shadow of a doubt that Johnny was on the other side of the Channel – in Dunkirk. And try as she might, she couldn't picture him stepping into one of the rescue boats. He would always see that others go before him – inherent in his medical training.

Maybe she was allowing her imagination to run wild. She turned the page, desperate to read more, but there were other stories of battles and no more mention of Dunkirk.

Maxine scanned the papers every day, obsessed with the story. It was the longest week and by the 4th June over 300,000 soldiers had been brought back to British shores. Lists of names of those rescued were published every day, but she never saw Johnny Taylor's name amongst them. Of course she had no proof he was even at Dunkirk. But she didn't need proof. His letters had stopped and, as far as she was concerned, that was enough. She was only thankful she'd never applied to St Thomas'. Johnny would need to know she was close by when he returned.

* * *

27

It was hard to push Johnny to the back of her mind and care for her patients. Injured men and women were coming into the hospital every single day, and every time she dreaded it would be Johnny they brought in on a stretcher. She was still convinced he was in Dunkirk and hadn't been rescued and tried to ask around on how she could find any information but no one seemed to have any idea.

'You could try the Red Cross,' Sister Marshall suggested when she came across Maxine in tears one day in the nurses' room. 'They are the ones who send information to families when British soldiers are injured . . .' she hesitated, 'or dead. I think they'd be your best bet.'

But she had no luck there either. Until a fortnight later when she received a letter from them. With a lump in her throat, she read:

Dear Mrs Taylor,

We are very sorry to inform you that your husband, Cpl. John L Taylor has been taken prisoner by the German Army at Dunkirk. He bravely volunteered to remain so he could attend to his wounded comrades. When there is more news we will, of course, let you know.

Yours sincerely,

Mary Jackson (Mrs)

Welfare Officer

Maxine swallowed hard, trying to dislodge the lump. She was right. He *had* been sent to Dunkirk. Dear Johnny. Whatever must he have felt, seeing the ships rescuing thousands of soldiers and he wasn't one of them. But it seemed he'd made the decision, just as she expected he would. Maxine felt a sting behind her eyes. Yes, he was brave, and she could well imagine him doing just that.

*   *   *

28

Another agonising fortnight passed with no more news. Maxine was in the ward helping a patient to walk to the toilet, grateful that she was a slight woman, though she still weighed heavily on her arm, when Sister Marshall came up to her, a look of concern in her eyes.

'I'll take Mrs Harvey, Nurse. There's a telegram for you in Matron's office.'

She knew. Cold sweat beaded her forehead. She didn't even have to open the telegram. She reprimanded herself. Until she heard otherwise she mustn't crumple. Mustn't think the worst. It might be him and he was writing to say he was safe. But she knew any form of contact from him would not be in the form of a telegram.

With hammering heart she half ran down the corridor.

'Nurse!' A Sister she didn't know held her hand in the air. 'I must remind you – you may only run for fire or haemorrhage.'

'I'm sorry, Sister.'

Her feet now feeling like lead, she knocked on Matron's door.

'Come in.' Matron looked up. 'Oh, yes, Nurse Taylor. Do sit down.'

Maxine's knees felt they would give way at any moment. Defeated, she sat and caught her breath.

'A telegram has arrived for you.' Matron handed her a blue envelope.

With trembling hands Maxine took the telegram. Even before she saw the word 'priority' written on the envelope, she knew . . .

'If you'd like to take a moment and read it quietly, I'll leave you to it.' Matron disappeared out of the door. 'Call me if you need me. I won't be far away.'

Her fingers could barely work under the seal to open it.

Heart pounding in her throat, she pulled out the sheet of paper with the printed message.

From Lieutenant-Colonel J. A. Donaldson
6th July 1940
Dear Mrs Taylor,
  May I be permitted to express my sincere sympathy with the sad news concerning your husband Cpl. John L Taylor. I regret to say that we have been notified today via the Swiss Red Cross of his death from pneumonia.
  Your husband was an exemplary soldier and his loss is deeply regretted by us all.
  When we receive any of his effects they will be forwarded on to you.
  Once again please accept the deep sympathy of us all.
  Yours very sincerely,
  J. Anthony Donaldson

The paper fluttered to the floor. Maxine couldn't summon the energy to bend down and pick it up. A terrible shaking took hold of her body. She dropped her head in her hands, gasping to hold back the sobs. She mustn't break down. She needed to look after her patients. They relied on her.

She heard the door open and the solid figure of Matron step in.

'Oh, my dear . . . it's bad news, isn't it?'

Maxine nodded, speechless.

'Your husband?'

'Yes.' It was a whisper.

'I'm sending you home right away. Take two days off.'

'Oh, I couldn't . . .'

'We'll manage, if that's what's worrying you.' Matron put a hand on her shoulder.

30

She looked up. Matron's face was creased in sympathy.

'Please let me go back to the ward, Matron.' Maxine forced herself to speak calmly. 'I'll be better if I can work. I'll have plenty of time to think about it when I'm off-duty.'

'Very well.' Matron became brisk. 'But I insist you go to the canteen and have a strong cup of tea with sugar. You're in shock, my dear, though you may not realise it. And if you are not feeling better tomorrow, please stay at home.'

Somehow she got through the day, even forgetting for a few minutes at a time about the telegram and the terrible news. And then it would sweep over her in a sickening cloud. Johnny – her dearest friend since childhood. She would never see him again. Never look into his twinkling brown eyes. Never laugh at his feeble jokes.

She delivered the last bedpan to an elderly lady who reminded her of her headmistress. A hard-faced woman with frizzy grey curls and bitter lines around her mouth, who was furious to be forced to use such an item for her private ablutions.

Maxine pulled the curtains around the patient and tucked the bedpan under the cover. 'There you are, Mrs Shepherd. I'll be back shortly.'

'See that you do, Nurse.' Mrs Shepherd looked at Maxine with reproachful eyes, as though it were her fault. 'I waited a full quarter of an hour this morning before someone came to take it away.'

That evening, Maxine stepped into the hall and her mother came out immediately, her face red, all of a fluster.

'My dear, was it bad news?'

Maxine felt caught off guard. How did her mother know something had happened before *she* did?

31

'The telegram boy brought it here and I told him you were at the Infirmary.' She took her daughter's coat and hung it on the rack. 'It's Johnny, isn't it?'

'Let me tell you and Dad together, Mum.'

'I'd better make us all a cup of tea.'

A brandy would be more like it, Maxine thought, but she simply nodded and her mother disappeared into the kitchen.

She found her father in his chair in the sitting room reading his newspaper, glasses slipping down his nose, his favourite slippers with a hole in each toe encasing socks which she'd had to snip the tops off to make room for his poor swollen ankles. He rose up with difficulty and gave her a hug.

'Your mother says a telegram came here for you, but she sent the boy to the hospital.'

'It's very bad news,' Maxine began as her mother appeared with the tea tray. She felt the tears prick at the back of her eyes. She must keep calm. Must let them know she was being sensible and not acting impulsively. 'Johnny's dead.' There was no other way to say it.

Her mother's hand flew to her mouth. 'I knew it . . . I just knew it. As soon as he'd been taken by those dreadful Germans. Didn't I tell you, Stan?'

Her father gave a long sigh. 'Yes, you did, dear.' He turned to his daughter. 'And I'm very sorry to hear it, Maxine. He was a good lad and thought the world of you. Did they give you any details?'

'Yes.' Maxine's voice was almost a whisper. 'Pneumonia.'

'Oh, the poor boy.' A tear spilled down her mother's cheek. 'Well, at least you've got us. We'll look after you at home and help you through.'

'Thanks, Mum, and I really mean it, but I've decided to apply to St Thomas'.'

'You're not going on about moving to London again?' Her mother's eyes were wide. 'You don't want to make a decision as important as this without more time. You've had a terrible shock, dear, and you're not thinking straight.'

'I am, Mum. Everywhere I look around here reminds me of Johnny—' She broke off, her voice trembling. 'I must go and see his parents. They'll be heartbroken . . . their only son. Oh, it's not fair. It's just not fair.'

Her eyes swimming, she banged her cup on its saucer and rushed out of the room, but not before she heard her father say, 'Leave her be, Edna. She's old enough to make her own decision. The change is probably just what she needs to take her mind off things.'

Maxine heard back from St Thomas' within a few days. They were interested! Because of the war, provided she had references from the hospital, they weren't going to waste time interviewing her. There was a desperate shortage of nurses so they would like her to start as soon as she could give in her notice. They had every reason to believe that her initial training at the Royal Infirmary was first class and that she'd be a real asset at St Thomas' as a nurse at their Nightingale School for the next two years. Would she let them know by return that she was still interested so they could prepare her paperwork?

It had happened. One letter to the hospital had led to her life changing – but only because her dearest Johnny had died. She swallowed. She was determined to do her best in this war, whatever the cost. She owed it to him.

As soon as she had given in her notice, Sister said in view of the circumstances she could leave as soon as she was ready. A fortnight later the arrangements were in place. And then it was her last day. Maxine had said her goodbyes to the other nurses and patients and as she was about to leave by the staff door, Sister Dugdale stopped her and put a small package in her hands.

'From all of us on the ward,' she said. 'You've worked hard,' she continued, her voice as crisp as her cap and apron. 'The makings of an excellent nurse so long as you don't get carried away with your emotions. It's difficult, I know . . . perhaps *the* most difficult, but it's vital you don't get personally involved with individual patients to the point where you can't do a professional job.'

Maxine knew Sister was referring to Robin, only six, on the children's ward. The child had been run over in the blackout and they said his injuries were so bad he probably wouldn't survive. But he had. Maxine had been determined that he would pull through. His parents were constantly at his bedside, but when they left for the day she would talk to him, give him sips of Lucozade, read to him. Her reward was that he slowly recovered and her favourite time of the day was when she came on duty and his face lit up in a beaming smile. She could have hugged him to bits. Three days before his discharge she'd come on duty to find his bed freshly made up.

'Have they already sent Robin home?' she'd asked, happy that the day had come, but disappointed she hadn't been there to say goodbye.

There was a few seconds' silence. A tension in the ward. Maxine looked at Fuller and White, the two other nurses. Then Fuller said in a low voice, 'He died in the night.'

She'd run to the toilets and sat on the seat, sobbing her eyes out. Eventually she got up and combed her hair and arranged her cap. She looked terrible. Eyes puffy and red. Sister was sharp with her, and she thought at the time what

34

a hard woman Sister was. But experience taught her differently. Sister was right. She probably didn't have the perfect temperament to be a nurse, but she'd do her level best, especially now they really were at war. And if one day she could become a children's nurse, it might be her salvation.

The night before Maxine left home for London there was something she needed to do. She knew it would take all her courage.

'I think I'll have an early night,' she told her parents after the three of them had spent an awkward evening in the front room, none of them knowing quite what to say.

'I don't blame you, love.' Her father smiled sympathetically, his eyes full of affection. 'You've got a big day ahead of you tomorrow, and an early train to catch.'

'I'll say goodnight then.'

In her bedroom Maxine reached for the top shelf in her wardrobe and removed a shoebox, laying it on the bed. She lifted the lid to reveal Johnny's letters in a neat pile – and a navy blue ring box. She took the ring box out, then gently removed her engagement ring, remembering when Johnny had first slipped it on her finger. Emeralds were said to be unlucky and it had turned out to be true, she thought sadly.

'Goodbye, Johnny,' she spoke aloud, the words almost choking her. 'I've loved you since I was eight, but I must leave you now to rest in peace.'

With tears streaming down her cheeks, she kissed the ring and pressed it in its slot. The lid made a final snap as she closed it and laid the little box on top of Johnny's letters. Satisfied, she slid the shoebox back on the shelf in the wardrobe. The ring would be safe there.

Chapter Five

London, July 1940

As Maxine hurried over Westminster Bridge, she tilted her head skywards to the faint sound of a plane, but there was nothing in sight except two contrails crisscrossing a flight path. The Battle of Britain had started a few days before, raging over Kent and the coast. Her mother had begged her to stay in Liverpool, but stubbornly she'd kept to her plan. Hardly giving the Thames more than a cursory glance, Maxine paused a moment on the bridge to check the folded letter in her hand. Yes, St Thomas' was directly opposite the Houses of Parliament.

A few minutes later she passed through the imposing front entrance of the red-brick hospital. No sooner had she stepped in and given her name at the front desk than a tall, thin woman with a blue and white uniform which crackled when she walked marched up to her. There was no smile of welcome and Maxine's heart plummeted.

'Taylor, I presume. I'm Sister Dawson, standing in today for the Home Sister, Miss Harley. We're expecting you. In fact,' she made a play of looking at the watch on her chain, 'you're half an hour late. I believe we said three o'clock.'

This wasn't a good beginning. Maxine was certain she

was no more than five minutes late, but it wasn't the time to argue.

'I'm awfully sorry, Sister,' she said. 'The train stopped even more times than usual, and I don't know London all that well so I got a bit confused.'

'Hmm.' The woman tossed her head in disbelief. 'You couldn't have a much better landmark than Big Ben.' She looked Maxine up and down, her lips tightening as though to say that Maxine wouldn't do at all. 'Well, you'd better come with me and I'll show you your room. You'll be in the West Wing – that's where the second- and third-year nurses live.'

Maxine followed her down long, gloomy corridors with so many twists and turns she had no idea which direction she was going. Finally Sister opened one of a dozen identical doors.

'You'll be sharing with Nurse Redding.' She glared at Maxine. 'And no smoking. That's an order.'

'I don't smoke,' Maxine said, feeling like a probationer instead of a second-year nurse.

'Be in my office in ten minutes,' Sister Dawson ordered, closing the door with a loud click.

Maxine sat on the furthest bed, where the area didn't appear to be occupied, and looked around. Except for a photograph and a book on the other bedside cupboard, and a cape flung over a chair to show some sign of life, the room was as gloomy as the corridors. The bedspread was a khaki colour and the curtains weren't much fresher looking. Even though it was still July the room felt cold. She shivered and unpacked her case, hanging up the few pieces on the wooden hangers provided in the shallow cupboard next to the other nurse's clothes, and berating herself. She'd made completely the wrong decision but there was simply no going back;

37

she'd have to live with it. She only hoped the other nurse would be nice.

Slowly Maxine unpacked her small case and undid the little parcel Sister Dugdale had given her. It was a small green Bakelite clock. She immediately wound it up and placed it on the bedside table. Somehow, its friendly little face and cheerful sound of ticking made Liverpool seem not quite so far away.

Suddenly the door opened and a slim young nurse, short in stature, with dark curls, her cap slightly askew, stood in the doorway smiling.

'Oh, good, you've arrived.' She came in and quickly closed the door behind her, then thrust out her hand. 'I'm Anna Redding. Welcome to the fray.'

'Maxine Taylor.' She took Anna's warm, strong hand in hers.

'I hate all this surname business even when we're off-duty,' Anna said, 'and I think we're going to be great pals, so let's always call one another Maxine and Anna. What do you think?'

'I'd really like that,' Maxine said sincerely. It was a long time since she'd had a proper girlfriend, and now that Johnny . . . She wouldn't allow herself to finish that thought.

'Have you been assigned a ward yet?' Anna asked.

'No. I've got to see Sister Dawson right away. I expect she'll tell me . . . or rather order me.'

'That's Dragon Dawson to a tee,' Anna laughed, her hazel eyes sparkling mischievously.

'Perfect name,' Maxine chuckled, as she opened their bedroom door.

'Good luck!' Anna called. 'And see you later in the canteen.'

* * *

38

Maxine's first day began at 7.30 on the dot in Women's Surgical with the Staff Nurse greeting her, 'Oh, not another new one. I'd hoped I was getting someone with experience.' She looked Maxine up and down and pursed her lips. 'I suppose you'll have to do. We're extremely busy, so buck up and set to. The doctors will be doing their rounds at nine and everything has to be spotless.'

Nothing Maxine had done had been right. She was spending too much time with one of the patients, Mrs Roberts, who had undergone the removal of her childbearing apparatus and could not stop crying; she'd missed a piece of fluff under the bed when she'd mopped there; she'd been about to give the wrong tablets to one of the patients with the same surname as the lady in the far corner . . . By the time Staff Nurse reluctantly said she could have her long afternoon break, Maxine was almost in tears.

'Two hours and not a minute longer. And before you ask – you'll finish at eight this evening.'

Maxine assured her she'd be back in the ward promptly.

In the canteen, she grabbed a bowl of soup and spied Anna waving for her to sit at her table.

'Good,' Anna said approvingly, looking at Maxine's bowl. 'I chose the soup to be fast as well. Let's hurry and then we can go to the park and have a natter – get out of this racket for an hour. I've done nothing but change beds and clean lockers and give out and empty bedpans this morning in Men's. Ugh!' She pulled a face, making Maxine laugh. 'And what have you been up to?'

'Nothing any more exciting than you,' Maxine admitted. 'The worst part is the Staff Nurse.'

'Jenkins?'

Maxine nodded.

'She's a tartar. Only been here a month and wants to

exercise her authority. Don't take any notice. Keep your head down and you'll be all right.'

The afternoon was even worse. Maxine had to sit at a table with two trainees and stitch sanitary towels. She thought she would scream with boredom, and the two young nurses looked equally fed up.

'Push that mop of yours right under your cap, Baker,' the Staff Nurse admonished one of them, a girl with beautiful red curls, as she swept by. 'You look like someone on the stage.' She hesitated and looked at Maxine. 'And you, Taylor, I need you to do the rest of the blanket baths we didn't get round to this morning because you spent too long chatting to the patients.'

Maxine bit back a retort.

That night in bed, tired out though she was, Maxine tossed and turned. A few feet away she could hear Anna's regular breathing. How she envied her new friend. All she could think about was Johnny. Johnny dying, with no one to hold his hand. She began to cry, softly at first, and then her body racked with her sobs, and her tears drenched the thin, flat pillow.

She sensed, rather than saw, Anna leap out of bed and rush towards her. A hand stroked her hair.

'Don't cry, Maxine. The first few days are always the worst.'

'It's not that.' Maxine's voice was muffled in her pillow.

'What is it then? You can tell me. I'm a good listener.'

Maxine struggled to sit up, tears still falling. 'You don't want to hear all my woes. Everyone's got troubles at the moment.'

'Let's make a pact right now,' Anna said. 'We'll always

40

trust one another to be able to say whatever is troubling us. Me, as well as you.' She stuck her hand out. 'Come on, shake hands.'

Maxine put out a trembling hand and Anna took it in her own warm one.

'Now, tell me what's the matter. It's bound to be a man, isn't it?'

Maxine nodded. 'I've lost my best friend.' She squeezed Anna's hand without realising. 'He . . . Johnny . . . I've known him since we were children and now he's *dead*.' She lowered her head as she broke into sobs.

'What happened?' Anna gently touched her shoulder.

'He was taken prisoner at Dunkirk, and then he died of pneumonia.'

Anna produced a handkerchief. 'Here, blow your nose.' Maxine blew. 'It's horrible. Women losing their men because of that rotten little man with his ridiculous moustache.'

Maxine turned her head to see Anna's own eyes fill. 'You sound like you've lost someone too.'

'My dad.' Anna's voice was flat. 'He was a fireman and he'd just rescued a family from a burning building and then . . . a piece of burning timber fell on him, killing him instantly.'

'Oh, Anna, I'm so sorry.'

'But we're not talking about me,' Anna said firmly, 'and it sounds trite, but the pain does lessen with time.' She looked sharply at Maxine. 'Did you fall in love with your Johnny when you were adults, by any chance?'

'I loved him deeply, but I'm not sure I was in love with him,' Maxine admitted. 'But he persuaded me to marry him because of the war.'

Anna's eyebrows shot up. 'Oh, my goodness. I should have realised – you're wearing a wedding ring. So you're now a widow?'

'I was married such a short time I hardly felt married, let alone widowed. I just feel a horrible black hole where Johnny ought to be.'

'Bugger this war,' Anna said, hugging her. 'No one can ever take the place of anyone, but I'll do my damnedest to be the best friend ever. You're not alone now. You've got me. Just remember that.'

Chapter Six

September 1940

If it hadn't been for Anna's kindness, making sure she wasn't left alone on her time off, and cheering her up with her impersonations of some of the senior staff, Maxine didn't think she would have made it through those first difficult weeks grieving for Johnny and feeling guilty for leaving her parents. But Anna, it seemed, refused to let anything get her down – not the notorious Sister Dawson who did her best to make the second-year nurses' lives as miserable as she possibly could, nor the complaining patients, nor the horrific injuries they were constantly faced with. And after her first month, with Anna's support, Maxine began to feel she might be a very small but worthy cog in the very large wheel that was St Thomas'.

At the start of the month she was sent to Female Chronic where the patients were mostly grannies who'd been put in cot-beds until they died. There was little to amuse them – they only lived for their sons' and daughters' visits that were all too brief, the grown-up children needing to get back to their own families before the blackout. Maxine felt sorry for the elderly patients, as many of them were having one-sided conversations with long-departed relatives. Most days

Mrs Jason conversed happily with her son who'd fallen in Flanders. Afterwards she would dissolve in tears and Maxine would sit with her and hold her hand, letting her ramble on, even though she knew she would be reprimanded for wasting time if Staff Nurse walked in. The old lady's only other bright moment was her nightly Ovaltine.

One evening Maxine was making Mrs Jason a cup, and one for herself and Bennett, the other night nurse, when she heard the distant throb of engines and at the same time the sirens went off. Her hand shook as though with the vibration and some of the liquid slopped over from Bennett's cup.

'German,' Maxine breathed.

'How can you tell?'

Even though it was almost dark, Maxine could see Bennett's face had grown pale.

'By the way the hum isn't one continuous sound,' Maxine answered, putting the cup down. As she did so there was the most tremendous bang, followed by the sound of an explosion and what sounded like the shattering of a thousand windows. Dear God, this was close. Her hand trembling, she banged the kettle down.

Elderly patients in their dressing gowns and slippers were wandering in from the ward next door, looking dazed. One man shouted, 'We've been hit!'

What should she do? If another bomb fell a fraction closer, it could wipe out the whole ward. Beads of sweat gathered on her forehead under her cap, and Maxine raised her hand to wipe them away. Her heart beat madly.

'Stay here, Nurse Taylor, and keep the patients calm.' It was Sister Mason. 'I'm going to see where the damage is.'

Ovaltine forgotten, Maxine and Bennett briskly did the rounds of those patients who were still in bed, helpless as babies as they lay in their cots. Just as Maxine was trying to comfort an agitated Mrs Jason, the Home Sister stuck her head in the doorway.

'I'm afraid the Nurses' Wing has been hit.' Her usual kindly expression was replaced by shock. 'I'm just going to let the other wards know.' She disappeared.

Maxine froze. Dear God, the Nurses' Wing. Anna! She would be sleeping in their room – not on duty until the morning. *Oh, Anna, please be safe. And the others.*

'Bennett, will you wait here in the ward while I go and see.' Maxine was galvanised into action as she tossed the words over her shoulder. Against all the rules, she flew down the unlit corridors, where a wall of dust greeted her, and managed to catch up with a crowd of hospital workers as they were speeding towards the West Wing.

'There may be people trapped,' one of the doctors said. 'We must be prepared for the worst.'

Smoke filled Maxine's throat as they came upon a scene of horror. The Nurses' Wing was a heap of bricks. She couldn't see over the top of the pile to what had been the far wall. There was no sign of life, no shouts or moans – nothing. Everyone stood, eyes wide, trying to take it in. Some of the women were crying. The stench of something burning which she dared not . . . could not name . . . filled her nostrils. *Anna!* She screamed her friend's name but no sound came from her lips, only the taste of dust on her tongue.

'They didn't stand a bloody chance,' one man finally broke the eerie silence, anger coating his words.

'Must have been a really high explosive to do so much damage,' said another.

Muffled explosions now barely registered, Maxine's head was so blocked with fear for Anna. In one of the corners where they were standing was a heap of fallen timbers, sparking and flaring even as she watched momentarily before she came to her senses and grabbed the nearest man's arm. She pointed, fear and dust choking her as she stuttered, 'Fire!'

'I believe someone's gone to call the fire department,' he said grimly, turning to her, 'but until they come we need to be sure there's no one still alive.' He lifted his chin. 'ANYBODY HERE?' he roared, his words bouncing on the rubble. 'ANYBODY HERE?'

To Maxine's joy, she heard female voices.

'Here! Please help! We're here!' They were calling from all directions.

It was as though a nerve force suddenly held everyone together, giving them a purpose. Maxine rushed forward with the crowd, tearing bricks and mortar away to get under and behind the ruin the explosion had left. *Anna, hold on. Hold tight. We're coming to get you. Don't give up, please, Anna. I'm here.*

As if they'd heard her shout the words aloud, the others began calling, 'Hold on, there. We'll get you out.'

Minutes later the first nurse stumbled out to a tremendous cheer, but this girl was too tall to be Anna. One by one the nurses worked their way through a gap which had been blocked by a huge storage cupboard. Surely Anna would be the next nurse. But no matter how Maxine peered, the thick black dust made the nurses almost unrecognisable. Blood stained their pyjamas and faces and hands. One girl, who she'd thought for a wonderful moment was Anna, was bleeding from her arm, but all of them shook their heads, warding off any concern.

'There are two nurses still left – they're in a bad way,' another nurse said, her short hair matted with blood. 'Please help them.'

'Have you seen Anna Redding?' Maxine pleaded, strangling a sob and coughing as the dust caught in her throat.

The nurse shook her head.

'They'll be on the other side of the gap.' A porter Maxine recognised sprang forward with two other men. She started to rush after them, but another man dragged her back.

'You'll only be in the way,' he said not unkindly. 'You'll be needed when they're all found.'

Maxine heard the pounding of feet. Men's voices. Oh, thank God, the firemen were here.

'Stand back,' one of them ordered. 'Clear some space.'

After what seemed like hours to Maxine, desperately trying to quell the nausea which threatened, the rescuers emerged carrying the two injured nurses between them. No sound came from the limp bodies. Neither of them was Anna.

'Redding.' Maxine's eyes swam in frightened tears as she shook the arm of a plump-faced girl. 'Anna Redding. Have you seen her?'

'I wouldn't know her.'

'There are others still missing besides Redding,' one girl with a gash on her forehead hissed.

Tears poured down Maxine's cheeks. The worst, it seemed, had happened.

Matron made an official announcement the following morning.

'Out of the thirty-two nurses who were sleeping in the West Wing last night when the bomb made a direct hit, I am thankful to announce that only four girls died, and one, Lois Jenkins, who is seriously injured but stable, and we are optimistic for her full recovery. That doesn't decry the sacrifice those girls made, but it could have been even worse. We could have lost all or many more of our wonderful nurses.' She paused. 'Here are the names of those who died.'

Maxine held her breath while Matron adjusted her glasses.

'Patricia Cooper, Jane Deveraux and Sally Grimshaw and Belinda Brown.'

Maxine stood alert, her nerves taut. Anna wasn't on the list. Why? Where was she? A flicker of hope died at Matron's next words.

'Unfortunately, we haven't found Anna Redding. We can only presume she died, as several of the nurses confirmed she was in the quarters with the others at the time the bomb went off. I will inform you when I hear of any further news. In the meantime, in case the Germans decide to have another shot at us tonight, I have asked the cleaners to prepare the basement. All of us, the whole hospital – except those on duty – and I mean doctors, nurses, cleaners, cooks, servicemen, and everyone in between – is to sleep down there tonight. I will inform you if there are to be any further changes.'

It wasn't until the afternoon that Anna was pulled out of the rubble. Like the other four nurses, she'd been buried alive. Maxine swallowed the bile that kept coming up into her throat before she fled to the toilet and vomited until her stomach had nothing left to bring up. And then she wept. She wept for Anna and she wept for Johnny. Two wasted young lives within months of one another.

'I'll never forget either of you,' she whispered, her hands folded together in prayer.

Maxine lay still, wondering why every bone ached. She stretched out her legs, grimacing as pain shot through them. She ran her tongue over her teeth. Her mouth felt gritty, dusty, stale. Where was she? What was that strange odour? Something rancid. So strong it turned her stomach.

She opened her eyes and lifted her neck, twisting it this

way and that, hardly taking in the sight that met her stare. Fully dressed bodies were lying inches away from her, still sleeping, some of them actually snoring. Of course. She was in the basement of the hospital. Matron had ordered everyone to spend the night here, leaving only a skeletal staff above.

Maxine managed to raise herself to a sitting position and took in the incredible scene. Surgeons were pressed up against tea ladies and maids; Dr Shaw, who always barked his orders and was often rude to the nurses, had his head on the shoulder of the young trainee nurse in her ward. She wondered what he'd think when he woke up and realised who he'd slept with last night. Maybe he'd get the message that he wasn't quite as important as he liked to make out. She couldn't help the smile which hovered over her lips . . . that is, until she remembered poor Anna. Her dear friend. How she was going to miss her.

It was still early but several people were stirring and Maxine struggled to her feet.

'What a night,' John, one of the porters said, flexing his arms above his head and yawning.

'Not the most comfortable, I have to say,' someone else said. 'But we're the lucky ones.'

'You can say that again.'

More staff were scrambling to their feet, giving one another wan smiles, probably feeling as foolish as Maxine that they'd spent the night in such proximity with one another, and now it was over they needed to get on with their normal duties.

And she needed to go back to her patients.

Two nights later, wailing sirens sent cold shivers down Maxine's back as she desperately tried to help the patients to safety before terrifying explosions wiped out two whole blocks of the hospital. Wards were totally destroyed and Matron ordered everyone to transfer what seemed like the whole hospital to the basement.

Everyone had to work at top speed with the blackout still in strict force, even in the basement. Carrying a pile of linen, Maxine had almost careered into a wall.

'It was those painted animals that saved me from a nasty collision,' she told Bennett at breakfast next morning. 'They certainly showed up in the dark.'

'Oh, you've spotted the White Rabbits,' Bennett laughed. 'Bloody ingenious, if you ask me. Some chap, I think it was, painted them on the wall for just that reason – to save us all smashing into it.' She swallowed a spoonful of porridge. 'I see you're down for the children's ward for the next month – rather you than me. I hear the Staff Nurse is awful.'

'I particularly asked for the transfer.' Maxine smiled at Bennett's raised eyebrows. The children's ward was always the least favourite among the nurses, mainly because of the children's distress caused by their parents either coming on visiting days and stirring them up, or not appearing at all. She didn't bother to explain that she'd always wanted to work with children.

Staff Nurse Mayfield ordered Maxine to bath the children who were able to get out of bed. Her first patient was a scruffy, undernourished waif who had just been admitted with a body full of scabs, looking suspiciously like the results of chickenpox. If it was, at least now the spots were scabs he wouldn't still be infectious. She would show them to Sister Mayfield after his bath.

'You're a girl and not s'posed to see my willy,' the child shouted when she pulled his filthy underpants down.

'I'm a nurse, so it doesn't count,' Maxine told him, biting her lip to hide a smile.

'Why doesn't it?' His round blue eyes regarded her.

'Because we're trained especially to help children to get better.'

'I don't wanna go in the water. Mum never makes me. I don't like it.' His eyes were wide with fear.

'We have to clean those nasty scabs or they'll get worse and start itching and spreading.'

She quickly lifted him into the bath, and taking no notice of his screams, she soaped and rinsed him.

'I can get out myself,' he said, his face contorted as he struggled to put his thin legs over the side of the bath.

'Well, you're a big boy.' Maxine smiled as she dried him. 'And you've done well.' She dabbed his tears away. 'Can you tell me your name?'

'Course I can,' he said scornfully. 'It's John Smiff – but Mum calls me Johnny.'

Her eyes filled as she heard the little lad's name and a tear rolled down her cheek. Quickly, she brushed it away.

'Why are you crying, Miss?' Johnny looked up at her, his eyes still wet. 'Have they said *you've* got to have a bath now?'

Chapter Seven

September 1941

When Mr Churchill had announced at the end of May that the Blitz was over, and the Luftwaffe no longer pounded London and the Docklands every night, Maxine had a desperately needed reprieve. She'd been working twelve-hour shifts, covering for a nurse on sick leave as well as doing her own duties, with little time off in between – not enough to do much more than write letters home, keep up her laundry, and occasionally go to the pictures with one or more of the nurses she'd come to know in other wards. A pleasant Scot called Gillian was now in the next bed but kept herself to herself and Maxine was grateful. It would be a very long time before she'd open her heart to anyone else.

Going through the Blitz with the constant bombing which had caused further destruction at the hospital, the strain of always showing a calm exterior so as not to unsettle the patients every time they heard the siren, and without Anna's cheerful approach to life, Maxine sometimes found the days difficult to get through.

Nevertheless, she'd looked forward to her few days off with her parents. They'd seemed pleased to have her home, but she could tell by her mother's glances to her father that she was still puzzled their daughter had left them to fend for themselves.

Feeling she was letting them down, but thankful her father was no worse, Maxine was glad to get back to London.

'Good to have you back, Taylor,' Bennett said, immediately she set eyes on Maxine. 'We've missed you with so few of us left.'

Maxine noticed the deep circles under the nurse's eyes and felt a pang of guilt. 'Oh, I'm sorry, Bennett, I shouldn't have gone – there was no emergency or anything at home.'

'Don't be daft. If anyone needed a break, *you* did.' She looked at Maxine under her lashes. 'Bit of a stir going on since you left.'

'Oh, what?' Maxine straightened her cap, barely summoning a grain of curiosity.

Bennett grinned. 'I expect you'll see soon enough.'

An hour later Maxine was chatting to Tom Jansen, a soldier who'd been badly wounded in the leg and had had to have it amputated. He'd been incredibly brave, keeping up her spirits every bit as much as she did his, and she was always impressed with his optimism.

'Enough of the chit-chat, nurse. This is a hospital, not a social club.'

She jumped. Spun round. Looked up to a powerful jaw, hard mouth, and straight into granite-coloured eyes. Strong nose. Dark auburn hair was brushed back from his forehead. A face that meant business.

'Excuse me, but—' Maxine began.

'Nurse was just—' Tom interrupted, struggling to sit further up in his bed. Maxine automatically went to help him. 'I'm all right, Nurse – honestly.'

The doctor whom she'd never seen before didn't give the

boy a glance. As if he'd never spoken. Instead, the steely eyes alighted on Maxine.

'No excuses – there's work to do, so get on with it.' He swung away.

Maxine stared after his departing figure marching along the basement corridor, burning with fury. Even Matron never spoke to her so rudely. Where was Matron this morning anyway? *She* knew, if anyone did, that Maxine barely wasted a minute. What an overbearing . . . She couldn't think of a strong enough word to describe him. Who did he think he was?

She tried to carry on with her normal duties but her heart quickened with annoyance every time she thought of the auburn-haired doctor. He obviously had no respect for nurses whatsoever, no bedside manner, no understanding that a little human contact which made them feel special and individual played a crucial part in a patient's recovery. She needed to find out if he'd been temporarily transferred to her ward or, God help them, was going to be there permanently. If so . . . She didn't want to think further, except that if he was, she was in for an even greater daily challenge.

But to Maxine's surprise, not everyone thought the same way about the new addition to the department.

'Isn't he a dreamboat?' Bennett's eyes danced mischievously as she was about to take temperatures. She looked at Maxine. 'You *have* met him, haven't you?'

'Met who?' Maxine replied innocently, though she knew perfectly well now who Bennett was talking about.

'Red.'

'Red?'

'You know. The new doctor.' Bennett looked surprised Maxine didn't seem to know who she was referring to.

'It's *Mr* Blake, as it happens,' Sister admonished as she swept past to supervise the new probationers.

The two young women grinned at one another.

'A surgeon, no less,' Bennett said, her hand to her mouth to stifle the ready laugh. 'Even better.'

'No wonder he's on his high horse,' Maxine commented.

'What makes you say that?' Curiosity flickered across her colleague's face.

'He told me off for chatting to Tom. And when Tom tried to stick up for me he completely ignored him and carried on at me in a most arrogant manner. I thought he was horrible.'

'Mmm.' Bennett shot a look at her watch. 'We need to continue this conversation this evening when we have some privacy.'

The buzz in the temporary canteen the Red Cross had organised after the bombings was even greater than usual. Maxine caught the name 'Red' several times from some giggling trainees at the next table.

'Wonder if he's as red hot as his name.' A girl with bright golden curls escaping her cap laughed and gave a huge wink to her colleague opposite.

Maxine glared at them before burying her head in her book at the same time as eating her stew and dumplings, though it was difficult to concentrate with the volume of noise around her.

'Is this seat taken?'

It was a deep voice, educated, richly coating the few words.

'No, please . . . She barely looked up beyond the white coat buttoned to the neck, recognising his voice. She dropped her eyes to her book again, hoping he would leave her in peace.

'Oh, didn't I meet you earlier . . . in the men's ward, wasn't it?' He set his tray on the table, removed the plate and cutlery, and propped the tray up against the table as he sat down, his piercing grey eyes fixed firmly upon her.

Damn. The arrogant surgeon. She was tempted to tell him it was the exact opposite of 'wasting time' that he'd accused her of, but she raised her head a few inches and looked directly at him.

'I believe you spoke to me when I was with Mr Jansen.' Ice dripped from the words as she made a pretence of dropping her eyes back to her book.

'And *your* name?'

What a rude man. She bit her tongue to stop herself from giving him a sharp reply. She must never do anything, say anything, to get in the way of her Nightingale Badge. *Be polite. However he tries to get your goat.*

She placed her finger on the paragraph she was reading to let him know this was only going to be a brief interruption. 'I'm Nurse Taylor.' Immediately the image of Johnny sprang to her mind. She blinked.

'Christian name?' he practically barked.

Her hands made a fist underneath the table. 'Maxine.'

'Maxine,' he repeated and jerked his head towards her book. 'What are you reading?'

She looked across at him, irritation bubbling to the surface. '*Out of Africa.*'

'Oh, Isak Dinesen's memoir. How do you find it?'

He would *know Karen Blixen's Danish name.* Try as she might, she could never recall it.

'I like to read about a determined woman who is doing what she loves most against all odds,' she returned coolly.

'Is that what *you* are? A determined woman?' He raised his eyes to the ceiling, then caught her eye and smiled in a self-satisfied way. 'Are you working at St Thomas' against all odds?'

How dare he?

'I don't think there's any comparison between a nurse in a hospital and Karen Blixen running her farm single-handedly.' She deliberately looked down at her book again.

Why doesn't he go away and leave me alone?

'Impossible to concentrate, I should say, in this madhouse.' He gazed towards the heaving tables.

The annoying thing was that this time he was right. She snapped her book closed.

'By the way, I'm Edwin Blake.'

If he thought she was going to curl up in deference to his godly presence, he was wrong. She hid a smile. She'd have a little game with him.

'How do you do, Dr Blake.'

Quick as a flash he answered, 'It's *Mr* Blake, actually.'

Maxine's hand flew to her mouth in mock dismay. 'Oh, I'm *so* sorry.'

If Anna had been with her at that moment and caught her eye they would not have dared look at each other for fear of breaking into giggles for pulling the great man down a few pegs. She looked innocently at him.

There was a moment's pause. Her heart beat a little too rapidly. *Have I gone too far?*

'I suppose I deserved that.' A smile hovered, softening the hard line of his lips.

She picked up her knife and fork again and made a pretence of finishing her meal, but each swallow stuck in her throat. This was awful. She wasn't enjoying the stew at all with him staring at her, while he hadn't even touched his food.

'You may begin, *Mr* Blake,' she emphasised, tackling a

piece of brownish potato. She looked up and smiled. 'Sorry, but you were staring.'

Her remark seemed to draw him back an inch or two. Then what looked like a flicker of respect passed across his face. 'Was I really? I didn't mean to.'

He began to eat, grimacing every so often and inspecting the contents of his fork before continuing. He broke the awkward silence.

'How long have you been at St Thomas'?'

Oh, no. He wanted to keep up a conversation. Surely her message was clear that she wasn't at all interested. He was just doing it to annoy her.

'A year. When it was a whole building.' She placed her knife and fork neatly together and made a great play of looking at her watch, 'Oh, it's later than I thought.' She jumped to her feet and tucked her book under her arm.

He immediately sprang up. 'But you haven't finished your—'

'I wouldn't want to be accused of wasting time *again*.' She threw him a cold glance. 'Good day, Mr Blake.' With that she turned and made her way through the narrow spaces between the other tables, inwardly seething.

Pompous prig. She thought of more words for Mr Edwin Blake as she tidied her hair in the small mottled mirror over the washbasin in the cloakroom before she felt ready to face her patients again.

'A word with you, please, Nurse Taylor.'

Sister Crook put her head round the tiny kitchen as Maxine was preparing the drinks on her ward. She immediately put down the cloth and followed Sister into her room.

'Sit down, please.' Sister Crook took her place on the opposite side of the desk. 'I'm most surprised,' the older woman began, 'to find that although you have not actually been *rude* to one of your superiors, you have nevertheless not acted in the required deferential manner to an eminent surgeon. So what do you have to say for yourself?'

A flush of anger rushed to Maxine's cheeks. 'I imagine you're referring to Mr Blake,' she said, barely trusting herself to speak.

Sister nodded.

By sheer willpower, Maxine stopped herself from saying anything that would get her into more trouble.

'What I'm saying, Nurse, is that you need to mind your P's and Q's when he's around. Mr Blake is an important man and we're grateful to have him here. And you don't want him putting any black marks against your Nightingale Badge, do you?'

'No, of course not.' Oh, how she detested such arrogance. Someone who put himself so far above the minions, he thought nothing of having the power to ruin her career if he so wished. Her hands clenched into fists.

'So will you in future give him the respect he deserves?'

Maxine only paused for a second. Sister's eyes were unusually stern. 'Yes, Sister, I'll do my best.'

'That will be all.' She let her gaze rest on Maxine a few moments more. 'You're an excellent worker, Nurse Taylor, but you have much to learn about men. Never forget – they can make us or break us.'

Chapter Eight

Maxine did her best to avoid Mr Blake whenever she could. Even glimpsing him in the distance along one of the corridors made her seethe that he'd reported her, but he seemed bent on seeking her out.

'Nurse Taylor, would you come over here and show the juniors the correct way to take a patient's temperature,' and 'Nurse Taylor, please show Nurse Johnson how to give a proper bed bath,' and 'Nurse Taylor, would you demonstrate hospital corners on this bed.'

Maxine would grit her teeth and carry out his instructions, which normally would have come from Sister, until it became obvious to her – and probably most of the staff, she wouldn't be surprised – that he was doing this on purpose, causing her a good deal of embarrassment. She knew she would have to speak to him about it.

Bennett had only said that morning, after Maxine had made an irritable comment about him, 'Taylor, you realise our dear Mr Blake fancies you.'

In spite of Maxine's denial, she couldn't help the warmth that seeped under her collar.

'Whatever nonsense are you talking about?' she demanded.

'He singles you out – nearly all the time. It's clear as daylight to the rest of us.'

'But I've done nothing to encourage him to single me out. I don't even *like* the man. I do respect him, having seen the results of his operations, but that's all.'

'Careful,' Bennett hissed. 'He's coming in and making a beeline for you.' She winked. 'I'm off.'

'Ah, Nurse Taylor.' Edwin Blake strode up to her. 'I'd like you to help me with old Mr Hodgkins in the far bed – if it's not too much trouble.'

'No trouble at all, Sir.'

She'd tackle *Mr* Blake later – when she'd got some food inside her.

Maxine drew in a deep breath before she raised her hand to knock on the door of Mr Blake's private office.

'Come in.' Edwin Blake looked up from his paperwork, an expression of surprise flitting across his face.

'Mr Blake, may I have a private word with you?'

'Of course. Please be seated.' He got up and walked to the door, clicking it shut.

'May I be frank?'

'By all means.' He leaned forward, steepling his hands. 'You sound as though you have something troubling you.'

'I do.' She kept her gaze steadily upon him. 'It's been remarked upon more than once that you are deliberately singling me out, and some of the staff, and even the patients, are beginning to gossip.'

'Really?' A dark auburn eyebrow shot up. 'What about?'

'That you're seeking me out . . . drawing attention to me in front of the others.' She looked him in the eye. 'If I'm honest, I've noticed you doing it myself, but I put it down to the fact that we got off to a bad start and you're asserting your authority . . . reminding me of my place.'

He caught her gaze and held it. Then he put his head

back and roared with laughter. 'You're even more innocent than I thought.'

He came round to her side of the desk and sat on the edge of it so he was facing her. He caught one of her hands, which she immediately snatched away.

'Can't you see? It's because I *like* you. I'd like to see more of you, and not just here in the hospital. I'd like to get to know you better.' He took her hand again and in her confusion she didn't pull away. 'You're lovely, Nurse Taylor – Maxine. Do you understand what I'm saying?'

She gave a start of surprise. She really hadn't been prepared for this kind of admission. 'Why are you interested in me?' She tapped the top of her apron with her fingertips. 'I haven't even got my full qualifications yet. I'm nowhere near your level and never will be. I don't understand.'

'I don't want anyone "near my level", as you so quaintly put it,' he said, smiling. 'I don't want you to alter at all. Why don't you give me a chance? Let me prove that I'm not the ogre you first thought I was.'

'What if I find my first thought was right all along?' She removed her hand and looked him directly in the eye. 'For instance, why did you find the need to report me? I thought that was totally unfounded.'

He frowned. 'What are you talking about?'

'You spoke to Sister Crook about me. That I'd been disrespectful to you. I suppose I have to be grateful you didn't go straight to Matron.'

'I haven't spoken to anyone about you. Why should I?'

'But Sister called me into her office and warned me that you'd—' She broke off. Sister hadn't actually said it was Mr Blake who'd reported her. It could have been anyone who'd overheard her. One of those nurses in the canteen, maybe. Heat flew to her cheeks. How stupid she'd been to assume . . .

'You're blushing, Nurse,' Edwin Blake said, laughing. 'I believe you've just realised I'm not quite so bad as you'd thought. But if you're still in two minds, I'll have to prove I'm not an ogre, won't I?' He looked at her. 'So, Maxine Taylor, would you consider having dinner with me?'

She'd jumped to conclusions. It hadn't been him who'd reported her. He gazed steadily at her, waiting for her answer.

Suddenly she wanted to go out somewhere nice. Eat a plate of delicious food, if that was possible these days. Forget about blood and vomit, groans and tears . . . just for a few hours. Forget this horrible war that had taken Johnny and Anna from her. For one glorious evening.

She permitted herself a half-smile. 'Thank you – I'd like that.'

He smiled. 'What about tomorrow evening? Can you get away?'

'Yes. I'm off duty at six o'clock.'

'We'll go out to eat then.' He wrinkled his brow. 'Where would you like to go?'

She'd never been given a choice. Johnny had always decided for her.

'I'd prefer you to choose,' she said. 'I'm sure you know London better than me.'

'Then I'll surprise you. But dress up.' He paused. 'I'll meet you by the South Bank lion at the foot of Westminster Bridge at six forty-five. That give you enough time?'

She nodded.

'By the way, don't mention this to anyone at the hospital. They frown on any kind of friendship between the doctors and nurses.'

'Does that go for surgeons too?' Maxine kept her face straight.

He smiled. '*Touché.*' He looked at her with something like a spark of admiration. 'However, no one's exempt.'

It was nearly half past six by the time she'd shed her uniform. Her temple had begun to throb, gently at first, and then more insistently when she started to panic. She didn't have the right clothes. She shouldn't be going out with him in the first place. But it couldn't stop the frisson of anticipation that she was going on a date with a man of the most impressive reputation. And looks. She grinned to herself as she removed a black straight skirt from its hanger.

Her Liberty-print blouse she'd made two years ago would have to do. It had a pretty bow at the neck and the small coloured flowers of pinks and reds and greens flattered her fair complexion and naturally gold-streaked hair. She added her pearl earrings and necklace, and slipped into her only decent pair of shoes, a pair of black patent courts she'd bought in Liverpool when she'd first got married. Immediately her thoughts flew to Johnny. By going out to dinner with Edwin, was she being unfaithful to his memory? Unconsciously, she twisted her wedding ring. It was only dinner.

She glanced at the clock. Twenty minutes to seven. She'd have to hurry. She threw on her only jacket, hoping it wouldn't rain, adjusted her neat felt hat and grabbed her bag and gloves.

He was waiting for her. She'd never seen him outside the hospital before. He wore a light grey pinstriped suit and bowler hat, with black polished shoes, and swung an umbrella from his arm, oozing self-confidence. She was sure he knew he looked good.

As soon as he saw her he said, 'Ah, there you are,' and

held out his arm for her to take. Awkwardly, she put her hand though the crook of his elbow, feeling strange. It didn't belong there. But not entirely comfortable in her high heels, she was grateful for his support.

'How was your day?' he said, glancing down at her, as they quickened their step over Westminster Bridge.

'Not very nice,' she admitted. 'Mr Kingston died.'

'Ah, yes, Michael Kingston.' Edwin Blake nodded. 'I'm afraid I didn't hold out much hope for him.'

'It was a shock for *us*,' she said. 'He seemed to be doing so well.'

'He hadn't heard from his wife for some time,' Edwin Blake remarked. 'I think he felt depressed about it, wondering what she was up to.'

'Poor man.' Maxine felt the all too familiar stinging behind her eyes.

She glanced up at the man striding alongside. He didn't usually make any personal comments about the patients, but obviously took it all in. He'd remembered Mr Kingston was a Michael, for a start. Maybe he was human after all. Maybe there was a beating heart underneath his strict exterior.

'Taxi!' He suddenly stepped into the road and held up his umbrella. A black cab pulled up and he opened the door for her. 'It's a pleasant walk on a summer's eve,' he said, settling down beside her in the soft leather seat. 'But not this evening.' He raised his eyes skywards. 'Looks like it could rain. Besides,' he smiled down at her, 'I want to pamper you.'

Inside the taxi, his fingers closed over hers. She didn't want this. It was too soon. But she didn't want to hurt him by snatching her hand away for the second time. After a few moments she gently extracted it as an excuse to look in her handbag for a handkerchief, and dabbed her nose.

'You haven't got a cold coming, have you?' He sounded concerned.

'No, no. Probably the dust in the basement.'

'Because I can't afford to catch one,' he said surprisingly. 'Too many patients relying on me.'

Was he just a little too full of his own importance? She quickly brushed the thought away. He was being sensible, that was all.

They chatted amiably enough until the taxi stopped outside the Ritz. Maxine gasped and Edwin Blake gave her an amused smile.

'Will it be to your liking, Miss Taylor?'

'I'm not dressed for anything so grand.'

'You look perfect.'

A man dressed in a bright red uniform stepped briskly forward and bent to open the car door. 'Madam,' he said, holding out his hand to help her out, 'welcome to the Ritz.'

She gave the man an uncertain smile, lost for words. But it didn't stop the tingle of excitement she felt as Edwin Blake took her arm and guided her through the door of what many people regarded as the best hotel in London.

Maxine gasped as she stepped into the enormous dining room. It was buzzing with people's chatter and laughter, but nothing could detract from the surroundings. Her astonished gaze soared upwards to the ethereal painted ceiling, the tall windows richly draped in shining gold-patterned fabric, the bronze chandeliers . . .

'Your table, Sir.' The waiter pulled out an upholstered chair from the table covered in a crisp white cloth and set with gleaming silver cutlery and crystal glasses. 'Madam.'

As soon as Maxine glanced at the menu, the heat rushed to her cheeks. There were dishes she'd never heard of, let alone could pronounce. Edwin Blake was going to think her such a fool.

As though he felt her confusion, he said, 'Will you allow me to order for you, Maxine?'

'I'd be grateful. They look like very fancy dishes with their foreign names.'

He chuckled. 'They have to keep up the pretence that they're still serving the finest food even though there's a war on and rationing. Mind you, they do manage to get good supplies most of the time.' He bent his head to scan the menu. 'I recommend the duck à l'orange.'

'It sounds wonderful,' Maxine said, not having a clue. She'd never eaten duck before . . . and with orange . . . it didn't sound that appetising. But she was thankful the problem had been taken out of her hands.

'So now you can relax.' Edwin Blake smiled at her. 'The Ritz will do all the work. All you have to do is sit there and look beautiful.'

It was meant to be a compliment, she was sure, but her skin prickled. She wasn't some empty-headed young girl, even though she'd pointed out she wasn't on his level. She'd meant he held a high position in the hospital, not that he was her superior in every shape and form. Whatever had made her make such a comment?

'Here's to a normal civilised evening in the madness of this bloody war,' Edwin said, raising his glass. 'And I say "bloody" as that's exactly what it is – in more ways than one.'

She raised her glass towards his and smiled. 'I second that.'

The wine tasted good even though she wasn't very used to it. She allowed the liquid to roll over her tongue, relishing such a delightful flavour of peach, as it slid luxuriously down her throat.

'Do you read poetry?'

His sudden question made her start. 'I did . . . at school.'

'It's good for the soul.' Edwin's eyes met hers. 'Have you a favourite poet?'

'N-no.' Desperately she searched her mind for a familiar name. 'Well, I did like Byron.'

'Ah, Lord Byron.' He kept his gaze on her. 'He was a rum cove. I'm surprised he's your favourite. Goes a bit close to the mark sometimes, in my opinion.'

'I'm not sure what you mean?' *Oh, God, what had she started?*

'Very *risqué.* Not sure young ladies should be reading such stuff.'

'I was far away from being a "young lady" at fifteen when I first read Byron,' she said, her tone a little more clipped than she meant. 'I don't suppose I understood half of it, but I remember we used to giggle over some of the passages.'

He raised an eyebrow and she was thankful when the waiter brought their soup. It was time for her to change the subject, even if only to comment on the food.

'It's delicious,' she said truthfully.

'One wouldn't expect it to be any different at the Ritz.' He smiled, dipping his spoon in.

'What made you come to St Thomas'?' she asked him, feeling on more familiar ground.

'It's a good teaching hospital – or was, what's left of it. That's really my forte – teaching. But they're talking of opening a place in Guildford – a medical school – so I'll likely be transferred.'

She felt a tiny quiver of disappointment. 'I imagine all the hospitals are finding it difficult. There's—'

'Let's not talk about work,' he cut in. 'I want to get to

know you, Maxine. And for heaven's sake call me Edwin – when we're off duty, of course.'

So he's expecting to see me again.

'Is there a young man in tow?' Edwin broke into her thoughts.

'I haven't a boyfriend, if that's what you mean,' Maxine answered quickly, her face feeling warm all of a sudden.'

'A pretty girl like you without a boyfriend?'

'Not exactly. I was married.'

'*Was?*' His eyes widened.

'He died,' Maxine said quietly, putting down her soup spoon.

'Oh, dear. I'm so sorry.' Edwin seized her left hand before she could retrieve it. 'I didn't notice your wedding ring. Clumsy of me. How did it happen?'

'He was one of the ones who had to stay behind at Dunkirk. A medic. They needed them to go off with those rescued, but they also needed medics to stay behind and look after the wounded. I understand he volunteered.' She wasn't prepared to go into any further details.

'How old are you, Maxine?'

'Twenty-one.'

'Too young to be a widow.' He gently squeezed her hand. 'I'm so sorry,' he repeated.

'He wasn't only my husband for a very short time but he was my best friend . . . from childhood. That's what is so painful. I've lost my best friend.' Her eyes filled with tears.

'Then let me try to make it up to you,' Edwin said.

'No one can make up for anything like that,' she said briskly, to hide the familiar ache in her heart.

'I'll damned well give it a good try.'

Maxine was keen to get off the subject and was grateful when the main course arrived. To her surprise she found the duck delicious. She also found she was beginning to enjoy Edwin's conversation about the places he'd travelled to before the war, though she couldn't add anything much except to nod and smile.

'What other books have you read besides *Out of Africa*?' he asked.

'*Rebecca.*' She thought a moment. 'I like Agatha Christie.' Her mind went blank and quickly she said, 'What about you?'

'Aldous Huxley's *Brave New World*, Evelyn Waugh – I've just finished *A Handful of Dust* – anything by Jean-Paul Sartre . . .'

He mentioned two or three more names but she'd never heard of any of them. She sipped her wine, hoping she looked interested, not knowing if she'd like the plays he now mentioned because she'd only heard of Noel Coward's *Private Lives*. But Edwin was nice. Attentive. Polite. Absolutely charming. Altogether different from when she'd first come across him in the ward.

'We must do this again . . . soon,' he said as he helped her on with her jacket an hour and a half later. 'I'm not going to keep you out late. None of us are getting a lot of sleep lately, and I need steady hands when I hold the knife.' He grinned at her.

'Put like that, I think you're very wise.' Maxine smiled back.

The taxi pulled up, as Edwin directed, in Royal Street, close to the hospital building. Edwin paid the fare and the cab disappeared into the dusk. He looked down at Maxine, a strange expression she couldn't fathom on his face.

'You're very lovely,' he said. 'Would you allow me to kiss you?'

She didn't know if she wanted him to or not. Before she could answer, he drew her into his arms and she felt his lips on hers. It buzzed through her mind how different he felt from Johnny, whose kisses were cheerful . . . friendly . . . Edwin's was more like a lover's kiss. For a few seconds she tried to wriggle free. It was too smothering. But then, against her will, she felt herself responding, felt her own lips start to kiss him back. How she'd missed this. But it was too dangerous. She didn't want to like him in that way. Dazed, she pulled away.

'I've had one of the best evenings in a long time,' Edwin said.

'Me, too,' she whispered.

'Then go, before you turn into a pumpkin.'

'Isn't that what the carriage is supposed to do?'

His teeth gleamed in the fading light. 'Yes, something like that.' He gave her a swift kiss on her lips. 'You'd better go in, Cinders. It's going to bucket down.'

Reluctantly she turned away, aware that he was watching her. Inside the hospital she removed her high heels, not wanting to wake anyone as she crept down the steps. It was only when she was safely in the bedroom, hearing Gillian's gentle snores from the other bed, that she realised she wasn't sure if she felt relief or disappointment at the sudden end to the evening.

Chapter Nine

'Come on, lazybones, wake up.' It was Walker, one of the three other nurses Maxine shared the room with, shaking her shoulders gently. She'd been dreaming about Edwin.

Her eyes opened wide as she jerked up.

'You were sleeping the sleep of an angel – even on your bed of straw,' Walker chuckled. 'He must be gorgeous.'

To her annoyance, Maxine felt her face redden.

'Oooh, look who's blushing. I'm pretty close to the nail, aren't I?'

'I'm not answering.' Maxine swung her long, slender legs off the mattress, laughing and shooing Walker away.

Somehow it seemed a little dull that morning without Edwin coming in and out of Men's Surgical. She rather missed him. This was ridiculous, to feel like this after one date, and probably the only date he would ever ask her on. She'd convinced herself that it was just an impulsive gesture on his part and he wouldn't be repeating it, when Bennett came to find her as she was washing a few cups whilst waiting for the kettle to boil on the Primus stove for their afternoon tea. The patients had had theirs and Maxine was looking forward to snatching five minutes with her feet up and a couple of Digestive biscuits.

'For you.' Bennett handed her an envelope.

'Me?' Maxine pointed to herself.

'Yes, love. It's got your name on, if I'm not mistaken – Nurse Taylor. *Private and Confidential,* so it says.'

Maxine took the envelope and shoved it in her apron pocket, ignoring the curiosity on Bennett's face.

'I'll read it later – *in private,* as it states,' she said with a grin.

'Fair enough, but you have to share it with us if it's something exciting.' She gave Maxine a sly look from under her lashes. 'I have a feeling I know who it's from anyway.' She winked and scurried out of the kitchen door, pulling it behind her.

There was no possibility of reading the letter now. She'd be in trouble if she didn't get back on the ward right away.

Immediately she forgot about Edwin as George Morton grabbed her attention. During the blackout he'd been knocked off his bicycle by a motorist and suffered internal injuries and a broken arm. Waving his good arm in fury, he cursed Hitler for causing the accident, which, Maxine supposed, indirectly Mr Hitler had.

The only bright spot was that today was payday. She joined the queue outside Matron's office to collect her wages – ten shillings more than she'd received at the Infirmary. 'London rating,' Anna had explained, her nose wrinkling that it wasn't nearly enough compensation. She could see her friend's expression now. How she missed her.

'I didn't break the bleedin' thermometer,' a young girl's voice came from behind her in the queue. 'Mr Gibson is a bit funny in the head, I reckon, and he snatched it from me before I could even see his temperature. And to cap it all, Sister said she'd deduct it from my measly four pounds.'

'Did you tell her what happened?' another girl asked.

'No point.'

Maxine wished she could block out their conversation and just collect her envelope and go. She was longing to read her letter, which was beginning to burn a hole in her pocket.

It was several hours later before Maxine fell onto her bed, exhausted. She took the envelope out of her pocket and tore it open. There was a single sheet of paper inside and when she unfolded it, there was his writing – not the usual scrawl of a doctor or surgeon, but beautiful italic writing that looked as it if had popped out of one of the history books.

Dear Girl,

I hope the wine didn't have any ill effects on you last night and that you had a decent sleep. I didn't. And it wasn't just the bombs keeping me awake. I kept thinking of your lovely face and how I couldn't wait to see it again, but it's my day off today and I have some errands to do.

When do you have some time off in the day? It would be nice to walk in the park, and maybe go to a matinée or something. I'll be back on the wards tomorrow so you can tell me then – discreetly, of course, but I know you always will be.

Until tomorrow, then.

Yours,

E

Maxine frowned and read it through a second time. What did he mean by calling her 'Girl', and signing off 'E'? Was that his way of being discreet? It sounded so impersonal. And yet the sentiment was there, staring her in the face. He wanted to see her again. He thought she was lovely. He was just very different from Johnny – that was all.

With a flutter of anticipation, she folded the letter and slipped it into its envelope and back into her pocket.

Edwin arrived on her ward the next morning and didn't show by even a flicker of an eyelash that he had a personal interest in her. She played along with it to perfection. But when they had less than a minute alone as he was frowning at one of the patient's medical sheets, and the two other nurses and Sister were at the other end of the ward, Edwin muttered, 'So when are you free, Nurse?'

'The day after tomorrow,' she answered, pretending to tuck in a corner of Sidney Johnson's bed. 'I'm off in the afternoon. From two o'clock.'

'Good. That will be all, Nurse.' He lowered his voice. 'Meet you at the same place at half-past two. Be prepared for anything.'

'Thank you, Mr Blake.' She wanted to giggle. He was such a respectable man, and there he was, making a date with her right under Sister's nose.

They did as his note suggested and meandered through Archbishop's Park. Even though it was right on the doorstep of St Thomas', Maxine had had little chance to enjoy it, except for an occasional sandwich at lunchtime with Anna.

'I wanted to take you to see a play, but I'm afraid they've already started. Half past two is pretty much the time for most of the matinées.'

'It doesn't matter at all,' Maxine said, taking his proffered arm. 'We're inside a stuffy building for too many hours, so it's wonderful to be out in the air. Most of the flowers are coming to the end, but I can still smell the last of the roses.' She breathed in deeply. 'Mmm . . . lovely. And just walking amongst the trees. We're so lucky in London to have so many parks.' She glanced up at the sky. 'Only the barrage balloons remind us there's a war on.'

He looked down at her, his eyes searching hers. 'If there *wasn't* any war, would you be happy right this minute?'

'I'm enjoying this,' she said, seriously. 'But I'm not sure what being happy feels like anymore.'

He tucked her arm in his a little tighter. 'You're not on duty this evening, are you?'

'No. No, I'm not.' Why did she feel uncomfortable all of a sudden? Was it that he seemed to know her schedule despite her only finding out about the alteration herself that morning?

'Because we can go and see a film if you like. Or a play. I haven't booked anything because I wasn't sure. We could get a bite to eat first, or afterwards – whichever you prefer. What would you *really* like to do?'

'I'd love to see *The Dancing Years*,' Maxine said tentatively.

'That's Ivor Novello.'

'Yes. I heard a programme about it on the wireless and made a note of it. It's on at the Windmill Theatre.'

'You can't go wrong with Novello.' He patted her arm. 'Look, why don't we have some refreshment and then see if we can book tickets.'

'Weren't we lucky to get such good seats?' Maxine said as they found their row just as the orchestra started up.

Edwin smiled and took her hand. She was conscious of his warm fingers linking with hers, stopping her from completely losing herself in the romance of the musical. She tried. How she tried to concentrate, but it was impossible. She wanted him to kiss her again. Hold her. She didn't dare look at him in case he guessed her thoughts.

76

Think her fast. She stared ahead, hardly blinking, hoping he wasn't aware of her turmoil.

He began to caress her fingers, one by one. A shiver ran through her body. She tried to think of Johnny. Keep loyal to him. But his face faded in and out of her vision and it couldn't take the place of this living, breathing man next to her, so close their shoulders were touching.

Her breathing became rapid and she forced herself to draw in a long, deep breath through her nose to steady her pulse. He must have heard the intake as he shot her a look as though to ask her a question.

The music came to a close. To her relief, the curtain fell down.

'Thank goodness it's the interval,' Edwin said. 'The space doesn't accommodate my legs at all. I've got cramp in one of them.' He rubbed his calf, then got up. 'We'll go and get a drink. Stretch our legs.'

She was thankful. The physical closeness of him was too dangerous. She needed to distance herself. She followed him out of the auditorium and into the bar downstairs.

The bar was jammed from end to end, but Edwin was half a head taller than most other men and Maxine noticed the blonde behind the bar served him sooner than she should.

'There wasn't any chance to ask you what you would like to drink,' he said, carrying two glasses of wine and pushing his way through to where the crowd had thinned, 'so I hope this is acceptable. Don't suppose you've seen a table?'

'No. I don't know how everyone got here so quickly,' Maxine said, looking round. People were lighting up cigarettes, and passing chocolates, pouring champagne and laughing at something that had been said. They all seemed to belong. Maxine looked away abruptly.

'We'll lean against the windowsill, if you can manage.' Edwin placed the glasses on the sill and glanced at her. 'Are you sure you're all right, Maxine? You look a little flushed.'

'I'm fine.' She gave him a wide smile. 'Isn't the show wonderful? Such lovely music. Almost makes me want to dance.'

Why, oh why had she said that? As though she was trying to hint where she'd like to go on their next date. Well, there wasn't going to be another date. She was acting like a star-struck girl and she didn't like herself one bit. But she'd made a decision. She wasn't going to put herself through all that emotion she'd felt sitting there beside him in the theatre. He'd laugh his head off if he had an inkling of her muddled mind. She'd feign a headache or something. Ask him to take her back to the hospital. But it was too late. The bell rang for everyone to finish their drinks and take their seats in the auditorium again.

'Drink up, sweetheart. We don't want to disturb everyone by being late.'

There was half a glass of wine left. She tipped it back and swallowed it without stopping.

'Don't want to waste it,' she told him, a little shame-faced. She clutched on to his arm and he laughed as she lost her balance. He put an arm firmly around her waist and led her back to their waiting seats.

She didn't remember one thing of the second half of *The Dancing Years*.

The rest of the evening seemed to melt away and they were on their way back to the hospital. Edwin was unusually quiet in the taxi, just holding her hand tightly as though he never wanted to release it.

Maxine's mind was in tumult. She hadn't even *liked* the

man when she'd first met him; now she couldn't stop the rush of feeling every time she looked at him. She mustn't let him know. He would think her a foolish little girl. After all, that's what he had called her – Girl. But she wasn't a girl. She'd been married to her dearest friend. She knew how it felt to be married. The intimacy. And she'd missed it more than she'd realised.

Once or twice she caught Edwin glancing at her in the taxi but she forced herself not to turn her head. He instructed the driver to drop them off in the same street as last time. He was protecting her reputation as much as his own – but she hated the subterfuge. It spoilt the ending to what she could only describe as a romantic day fuelled by her longing. But now she would go down to the basement and he would go to his quarters, wherever they were.

As soon as the taxi had moved off, Edwin reached to take her in his arms and laid his cheek against hers. Then his lips sent kisses down her neck, thrilling her. His fingers undid the buttons of her jacket. His hand cupped her breast over her blouse. Then his fingers found bare skin. He began to stroke her and she moaned.

'Maxine. Oh, Maxine, you dear girl. I want you so much. Do you want me too?'

She couldn't fathom the expression in his eyes.

'I think I'm falling in love with you.' His voice was husky.

'It's too soon,' she whispered.

'Not for me, it isn't. I think I fell in love with you when you put me in my place that first day.'

She caught a flash of his gleaming white teeth as he smiled.

'I don't want you to leave just yet. What say we have a nightcap in my room?'

She had no idea what a nightcap was but imagined it was a drink of some kind.

79

'A cup of cocoa would be nice.'

He threw his head back with a roar of laughter. 'Then it's cocoa you shall have. But we must go separately. I'm in that far wing . . . the one still standing,' he added with a grimace as he pointed. 'I'll leave the door open for you. Then go up the stairs and mine is the second door on the left. Follow me after two minutes.'

She felt awkward as soon as she glimpsed the double bed through the open door from a small sitting room. Trying not to be caught staring, she looked around. It was as neat and spotless as Edwin himself.

'Take your jacket off,' he said, slipping off his own and draping it over the back of one of the chairs.

'Edwin, I—'

But she was already in his arms. His lips were on hers.

Then without speaking, and before she could protest, he picked her up as though she were as light as a ballet dancer and carried her into the bedroom.

'Get under the sheets,' he murmured.

She obeyed.

It hurt. She was so tense it hurt terribly. She called out for him to stop, but he didn't seem to hear. Tears poured down her cheeks. This wasn't how it was meant to be.

He finished and fell onto his side, smiling at her. Then his smile faded.

'What's the matter, darling girl? Did I hurt you?'

She nodded, desperately embarrassed.

'I'm so sorry. Forgot to warn you I'm a big bloke. It won't be so painful next time, I promise. In the end you'll accommodate it more easily . . . speaking as your surgeon.' He grinned. 'I want you to enjoy it as much as I did.'

He kissed her bare shoulder. 'Did you enjoy it just a little?'

'Yes,' she whispered, but it wasn't really the truth.

She felt ashamed that she hadn't been able to give more of herself, but the pain had been very real. She thought how very inexperienced she must seem to him. But she'd been married, for goodness' sake. She ought to know what to expect. Then, without warning, she heard Johnny's voice in her head after she'd accepted his proposal.

'Even though there's no doubt we'll soon be at war with Germany, we'll save ourselves until we're married. I respect you too much to make love to you before the wedding, Max, darling.'

But Edwin hadn't waited. And she hadn't stopped him. She wasn't certain the feelings she had for him were love – not yet anyway. And Edwin? Was he genuine? Or was she just a war-time diversion? She cringed at the thought, and as though Edwin had read her mind, he held her close, whispering how much he adored her. She breathed out a happy sigh. He did care for her after all.

Chapter Ten

A fortnight flashed by. Maxine and Edwin had managed to snatch a couple of hours together here and there, mostly for an occasional meal. She felt she was beginning to get to know him, but his next proposal took her by surprise. He insisted upon giving her some money to buy an evening dress and a pair of shoes.

'You always look beautiful to me – you know that – but you'll feel a million dollars in a new dress. And I have somewhere really special I want to take you.'

'Nowhere can be more special than the Ritz.' Maxine smiled.

'Hmm. It's not the only special place,' he said, counting out some pounds from a bundle of notes. 'Here . . . this should do it.' He pushed the money into her reluctant hands. 'Some of the stores in Oxford Street were badly damaged last year in the Blitz, but Marshall & Snelgrove escaped much of it, so I'm told.' He closed her fingers over the notes. 'Try them first.'

'Are you absolutely sure?' She looked up at him, her eyes anxious.

'Absolutely, poppet. Go and enjoy yourself. And have lunch out. Take a girlfriend.'

But in the end she went on her own. Somehow she didn't

feel like explaining to any of the others how she had come by all this extra money. She might have told Anna, but there was no one else she would confide in. But did that mean she was doing something she wasn't proud of? She didn't want anyone to think she was after his money. But it might look just like that to them. Surely it was natural that Edwin wanted her to look nice. And *she* wanted to look nice for him. Was that so terrible?

She shrugged and tried to put the question out of her mind, but she couldn't shake off the edge of guilt she felt that Johnny wouldn't have approved at all.

She had to admit it was heaven to have a whole day off to herself, wandering around the shops, knowing if she saw something she liked she'd be able to buy it – within reason, of course.

She settled on a dress the colour of a shimmering turquoise sea she'd once seen in a holiday brochure. Immediately as she put it on her skin glowed, the colour of her eyes took on almost the same turquoise, and her hair glinted like gold under the lights. Although it was strapless she knew she could make it more of a versatile outfit with the little short jacket she'd made for her wedding dress. She smiled at herself in the mirror, and almost to her surprise, the attractive young woman smiled back.

She was sure Edwin would love the sea dress as much as she did.

Now to the shoe department. She was alarmed to see that many of them cost as much as her dress. Her eyes fell on a pair of dark green suede shoes with a bow on the front and a black patent heel. She turned the shoe over. Three pounds nineteen and eleven. Nearly four pounds. That would make it twelve pounds eight shillings out of the fifteen pounds he'd given her. She tried them on.

'They fit you like a glove, don't they, Madam?'

'I can't feel them at all.' Maxine smiled up at the young girl.

'This make is very high quality,' the girl said. 'I think you'll enjoy wearing them and I'm sure you'll have a lot of compliments. They're very special.'

Maxine couldn't refuse.

The girl put them in a shoebox lined with tissue paper and tucked it into Maxine's carrier bag.

There was enough money over to buy a pair of cami-knickers and a pretty brassière. It was no good wearing a beautiful dress if she only had tired undergarments beneath. She couldn't wait to show Edwin her purchases.

She was too excited to sit for a proper lunch, as he had suggested, but she had a cup of tea and a fruit scone in the store's café, all the while thinking of him. Why had he singled her out? An eminent surgeon, he could have anyone he wanted. What was it about her that he liked so much? He was a bit serious compared with Johnny (though she knew she mustn't compare the two men), but she supposed he'd have to be with his kind of responsibility. He must feel so satisfied at the end of each day saving lives. She wished she could do more herself.

Was she falling in love with him? She couldn't help a wry smile. She was running ahead. It was far too soon to be posing such a question.

Yesterday's treat on her shopping day seemed an age ago when Maxine was plunged into a nightmare at the hospital. Eleven people, four from the same family, had been brought in during the night, wounded from a bomb which had exploded in one of the streets uncomfortably close to St Thomas'.

'Did anyone die?' she asked Staff Nurse, dreading the answer.

'Three.' Staff Nurse Williams' tone was abrupt as she glanced towards the door. One of the orderlies was pushing a man in a wheelchair. The patient's hair and face was thickly coated with dust, and he was muttering obscenities under his breath.

'Calm down, Sir,' the orderly said, not unkindly. 'You're safe now. We'll soon get you put right.' He helped him out of the chair and managed to get him into bed, with more curses emanating from the patient's mouth.

Maxine's heart went out to the poor man.

'I'd like you to give him some special attention while you're on duty,' Staff Nurse Williams said. 'You'll be able to keep a strict eye on his daily improvement . . . or not.' She left her to it.

Maxine helped one of the nurses to get him undressed and into the bed. The man groaned as the nurse knocked his leg by mistake.

'I'm so sorry, Mr—'

He looked up, a faint expression of surprise on his face. 'Bill . . . Bill . . . oh, God, I can't remember my name.' He tapped the side of his head.

'Mr Chorley?' Maxine broke in, reading from his notes.

'Yes, yes, that's it . . . Chorley.'

He looked relieved that he had a full name, but Maxine wasn't convinced. She was sure he'd clung onto 'Chorley' without any real conviction. It looked like she had plenty of work to do with Bill Chorley, but she was glad. She needed to keep busy. Keep her mind off Edwin. And their next time together. She hugged herself at the thought that there would definitely be a next time.

* * *

85

Bill Chorley was a difficult patient, right from the start. But it didn't bother Maxine one bit. She took him his noon meal on his second day.

'What's this muck?' He looked up at her as she placed the tray on his bedside table and helped him into a seating position. When she didn't respond, he banged his spoon down on the plate like a toddler having a temper tantrum.

She refused to rise to his bait.

'You seem very pally with our charming Mr Blake,' he remarked.

Oh, why did she always have to blush whenever Edwin was mentioned or when he came into the ward?

'Yes, I thought so,' he chuckled. 'You've got "guilt" written all over that pretty face of yours.'

'You need to concentrate on getting well, Mr Chorley,' Maxine said, frowning at him, 'and not concerning yourself with the latest gossip.'

'Oh, I don't think it's gossip,' Chorley said annoyingly. 'I watch things. You and Blake are having an affair – it's bloody obvious.'

'Don't be ridiculous.' Her blush deepened.

'Then why are you turning so red?' he asked, a grin spreading over his face. 'And by the way, you can call me Bill. I'm not at all sure I recognise the name of Chorley anyway.'

'When you come up with one you *do* recognise, then let me know,' she quipped, trying to change the subject.

'He's not good enough for you,' Bill said, out of the blue.

She gave a start. 'I'm not prepared to discuss it.'

'Just wanted to warn you, Nurse. I don't trust him. His eyes are cold. They give nothing away. I've seen his type before.'

'You don't know him. I thought he was a bit abrupt

when I first met him, but he mellows when he's out of the hospital.'

'So I'm right. You *are* going out with him.' He gave a triumphant smile.

Blast. She should never have admitted to anyone, let alone a patient, that she was seeing Edwin outside the hospital.

'Please hush, Bill,' Maxine said, desperate to change the subject. 'How's your dinner?'

'Give me a chance.' He cut up a piece of meat and looked at it before he put the fork in his mouth. 'Bloody hell, that's tough.' His jaw went up and down and side to side in such a comical fashion she couldn't help smiling, until he spoke once more. 'Be warned, that's all.'

Chapter Eleven

'We're going to a dance,' Edwin managed to say in an undertone to Maxine when she was in the sluice, washing the bedpans. A horrible job which brought back memories of her first year at the Infirmary, but it had to be done.

Maxine had never learned to dance properly and awkward male partners hadn't helped, but looking at Edwin she was sure he'd be a good dancer.

'I've looked up when your next day off is, and managed to change mine to coincide,' Edwin went on. 'We should go the evening before and then we can spend all day together the next day.' He looked at her. 'Would you like that?'

'It sounds lovely, but—'

'I'm going to book a hotel for the night so we can relax and not have all eyes on us as we do at the hospital. I don't want to let you out of my sight for a moment, so pack a small overnight bag.'

Her heart gave a little flip. Making love that first time had been in the heat of the moment, but this time she knew it was his plan. Was she ready for such a leap?

'And you can wear your new dress,' he added.

'Where are we going?' Maxine asked as they approached Covent Garden, her hand feeling more familiar in the crook of his arm. How nice it was to have a boyfriend she could be affectionate with. Something she'd missed terribly since Johnny died. Thinking of Johnny she felt a twinge of guilt. But she couldn't go on forever without enjoying another man's company. Surely Johnny wouldn't want her to. She glanced up and caught Edwin's eye and he smiled. She smiled back.

To have an evening and a full day ahead of them was almost unheard of since the war started. Edwin had obviously organised it, but how, without raising suspicion? She was truly grateful; however, it had come about after another harrowing week. And Edwin would have had the same exhausting week given the wave of new patients who'd been admitted, nearly all requiring surgery.

This time on their own would be a good opportunity to get to know one another better. She gave his arm a daring little squeeze and he looked down at her and smiled.

'It's a surprise. But I've booked us into a hotel close to where we're going, so we can register first and put our things in our room – have a wash and brush up, if we need.'

'Sounds a good idea,' she said, more for something to say. Unexpectedly, she began to feel nervous.

The hotel was small and non-descript which suited her perfectly. Inside, a grey-haired woman at the reception desk regarded them keenly through thick lenses.

'Mr and Mrs Edward Brown,' Edwin announced firmly.

This time she understood his discretion. Until the world knew they were courting it was best kept a secret to protect them both.

'Sign here, please, Mr Brown.' The receptionist slid an open book and pen towards him, at the same time glancing at Maxine's left hand as though suspicious the third finger would be bereft of the necessary gold band. She gave a nod almost of disappointment, her bun so tight the skin tautly stretched around her face and eyes under the strain of her hairpins. Her prim expression reminded Maxine of her mother. If her mother could see her now with a man who wasn't her husband, booked into a hotel in the same room, she'd be horrified, no matter how famous a surgeon he was.

'No, thanks,' Edwin was saying. 'We've only got a couple of small bags with us, so I'm sure we can find our way.'

'You're on the second floor,' the woman told him, 'and I'm afraid there's no lift.' She seemed momentarily taken aback when Edwin treated her to one of his charming smiles. 'But then you're young,' she said, 'so I'm sure you'll manage.'

Maxine bit back a giggle.

'Old bat,' Edwin said when he unlocked the door to their room. 'Don't suppose she's ever known a night of passion in her life.'

'You don't know that,' Maxine retorted. 'That's the thing with people. You never know what they're capable of until you get to know them. Or they tell you things and it might not be the truth, so you still don't know them.'

Edwin threw her a questioning glance. 'You're very deep, all of a sudden,' he said, frowning.

'She might have lost someone in the war and she doesn't have much reason to be jolly,' she told him crisply.

'Last war, more like.'

'Even if it was, you don't get over that sort of thing easily or quickly . . . or ever.'

Damn. She hadn't meant to say that at all. What was he going to think, her bringing up her dead husband just when he was treating her to a wonderful time? She opened her mouth to apologise, but he stopped her with his arms, holding her tight against him.

90

'I'm sorry, poppet. Of course you don't. You're thinking of your husband, aren't you? What an insensitive cad I can be sometimes.'

He bent his head and kissed her lightly, then again, only deeper this time.

'I want to make love to you right now,' he said. He was breathing fast. 'Let's not bother with dancing. We can go straight to bed. Then have a quick supper afterwards – if you're hungry then, that is. If not, we'll skip it and make love again.'

'We're definitely going dancing,' Maxine said, smiling, trying to lighten the tone. She didn't want to admit to herself that she was putting off the moment when Edwin would make love to her again. 'You haven't bought me a new dress for nothing.' She ducked out of his embrace. 'I'll go and change. Won't be ten minutes.'

'You'll be the first woman I've ever known to be that quick,' he said, shrugging. 'I'm ready, so I'll wait for you downstairs in the bar.'

Swiftly, she removed her blouse and skirt, splashed under her arms at the washbasin, then eased the sea dress over her head and hips and slipped on the new green suede shoes. How lucky to have found the dress, what with the shortage of ready-made clothes, and material about to be rationed. Picking up the brush, she ran it through her hair and touched up her lipstick. She was ready.

'Well done,' Edwin said, scrutinising his watch as soon as she entered the bar. 'Not even a minute late.' He tipped the rest of the golden-brown liquid down his throat and smacked his lips together, then looked her up and down. 'Is that the new dress?'

'Yes. Do you like it?' She gave a twirl, feeling a little self-conscious.

'It's gorgeous. *You're* gorgeous.' He glanced at his watch again. 'Right. Are you ready?'

He took hold of her hand as they walked past the reception desk.

'Where are we going?' she asked.

'The Royal Opera House,' he said. 'It's not far. Covent Garden.'

'Oh, I thought you said we were going dancing.'

'We are. They changed it into a dance hall at the beginning of the war – more likely to raise people's spirits than going to the opera. They hold dances every night and it's usually packed. Amazing, considering a bomb could drop on them any time.'

He must go quite regularly, she thought. She wondered idly who he'd brought, then decided it was none of her business, and in any case it would have been before they'd started going out together. What was in the past had to remain in the past.

She'd never been inside the Royal Opera House before, though she'd always given more than a glance at the columned façade when she'd passed in front.

'I didn't think there'd be quite this queue when we've come so early,' Edwin grumbled.

'It shows it must be good,' Maxine said mildly, wondering if it stretched to the other side of the building. If so, they were in for a long wait.

But fifteen minutes later they'd stepped inside. She drew in a quick breath, totally unprepared for the sight and sound that engulfed her. What had once obviously been a sump-tuous interior had given over to a heaving mass of bodies. On the bandstand she was thrilled to see a group of female musicians belting out a swing number, and a glamorous woman leading on the saxophone.

'Ivy Benson and her all-girls band,' she breathed. 'Oh, Edwin, I've always wanted to see them.'

Edwin nodded with no seemingly particular interest. 'Keep your eyes open for a table.'

She followed him as he forced his way through the crowd.

'Goodness, however many people have they packed in here?' she asked as he took her jacket, somehow having managed to find a table to share with another couple. He draped her jacket on the back of one of the chairs and she removed her hat and balanced it on top.

'They say the place holds fifteen hundred,' Edwin said, eyeing up the floor and the people sitting high in the balconies.

He was shouting above the cacophony and she barely caught his words. It was certainly not the right place to have a conversation.

'What would you like to drink, poppet?'

'A glass of white wine would be lovely, thank you.'

After their drinks, he led her onto the dance floor. He was an excellent dancer, but she couldn't relax, so terrified was she of making a wrong step.

'Listen to the words,' he whispered when Ivy Benson was singing 'I'm Getting Sentimental Over You'. He gave her hand a squeeze, his breath tickling her ear.

After two or three more dances – one being the jitterbug, which was the latest craze from America that even Edwin couldn't master – he led her back to the table, where another couple had taken their places.

'Excuse me,' Edwin began, pointedly looking at them, pink with annoyance.

'Oh, was this your jacket?' A scarlet-lipsticked woman looked up at Maxine who nodded. 'I had to sit down, love – my feet were killing me.'

'Don't worry.' Maxine smiled. 'We'll find somewhere else.'

'If you're sure . . .'

'Maxine!' Edwin's tone was a little irritable.

'Come on, Edwin. People are coming and going all the time. There's bound to be something.'

But since they'd been on the dance floor, many more couples had come in and grabbed the few remaining tables.

'Are you feeling tired?' Edwin asked as they trailed round trying to spot a couple of spare chairs.

'Not really.'

'Incorrect answer,' he said, chuckling, his happier mood seemingly returned. 'You're supposed to say, "Yes, darling, I'm tired out and all I want to do is go to bed – with you."'

Now it was her turn to flush.

He pressed her hand. 'Shall we go?'

She hadn't known how to broach the subject of Edwin wearing something to protect her, but to her relief he brought out a small packet and swiftly covered himself. It was almost as painful the second time, mainly because Maxine was tense once more, made worse by Edwin telling her to relax and enjoy it. She tried to concentrate on him and his pleasure and was thankful the searing, throbbing pain began to subside the moment he pulled out of her.

'You're still as tight as a virgin,' he said as they lay together afterwards. 'It's exciting for me but probably not so much for you.' He kissed her swiftly on the lips. 'You wouldn't think you'd been married to your Johnny – for how long was it?'

She was glad it was dark in the room and he couldn't see the warmth rise to her cheeks. She wished he hadn't mentioned Johnny.

'He was away a lot and he was killed early on.' She really

didn't want to talk about it; it made her feel she was being disloyal to Johnny's memory.

'It must have been awful for you,' he murmured, 'but I'm here now.'

In the morning he made love to her again, and finally she told herself she was almost enjoying it.

'It's our secret, poppet,' he said more than once. 'Let's keep it to ourselves. There's too much gossip by far at the hospital and we both need to concentrate on our work.'

Chapter Twelve

She was only five days late. It was nothing, Maxine told herself. What with the war on and everyone's energy about to snap at any moment through lack of sleep and too few staff, she shouldn't expect to be on time, every time.

But you're never late.

They'd managed several more dates, mostly ending in his bed, but Edwin had always been careful to use something.

Except that very first time.

Several more days passed. Maxine tried to put the worry to the back of her mind, but however busy she was, however demanding the patients, however rude Staff Nurse Johnson, it was always there. Was it possible . . .?

And then one morning before breakfast she was sick. The suspicion, now confirmed, struck her with such force she almost reeled as she pulled herself up from the toilet bowl. She was going to have a baby. She felt sure of it.

She rinsed her mouth and caught sight of herself in the mirror. She looked more like a patient than a nurse – her skin pink and blotchy, her eyes anxious. Despite her fears she smiled at the image. Everything would work out just fine. She loved him and he loved her. Being fourteen years older, he'd be thrilled to become a father at last. She hugged the thought to her. A baby. A baby with Edwin. Would it be a boy or a girl? She didn't care, so long as it was healthy. He'd probably want a boy. Most men seemed to. But perhaps he wouldn't care either.

Now that it was real and she'd accepted the truth, she couldn't wait to tell him the news.

But she had to wait two more days as Edwin had gone to see his parents. He rarely spoke of them, and when he did it was usually not very complimentary, so she was rather taken aback that he was going to spend a whole weekend with them. But they were elderly, which pleased her, really, that he was keeping an eye on them.

Edwin looked strained around the eyes and mouth when he came back to work on the Monday. Maxine wondered if he'd had a difficult time with his parents but she decided not to question him as the subject always seemed to put him in an irritable mood. Well, she was about to change his mood completely – change his life forever. And for the better.

She went to the kitchen to put the kettle on, hoping he would follow her. He did.

'Would you like a cuppa, Mr Blake,' she teased, loving that she had to pretend there was nothing between them in front of the others, although she couldn't help the image of their last time in bed together. Was he thinking of it too? She felt a stab of excitement at the memory of their arms and legs entwined . . .

'Later.'

His abrupt tone made her jump. She gazed at him curiously. He must have something important on his mind – one of the patients, no doubt.

'Sorry, Max. I'm not thinking straight. There's something

I need to talk to you about.' He looked at her properly for the first time, his expression serious. 'When are you free?'

'Um – six o'clock.'

'Good. We'll go and have a quiet meal. See you at the lion at six forty-five.'

Before she could suggest a more private place, Sister Crook bustled in and gave Maxine a sharp look with her gleaming brown eyes.

'We're all desperate for a cup of tea, Nurse, so when might we expect one?' There was more than a hint of sarcasm in her tone as her curious eyes alighted on Edwin.

'I was just coming to tell the others, Sister.' Maxine stirred the teapot. 'It's all made.'

A tingle ran through Maxine several times as she went about her business seeing to the patients. Was Edwin about to ask her the question she dreamed of? Was his abruptness earlier because he was worried she might say no? She couldn't help smiling. He really was rather sweet.

That evening by the gate he took her arm and hailed a taxi. He seemed more attentive than usual, checking if she was warm enough, if she felt hungry, if she'd had a good day. If she wasn't mistaken, he seemed nervous, but he'd be fine when she said yes, she would marry him. They'd have a drink to celebrate. And then she'd tell him it wasn't all. That she had her own important news. Oh, she couldn't wait to see his face light up.

Even in the midst of this terrible war, life was wonderful.

He'd never taken her to this restaurant before. It was an Italian place and the waiters were Italian, so she presumed, with their smiles and arm wavings, and gesturings for them to take a seat at a table for two, tucked into the corner at the back. Perfect, Maxine thought. They wouldn't be disturbed by the other diners.

She ordered spaghetti and Edwin asked for a steak, but the waiter told him they hadn't had steak in for the last year. She excused the flicker of annoyance in his voice when he said he'd have spaghetti as well. His very position told her he was used to such a standard and she threw him a sympathetic smile. But he didn't smile back and seemed reluctant to start the conversation, just mentioning the patients and a particularly nasty operation he'd had to perform, only breaking off when the waiter poured their wine.

'But it went to plan,' he said, looking at her across the small table.

She reached for his hand. 'Of course it did. I have every faith in you.'

'Maxine, we need to talk. I have something I must say. And please don't interrupt me.' He squeezed her hand, then dropped it to pick up his glass. 'Cheers,' he said, his face flushing.

She hid a smile. He was going to explain how they would make an ideal couple but his parents might not approve because of the difference in their backgrounds. She wouldn't worry too much about that. She'd had her share of a particularly difficult mother. He'd go on to say that of course she could still continue her nursing but that one day he hoped she would consider giving it up so they could start a family.

'So you see, Max, darling, we can't go on seeing one another like we have. I just hope you understand.'

Dear God. What had he been saying?

She'd been so wrapped up in her thoughts she hadn't heard him. Or she hadn't heard him right. What was she supposed to understand?

'Wh-what did you say?'

Edwin had had his head down, but now his eyes gravely met hers. 'Have you heard a word I've been saying? Do I have to repeat it?'

She nodded dumbly.

'I was falling in love with you – and I can't. I mustn't.'

She needed to put things right. Quickly.

'Darling, it's all right,' she said smiling. 'I agree it's sudden, but I feel the same way about *you*. I'm falling in love with you too, and I keep telling myself we don't know each other very well – but we will. And there's something I have to tell you that will bring us even closer together.' She put her hand out to cover his. 'You see, I'm – we're – going to have a baby!'

She looked at him tenderly across the table. Her smile faded. Where was the joy lighting up his face? Where was his grin of delight? Instead it was as though he'd recoiled from her words. The silence was palpable. He must be in shock. She'd give him a few moments to take it in. For some reason, Bill Chorley's face loomed in her vision and she felt her heart quicken. Then a feeling of doom descended upon her, smothering her.

Say something, Edwin. Please say something.

'Are you sure?' His voice was tight, dismayed rather than shocked.

'Yes, I'm sure.'

'Oh, Maxine, I'm so sorry. It must have been that first time.' He squeezed her hand. 'I was so caught up with your beauty, your sweetness. Bloody thoughtless of me not to have used a French letter.'

'But if we love each other, it's not such a disaster, surely?' Maxine hated the imploring tone in her voice. 'We can get married soon and have the baby just like any other married couple.'

He shook his head. 'It's impossible.'

It was as though a curtain had been pulled aside, revealing the horrible truth. She swallowed hard, waiting for it to hit her.

'Maxine, I did . . . do love you. Please believe me. At first I admit it was just a diversion in this rotten war, but then we became close and it got more difficult to break up with you. But the truth is . . . I'm married – with two sons. I can't afford to bring this upon my family.' He ran his hand through his hair, not looking at her.

Shock waves pounded through her head until she thought she would faint. She clung on to the edge of the table.

'Your pasta, Madam . . . Sir.' The waiter put two steaming plates in front of them.

The sight of the pale strands of spaghetti, the white creamy sauce and the cooked green spinach turned her stomach. Her head roared and her grip on the table tightened.

'Are you all right, Maxine?' His voice came from far away.

She stumbled to her feet and he shot up and put a protecting arm around her.

'Is something the matter?' Another waiter rushed forward.

'She needs some air,' Edwin said. 'It's a little stuffy in here.'

The waiter opened the door for them and Maxine stood for a few shaking moments in the cold of the night, aware of Edwin standing behind her, his hands gripping her shoulders.

'Breathe very slowly and deeply,' Edwin ordered. 'In – out, in – out. Keep doing it until you feel calmer.'

Hardly conscious of what she was doing, Maxine obeyed, but her breaths were shallow and angry.

'Come on back in,' Edwin said quietly after a minute or two. 'I don't want you to go down with pneumonia.'

Like Johnny. Her eyes filled with tears. Sweet Johnny, who had never done anything but love and cherish her.

Edwin took her arm and led her back to the same table, but the plates had gone.

'We didn't want food to become cold,' the waiter said, smiling. 'I bring it now.'

'I couldn't eat a thing.' Maxine's voice was hoarse.

'Could you bring us both a brandy?' Edwin said.

The waiter nodded and disappeared.

'I hoped you wouldn't take it this badly.' Edwin looked everywhere but at her. 'But, of course, I didn't know about the baby.'

She stared at him so hard he was forced to look at her.

Bill Chorley was right. Edwin's eyes were cold.

'I never dreamed this would happen, Max. You do believe me, don't you?'

'Yes, I believe you.' Maxine jumped to her feet at the same moment the waiter arrived and put the two glasses of brandy on the table, then quickly backed away. 'I believe you are the most deceitful and despicable man I have ever met. I believe you don't deserve your wife, who I'm sure is very nice and much too good for you, and your two lovely sons. I believe I wish I'd never set eyes on you.'

'Steady on, Max.' His eyes darkened. 'It takes two, you know. And I never said I was serious . . . or promised you a future.' He took a swallow of brandy. 'I thought we were just enjoying one another.'

'Enjoying!' Maxine spluttered. 'I *loved* you . . . at least I thought I did. And I thought you loved *me*.' She stood over him glowering, raising her voice. She could see the other diners turning in their direction, but she didn't care.

'If I can do anything . . .' Edwin tapered off weakly.

'Money. I can give you money. You don't have to keep it. You can't bring it up on your own.'

'It's not an "it". The baby's a he or a she. *Your* child as well as mine.'

'I didn't mean—'

'Of course you didn't. You didn't mean anything. And I don't mean this.' She picked up her untouched glass of wine and threw the contents in his face. He blinked and the liquid fell down his forehead and cheeks.

'Now you're being childish.' He wiped his face with his napkin and scrambled to his feet.

'Please don't come anywhere near me. I never want to see you again as long as I live.' Tears were streaming down her face but she was unaware. She grabbed her bag and rushed towards the entrance.

One of the waiters beat her to it, holding out her jacket and slipping it over her shoulders. 'I call you a taxi,' he said.

'No, no, thank you. I'll get one myself.'

She had to escape from that horrible restaurant.

Please let a taxi come soon. I don't want Edwin to follow me. As though in answer to her prayers, a black cab pulled into the curb. She flung open the door.

'St Thomas' hospital, please.'

The driver looked round at her. 'Are you all right, Miss?'

'Just tired – like everyone.'

She wiped the tears with the back of her hand. She'd been so happy. How could that have changed so quickly? Edwin should be by the side of her, holding her hand, telling her how proud he was that they were going to be parents. And then a thought struck her. She had no idea if she had enough money to pay the fare. Edwin always paid and she hadn't thought to check her purse to see how much change she had. With shaking hands she opened her bag and took out her purse. It was impossible in the dark to see exactly how much was there. She tried to remember if Edwin had handed the driver a ten-shilling note on the ride over. Surely not. Her fingers found a half-crown, a sixpence and a few coppers. It didn't seem nearly enough to get her as far as the hospital. She'd have to watch the meter. Ask the driver to stop no later than when she'd used up three shillings. She'd walk the rest of the way.

'We can't go the direct route because so many streets are blocked,' the cab driver half turned his head towards the back of the cab. 'We'll have to do a detour.'

Her heart sank. If he had to go much out of the way, then the fare would go up and she'd be further away from the hospital. She leaned forward, heart beating too fast, squinting at the meter, which was turning with frightening rapidity. She didn't recognise where they were and the meter was up to one and six already. She swallowed hard. The meter turned to one and nine. Only a few hundred yards or so and it would reach two shillings. The ticking of the meter began to get on her nerves. Her purse was still open and she reached in again, but no, there was only the one half-crown. She could feel its edges. Two and thruppence . . . two and six . . . that was her half-crown gone.

'Please would you stop right here.'

The driver looked round. 'We're not there yet, love. Only just coming up to Westminster Bridge.'

'No, put me off right now. Please, now!'

She could feel the panic in her voice. Just as she thought she would scream, the taxi slowed down and stopped.

'All right, love. If you insist.'

She opened the door and he rolled down the window.

'Thank you. How much do I owe you?'

'Are you a nurse at the hospital?' He jerked his head towards St Thomas'.

She nodded. She'd lost the power of speech.

'I wouldn't dream of charging you, love. Not with the sort of work *you* have to do every day.' He roared off.

Her jaw dropped. She could have gone all the way to the hospital without the worry of not having enough money. What a kind, kind man. If only he knew. She drew in a deep breath. She supposed the walk would do her good after being in that horrible stuffy restaurant and then in the back of the taxi. Maybe it would clear her whirling head and give her the chance to work through what had happened.

The blackout made everything distorted. She nearly slipped down a curb she hadn't expected. A cyclist shot by, making her jump. She stuck her hands in her pockets and started to walk, willing herself not to think – to keep putting one foot in front of the other. Although it was dark, the moon beamed down over the Thames like a searchlight, making the water shimmer. Bomber's Moon, they called it. But she mustn't dither. It wasn't safe to be out so late. There were only a few figures on the bridge, some of them coming towards her, most of them with their heads down, just wanting to get home—

The wail of a siren. *Dear God.* Where should she run? Panic-stricken, she was only halfway over Westminster Bridge. She screwed up her eyes. *Keep calm, Maxine.* She must reach the other side of the river. Run. But her legs refused to work. People were running past her. The thunder of an enemy plane. She looked up at the sky. More than one . . .

'Don't just stand there!' someone bellowed. 'Get to the shelter!'

She heard a whine and then an explosion. It seemed to be coming from the direction of St Thomas'. She smelled fire.

Please don't let the hospital be hit again. She couldn't bear it. Her heart pounding in her throat, she began to run. No one was on the bridge now. She was alone. No idea where the nearest shelter was. She couldn't die. Another bang – she couldn't tell from which way. Dear God, she was going to be caught. She mustn't die. *Run further. Get to that lamppost on the far end – the lion – almost there.*

The moon threw its light over the outline of the hospital. She couldn't make out any flames. Panting now, her heart thumping against her ribs, her throat raw, she'd got to the end. She was off the bridge. There was her lion. Sobbing with terror at the sound of another explosion, she ran with her hand on her stomach. She ran until she could run no more.

Chapter Thirteen

The next morning she was late for duty for the first time. She'd lain awake all night sobbing quietly so as not to disturb the others, angry with herself that she'd been such a fool. She should have known a handsome man like Edwin Blake – a well-known surgeon – wouldn't be single. But the possibility had simply not crossed her mind.

Married. All the times they'd made love he was married. How could he pretend? Even poor old Bill Chorley who doubted even his own name had seen through Edwin and had warned her, but she'd taken no notice. She felt a flicker of sympathy for Edwin's wife. Well, the wife could have him as far as she was concerned. He was a weak and dishonest man who should be thoroughly ashamed of himself. But she blamed herself far more. She'd been grief-stricken and starved of Johnny's love and along came Mr Edwin Blake. She'd been flattered by his attention. And then she'd begun to care for him. Or was it, after all, just infatuation?

Edwin didn't make an appearance all day, although she was sure he was on duty. She dreaded yet longed to see him.

That evening she couldn't face the small room the nurses usually gathered in as they were changing shifts. They'd see immediately what a state she was in. Sister had already admonished her for not concentrating and neglecting to bring Mr Chorley a bedpan. She'd go straight to her room and pray none of the others were there. She badly wanted to be alone.

An envelope had been slipped under the door. She bent to pick it up and saw it was addressed to her. Edwin. She tore it open and pulled out the single sheet.

My dear Maxine,

We must talk. I've worked out something. Please meet me in our usual café as soon as you read this. I'm banking on it not being too late when you go off duty. Time now is 8.15 p.m.

E

Couldn't he even sign his name? Maxine's mouth was a grim line as she ripped the letter into four and threw the pieces into the fireplace, then lit a match and watched the flames curl round and immediately devour them. But was she allowing her pride to make a momentous decision never to see him again? Never to let him set eyes on her baby? Maybe he'd had second thoughts. He said he'd worked out something. She glanced at her watch. Just coming up to nine o'clock. She owed it to her unborn child to at least listen to what he had to say.

He was there sitting at a table in a corner of the café with a glass of beer in front of him, though it looked as though he'd only had a few mouthfuls. When he saw her, he sprang to his feet and tried to kiss her cheek, but she turned away and sat opposite him, her hands twisting together in her lap.

'What will you have to drink?'

'Just an orangeade, please.' The thought of alcohol turned her stomach.

Edwin shifted in his seat. He kept glancing at her, then looking away, as though he'd rather be anywhere but here in the café with her. She wasn't about to help him.

'Max, give me your hand. I can't talk when you look so angry. I only wish we could discuss this in private, but it's not possible.'

She immediately pulled her hands out of his view. 'I'm not angry, I'm upset, which is very different.' She swallowed hard. 'Tell me something, Edwin – if I'd asked you at the beginning if you were married, would you have told me the truth?'

'I don't know.' He tilted his head upwards and fingered his throat.

'It's a bit fundamental to a relationship, don't you think, for each party to know where they stand?' Maxine glared at him. He had the grace to lower his eyes.

'I can't tell you how sorry I am. I have no excuse. I have a wonderful wife.'

'Does she know you're a philanderer?'

'She doesn't ask those sorts of questions.' His voice had a distinct edge, as though warning her not to go further.

'Then she's as much a fool as I am,' Maxine said, ignoring his tone, her face flushing with suppressed anger.

'Maxine, I don't want us to quarrel. I admit I've been a selfish bugger, but I do want the best for you . . . and the baby,' he added.

'Well, that's something.' Maxine nodded her thanks to the waiter who set down her orangeade and disappeared.

'I have good contacts in the medical world,' Edwin went on. 'One of the advantages of being a surgeon – I know who's a good doctor and who isn't. I want you to have the very best attention, so I've made an appointment for you to see an excellent doctor in Harley Street. You'll be seeing

Dr Langley this Friday at ten o'clock. I'll arrange for a taxi to pick you up.'

'I don't need to go to Harley Street,' Maxine said. 'For one thing it's expensive, and entirely unnecessary. I can go to one of the doctors at St Thomas' for any check-ups.'

'That would be very unwise,' Edwin said, and Maxine noticed a flicker of unease in his eyes. He pressed her hand. 'I don't think you understand what I'm getting at. Dr Langley will take care of your situation and I will obviously pay the bill. He's a top man for this sort of thing.'

Maxine stared at him in horror. He wanted her to have the unthinkable. Then he could go back to his wife and sons knowing that he'd done the 'decent thing' and could put the whole sorry business behind him. She snatched her hand away.

'I didn't get caught up on Westminster Bridge and almost killed by a German bomber last night for you to say you want to kill our baby.'

It was Edwin's turn to gasp. 'Oh, my God, Max, I heard it. I hoped you'd already got back to the hospital safely. You poor darling. Thank God you're all right.'

'I'm in one piece, if that's what you mean,' she snapped.

Edwin was silent. He picked up his glass and took a deep swallow. 'Look, Max, I'm as upset as you—'

'Really?' Maxine kept her gaze on him.

'Just hear me out.' He wiped his mouth with his napkin. 'You're young and very lovely. You're about to take your finals. If you toss that opportunity away, you'll be a fool, sacrificing all your hard work for a life of drudgery. You have everything ahead of you and the chance to meet a man who'll be only too eager to get married. But not quite so eager if there's a child around. You can't bring up a child on your own, and from what I know of your parents' situation they can't help you while you go to work. The baby is not a true being in the first eight weeks – take my word for it. You'll be in safe hands with Dr Langley and it will all be over quickly and you can put it out of your mind.'

'Out of my mind,' Maxine repeated, springing to her feet. 'It's *you* who's out of your mind. Keep your blood money. I haven't changed *my* mind from yesterday. And as far as the baby's life is concerned, he or she is very much a "true being", as you so quaintly put it. But that's something you'll never understand.'

She mustered every shred of courage and dignity as she left the café.

No matter how bad things were, she would never ever get rid of her baby. In the midst of all the death and destruction around her, the baby felt like a precious gift of life.

Maxine made up her mind to avoid him, but a week flew by and there was no sign of Edwin. Perhaps he was on holiday. Gone to see his family, she supposed. Maybe he would tell his wife about some silly little nurse who'd had a crush on him. She imagined the wife laughing that a girl in such a lowly position should even imagine herself to be in love with such an important surgeon.

Finally, Maxine plucked up courage when Sister Lawson was handing out the medicines. 'Sister, what's happened to Mr Blake? He hasn't been on the ward lately.'

Sister Lawson threw her a knowing look. 'Why do you ask, Nurse? Is it a personal reason?'

'N-no.' Maxine was thrown off guard, wishing she'd never asked.

'Well, for your information he's been transferred to Sunnydown School, the new medical school just opened in

Guildford.' She shook her head. 'It might be just as well, as far as you're concerned.'

Heat flew to Maxine's cheeks and she knew she'd gone bright red. She bent down, pretending to tighten her shoelace, and blinked back the tears. He hadn't had the decency to say goodbye.

She stretched upright and pulled her shoulders back. Somehow she'd cope – without any help from Edwin Blake.

'I'll go and give Mr Carter his pill, Sister.'

'You do that,' Sister Lawson said, not unkindly. 'Work's the best thing.'

Maxine's misery turned to fury. Fury with Edwin and fury with herself. Through her own stupidity she had put herself in a terrible situation. In a few months she'd start to show. She'd have to give her notice in before that happened as she wouldn't be able to bear the humiliation of one of the staff guessing and reporting her. No, it was better to tell Sister that her father was worse and she was needed at home. She hated the thought of telling a lie, particularly where her parents were concerned, but she couldn't think of a better excuse.

Her heart sank when she thought of her parents. When she had to tell them. They'd be heartbroken. They'd wanted her to have a baby when it was with her husband, but to think that their daughter had had an affair with a married man, who turned his back on her, and she was left with an illegitimate baby would be too much for them. And she would be leaving St Thomas' without her coveted Nightingale Badge – her mother's dream ever since Maxine explained it was a special award in place of a Nursing Certificate, and only given by St Thomas' in recognition of Florence

Nightingale's outstanding contribution to nursing which had taken place at that very hospital.

The only way not to hurt them would be to keep the baby a secret. Her stomach clenched at the thought. How could she deceive her parents? But how could she risk her father's bad heart. If he had a heart attack with the shock, she'd never forgive herself . . . neither would her mother. She could picture her mother now, her expression tight, exclaiming what shame Maxine had brought to the family. As if it wasn't enough with Mickey in prison. How she'd let them down after all their scrimping and saving for her to learn a decent profession.

A wave of nausea swept through her and she couldn't guess if it was the baby or the thought of her parents' distress. But if she really was going to keep the baby a secret she needed help. She'd have to go back to Liverpool, the place she knew best.

That evening Maxine prepared for the night shift, welcoming it in a way. It was usually peaceful and she could attend her duties with the least amount of interruptions and chatter. She might get a chance to think this through in the middle of the night.

But the patients were restless, demanding and calling the two nurses for one thing or another. Three people from the same family were admitted with wounds from an explosion. It was becoming more common to have these multiple admissions of mothers and fathers, brothers and sisters, she thought, as she hurried to settle them. She wondered how long she could stand the constant smell of vomit and sweat and disinfectant. The baby seemed to have heightened her smell to such a level that some days she didn't think she could carry on any longer.

Maybe it was better to give in her notice sooner rather than struggle on, feeling worse by the day. If she could just last until Christmas – she'd need every penny.

'Please, Sister, may I see you in private?'

Maxine had managed to overcome her nausea and Christmas was only nine days away.

Sister Lawson scanned Maxine's face with her usual thoroughness.

'What are you in the middle of?'

'I've just finished cleaning Mr Draper's leg wound.'

'Then come to my office right away.'

Maxine followed the solid figure of Sister to her office, shutting the door behind her.

'Nothing wrong, I hope, Nurse.' Her sharp eyes alighted on Maxine.

Did she imagine it, or did Sister's eyes drop to her stomach? Maxine shifted on one leg, then moved her weight to the other.

'Do sit down. Now, what is it?'

Maxine drew a deep breath. 'There *is* something wrong, Sister. I've heard from my mother. My father's been unwell for some time – it's his heart – and Mum says could I please come home and help her to care for him. So I'm afraid I'll have to give in my notice.'

'I'm sorry to hear about your father,' Sister said, steepling her hands and cupping her chin. 'Can they not get someone locally – from the Royal Infirmary – to help out?'

'By the sound of her letter, Mum needs me right away.' Maxine's cheeks flooded with colour.

'Well, of course you must return home,' Sister Lawson said. She looked across her desk at Maxine. 'And you're sure there's nothing else – no other reason for suddenly leaving?'

'N-no, nothing.' Maxine felt the sweat trickle down the back of her neck. Sister was too observant by far.

'And you won't give up your nursing when anything happens to your father?'

Oh, how she hated this. One lie and it led to a complete conversation that was dressed in lies.

'I won't give it up,' she said. 'It's in my blood now.'

'What about your finals?'

Maxine swallowed. 'I still intend to take them.'

'You'll have to come back here to do so.'

'Yes, I realise.'

'Then, if you're absolutely sure,' Sister said, 'would you like to be released by the end of this week?'

'I would.' Maxine scrambled to her feet, grateful the interview was at an end. 'Thank you for being so understanding, Sister. I won't forget it.'

'You may go, Nurse Taylor. You have a lot to do before Saturday. And whatever you do, don't forget your promise to me. You have the makings of an excellent nurse.' She rose from behind her desk and held out her hand. 'Good luck, Taylor.'

They all said they'd miss her, but Maxine was aware she hadn't forged strong enough relationships for anyone to keep in touch with her. Her only close relationship had been with Anna. And Anna was gone. Then Edwin. But he was gone too. Maxine held back the bitter tears. She was alone. Abandoned. As though she never existed. But she was going to have a baby. The baby existed. Even if she couldn't let anyone else know.

She put a hand on her stomach. It felt exactly the same. She thought there might have been a slight swelling by now. Maybe it wasn't true. Maybe she'd jumped to the wrong conclusion. After all, she'd never been to the doctor's to have it confirmed. But if she were honest, she didn't need to. She knew she was going to have a baby with every beat of her heart.

Christmas was very quiet. Her mother seemed pathetically grateful that she was home, and as far as her father was concerned, he had actually improved since Maxine had last seen him. Of course she was relieved and pleased but it made her feel even more guilty that she'd used him as an excuse to return to Liverpool.

'I don't like to ask, dear, when you've only been home a week, but when do you have to go back to London?' Her mother busied herself wiping down the stove where some porridge had dripped.

The question Maxine had been dreading.

'I've got a little time yet.' She stumbled over the words.

Her mother looked at her sharply. 'Is anything wrong, Maxine? You don't seem your usual self. And you're looking very pale. You haven't even drunk your tea.'

'I'm all right. We don't get a lot of sleep at night with the bombing and night shifts, and we're always short-staffed so we have to work twice as hard.'

'Yes, your father and I listen to the wireless,' her mother said, 'though it's been terrible here, too. Those Nazis are determined to destroy our docks.'

'Have you heard from Mickey lately?' Maxine needed to change the subject and her parents hadn't even mentioned her brother since she'd been home.

Her mother's face closed. 'He doesn't write much. Only when he wants us to bring him something, poor lad.'

'Do you know when he'll be out?'

'No.' A tear dripped down her cheek. 'I know my boy

didn't do those terrible things, Maxine. He's not a bad boy, really.'

Her mother was kidding herself. Maxine wanted to remind her that the police had found all the evidence they needed of his robberies, and since the war started he'd even been involved in black marketeering. Again, he'd been caught. It seemed disloyal to admit it – if only to herself – but she'd been relieved when he'd been put in jail. He wouldn't be able to ruin anyone else's life whilst he was behind bars.

But there was no point in making any comment. Instead, she rose from the table and gave her mother a rare hug.

Her mother gave her a small squeeze in return, then, as though embarrassed she'd gone too far, she began to clear the kitchen table. Maxine watched her for a few moments before taking up a tea towel and wiping the breakfast dishes, already washed and turned upside down on the draining board.

The few seconds of closeness had gone. Maxine had almost blurted out that she was going to have a baby, but stopped herself in time.

Upstairs in her old bedroom, Maxine lay on top of the bed, tucking an extra pillow under her head. Feeling a little disloyal, she couldn't help comparing the comfort to her straw mattress at the hospital. She needed to think. Think what her next step should be. Where should she go before she had the baby? Who could she trust to ask advice?

The answer came in a flash. Pearl! Her cousin. Pearl wouldn't judge her. Maybe she could even stay with her when she started to show. And then afterwards . . . afterwards . . . then what? She couldn't think beyond bringing the little one into the world.

She'd write to Pearl straightaway.

*   *   *

117

She began the letter three times, but in the end decided it would never be perfect. She simply needed to let Pearl know what had happened and if she could come and visit her for a few days.

A letter came back by return.

Dear Max,

My goodness, you have got yourself into a right pickle, haven't you? I can perfectly understand why you don't want to tell Aunt and Uncle. They'd be so upset. Well, you know my flat. It's very small, even for one person. But if there's room in the heart, there's room in the home, Mam always said. So, yes, of course you can stay. And not just for a few days. You'll need longer than that. Stay as long as you like. I'm away quite a bit anyway with the rep company.

Let Aunt and Uncle think you've gone back to St Thomas'. With a war on they won't expect to see you that much. Then when it's all over you can tell them you missed Liverpool so you've come back but you want to find your own place. After what you'll have gone through you won't want to live with them again, that's for sure.

I expect you plan to have the baby adopted.

Much love,

Pearl xx

It was Pearl's last sentence that made Maxine's insides tremble with the enormity of her mistake.

Chapter Fourteen

Liverpool, January 1942

Living with her cousin was the very opposite of living with her parents. Pearl had no rules at all. Maxine could come and go as she pleased. If she wanted to cook that was fine with Pearl. If she didn't feel like, it she and Pearl would have a meal at the local café. Occasionally Pearl took her to the café near the theatre where she met her theatre friends, but Maxine felt uncomfortable not being able to join in properly with the conversation.

'You *will* meet someone again, Max,' Pearl said one night as they sat together in the flat. 'They're not all like that bounder.'

'Maybe not.' Maxine swirled the contents in her glass. Pearl's words still cut through her. How could she have ever thought she loved him? She looked across at her cousin. 'I need to get a job, Pearl, even if it's just temporary, so that I can pay my way. It's not fair to you to keep me.'

'I owe you a favour . . . remember?'

'You don't owe me anything. I was glad to help.'

'I couldn't have given up my job without that money, Max. You helped me change my life. So it's up to me to help you change yours.'

Maxine threw her a wan smile. 'You've more than done that by offering me a home. No, Pearl, it's up to *me* to take control . . . but you know I'm really grateful for all you've done,' she added hastily. 'If I can just find something part-time to give me some cash and stop me going cuckoo on my own.'

Pearl nodded. 'I can see that. But it'll have to be somewhere where Aunt and Uncle never go, and don't have any friends who ever go either.' She looked thoughtful, then suddenly brightened. 'I've got it! They're advertising for someone to help in the bar at the theatre. You could make a few bob there and apparently the tips are good, too.' She got up to poke the fire which was in danger of dying out.

Maxine's heart plummeted. This was not what her parents had scraped and saved for. Their daughter behind a bar. But what choice did she have? No one would take her on permanently when she told them she was going to have a baby in a few months' time. Serving in the bar she could probably get away with another three months before she showed, and she'd be able to give Pearl some money for her food and lodgings.

'What do you think, Max?' Pearl turned her head from the fire.

'I think it might be the answer for a few months. Can you tell me who I need to talk to?'

Pearl rewarded her with a beaming smile.

Maxine was offered the job immediately.

'You'll need a bit of training if you've never done this sort of work before,' her new boss, Graham Grant, said, a knowing smile hovering over his too-full mouth. 'But with your looks, you're bound to bring them in.'

He really thought he was paying her a compliment,

Maxine realised, pushing down the surge of anger that threatened to bubble to the surface. But she pressed her lips together. It wouldn't do to cheek him. She needed this job more than he needed her.

'I'm a quick learner,' she said mildly.

Training was all of half an hour and that was done by Betty, the other barmaid. She had long bleached hair and dangling earrings and wore a thick coat of make-up.

'You want to make more of those eyes of yours, love,' she said. 'Here, I'll lend you my charcoal eyeliner.'

'No, really, thank you – you're very kind.'

'You want to take my advice,' Betty said, her crimson lip curling as she slotted a clean glass into the rack above. 'The boys love it. You'll make lots more tips if you let them think you're interested.' She paused and looked Maxine up and down with a complete disregard for manners. 'Have you got a feller?'

'No. No one.' *Please don't let her ask anything more.*

Betty's eyes widened in surprise. 'What? A nice-looking girl like you.' Her mouth formed into a wicked smile and she gave Maxine a theatrical wink. 'I take it you do like men – in the right way, I mean?'

'Yes, they're all right,' Maxine said, ignoring Betty's last remark. She'd have to say something. 'My husband was killed at the beginning of the war.'

Betty's hand flew to her mouth. 'Oh, I'm sorry, love. That's me all over. Only open my mouth to change feet, is what my Albert always says.' She gazed at Maxine. 'You look so young to be a widow.'

'There are thousands like me,' Maxine said.

'You must come and see me in *Lady Behave*,' Pearl said when she slipped into the bar one lunchtime. 'This week's our last week and then we move on to Manchester. You could come Friday on your day off.'

'Oh, I don't know . . . I'd love to see you but—'

'No buts,' Pearl broke in. 'It's set in Hollywood. Take your mind off things for a bit – you never go out.' She reached for her handbag and pulled out a leaflet. She handed it to Maxine. 'This'll tell you a bit about it. I won't spoil it by giving you too many details. I'll get you a couple of free tickets. Bring a friend.'

Maxine swallowed. 'Just one ticket will be lovely, Pearl. Thank you. I'll look forward to it.'

It would probably be the last time she'd be able to go out without anyone suspecting her condition.

It was strange to be getting ready to go to the Pavilion Theatre but not having to work in the bar as she'd been doing for the last month. Maxine took a last glance at herself. She had to stoop a little to see a head-to-toe image. She could hardly recognise the serious, sad face. How had her old self vanished so quickly? A young woman who was determined to live life to the full, even with a war on. The war hadn't slowed the British one bit. They still came out with their usual irony and good humour.

She forced a smile and the woman in the spotted mirror smiled back. Could anyone tell? She turned sideways, noticing how the turquoise dress she'd only worn that one time still skimmed lightly over her stomach and floated past her knees to the dark green suede shoes. She'd felt so wonderful in the dress when she'd worn it for Edwin. How happy she'd been. Now everything had changed. She wished she wasn't wearing the dress with all its memories, but she had nothing else nice enough for the theatre. She made a grimace and picked up her coat, wishing she could turn back the clock.

But it was time to leave and she didn't want to miss a minute of Pearl's show.

Every day she went to her job at the theatre, Liverpool appeared worse than the day before. There'd been another bad raid only a few days ago, destroying more shops and people's homes. Buildings that were left standing had their windows taped to stop people getting cut from flying glass, and sandbags were piled high outside, though Maxine always wondered if they really worked when the bombs rained down.

It was heartbreaking to see two young men, one with a bandaged eye and his arm in a sling, the other on crutches with a leg missing, making their painful way along the broken pavements. She watched them peering at the ruins with the same puzzled expressions, as though to ask if it was all worth it. She swallowed as Johnny's face flashed across her mind. At least these men were alive.

Politely, she pushed her way through a crowd of men in expensive-looking coats and hats, standing in front of a heap of smashed offices. They were talking animatedly, some of them jotting down notes, puffing cigarettes as they spoke. As she passed by, Maxine heard one of them say, 'Nice to do business with you, Harry,' and the two men shook hands. She couldn't help a wry smile. Liverpudlians were proving more resilient than Hitler had bargained for.

Trams carved their way slowly through the wreckage. She inhaled deeply and hopped on one for the nearest stop to the theatre.

She was in plenty of time. Enough to have a drink this side of the bar, but she didn't want anyone who knew her to think she had no other life but the theatre. She decided to find her seat and peered at her ticket.

'May I help you, Madam?' Barry, too young to be called

up, looked at her ticket. 'You're in the balcony,' he said, pointing upstairs. 'Second floor. Someone will show you your seat.'

She climbed the two flights of stairs with a dozen others, all defiantly wearing their best clothes, in contrast to the drab daily wartime wear, chatting and laughing. They seemed to be the lucky ones. No one here with missing limbs or scarred faces. Everyone seemed to be with someone and Maxine felt self-conscious, as though people were staring at her.

Telling herself not to be so ridiculous, she smiled at an elderly woman who was directing people to their seats. The woman pointed to the front row, a third of the way along, where there was only a low barrier between her and a long drop into the audience. Alarm flooded through her. Her head swimming, she sat down on her designated seat and pushed her back further into the chair, trying to put as many inches from the barrier and herself as she could.

She took a deep breath, her hand on her stomach. Her heart felt like it was beating out of control. A column in front of her didn't help. She twisted her head to see what angle was the best to get the full effect of the whole stage, but wherever she turned the view was no better.

The lights dimmed and a couple arrived just as the curtain rose. They squeezed past, apologising profusely, as they made their way to seats on the other side of her.

It was a light comedy with some good lines and a few pretty songs she'd never heard before. Pearl had a bigger part than she'd let on, and at one point had the stage to herself, where she sang a song recalling a fond memory of a man she'd loved and thought she'd lost. She had a surprisingly strong pure voice which Maxine had never heard. She clapped loudly with the others on Pearl's last notes, but as soon as Pearl vanished into the wings, Maxine found it almost impossible to concentrate, she was so aware of the dizzying height of the balcony.

Just at the point where she thought she would have to escape for some air, the lights went up for the interval. Maxine's mouth was dry. She rose to her feet and followed a thick line of people through the exit and into the bar queue.

As luck would have it, George was behind the bar; they usually worked together on the day shift.

'Can't keep away?' he said, grinning.

'My cousin's in the show,' Maxine said. 'I promised her I'd come and see it before she moved on somewhere else.'

'You're a dark horse. You never said you were related to one of the stars. What's her name?'

'Pearl Love—'

'Pearl? She's your cousin? We adore her.' He gave a nod of approval. 'Now, what can I get you?'

'A glass of lemonade, please.'

George raised a brow. 'Nothing stronger?' He looked more closely at her. 'You're a bit pale. Are you all right?'

'I am now.'

George poured the lemonade. 'What do you mean?'

'My seat. It's so high up. I didn't realise . . .' If she was honest, she didn't think she could go back to that horrible seat. She took some greedy swallows of the sharp lemonade.

'There are some empty seats in the stalls and you'd get a much better view.' George flipped the lid up from the bar and came through to her side, saying over his shoulder, 'Josh, I'm just going to change Maxine's ticket. Back in a mo.'

The exchange took less than a minute.

'I'm not going to charge you extra as you're staff,' the man at the ticket counter said, 'even though this seat is nearly double the price.' He winked at her.

A bell rang.

'Off you go,' George said, smiling. 'I think you'll enjoy the show better now.'

'Thank you so much, George. I know I will.'

Her seat was only five rows from the front and only one empty seat away from the aisle. In fact, she'd take the aisle seat to stretch her long legs and put her coat on the other. Immediately she relaxed as she sat down. She could easily escape if she needed to. It was probably being pregnant that had made her feel so faint. The bell rang again, more urgently.

'Excuse me, I believe you're in my seat.'

She was conscious of a musky masculine smell. The faintest whiff of tobacco. Without apologising, she moved into the seat that should have been hers and stared ahead, glad she'd moved nearer to the stage. The figure sat down.

'Sorry about moving you, but it was probably easier than me trying to step over you,' he said in a low tone. 'You missed the first part. What a shame.'

She turned her head towards him. A man, maybe in his late twenties, with thick, dark brown hair, gave her a sympathetic grin and she noticed his eyes crinkle in the fading light.

'No, I saw it, but I was up there, at the very top.' She gestured to the balcony. 'I forgot how much I hate heights, so I changed my ticket.'

'Well, you were right up with the gods.' He shook his head, still smiling. 'Not the best seats with all those pillars in the way.'

She liked the sound of his voice. It was low and warm but had a ring of authority as if he was used to giving orders. He had a nice face. Not strictly good-looking. Craggy features. But a face that inspired confidence. He was dressed casually in dark trousers and a tweed jacket as though he'd only just made the decision to come to the theatre. She wondered idly if he was in the forces. He must be, she decided. He was the right age. She tried to picture him in the different uniforms, then shook herself. He was of no interest to her.

'Name's Crofton Wells.'

'Unusual,' she murmured.

'I'm used to it now,' he grinned easily. 'And you are . . .?'

She didn't want to tell him her name but it would seem awfully rude if she simply ignored him, and she couldn't think of an excuse not to. 'Maxine . . . Taylor,' she said reluctantly.

'Maxine,' he repeated, and it sounded special when he said it.

'Shhhhh!' someone near them admonished as the lights went out.

The orchestra struck up. She felt, rather than saw, Crofton Wells glance at her.

'Are you feeling all right now?'

'Much better, thank you,' she whispered. 'This is a wonderful seat.'

Then she blushed, grateful for the darkness, not wanting him to think she thought it wonderful because he was sitting next to her.

'I'm glad you changed your ticket,' he said softly.

A rare feeling of contentment stole round her heart and she settled back.

Disappointingly, Pearl didn't appear again until almost the end. Then, after a rousing finale, the curtain came down, then immediately rose again to wild applause. Maxine's hands stung with clapping. She stole a glance at Crofton Wells, who caught her looking and smiled. She smiled back, pleased to see he was clapping just as enthusiastically.

'Did you enjoy it?' he asked, looking at her as the lights came on.

'Very much. This half was even better, although my cousin wasn't in it as much as the first half.'

'Ah, you have a cousin in the show. Who is it?'

'Pearl Lovelace.'

'Lovelace?' Crofton Wells grinned broadly.

His eyes were a warm brown, reminding her of Johnny's, though Crofton's had amber flecks in them. She inwardly shook herself. She shouldn't be studying him so closely – he might get the wrong impression.

'Talking of unusual names . . .'

'It's her stage name,' Maxine said laughing. 'Although "Pearl" is real.'

She couldn't help thinking what a nice man he was. The sort of man she would have liked if she hadn't been such a fool. Her stomach turned over at the mess she was in. Who would want her now she was carrying another man's baby? She could tell Crofton Wells liked her – maybe even found her attractive – but he'd run a mile if he knew.

'Beautiful dress,' he said, an appreciative twinkle in his eyes as he stood in the aisle and helped her on with her coat. 'Seems a pity to cover it up.'

She felt the briefest touch of his fingers on her shoulders.

'Thank you.' She smiled as they joined the crowd towards the exit. In the foyer she held out her hand. 'It was nice to meet you,' she said.

'But this isn't the first time we've met,' he said, taking her hand, and the words were so unexpected she took a step back. 'I know it sounds like a bad pick-up line, but it's true. I saw you on a tram once in town. It was only through the window, but it *was* you, wasn't it?'

She gave a jolt of recognition. The man with the books

under his arm who'd tried so hard to catch her tram. She remembered the odd feeling of disappointment as he'd receded into the distance.

'I remember,' she said, her face glowing, savouring the warmth of his hand, 'though it must be a couple of years ago now. Fancy you recognising me.' She tried to ignore the way her heart was beating a little faster than normal. 'You looked very cross when the tram doors shut.' She sent him a mischievous smile.

He grinned back and she noticed how his face lit up. 'Yes, I was very annoyed. I'd promised a friend I'd go and see him in hospital and I didn't have much time.' Her hand was still in his and reluctantly she drew it away. 'I had a feeling you were heading for the Infirmary as well . . . were you?' She nodded. 'In fact, when I finally got there I kept a lookout in case I saw you again,' he chuckled.

Maxine's eyes widened in astonishment.

Before she could reply he said, 'Look, as we've ascertained we're not strangers, would you like to have a drink somewhere?'

His words took her by surprise. She would love to, more than anything. Pretend they were a couple. Like all the other couples around her. But it was impossible. She wasn't going to risk it. To give herself a few seconds to think, she pulled on her gloves.

'I-I can't,' she stuttered. 'I told Pearl I'd meet her afterwards.'

His face fell. Then brightened. 'You could introduce me to your cousin. I'm sure she'll be ready for a drink after all that singing.'

He'll be married, of course. Another one, full of lies.

But what would be the harm? One drink and then you need never see him again. One drink to pretend you're normal.

To have a husband like other women who are going to have a baby.

Except he wasn't her husband. And it wasn't his baby growing inside her.

'I'm sorry.' She turned abruptly and felt him staring after her.

Chapter Fifteen

He hesitated. Let her go or run after her?

Stopping to think had lost him precious moments. He ran after her, but she'd disappeared into the crowd. He turned his head this way and that. She was a tall woman. He should be able to spot her. But she could be anywhere. Maybe jumped into a taxi, or a bus had just come along, or she'd nipped into one of the restaurants. Wherever she'd vanished, she'd made it perfectly clear that she wasn't one bit interested and couldn't wait to escape. The first time he'd set eyes on her through the tram window, even though it was only the briefest of moments, he'd been more certain than anything in his life that this was a woman he wanted to know. And now he'd spent time in her company he was even more certain. But he'd lost her for the second time.

Maxine Taylor was the first woman he'd been immediately attracted to since the divorce. Her face, not pretty in the classical sense, yet there was something even more lovely about her. The look of sadness in her beautiful turquoise eyes. Her mouth was made to smile, but he didn't think she did much of that lately. She'd told him nothing about herself, only her name. And that might not be real. She'd even admitted her cousin's name 'Lovelace' wasn't.

Worst of all, as she was putting on her gloves, he'd noticed a shiny gold band on her wedding ring finger.

Just his luck.

He sighed. He'd feel better when he was back at the camp with a cigarette and a glass of whisky in his hand.

*   *   *

She'd planned to find Pearl after the show. Congratulate her. But all she could think of was to get out of the theatre as fast as possible. What a fool she'd been.

In bed that night her mind whirled. She realised it was hopeless, thinking she could have just one evening out amongst people and forget. Pretend she was the same as everyone. It would get her into trouble if she talked to strangers, joined in conversations . . . Someone was bound to discover her secret. Tell her parents. The realisation swept over her once again of how easy it would be for them to find out. Her mother would never forgive her.

She couldn't get comfortable. Pearl's little put-up bed was narrow and hard, though she hadn't noticed it until tonight.

Her head throbbed. Only Pearl. No one else must know. Without warning, the image of Crofton Wells flashed in front of her. She had to admit she would like to have got to know him a little more. Funny how they'd been aware of one another all that time ago through a tram window. His brown eyes, warm with concern. So different from the uncaring grey eyes of Edwin Blake. Tears poured down her face and she angrily brushed them away. She plumped up her pillow and turned over to block him out, but the pillow was still not enough to muffle her sobs.

She heard the front door open and slam shut. Footsteps

on the stairs. Pearl called out her name. Her door opened and Pearl's head poked round.

'Are you still awake, Max?'

'Yes. Come in. I was hoping you'd be back before I went to sleep.' Maxine sniffed and felt for her handkerchief underneath her pillow.

'What's wrong?' Pearl's smile faded as she looked at Maxine's wet cheeks. 'You've been crying. Was I really that bad?'

'No, of course not,' Maxine smiled weakly. 'You were marvellous. You lit up the stage and your voice carried right up to the second-floor balcony.'

Pearl's eyes gleamed with pleasure. 'I'm sorry you didn't have the best seat,' she said, sitting on the edge of Maxine's bed and unclipping her earrings. 'Oh, that's better. They were killing me.' She threw a glance at Maxine. 'Did you really enjoy it?'

'I *really* enjoyed it,' Maxine said truthfully, on the brink of telling her about Crofton Wells.

'Then what happened? Why were you crying when I came in just now?'

'Because . . . because . . .' How could she explain to Pearl?

'You had a nice evening and then everything came rushing back to you when you came into an empty flat. Is that it?'

Maxine nodded. Pearl had been unexpectedly intuitive and she felt closer to her cousin at that moment than she had since they were children.

'You know,' Pearl said, shifting herself closer and taking Maxine's hand, 'I do understand.' She said the words so quietly that Maxine had to strain to hear them. 'More than you might think,' Pearl added.

'What do you mean?'

'No one in the world knows this,' Pearl whispered. 'But I had an abortion two years ago.'

133

Maxine's hand flew to her mouth and her eyes went wide. 'Oh, Pearl. It's illegal. How did you—?'

'Somebody, a friend of a friend recommended. But it was a botched job and I thought I was going to die. It was terrible. The baby's father scarpered. He was a rotter. I knew it, but I'd had a bit too much to drink that night and ended up . . . well, I don't have to tell you the gory details.'

Maxine was numb with shock.

'Pearl, I had no idea—'

'No one did. That was the whole point. Can you imagine my dad? He'd have turned me out of the house. And Mam wouldn't have been able to stand up to him. That's why I had to get out – get a place of my own before I showed.'

'I wish I'd known. I would've helped you.' She looked at her cousin. 'Did you have anyone?'

'Yes, one of the girls at Woolies. I kept being sick and she guessed what was the matter. Luckily she had a couple of rooms in a boarding house and offered me a roof. She looked after me.' Pearl gave Maxine an unwavering look. 'I owe dear Jean my life.'

'I'm so lucky to have you,' Maxine said, her voice trembling with emotion.

'And I'm glad you're here and that I can help,' Pearl said simply. Then she grinned. 'But you'd better make the most of it. I'm off the day after tomorrow and won't see you for a whole month. So you'd better be good.'

Maxine swallowed. She hadn't realised Pearl would be on tour for such a long time with her new show. There was no point in telling Pearl about her meeting with Crofton Wells after all.

Maxine needed to make some plans. Make an appointment at one of the maternity hospitals to see a doctor to check that everything was all right, and to confirm she would be able to have the baby there. At least Johnny's wedding ring would save her from one of the Salvation Army homes for unmarried mothers, or worse, The House for Fallen Women. But she'd have to tell another lie at the hospital – that her husband had only recently died. Thank goodness her mother rarely went into town, her father never, and Liverpool was a large enough city to swallow her up.

But it was February and she was starting to show. She could wear loose clothing for a couple of months more, but in her last two months she'd have to remain a prisoner in Pearl's flat. And if Pearl was away during that time she wasn't sure how she'd be able to cope.

She also needed to change her ration book to a green one for pregnant women. It would allow her extra fruit and eggs and a free full pint of milk a day, and cod liver oil and orange juice. Her cousin, thinner these days, would appreciate some extra rations when she came home.

Maxine sent a letter to the Liverpool Maternity Hospital in Oxford Street and within three days she had a reply telling her to report to Dr Hall the following Friday for an examination.

'All is well,' he said after an interminable examination. 'We'd better put you down for 20th June.'

Maxine managed to hold her job until the middle of March when she couldn't disguise her pregnancy any longer. At first Betty had remarked that Maxine was putting on the pudding, as she called it, but when March turned to April Betty remarked, 'If I didn't know you, I'd say you were up the duff, my girl. But if you are, you're keeping the father very quiet.'

Maxine immediately flushed. 'It's all that Guinness you keep making me drink.'

Betty gave her a narrowed gaze. 'Hmm.'

She didn't say more, but Maxine knew she couldn't carry on. She was always terrified that someone she knew would come in and go straight to her parents. But even that terror diminished when she thought of another person who might stride in at any moment. A tall man with dark brown hair and twinkling eyes who would look aghast when he saw her protruding stomach.

It was time to give in her notice. Graham Grant didn't try to persuade her to stay and Maxine thought it likely he'd guessed her condition. Smarting with embarrassment, she muttered goodbye to Betty and George and escaped as quickly as she could to the relative privacy of Pearl's flat – her life for the next few months. Relying on Pearl who was away half the time. All her own stupid doing. But there was no going back.

The thought of having to lie to her parents made Maxine's cheeks flood red with shame. In the end she wrote to them saying she'd taken a few weeks' leave from the hospital because tending to patients with such terrible injuries day after day was making her a nervous wreck. She was staying with her cousin for a rest but planned to go back to nursing as soon as she felt strong enough.

She wasn't surprised to receive a letter of deep disappointment from her mother, but her father had scribbled a few lines on the end and told her not to worry, and to get better soon and come and see them. If only she could, but she was getting heavier by the week and only went out now to the small parade of shops nearby for essentials. She was desperately lonely, but she tried to keep busy by sewing nightdresses and blankets for the baby out of an old sheet and moth-eaten blanket of Pearl's as she listened to the latest news on the wireless. Trying to get food down was a torment. She had to eat sensibly for the baby's sake, even though she often thought she would choke. And when she couldn't stand life trapped in Pearl's rooms any longer, the baby would give a kick as though to tell her to buck up. That she'd get through it.

It was worse than she could possibly have imagined.

'Pull your knees up. Breathe slowly. Don't fight the pain. Push.'

A woman barked out orders, but Maxine kept getting muddled and forgot which instruction she should be following. If only Pearl hadn't been away again. She'd never felt so alone.

A whole night rolled by. Maxine tossed and turned, the mound of her stomach making it almost impossible to get comfortable. She heard screams. Some other poor woman close by – until she realised it was herself.

When she felt she could bear the pain no longer she was faintly aware of someone who took her hand.

'Doctor Williams here. You're doing very well. The head is almost through. Try to push hard next time the pain comes.'

The pain's never gone, she felt like yelling back.

But she did as she was told and pushed as though her life depended on it, and less than a minute later Edward Taylor came rushing into the world with his mother's last effort.

'It's a boy!'

She'd known all along the baby would be a boy. She'd never imagined him otherwise.

The sound of a smack. A thin wail. And then as though

the baby had gathered every shred of energy, came loud crying.

'He's got a good pair of lungs,' the midwife remarked as she wrapped him in a sheet. 'I'll take him to be cleaned up and then you can see him properly.' She disappeared with the baby before Maxine could beg her to stay.

But I wanted to see him now. *See who he looks like.* She folded her hands together as though in prayer. *Please don't let him look like Edwin.*

She broke down in sobs.

'What's the matter, young lady?' Dr Williams said. 'It's all over. You have a fine baby boy. We must let your husband know.'

'He's dead.'

'I'm sorry,' Dr Williams said, his eyes sympathetic. 'Happens all the time. Trouble is, there'll be thousands of poor little buggers – excuse my French – that their fathers will never set eyes on. But at least he'll be a comfort to you. Remind you of your husband.'

She managed to stop herself from retching by clawing at her handkerchief and practically stuffing it into her mouth. Under her eyelids she noticed Dr Williams regarding her with suspicion. He opened his mouth to say something but must have thought better of it, as he merely said, 'I'll be round to check on you tomorrow morning.'

'You'll be ready for a nice cuppa, love, I'm sure,' said a short dumpy woman in a pink overall wheeling a tea trolley towards her.

'I believe I am.' Maxine smiled weakly as the woman poured her a cup and popped two lumps of sugar in without asking before she handed it to her.

'Thank you, Mrs—'

'Call me Doreen, dear. Everyone does.' She gave Maxine a gummy grin. 'I'm here most days. The mums are always pleased to see me as they say I make a better cup of tea than the nurses.' She let out a peal of laughter which jarred Maxine's ears, the sound was so incongruous amongst all the groans of pain and screams of babies.

Doreen bustled away, still chuckling.

When the midwife returned with her baby swaddled in a shawl, Maxine noticed his hair was exactly the same dark auburn as his father's – and he looked the image of him. She swallowed the tears. There was no denying that he was the son of Mr Edwin Blake. The baby opened his mouth and howled.

'It's his feeding time,' the midwife said. 'Why don't you sit up a bit more and undo your nightdress.'

Fear shot through her. Being a nurse hadn't helped her for this moment. But she did what she was told, then opened the front of her nightdress. The midwife placed him on her right breast and immediately he began sucking.

Maxine looked down at her baby taking her milk, and without any warning a torrent of love flooded her whole being. She loved him. More than she'd ever loved anyone. And she would always love him, regardless of who his father was.

'Best thing for you now, Mrs Taylor, is sleep,' the midwife said briskly after some minutes, 'and in the morning the doctor will come and stitch you up.' She leaned over and picked up the baby, who wailed in protest. The next moment they'd both vanished.

Teddy, Maxine thought. *His name is Edward Taylor but he'll be known as Teddy.*

Despite the cries and screams and sobs of the other mothers, Maxine slipped into a deep sleep and was surprised when she woke up and it was morning.

'Breakfast, Mrs Taylor.' A young nurse put a tray on her bedside table and helped her into a sitting position. 'I've a nice cup of tea for you and some porridge. Afraid there's no sugar, but I managed to find a teaspoonful of treacle. And a piece of bread and marg.'

'Thank you, Nurse,' Maxine managed. 'You're very kind.'

'That's all right, Mrs Taylor. Just eat it up and then you can see your baby. I expect his father is away like most of the fathers. Such a shame they can't see—'

'His father is dead.'

'Oh! Oh, my goodness.' The young nurse's hand flew to her mouth. 'I'm so sorry. I should have checked. I—'

'There's no need to apologise, Nurse. You weren't to know.'

'I'll be off then.'

Maxine drank her lukewarm tea gratefully. This time there was no sugar in it but she was used to that. She picked up her spoon and dug it into a hard mass of porridge. She took a mouthful, then put the spoon down. She couldn't eat it. With a sigh, she folded the slice of bread and margarine in two and took a reluctant bite.

She could have changed her mind – even at such a late stage. She wasn't in a home for unmarried mothers and children where she'd be *forced* to give up her baby for adoption; she was a widow and it would have appeared perfectly natural for her to keep the baby. But how could she make sure Teddy had a happy life – give him the best education, be both father and mother, always there for him, when she had to work for a living?

After all the agonising she'd made her decision, for better or worse, and she just had to stick to it.

It was far worse when they gave her Teddy to hold. To feel his warmth – his baby milky smell – see his blue eyes, unfocused, but looking just as though they were watching her. Maxine was as certain as the fact that she was holding him that he knew she was his mother. He sucked her nipples greedily until they were so sore she could barely stand the sensation of her thin cotton nightdress when the fabric brushed against them. How he howled when the nurse would take him away from her. She was proud he had good lungs. He wasn't going to be a weakling – not like his father.

What kind of man would he become? she wondered. Would he make a difference in the world? She only hoped he would never see a war – or have to go to war. She thought of all the mothers who had lost their sons in the last one – the war to end all wars, they said – but it hadn't. She couldn't bear to lose Teddy. But she *was* going to lose him. Any week, any day, he'd be snatched from her. She shut her eyes tightly as the agony of having to let him go washed over her once more.

Every time she wavered she only had to re-read the closing lines in the letter the man from the agency who had found the couple to adopt Teddy wrote.

I know it will be very painful for you, Mrs Taylor, but rest assured it's the right thing to do for the child. If you love your child, as we know you do, you'll want the best for him. Even if it means giving him up for adoption. And we couldn't have found a more suitable couple. They lost their only child, a daughter, through illness and are heartbroken. We are sure Teddy will help them to heal, while they give him a loving home in return.

Maxine dropped her head in her hands and the tears ran between her fingers. She couldn't help but wonder who would help *her* heal.

No matter how she tried, Maxine couldn't sleep. Tomorrow was when she would hand her precious baby over to strangers – praying the adoption centre had thoroughly vetted the couple who were to take Teddy home. Tossing and turning,

141

she finally put the bedside lamp on and looked at the clock. Ten past three. She hadn't slept a wink. She'd sobbed her heart into her pillow the first hour, then tried to think if there was any possible way she could keep the baby. Her mother wouldn't turn her out like Pearl's mother, she didn't think, but she would tell Maxine she'd have to stay at home and look after him. She knew her parents couldn't afford an extra mouth – two, when Teddy was a few months older, but worse . . . her mother would say she couldn't face the neighbours knowing what shame her daughter had brought upon them. And she'd say how Maxine was placing an extra burden on her father with his bad heart. He needed his rest, she could hear her mother saying, and wouldn't be able to tolerate a screaming baby. It would kill him.

Did she really want Teddy to grow up in such an atmosphere of resentment? She tried to close her eyes again but the demons had taken over.

No one was with her at ten o'clock next morning when she signed the register under the watchful eye of Mrs Lidbetter at the adoption centre. The last sight Maxine had of her son was his tuft of red hair peeping out of his bonnet, his blue eyes looking up at her with such trust, as the woman gently took Teddy from her. Immediately, he screamed as Mrs Lidbetter hurried him through the double door.

It had taken every bit of Maxine's self-control not to go rushing after them, telling the woman she'd changed her mind. Blinded by tears, she stumbled out of that hateful building, her arms now empty, knowing she would never again hold that precious body close to hers.

142

Chapter Sixteen

She would have to find a job. Pearl had been wonderful these last two months when thankfully she was rehearsing a new show in Liverpool, so came home every night, but now it was September and Maxine couldn't encroach on her cousin's good nature any longer. Although she'd visited her parents a couple of times and her mother in particular had begged her to come home, Maxine wanted somewhere of her own. But with no money and no job it was going to be a problem.

'Have you got any idea what you want to do?' Pearl said when Maxine brought her in a cup of tea one morning. 'Oh, what a treat. Thanks, Max.' She stretched her hands out to take it.

Maxine sat on the dressing-table stool and sipped her tea. 'I need somewhere I can live in – kill two birds with one stone. The hospital was easy. I was living with Mum and Dad, and if I hadn't had them I'd have lived in, like I did at St Thomas'.' She swallowed, remembering Anna.

'And you don't want to go back to nursing?' Pearl asked.

'Not at the Infirmary. I couldn't bear that. I must go somewhere where no one knows me.'

'Hmm.' Pearl furrowed her brow. 'There are other hospitals in Liverpool, Max. Why don't you try them?'

'I want a change. Did I ever tell you I really wanted to teach children? It was Mum's idea I should do nursing. They were so set on it – well, Mum was – and because Mickey's such a wash-out, I tried to do what they thought was best for me. And ended up really liking it.'

'So get a job in a children's hospital,' Pearl said. 'You'd have the best of both worlds.'

'It's an idea, but there isn't one locally, I don't think. And I want to keep close to Mum and Dad. He's not been quite so good lately.' She drained her cup and rose to her feet.

'Something will turn up,' Pearl said. 'It always does.'

Pearl's idea was a good one but there would be babies to look after in a children's hospital. And Maxine knew she could never work on the babies' ward. It would break her heart.

Joining up seemed the only sensible option. They always needed nurses and were talking about conscripting women with no children. If she didn't soon volunteer, she wouldn't have any say in it. She could easily be sent abroad and with her father becoming weaker she didn't want to leave him.

She'd go to the library. They would have details of the different forces and how to join up. It would give her something definite to do. Teddy's little face swam before her and she blinked back the tears, wondering how there could be any more left inside her. Her only consolation was that she was sure the couple could give Teddy a better life than she would be able to give him. She'd done the right thing for her beloved boy and if she needed to remind herself a hundred times a day, then she would.

The young man behind the counter of Liverpool's library gave her a welcoming smile when she walked in. He chose a few leaflets.

'You'll have most of the answers to your questions here,' he said. 'It should help you make up your mind which branch you'd be interested in joining.'

Maxine folded them in two and tucked them into her handbag. She noticed a pile of local papers on one of the tables nearby and an elderly man was reading one of them. It would be good to catch up with the news as Pearl rarely listened to the wireless and wouldn't allow a newspaper in the house. She said it was all too depressing for words and she didn't need any more unhappiness in her life.

Maxine nodded to the man at the table and picked up a spare paper. She sat down and flicked through it. When she came to the Situations Vacant page, she skimmed down the column. Something caught her eye.

Children's nurse required for Dr Barnardo's home, nr Liverpool. Must be fully qualified. Children's experience desirable. Live-in and all found. Please apply to Matron, Bingham Hall, Bingham.

Bingham Hall was just a few miles away. For the first time since losing Teddy, Maxine felt a twinge of hope. She read the advertisement again and immediately the hope dwindled. *Must be fully qualified.* She'd had the date of her finals just before she'd found out she was pregnant. How could she explain to them why she hadn't sat her exams? It was no good. She threw the paper to one side, and the elderly man gave her a quick glance before he returned to his reading.

She still had the leaflets about the various forces to read and ponder over, but the job at Dr Barnardo's – that was the one she'd really like. She wouldn't have to worry about being sent abroad, so she could keep an eye on her parents,

145

particularly her father. But the best thing of all was that she wouldn't have to cope with any more badly injured soldiers and so many deaths, which brought her to tears every time another young man slipped away. She knew she was being a coward, but losing Teddy . . . She gulped. Losing Teddy was worse than anything she could ever have imagined, but if she could put her heart and soul into a job for needy children, it might somehow help to ease the unbearable band of pain which gripped her heart every moment of every day. And they'd be children at Dr Barnardo's. She wouldn't have to face any newborn babies.

But it was wishful thinking. However Maxine looked at it, there was no getting round the fact she didn't have the necessary requirements.

Maxine thanked the young man behind the library counter. She needed a cup of tea. She walked down the street and into the first café she came to. It was full of men smoking, but she ignored them and sat at a small table to one side where she ordered her tea and a bun and began to read the first leaflet about the WRNS. There was a photograph on the front of a pretty girl in her smart uniform, and a description of the interesting life you could have.

But all the time Maxine read, her mind wasn't properly taking it in. If only the job at Dr Barnardo's hadn't stated so firmly that the nurse must be fully qualified. But suppose no one else applied for the job. She knew nurses were short because of the war. The matron might make an exception if she liked her. The more she thought about it, the more she knew she would do anything in her power to get this job.

She didn't want to write. She'd have preferred to speak to the matron on the telephone but there was no number. She could find it out, but it was probably a deliberate omission because the matron wanted to get a feel of the applicants before she began the interviews.

But what if she beat the other applicants? What if she presented herself in person at Bingham Hall before the interviews were even arranged? Matron could only turn her away. She'd be no worse off.

She set her chin determinedly.

Maxine alighted from the bus and made her way down the lane where the conductor had pointed and then left up a long, steep drive. Her heart was beating rapidly, but this time it wasn't so much from nerves as anticipation. She allowed herself a smile. She was finally doing something. Taking her life into her own hands. Even if she wasn't offered the job, she was pleased she'd made the decision to come here. If it wasn't to be this one, there was likely to be another orphanage in the area.

Just as Bingham Hall came into view, the sun came out. The house reminded her of a castle with its crenellated exterior. Tall chimneys sliced through puffed-up white clouds in a clear blue sky, glinting on the stained-glass windows of a turret-shaped building attached to the left-hand side. She wondered who cleaned the hundreds of leaded light windows, but the whole effect was charming and Maxine instantly knew this was the place where she wanted to work. And call home.

With a firm hand she grasped the bell cord by the huge oak door at the entrance and pulled. She stepped back and waited. A housemaid opened the door.

'Yes, Miss?'

'May I come in? I would like a few words with Matron.'

'Is Miss Lavender expecting you, Miss?'

'Not exactly.' Maxine managed to step round her and into the massive baronial hall.

147

Before Maxine had a chance to take in the surroundings, the maid said, 'May I ask who's calling, Miss?'

'Mrs Taylor.'

'May I tell Matron what it's about, please, Mrs Taylor?'

Maxine hesitated. She didn't want to discuss the vacancy with anyone but the matron.

'Who is it, Beth?' A stocky young girl dressed in a grubby pale blue overall appeared from one of the doorways.

'The lady's come to see Matron.'

'Do you have an appointment?' the stocky girl asked in a belligerent tone.

'No, but—'

'Then you can't,' the girl said, a gleam of power in her gaze. 'Matron never sees anyone without an appointment. It's the rule. So you can show the lady out, Beth.'

Somewhere near, there was the squeak of a door opening.

'Just a moment.' Maxine's voice was firm. 'I would like to have the chance to speak to Matron for a few minutes.'

'What about?'

This girl needed some training in manners, Maxine thought, a prickle of annoyance threatening. She forced her voice to be calm.

'I'm afraid it's personal. If you'll just—'

'Hilda!' A young woman appeared in the hall, tendrils of fair hair showing beneath her cap. With hurried steps she approached the little group by the front door.

The woman looked to be only about the same age as herself, Maxine thought. But although she was several inches shorter, she had a quiet voice of authority. Maxine hoped it might be one of the teachers. Whoever she was, it brought the stocky girl instantly to attention.

'Oh, Matron, I—'

'That will be all, Hilda. You may carry on.' She glanced

148

at the maid. 'And you, too, Beth, thank you both.' She looked at Maxine with a steady gaze. 'I believe you've come to see me. Would you like to step into my office?'

What a stroke of luck! This sweet-faced young woman, hardly more than a girl, was actually the matron. Maxine briefly wondered how she had been given such a responsible position, yet she seemed to be completely in control.

Once inside her office, the matron gestured towards one of the visitor's chairs, and Maxine gratefully sat down. 'First, may I ask your name and address?' She opened a drawer and took out a notepad.

'Maxine Taylor. I'm staying with my cousin at the moment in town.' She gave Pearl's address.

The young woman made a note and looked up, her eyes alert. 'I have a feeling you're here about the position of children's nurse.'

'Yes, I am.' Maxine leaned forward eagerly. 'I saw it earlier on today in the local paper, and to tell you the truth, I thought it was the answer to my prayers.' She hesitated. 'I'm sorry to barge in without an appointment but I was so sure I'd love this job . . . if you liked me, that is.'

'You might be the answer to *our* prayers.' The young woman smiled, which made her green eyes shine. 'But let me introduce myself. I'm June Lavender – well, for a little while longer anyway.' She flushed slightly and held out her left hand, where a beautiful emerald sparkled.

'Congratulations,' Maxine said warmly, pushing away the image of her own emerald engagement ring and a stab of guilt that she'd taken it off. 'It matches your eyes.' Maxine made herself return June Lavender's smile.

'Thank you.' Miss Lavender gazed at the ring for some seconds as if she couldn't believe it belonged on her finger. She looked up. 'Before we talk, may I offer you some tea?'

'That would be lovely, thank you.'

June Lavender told her a little of the background of Bingham Hall. She explained there were thirty-six children, only eight of them girls, ranging from four to fourteen.

'We used to have forty-one,' the young matron explained, 'but the evacuees, all but one, have gone home – probably too early, in my view, but it must have been hard for the parents.' She looked at Maxine. 'You can cope with the usual childhood diseases.' She made it sound a statement rather than a question.

'Oh, yes,' Maxine said. 'At the Infirmary and St Thomas' we had the full range – diphtheria, measles, mumps, polio—'

'So you can recognise the various symptoms?'

Maxine nodded. 'Yes. I'm good at spotting things, even if the patient hasn't come to me with any early illness.'

June filled her in with a few more details about the teachers and what classes they taught until the same maid, Beth, knocked and came in with a tray of tea. Miss Lavender poured out two cups and handed one to Maxine.

'Now tell me a bit about yourself, Miss Taylor.'

'It's actually "Mrs". I'm a widow.' After all this time it still felt odd saying the word.

'I'm so sorry.' June Lavender gave her a sympathetic glance.

Maxine explained how she'd trained at the Royal Infirmary in Liverpool and then transferred to St Thomas' in London after her husband had been killed.

June Lavender nodded. 'Work is always the best cure in these dreadful times,' she commented, scribbling some notes. She caught Maxine's eye. 'Have you any children?'

Maxine drew in a jagged breath. She should have expected it but somehow the question took her by surprise.

'We weren't married long enough. He was killed very soon

after we were . . .' She broke off, sickened. Teddy. She was pretending he didn't exist. Her darling baby. She felt a light touch on her arm.

'I'm so sorry,' Miss Lavender repeated. 'This must be very painful for you, but I hope you understand I have to ask these questions.'

'Yes, of course.' Maxine hunted for her handkerchief and blew her nose.

'Would you like a glass of water?'

'No, thank you. The tea is just right.' She took a deep swallow and gave an apologetic smile.

'Shall I carry on?'

Maxine nodded.

'Have you worked specifically with children?'

'In my last year of training I was often sent to the children's ward, which I loved. I always wanted to be a teacher, but my mother's dream was that I should become a nurse. Then the war started and it was terrible day after day nursing young men who were smashed to pieces, then seeing them patched up and sent off to the front again. I did it as long as I could, but it affects you after a while.' She caught June Lavender's eye and the young woman nodded. 'I needed a change,' Maxine went on. 'And if I'm working with children . . . well, that's the best of both worlds.'

She knew she was gabbling, but she wanted this job badly.

June Lavender bent her head to jot down a few more notes, then looked up and smiled. 'You're just the kind of person we're looking for,' she said, her smile broadening. 'I feel confident you can do the job. So all we need now is your Nursing Certificate, and then I can put you forward as a strong recommendation to Mr Clarke . . . he's at Dr Barnardo's headquarters. He'll have a chat with you, but he usually goes on my judgement, so I don't think there'll be any difficulty.'

151

Maxine forced herself not to show any anxiety. She'd practically been offered a job that sounded perfect, and now it would be snatched away from her because she hadn't done her finals. Because she'd been such a fool. The irony was that in the last month at St Thomas' the third-year nurses had been told there was little new to learn; it would all be just revision. Making sure she knew all she'd be tested on. And if previous tests and exams were anything to go by at both hospitals, she'd have passed with flying colours. When she next looked across the desk, she saw June Lavender's eyes watching her intently.

The young matron's smile faded. 'Is anything wrong?' Without pausing, she said, 'Oh, the salary. I haven't mentioned it yet.'

'No, it's nothing to do with the salary.' Maxine's voice was quiet. 'I'm sure it's fair, whatever it is.' She inhaled a deep breath. 'I hope you won't think I'm here under false pretences, Miss Lavender, but I haven't taken my finals. I completed almost the full term and had the date of the exams, but my father wasn't well and I was needed at home.'

Such a very small lie. Please, Miss Lavender, bend the rules this once.

There was a silence. Grass-green eyes looked steadily back.

Maxine's hands dug into the sides of the chair. She willed the matron to say something.

'The rules for hiring staff at Dr Barnardo's are strict,' June Lavender finally said. 'And nurses more than anyone, for obvious reasons.'

Maxine opened her mouth to say she did understand, but June Lavender gently put her finger in the air.

'But I like you. I think we'd get along well and I think

you'd fit in with the rest of the staff. I can't promise anything, but leave this to me to speak to Mr Clarke. I can only promise I will do my best.'

Maxine sprang to her feet and extended her hand. 'You've been more than kind, Miss Lavender . . . Matron. I'm very grateful.'

'Are you on the telephone?'

'I'm afraid my cousin isn't,' Maxine said.

'Then I'll write to you.'

Maxine tried to remain positive but in truth she could have wept with disappointment. If she'd had her certificate she was sure June Lavender would have hired her on the spot. There seemed to have been an immediate empathy. She didn't doubt the young matron would keep to her promise and do her best to convince Mr Clarke, but Maxine knew how strict hospitals were about rules and an orphanage would likely run along the same lines.

She could only wait . . . and hope.

Chapter Seventeen

Five interminable days later, Maxine picked up a narrow white envelope with her name on it from the small table in the entrance lobby of Pearl's flat.

'Is that you, Max?' Pearl's voice floated down the two flights of stairs. Her cousin stood at her door in a film-star negligee.

'Yes, I'm just collecting the post.'

'Anything for me?'

Maxine ran up the stairs and joined her. 'It's actually for me.' Pearl knew about the interview at Bingham Hall, and Maxine tried her best to hide the nerves in her voice.

'Don't open it until I get back,' Pearl called as she scurried to the kitchen to make the tea.'

She couldn't wait that long. With Pearl chattering as she rattled the cups and saucers and filled the kettle, Maxine sat at the small breakfast table and used a knife to slit the envelope.

12th September 1942
Dear Mrs Taylor,

I understand you have had a conversation with Miss Lavender, the matron at Bingham Hall, recently, about the position of children's nurse. Matron has strongly

recommended you to me although you do not yet possess
a Nursing Certificate.

Nurses are in short supply these days with the war, so
I am prepared to offer you the job if you will endeavour
to take your finals before spring of next year, 1943.

If you are able to accept this, Matron would like to see
you again to discuss the terms and show you your room
etc. so you have all the facts before making your decision.
If you accept, then I would like to meet you at Bingham
Hall in the near future, but it would merely be an informal
chat.

There is no need to reply to me as your next step
is to contact Miss Lavender as soon as possible. She will
then advise me of your decision.
Yours truly,
A J Clarke

'Anything exciting, Max?' Pearl said over her shoulder as
she poured the boiling water over the tea leaves in the
warmed teapot.

'It's from Mr Clarke at Dr Barnardo's.' Maxine skimmed
the letter again in case she'd misunderstood it. No, it was
definitely an offer. Her face broke into a smile that nearly
split her face in two. She'd done it.

'Well?' Pearl brought the tray over to the table and sat
down.

Maxine read the letter out loud, laughing at her cousin's
shout of delight.

'Oh, that's wonderful, Max.' Pearl jumped up and hugged
her.

'Yes, but it won't be permanent unless I can take my finals,
and because I haven't been in nursing for several months,
it could be tricky.'

'One day at a time, I always say.' Pearl poured the tea. 'You'll find a way. As for now, have your breakfast and go straight to the phone box and ring Miss June Lavender and say, "Yes, please". From what you've told me, I think working at Dr Barnardo's will restore you.'

A week to the day of her first meeting with June Lavender, Maxine was ushered into the Great Hall, but this time she was carrying her suitcase.

'Let me take that for you, Miss.' A sprightly man of about fifty dressed in a shirt and tie and braces tucked into work-worn trousers stretched out his hand for Maxine's case. 'I believe you're on the third floor.' He gave her a glance. 'I'm Charlie, by the way. Maintenance man extraordinaire.' He grinned.

Maxine hadn't had a chance to see her room as Miss Lavender had said on the telephone that it wouldn't be necessary for her to come for another interview. They were already short-staffed and two more children were due to arrive in the next few days, which would keep everyone busy. She would go over the terms with Maxine as soon as she was settled in.

Maxine followed Charlie with her case. He knocked on the door. A little odd, she thought, but as soon as she saw the twin beds and someone's belongings scattered on the bed by the window she understood. She was to share with one of the teachers or maybe the other nurse. Disappointed, though not surprised, she turned to Charlie, who set her case on the floor. 'Thank you very much.'

'I hope you'll be happy here, Miss.' He nodded and disappeared.

Maxine sat down on the edge of the bed. Happy? When was the last time she felt happy? For an instant, Crofton

Wells flashed in front of her. His craggy features, the warm smile, his shiny brown hair. Brown eyes that crinkled when he smiled. No sooner had his face appeared to her than it vanished. She was on her own. Her eyes stung. No, she'd never be happy again all the time she had no idea where little Teddy was. One day she'd find out about her baby. Make sure he was safe and well and happy. But for the moment she was content . . . and that was enough.

It had taken all of ten minutes to unpack her things and make her way downstairs. She could hear the sounds of children changing classrooms. Bells clanged and doors opened and banged shut.

'Stop that shouting, Harvey,' someone called.

'It weren't me, Miss,' came an instant reply.

'Don't answer back, please. And it's "wasn't", not "weren't".'

The sound of giggling.

'Everyone who is in my painting class please go to the art room.' A tall, large-built woman, her light-brown hair rolled back at each side of a plain face, appeared at one of the doorways. She glanced over at Maxine. 'Oh, hello. Are you the new nurse?'

Maxine nodded. 'Yes. Maxine Taylor.'

The woman extended a plump hand and smiled. 'Barbara Steen – call me Barbara – and very pleased to meet you. We certainly need you with only Kathleen now.'

'She's the other nurse, isn't she?'

'Yes, and although she's extremely knowledgeable she's really an assistant nurse. So that's why it's so important to have *you* with us.'

Maxine made her mouth smile but inwardly she quaked. Another nurse who wasn't qualified. And working so closely

157

with only a few adults was going to be difficult. She needed to keep her distance. Oh, she'd be friendly enough, but she mustn't get close to anyone, however nice they seemed. If they found out she, too, wasn't fully qualified they'd start probing deeper. And that would be dangerous.

June Lavender appeared from her office and smiled at Maxine, extending her hand. 'A warm welcome to Bingham Hall,' she said. 'I'm sure you'll soon settle in. And by the way, when the teachers and nurses are together, we go by our Christian names. It's only in front of the children that we're formal. So do call me June.'

'Thank you . . . June.'

'I'll introduce you to Cook. If you get on the right side of her everything else falls into place.' She chuckled at Maxine's worried look. 'I'm only teasing. Bertie is lovely.'

Bertie's kitchen was large and cluttered with pots and pans and bowls. A huge dresser held masses of plain white china plates, cups and saucers stacked up in piles on the main surface. A kitchen maid was at an enormous enamel sink, tackling a huge pile of washing-up.

'Will you be wanting a cup of tea, hen?' Bertie asked, wiping her hands down her apron before putting a hand out to shake Maxine's.

'I don't think I'd better.' Maxine cast an anxious glance at June Lavender. 'I've not come far and I think Matron is ready to show me the ropes.'

'By all means have a cup of tea,' June told her. 'Get to know Bertie. And any questions you might have, ask Bertie if I'm not around. She normally knows the answer, don't you, Bertie?' She turned her head to the cook.

'I try,' Bertie said, giving a modest sniff. 'Now for that tea.' She glanced at June. 'Will you have a cuppa, too, Matron?'

'I can't stop,' June said. 'One of the two new children is

arriving later this morning and I want to make sure everything's ready and I'm here to settle him in.'

'What's his name?' Bertie asked, filling the kettle and putting it on the stove.

'Peter Best.' June lowered her voice as though someone might be eavesdropping, 'He's actually half German.'

'Well, he's not the first one we've had.' Bertie set out the cups and saucers and poured milk into a large jug, all the while explaining to Maxine, 'We had a boy called Joachim last year and his parents sent him here for safety. Turned out to be a child genius in music, didn't he, June?'

June smiled. 'He could certainly play the piano and the violin beautifully. Luckily we had a wonderful music teacher called David who spotted his talent and Joachim is now in London studying classical music, but sad to say we've lost David . . . and Iris, our nurse who you're replacing. David and Iris fell in love,' June smiled, 'and they've moved to London to be nearer Joachim so he doesn't feel so alone. They've taken him under their wing.'

'What a wonderful story,' Maxine said.

'Not so wonderful about Joachim's sister and parents,' June said somberly. 'They were all sent to one of those dreadful camps. We don't know what happened to them but we have our suspicions. The trouble is, children can be very cruel, so they don't need to know about Peter's German side. We're told Peter speaks excellent English.' June looked at Maxine, her smile back. 'Come and see me in the office when you've had your tea and I'll show you the ward and introduce you to Kathleen, our other nurse.'

June chatted about some of the children as she led Maxine down a short flight of stairs to a lower floor later that morning.

159

'We're not at basement level,' she said, 'but at least any child who's sick or had an accident is safe and can get well in peace. And, of course, if there was an outbreak of any diseases, the patients are more contained away from the others.'

'It makes sense,' Maxine murmured.

June tapped lightly on the door which said 'Hospital Ward' and immediately it opened. A young woman, her curves firmly held in by her crisp nurse's uniform, with white cap partly covering her bright red curls, broke into a smile when she saw the two women.

'Oh, thank goodness you've arrived. You must be Nurse Taylor.'

'Please call me Maxine.'

'And I'm Kathleen. Nurse Manners to the kids. Pleased to meet you.' She pumped Maxine's hand up and down. 'It's been very difficult since Iris left. We've had two nurses from the agency but neither of them worked out, did they, June?'

June shook her head. 'It's difficult to get the right person.' She turned to Maxine with a warm smile. 'But I believe it's third time lucky.'

'And you'll be sharing my room,' Kathleen said, smiling. 'Hope you didn't find it too untidy. I did make an effort and we shouldn't get in each other's way too much as we'll be on different shifts.'

'Everything was fine.' Maxine returned the smile, grateful Kathleen seemed so nice.

'Come on in.' Kathleen stepped aside to allow the two women in.

The familiar smell of disinfectant filled Maxine's nostrils, reminding her of St Thomas' – of Edwin. She brushed the thought away.

'How's Bobby getting along?' June raised an enquiring eyebrow.

'Come and say hello to him. He's opted for a bed at the far end.'

Maxine noticed there were only three children occupying the twelve beds as they made their way towards Bobby.

June stopped by a boy who was sitting up in bed reading a comic.

'Jack, this is Nurse Taylor,' June said. 'She's here to help you get better.'

'I liked the other nurse,' he said with a determined look in his dark eyes.

'She was only here to fill in until Nurse Taylor came,' June said, throwing Maxine an apologetic look, 'and we must make her welcome. Can you do that?'

Jack was silent, his eyes defiant.

'What's your full name, Jack?' Maxine smiled at the boy.

'Jack Ronald Barrow, Miss.' The boy threw a swift look in Kathleen's direction. 'Nurse says I can go back to classes tomorrow.'

'That's marvellous,' Maxine said. 'We'll soon see you upstairs then.' Turning to Kathleen, she asked under her breath. 'What's the matter with him?'

'He gets sick headaches a lot,' she replied. 'The doctor's checked him and can't find much wrong. So we've had him in the ward for a couple of days . . . keeping an eye on him.' She looked at Maxine. 'I'm afraid all the children have problems of one kind or another – very often it's a mental thing and you can see why when you hear their stories, poor little devils.'

They walked past a child who was curled up in her bed fast asleep.

'That's Pamela,' Kathleen said under her breath. 'She cut

161

her hand on a piece of glass in the garden – turned out to be a stray piece from when the greenhouse got hit last year by Jerry.'

Maxine sent a sympathetic look to the child but Pamela didn't stir.

Bobby was already sitting up in bed watching them approach.

'How are you today, Bobby?' June asked.

'A bit better,' he croaked.

'Tonsillitis,' Kathleen said. 'You're doing really well, Bobby. Our new nurse and I will soon have you out of here.'

'Are you going to stay?' Bobby asked.

'I hope so, Bobby,' Maxine said fervently. 'If you and the other children will have me.'

Bobby gave a mischievous grin. 'I expect we will, won't we, Matron?' He gave a terrible wink.

'We certainly will, Bobby,' June laughed. 'And now you have two nurses to see that you're back in class in double-quick time.' She glanced at her watch. 'Well, I'll leave you both to it,' she said. 'Peter Best will be here any minute.'

When Kathleen had given Maxine the files to read on the children who had either attended the clinic, or stayed on the ward in the past month, and a few who had seemingly permanent problems, and shown her the storeroom where the various nursing equipment was kept, she announced it was time for a coffee.

'We can make a quick cuppa in what's laughingly known as the kitchen,' she told Maxine, 'but it's only a cupboard . . . Come and see.' She opened a door off the storeroom to reveal a single cupboard above and, below, a small sink flanked by a piece of wooden worktop no more than eighteen inches across, and an electric socket. 'We're very proud of our new kettle,' Kathleen said, brandishing a shiny copper kettle with a protrusion at the bottom. She plugged it into the socket and pressed down the button to demonstrate how it worked.

'I must say, I've never seen one before,' Maxine said, impressed as the kettle took no time at all to boil. 'The Royal Infirmary and St Thomas' in London never had anything this sophisticated.'

Kathleen grinned. 'So you worked in London as well as Liverpool,' she said. 'How did you like it? I bet it was a dangerous place to be, with all the bombing.'

'Liverpool's had its own Blitz,' Maxine said. 'It's taken the worst beating next to London, so it felt about the same.'

'I'd love to go to London,' Kathleen said wistfully. 'Maybe not until the war is over, but when we have time, I want to hear all about it.' She measured a teaspoon from the bottle of Camp coffee into each cup and poured the boiling water.

London was the last thing Maxine wanted to talk about. With a pang, she remembered dear Anna and was silent.

Kathleen gave her a rueful grin. 'Hark at me going on.' She handed Maxine a cup. 'We can't both leave at the same time, so I suggest when you've finished your coffee you go on upstairs to the dining room and meet some of the others. One of them will show you where everything is.'

'Can I bring you anything?' Maxine said, after she'd drained her cup.

'No, no. I want to have a flick through *The Lady* while the children are quiet for once. And don't rush back. June will no doubt need you if the new boy's arrived. I'll expect you when I see you.'

Maxine murmured her thanks and shot up the stairs before Kathleen pumped her any further about her past.

Upstairs was chaos. Children were rushing to the tables

for their favourite seats and devouring glasses of milk and their ration of two biscuits each. Two little girls, twins, by the look of them, were holding hands and giggling, but another child was crying her eyes out. Three women of various ages – Maxine presumed they were teachers – scurried around, trying to maintain some control, and barely giving her more than a glance. So much for being looked after, Maxine thought, smiling to herself. But that was all right with her. She found herself pulled into the queue.

One little boy with pale skin and ears which stood out like jug handles looked round at her with curious eyes.

'Are you new, Miss?'

'That's enough, Eric.' One of the women nearby smiled at Maxine. 'I'm sure we'll all be introduced to the new lady in good time.'

The little boy shrugged and shuffled forward.

A strangled sob came from behind her in the queue. Maxine turned to see the same sulky girl, Hilda, who'd tried to send her away on her last visit, grasping a young lad's hand. He was struggling to pull away and she could see the girl's grip tighten. The child looked to be eight or nine, with lank brown hair badly in need of a haircut and the same expression of despair in his startling blue eyes that Maxine had seen over and over again in the wounded soldiers who were brought into St Thomas' on a daily basis. It was a bad enough expression on those poor boys, let alone a child. Her heart went out to the lad.

'You're not going anywhere, you little pest,' Hilda said to him in a sharp tone.

'Thank you, Hilda. I'll take him now.' The matron's tone was firm as she took him by the hand.

The girl's a bully, Maxine thought. *I wonder why June keeps her on.*

'This is Peter Best,' June told her. 'He's just arrived.' She looked down at the boy. 'Peter, this lady is the new nurse. You may call her Nurse Taylor. She started work here at Bingham Hall this morning, so she doesn't know anyone – the same as you. I'm hoping you'll be able to help one another.'

Peter's expression was blank. He gave a violent sneeze, followed by two more. Maxine saw his nose drip.

'Have you a handkerchief, Peter?' she said, feeling in her apron pocket.

The boy shook his head.

'Here.' Maxine handed him a clean white handkerchief. 'Use this.'

He snatched it and blew his nose, then offered it back to her.

'Keep it until the end of the day and then we'll get it washed,' Maxine said, an amused smile hovering over her lips.

'Can I leave you with him?' June asked in a low tone. 'I had no option but to ask Hilda to show him the dining room and help him.'

'Of course.' Maxine put her hand on the boy's arm but he shrugged it off. 'Keep close to me and we'll find out what we have to do together. I'm as much in the dark as you.'

Maxine made sure Peter sat next to her and that he had his ration of milk and biscuits.

'You're new,' piped a little golden-haired girl sitting on the other side of him. 'What's your name?'

Peter ignored her and gulped his milk in one go. He set his empty glass down and Maxine noticed his hands shake and his bottom lip tremble. The poor child was terrified. She needed to get him out of the noisy dining room and into one of the empty classrooms. Talk to him quietly. He'd obviously gone through a difficult time before he arrived here. She wondered if Peter's story was similar to that other little boy June and Bertie had spoken about.

'Peter, if you've finished, why don't you come with me?' Maxine suggested. 'I don't know the building very well yet, but I can show you some of the rooms I've discovered and where you need to be after the break.'

Immediately Peter sprang to his feet and darted towards the door.

Maxine rushed after him into the Great Hall. 'Peter.'

He turned. His face was unnaturally flushed. He sneezed again.

Maxine bent down to him. 'That sounds like a nasty cold.'

She tried to put her hand on his forehead but he twisted away from her, pulling her handkerchief out of his grey shorts.

'I think we'll get you into the ward downstairs and tuck you up with a hot-water bottle. I'm sure it's only a cold, but we don't want it to spread to the other children.'

She could hear him sniffing as his shoes clattered on the steps behind her.

All this time Maxine noticed Peter hadn't uttered one word. Well, it wasn't surprising what with the way that girl Hilda had treated him.

As soon as the two of them appeared in the ward, Kathleen came over. 'Have we another patient?' she asked, glancing at Peter.

'Yes. He's our new boy, Peter Best,' Maxine said. 'He has a cold, so I'm going to take his temperature.'

'He can have that bed,' Kathleen pointed to one in the centre of the room. 'It's far enough away for no one else to catch it.' She put her hand out to Peter. 'Let's get you undressed and into some pyjamas.'

When Peter was tucked into bed, Maxine held out her thermometer.

'Can you put your tongue out for me?'

Peter did what he was told and she slipped the thermometer underneath. He lay perfectly still, his eyes locked on to the ceiling.

After half a minute Maxine removed it and held the glass tube up to the light.

'As I thought,' she said. 'A little above normal but nothing to worry about. The sooner you rest and keep warm, the sooner you'll be up. I'll bring you your dinner later.'

There was no response.

She smiled at him. 'Would you like some orangeade?'

He shook his head, his mouth firmly shut tight.

'I'm not taking any notice,' she told him. 'You need to keep drinking when you have a cold.'

His blue eyes fixed on hers, giving her the feeling he noticed everything.

'It's all new to you, as it is with me,' Maxine touched his arm, 'so I'm hoping we can help one another, as Matron said. Do you think we might?'

The boy looked at her without blinking. His eyes and nose were both running and she found him another handkerchief.

'You'll be safe here,' Maxine said. 'I promise.' She gestured for Kathleen to go into their little back room, and followed. 'Kathleen, can I leave you with him for the time being? I'd like to try and get my bearings and meet the teachers.'

'Of course.'

Maxine looked towards Peter's bed. 'I'm a bit concerned that he hasn't said a word since he arrived. Nothing at all.'

'Don't worry,' Kathleen said. 'I should think he's probably just worn out.'

Thank goodness Kathleen was an understanding and sympathetic nurse, Maxine thought. But Hilda . . . she was another matter.

Chapter Eighteen

'Would the teachers and Nurse Taylor please come to my office as soon as you've eaten,' June announced after Grace that evening at dinner.

Maxine intended having a private word with June about Peter, but maybe it was a good thing to be introduced to the teachers first.

Charlie brought in some extra chairs and somehow they all squashed inside Matron's modest office.

'I'd like to introduce you to our new member of staff, Nurse Maxine Taylor,' June said, smiling round at everyone. 'We've had some difficulties getting the right person, but I think Maxine is going to fit in really well with us, so please make her welcome.' Her eyes fell on Maxine. 'I'm sure you'll be happy here with us.'

'Thank you, Matron, I'm sure I will,' Maxine said.

'Barbara Steen. We've already met,' the art teacher said, smiling broadly.

'Athena Graham – English and Mathematics.' A young woman, her strawberry-blonde hair in a smooth shining Victory Roll, grasped Maxine's hand and pumped it up and down. 'Very pleased to meet you.'

'And this is Judith Wright, our temporary history teacher, though we're trying to persuade her to stay on.' June nodded to a stocky middle-aged lady with long tweed skirt and cropped non-descript brown hair with a side parting, firmly pulled back by a tortoiseshell hair slide.

Judith nodded, but there was no welcoming smile like the others. 'How do you do?' she said.

June came from behind her desk and stood with her back against it. 'I'll leave it to you, Maxine, to tell Kathleen about this meeting, so let me start. I want to put you in the picture about Peter Best. He has a German father and an English mother.'

Maxine heard an intake of breath from Judith Wright.

'But the father is Jewish, presumably,' the history teacher said, 'and they must have changed their name to "Best" to sound English.'

Maxine gave her a sharp look. There was something in Judith's tone that rankled.

'I imagine that's the case,' June said. 'We don't know much about him except that the boy came here from Germany just before the war with his mother, but she became ill and died, so he was sent to his grandmother's. Then one day this summer he came home from school to find the house a pile of rubble, poor little chap. His grandmother was inside at the time. She was killed instantly. He's been with foster parents since then, but they can't keep him any longer, so Dr Barnardo's agreed to take him in.'

'Peter doesn't look Jewish.' Judith's eyes swept round the room as though looking for affirmation from the others. 'He's got blue eyes, for one thing.'

'I wouldn't really know about that,' June said, giving Judith a steady look, 'but I expect he takes after his mother.' She paused. 'As you all know, Dr Barnardo's creed is to accept every child of every religion and race and colour – and treat them equally.'

170

Maxine noticed Judith purse her lips.

'Do we know if the father is alive?' Barbara asked.

'We haven't any precise details about him. He was probably sent to the concentration camp, the same way Joachim's family went,' June said soberly.

Maxine's blood ran cold at the thought.

'Look, I don't want to make a big thing of Peter coming from Germany,' June went on. Maxine noticed her eyes linger on Judith Wright a fraction longer than the others. 'Because we don't want the boy to go through the same bullying that Joachim went through. The children quickly realised he was foreign because he didn't speak perfect English, but Peter does, apparently, though we haven't heard anything from him yet.'

'I've tried to get him to talk,' Maxine said. 'But he just shakes his head. It's as though he can't trust himself to say anything, so he keeps quiet. Poor little lad. I'm glad we know something about his background so we know how to help him.'

'I agree,' June said, glancing at her. 'The boy is still in shock, so if it's all right with you, Maxine, I'm putting you in charge of him. You're a nurse so you'll know best how to handle him, and I'm hoping he'll learn to trust you.' She gave a slight smile. 'However, I don't think it will be an easy task.'

'I'll be very happy to look after him,' Maxine said quickly. 'He's in the ward at the moment with what appears to be a heavy cold. Kathleen got him ready for bed and I'll go and see him after the meeting. We need to find something he can be part of when he gets better, so he can make friends with some of the other boys. Maybe a singing afternoon that they can all join in.'

'That's an excellent idea,' Barbara said. 'We used to do that sort of thing often before the Fierce One came.'

171

'So we will resume them,' June smiled, turning to Maxine. 'The Fierce One was the matron when I first came here.' She looked round at the small group. 'What a shame we've lost David. He would have helped the children with the songs and played the piano.'

'I could probably manage to accompany some simple songs,' Athena said.

'The job's yours.' June beamed. 'Maxine, would you please tell Kathleen what we've talked about and report any progress or otherwise with Peter back to me?'

'Yes, of course,' Maxine replied.

'Any other questions?' June's eyes sharpened as they fell on Judith Wright. Everyone shook their heads. 'That's all, then. Any problems concerning Peter, please see me – and if I'm not around, then Maxine.'

Maxine told Kathleen in the small nurses' room the little they knew about Peter.

'Have you got any words out of him?' Maxine finished.

'Not a dicky bird. He's in shock, no doubt about it. But he'll come round. He's asleep now . . . went off straight away. Tired out, poor little blighter. But when he's recovered – we'll let him take however long he needs – I think the sing-song is just the ticket.'

Peter stayed in the ward four more days as he began coughing and complained of a sore throat. He did what he was told but clammed up when Maxine gently asked him how he felt, and did he want to talk about his mother and grandmother.

'Leave me alone!' he shouted once, then bit his lip so hard Maxine had to wipe away the blood spots.

It was sad they were the first words he'd uttered to her.

When Peter was over the worst of his cold and ready to

172

go to classes, Maxine saw Bobby was sitting up in bed reading *Beano*. She brought a chair over and sat by the side of him.

'How are you feeling, Bobby?'

'All right, Nurse.' He kept his eyes on his comic.

'Can you put your comic down a minute?' Maxine asked. With an exaggerated sigh, Bobby laid it on one side. Maxine lowered her voice. 'Have you spoken to Peter yet?'

'I asked him this morning if he was better and he just said yes. I don't think he wants to talk.' Bobby looked directly at her as he asked, 'Is he an orphan?'

'His mother and grandmother died, so he's come to us.'

'Oh.' Bobby went quiet for a few seconds. 'Where's his father? Is he dead too?'

'We're not sure, but I'd rather you not question Peter about that at the moment. He's only eight. He's had a lot to contend with. All I know is that he's had a very difficult time.'

'Yeah, well all of us here have had a difficult time,' Bobby said, picking up his comic again.

Maxine could see it was going to take a huge effort to win the children round.

'You should be well enough to go back upstairs soon,' she said, as she stood up.

Bobby nodded and carried on reading.

Day by day, Maxine was beginning to get the feel of the orphanage. Everyone had been too busy to take her round the whole building, more sprawling than she'd first imagined, but she'd enjoyed wandering on her own. Although it was large, it somehow felt homely.

She put her head round the door of the laundry to say hello to the two girls who called out their names through the steam – Lucy and Mabel. She knew now where all the classrooms were on the ground and first floors, the children's dormitories on the second floor, various bedrooms for the live-in staff on the third and the nursery at the top, together with some other doors which were locked. For storage, she guessed. There was the staff common room and the warm and welcoming kitchen where Bertie always invited her to sit and have a cup of tea if she wasn't too busy. But her favourite room was the library. With its timber vaulted ceiling and gallery, it housed the largest collection of books she'd ever seen.

'It was Lord Bingham's personal collection,' June said when they stood together one evening eyeing the overflowing shelves. 'We're safeguarding them for him, but we've never heard anything from him since Dr Barnardo's took over the house just before the war.'

'It's an impressive collection,' Maxine said, running her fingers lightly over some of the spines, inhaling the pleasing combination of leather and dust. 'I'm sure he'll come back for them after the war.'

'Maybe.' June didn't sound convinced. 'We've had some wonderful evenings in the library,' she went on. 'It lends itself somehow, especially to musical events, and the children love it. The books are a bit high-brow for me, though.' She gave what seemed to Maxine an almost embarrassed smile. 'I usually get my books from Brown's in town. In fact, it's where I first met Murray,' she broke off, beaming. 'Well, the first time properly.'

'Sounds intriguing. I'd love to hear more.'

Maxine hoped she had most of the children's names in her head and was determined to conquer the last few in the next two days. Everyone was very kind to her, enquiring whether she was settling in, and although she responded with a smile and said she was, if she was honest with herself, she was lonely. Pearl was spasmodic in her letter-writing, and although her mother wrote regularly, it was usually moaning about something or other. The only bright bit was the long PS at the bottom which her father added – usually some little anecdote about one of their various visitors to make her smile.

She couldn't bear to think of Teddy, but she couldn't bear not to either. If she dwelt on how she'd given her baby away to strangers, she carried the lump of guilt with her all day. And if she managed to . . . well, not put him at the back of her mind – she could never do that – but lose herself for a few hours in her new surroundings and get to know the children, she felt guilty that she'd forgotten Teddy already. It was beginning to have an effect on her sleep.

She would love to make a friend of June, but whenever their conversations became more personal, she had to hold herself firmly in check. It wouldn't be professional, for one thing, and she was too new for June to cope with any outburst. The last thing she could afford to lose was her job. Since Teddy, she'd cut herself off and felt so awkward every time she visited her parents, she'd made the visits longer apart. Her mother's face flashed in front of her as she remembered telling them she was going to be working at Dr Barnardo's.

'You don't know anything about children,' her mother had said, and it was like a stab in Maxine's heart. 'I'm sure you'll meet someone one day and have children of your own, but you'll never meet anyone stuck out in the wilds in an orphanage. No, it will be much better for you to go back to the Infirmary and then I'm sure you'll meet a nice doctor.'

Oh, if you only knew, Mum, about nice doctors.

'I've made up my mind, Mum.'

Yes, if she could have a real friend, like Anna, it would be June, Maxine decided, stirring her cocoa in the common room late one evening after she'd been studying for her finals over the last two hours, grateful that Sister Lawson was kindly keeping her informed by letter as to what would be expected of her. She glanced across at June, wondering not for the first time how such a young woman had become the matron of Bingham Hall.

June caught her eye and smiled. 'I know what you're thinking,' she said. 'You're wondering how I'm the matron when I'm so young, aren't you?'

'Well, yes, I was,' Maxine admitted. 'Any matrons I've come across in hospitals have always been at least sixty, usually on the plump side, and very, very fierce.' She smiled back at June. 'And I'm delighted to say that none of those attributes describes you.'

'I should hope not.' June laughed. 'I'll tell you how it came about one day – when we have time.'

'Sounds like a long story.' Maxine smiled. 'But tell me one thing. Are you happy here?'

'Very happy. I came here under sad circumstances and the orphanage has been a great healer. Of course, it's the children who are the ones who do the healing. Just by getting to know them and helping each child with their problems and pain and seeing an improvement in them helped me tremendously.' She gave Maxine a steady look. 'I think you're in need of some gentle healing too, Maxine. I don't want to pry, but I think you've come to the right place.'

'No, no, I'm all right, really I am. Everyone has problems, don't they?' Maxine felt her heart beat a little too rapidly.

June nodded and looked at her watch. 'Gosh. Twenty to

176

eleven. 'Where does the time go?' She stretched her legs and linked her hands behind her head, stifling a yawn. 'Freddie will wonder what's happened to me.'

'Who's Freddie?'

June smiled. 'Only the best dog in the world.'

'Ah.'

'Do you like dogs?' June asked.

'I love all animals. But we never had pets at home. Mum's rather house-proud and hates the hairs. But I didn't realise there was a dog here.'

'We have a "no pets" rule,' June said, 'but I was very lucky. When I became matron, I had the previous matron's little cottage, so I could take Freddie with me. We had to hide him in the barn before then. That's another story.' She grinned, and her face looked like a naughty schoolgirl. 'Fran, the gardener's wife, looks after him in the day, and I'm with him after supper in the cottage, and then I come back to the house last thing to make sure everything's all right and have a chat with anyone who's in the common room.' She looked steadily at Maxine. 'And I felt you've needed a bit of company in the evenings.'

'It's been wonderful these few days getting to know the children, and Peter is a particular challenge, but when they're all tucked up in bed . . .' she broke off, a little embarrassed.

'That's when you feel it,' June finished.

'Yes. All the problems seem to be twice as bad last thing at night and in the early hours.' As soon as she'd voiced the words she wished she could take them back. It would open up a whole lot of questions that she wasn't prepared to answer.

June sent her a sympathetic look. 'Well, you know where I am if you ever want to talk about anything,' she said quietly.

'I remember how I was when I first came here. But Iris, the nurse before you, was so welcoming and so down-to-earth and used to make me laugh. She wouldn't allow me to be unhappy or lonely. And Bertie helped as well. She's lovely and has a broad shoulder to cry on.'

'She is a dear, but I hope it doesn't come to that.' Maxine pretended to laugh it off but June was getting a bit too near the truth.

'So you think you'll stay with us?'

'Oh, yes. I'll definitely stay if you'll have me.' Maxine drained her cup. 'It's already starting to feel like home and you and the others have been so kind.' She wanted to add, 'Except Judith Wright', but thought better of it.

'I'm glad.'

The door opened and Athena's strawberry-blonde head appeared, as usual pinned in a smooth Victory Roll. 'Oh, sorry, am I intruding?'

'Of course not,' June said. 'Come on in. We've had our cocoa, but we can stay a few minutes while you make yours.'

Athena made herself a cup and pulled up a chair. 'It's a bit late but I couldn't sleep.' She took a sip of her drink. 'How do you think our new boy's settling in?' She directed her question to Maxine.

'It's very difficult for such a young child to have gone through what he has and behave like a normal child. He hardly speaks, although he understands English perfectly. He did tell me yesterday that his mother used to speak to him in English and make him answer in English, and then he broke down.' Maxine swallowed hard as she remembered the look of utter despair on the child's face.

'How are the other children reacting?' June asked Athena.

'They ignore him,' Athena said. 'I try to bring him into the rest of the class but he sits there without saying a word.'

'But they don't realise he's German,' June said.

'Oh, no. But because Peter won't speak or join in, they just leave him to himself. We're going to have to think of something which piques his interest.'

'I didn't want to probe on his first few days,' Maxine said, feeling she should have thought of ways to help Peter by now. 'He needs to get a bit more used to being here amongst such a lot of strangers.'

'I think that's very wise,' June said. 'When I first came here I saw a little girl, not four years old, in Bertie's kitchen. She was curled up in a corner with her fingers stuck in her mouth, and she wouldn't speak. Bertie said the child had come to the home several weeks before but was dumb – not born dumb, but her house had been bombed and her mother, father and brother were burned alive.' June shuddered. 'She'd been staying at her grandmother's or else she would have died in the fire too. It took time for her to trust me and it took a puppy—' she broke off, smiling, 'Freddie, who I've just been telling you about, Maxine, to help her begin to talk and act like a normal little girl again. But it was a very slow process.'

'Is she still here?' Maxine asked, blinking back the tears that threatened at June's story. Any story, sad or happy, these days, caught her unawares and made her want to cry.

'Yes,' June smiled. 'It's Lizzie.'

'Lizzie?' Maxine was astonished. She was the last child who would have sprung to mind.

'And now she's the most precocious of all the girls here,' Athena said, grinning. 'More so than some of the boys.'

'She is, isn't she?' June said proudly. 'She's a completely different child. You should have seen her when she first came here, Maxine. She was in a bad state, but all she needed was lots of love and patience and understanding. And it will be the same with Peter . . . I'm sure of it.' She looked at her watch. 'Gosh, it's nearly midnight. Let's call it a day. We've got a full one tomorrow with the air-raid practice.'

Chapter Nineteen

Maxine felt better after the conversation with June and Athena, especially with June's story about Lizzie. It gave her hope that Peter would, over time, begin to heal and join in with the others.

The next morning, she stopped June on her way to her office.

'June, may I have a few moments?'

'Of course, Maxine. Come on in.'

'Peter has hardly any clothes,' Maxine began, 'and I wondered if there is an allowance for him and enough coupons so we could buy him a few things. He needs some underwear and trousers, at least one shirt and a pullover . . . oh, and new shoes.'

'Yes, of course,' June said immediately.

'Is there a separate ration book for each child?'

'Yes, though Peter's hasn't come through yet, but I always have some spare coupons.' She unlocked her desk drawer and brought out an envelope. She quickly counted a few coupons and made a note in a red book.' She looked up. 'How much money do you think you'll need?'

'I'm not sure.' She'd never bought any children's clothes. She swallowed hard. Teddy. She should be making him his first little romper suit, and buying him his first soft baby shoes.

'I can give you five pounds. Do you think that will be sufficient?'

'I'm sure it will,' Maxine said gratefully. 'I'll try to bring back some change. Is it all right if I take him into town this morning as it's a Saturday?'

'I've left Peter under your care.' June looked at her and smiled. 'Please do what you think best for him, but I'm always here if you need to discuss anything. Two heads in this case might well be better than one!'

Maxine's feet were lighter as she ran up the stairs to fetch her jacket.

A flicker of interest actually crossed Peter's face when Maxine told him they were going into Liverpool to buy him some clothes.

'Are we going with Harold?' he asked.

She blinked, surprised that Peter was already acquainted with Harold, the chauffeur. The boy must be used to this kind of service, Maxine thought, wondering what his life had been like before he and his mother came to England. She looked down at him and made a vow to do everything in her power to help him. Goodness knew, she was well aware of how difficult it was to shake off the misery, even for only an hour or two a day. But she'd try. And this outing would at least give him a change of scenery.

'No, Peter. I think that being taken in the motorcar is only for emergencies or if Mr Harold is going to town anyway.'

'Oh.' Peter looked up at her. 'Must we walk?'

'No, no.' Maxine smiled at him. 'That would take far too long. But we'll walk down the drive and catch the bus straight into Liverpool. And then we'll have some fun choosing some new clothes. And I'm going to buy you an ice cream. Would you like that?'

182

'I don't like the English ice cream,' he said, his mouth turning down at the corners.

'Ah. That makes it difficult as we can't go to Germany just for ice cream,' Maxine chuckled, but Peter, she noticed, didn't even smile.

'Can we sit at the front?' he asked when the bus arrived.

Before Maxine could answer he'd bounded ahead, but unfortunately the conductor didn't give her enough time to get to her seat before he rang the bell. The driver started off with a mighty jerk, throwing her off balance. She managed to grab the rail as she tipped forward, but scraped her shin on someone's basket left in the aisle.

'Steady on, Miss,' the conductor called.

Bit late for that, she thought, annoyed when she noticed she'd torn her only pair of stockings as she sat down beside Peter. *Blast.* It was in such an obvious place. Well, she couldn't do anything about it – she was here for Peter, not shopping for herself.

The boy gave her a quick glance but didn't say anything and stared resolutely ahead through the grime-splattered glass.

Liverpool was quieter than she'd expected for a Saturday. She decided to take Peter to Morrows on Dale Street. The store was more expensive than Lewis's department store, but that iconic building had been bombed almost to a shell the previous year. Maxine swallowed as she saw more devastation than when she'd last been in town, just before she'd taken up her new post. At Bingham Hall she would hear bombs falling in the distance, but they were usually far enough away for the children not to be frightened.

She took Peter's hand but immediately he pulled it away.

'Peter,' she said, looking down at the child who was

expressionless. 'I'm responsible for you. If you had an accident *I* would be the one in trouble, not you. So please—'

'I won't run away,' Peter said. 'I'm not a baby. I don't need you to hold my hand.'

His words took her by surprise. It was probably the longest speech he'd made since his arrival. She saw in his expression he was challenging her. All right. She would challenge *him*.

'So long as you promise to keep by my side and watch out for the traffic.' She gave him a long look. 'Do you promise?'

'*Ja* . . . yes, I promise.'

'Good.' She paused. 'Peter, it might be best not to say any German words to anyone. You understand why, don't you?'

He gazed up at her and nodded. She had to turn away. She couldn't bear to see such fear in a child's eyes. In her mind she saw Teddy in a few years' time. His adoptive mother telling him his real mother didn't want him. Had given him away to strangers. Her eyes brimmed and she swallowed hard. When would this nightmare ease? But it was Peter who needed her now.

They turned down a side street into Hackins Hey. In spite of its narrow space, the street boasted some imposing old buildings jostled together, many of them housing half-empty shops. Maxine slowed her pace, keeping an eye on Peter, who didn't seem to be interested in anything, kicking a pebble along, his hands in his pockets and his mouth turned down. She glanced in the windows as they picked their way through the debris, but there was little to catch her attention.

She stopped, Peter almost bumping into her, as she stood, disorientated. Many streets now were unrecognisable with the buildings razed to the ground. Which way now? They walked on, and round the next corner she was relieved to see they were at the junction of Dale Street and Georges Road where the department store squarely faced them. It wasn't a particularly attractive building, but the window display showed a reasonable variety of men's, women's and children's clothes. She should get everything Peter needed here.

She opened the door and they stepped inside. Immediately, a smartly dressed woman approached them.

'May I direct you to the right department?' A saleslady's smile flashed across her face.

'We're looking for children's items,' Maxine said.

'Upstairs. First floor.' She pointed to a wrought-iron curved stairway.

Where was everyone? Maxine wondered as they reached the first floor. There were only a dozen people by the looks of it. Maybe it was too early.

She approached a saleslady at the nearest counter who beamed at them. This one was not much older than herself, with dark hair rolled back off her face, and wearing bright red lipstick.

'Good morning, Madam. What can I do for you?'

'I need to buy some clothes for this young man.' Maxine glanced down at Peter who was looking anywhere but at the lady behind the counter.

'What exactly are you looking for, Madam?'

'Um, some short trousers, and shirts . . . a pullover . . . oh, and school shoes.'

'The pullover will be difficult,' she said. 'People these days are having to knit their children jumpers and pullovers . . . even socks. We have some wool for sale on the ground floor, but it's mostly grey and fawn.' She wrinkled her nose in disgust. 'With the rationing it's as though they've decided not to give us a bit of colour.' She looked Maxine up and down as though assessing her knitting skills. 'Are you a knitter?'

'Not since I left school. I'm better at sewing.'

'Well, I'm sure you can make your son a pullover with a simple pattern.'

'*She's* not my mother.' The colour rushed to Peter's cheeks.

'Peter! Please don't speak so rudely.'

'But it's the truth.' Peter stared up at Maxine, a challenging light in his bright blue eyes.

'I'm his nurse,' Maxine explained.

'My mistake.' The young woman's smile vanished as her narrowed eyes flicked over Maxine again. 'Come this way.' She emerged from behind the counter and gestured them to follow. Maxine noticed the woman's shapely legs were clad in beautiful silk stockings set off by black patent high heels which clicked importantly over the linoleum floor. She was immediately conscious of the tear in her own stockings, only hers were cheap lisle. She bit back a twinge of envy.

They walked over to where a girl was polishing the glass top of a much longer counter. After a short word, the blonde woman pulled out a drawer and set it on the top of the counter and brought out a couple of shirts. She carefully unfolded them and spread them out so her customer could get the full effect.

Maxine picked up a blue shirt and held it under Peter's chin.

'It matches your eyes, love,' the blonde woman said, smiling again.

Peter simply stared at her.

Feeling embarrassed at the boy's rudeness, Maxine said, 'Does it come in another colour?'

'This is the only one we have in his size, I'm afraid,

Madam. We can't get all the sizes or the variety with the shortage.'

'Of course.' She should have known. 'We'll take this one anyway.' Maxine darted a glance at Peter but he was making faces at a little girl a few feet away who had hold of her mother's hand and had started to cry.

By the time Maxine had bought Peter the shirt, short trousers, two pairs of socks and some fawn wool the lady in that department had said would be enough for a sleeveless pullover, she'd used up nearly all the coupons and was at the end of her tether. She longed to sit down and have a cup of tea, but there were still his shoes to buy. If she had enough coupons, that is.

Why was she so tired? Was it because Peter refused to take any interest in anything at all? She sighed. It wasn't his fault.

Hoping that buying his shoes would be easier with so little choice, Maxine guided Peter over to the children's shoe section. It was still deathly quiet for such a large shop, although there was one customer, a man in a smart uniform, sitting on the edge of his chair, head bent low, trying on a pair of brogues a few feet from where she and Peter stood.

She glanced at him as he stood up and walked a few steps, and smiled at how odd the shoes appeared against his uniform. Then she jerked her head away and gave a sharp intake of breath. She could only see his profile, but she'd seen that profile before, she was certain of it. Months ago . . . before Teddy. She swallowed, wishing she was anywhere but in Morrows' shoe department, but Peter had actually picked up a shoe and was inspecting it. Maybe she was imagining things. She'd only seen the man in the dim light of the theatre. But that wasn't true. They'd had a conversation in the foyer afterwards and she'd seen him clearly.

His image had flashed in front of her eyes more than once after that evening but she thought by now she'd forgotten him. She glanced his way again. If he looked round, she'd know for certain.

As though he felt her eyes upon him, he turned. For an instant their eyes locked. And then his face broke into a wide smile.

'Goodness, if it isn't Miss Taylor.'

He'd remembered her name. She felt herself flush and was thankful that Peter had picked up another shoe and a saleslady was approaching him.

'It's . . .' For a split second she forgot his name. 'It's Mr Wells, isn't it?'

'Crofton, please,' he said firmly as he quickly closed the space between them. 'But only if I'm allowed to call you Maxine.' He grinned. 'Do you know, I so hoped I'd see you again. I ran out after you at the theatre but you'd disappeared into thin air – for the second time. How lovely to see you.'

She held out her hand and he shook it. She remembered the warmth of his hand in hers when they'd shaken hands that first time, and the memory made her ashamed all over again. She'd been carrying Edwin's baby and had tried to pass herself off as a normal single girl having a pleasant evening. But it had all been a delusion and she'd rudely left him standing when he'd asked if he might take her for a drink. But he'd tried to find her. She hugged the thought to herself.

'I'd like to try these shoes.' Peter pulled on her arm and held out a pair of brown leather shoes. 'Please,' he added.

'Why don't you ask the lady if they have your size, Peter, then come and tell me if they're comfortable. But first I want to know the price.'

Peter turned one of them over. 'One guinea.' He frowned. 'What's a guinea?'

'One pound and one shilling,' Maxine said.

'Oh.' He shot off with the shoes before she could say anything further.

'That was very naughty of him,' Maxine said, looking at Crofton. 'I'm sorry.'

'No need to be. He's just a lad. But I'm surprised he hasn't learned at school how much a guinea is.'

Should she tell him? Explain? No, it was too complicated.

'Is he your boy?' he asked.

'No.' She swallowed.

'But you *are* married.' His eyes dropped to her left hand where her gold wedding ring steadfastly glinted.

'Widowed,' she answered quietly.

'Oh, I'm so sorry.' Crofton briefly closed his eyes as though to kick himself. Then he said, 'Look, can I take you for a coffee or something. It's getting on for eleven and I'm sure Peter would like a drink and a bun. Boys are always starving hungry.'

Maxine paused. There was no denying – he was an attractive man. She'd thought the same when she'd first met him . . . and that strange moment of recognition when they'd looked at one another through the tram window . . . but what was the use? No man would ever want her when he knew the truth. But he wasn't asking her to marry him, for goodness' sake. He was merely asking if she'd like a coffee. And she was thirsty. She couldn't dash off for a second time, especially after she'd told Peter off for doing just that.

'That would be most welcome,' she said.

'Good.' He smiled at her and she was caught in those twinkling brown eyes. She noticed they had amber flecks in them and shook herself as Crofton said, 'Let's go and see how the lad is getting on with those shoes.'

* * *

When they were all settled in Morrows' café and Peter was attacking an iced bun and a lemonade, Crofton looked across the small table at her.

'I'm curious.' He nodded surreptitiously towards Peter.

'I work at the orphanage in Bingham.' What could be the harm in telling him that? 'It's a Dr Barnardo's home.'

'I've heard of it.' Crofton leaned back in his chair, a thoughtful expression crossing his face. 'Are you a teacher there?'

'A nurse,' she said, 'but strangely enough, I always wanted to be a teacher.'

Oh, why had she said that? It was much too personal and she'd told herself she would only stick to the facts. She didn't want him to start peeling any layers.

'So why didn't you?'

'Didn't I what?'

'Become a teacher.' He looked at her expectantly, as if her answer was important to him.'

'My mother wanted me to be a nurse. It was her dream.'

'But not yours?'

'No.' She looked away. 'Though I liked it in the end,' she added defensively. 'And now I have the best of both worlds – I'm surrounded by children, which is what I always wanted – even though they're a challenge.'

'I bet.' He grinned, then became serious. 'Especially when they must all have horror stories to tell, poor kids.'

She shook her head in warning and glanced at Peter who was scraping up the last crumbs of his bun.

'I understand,' he said in an undertone. His voice became brisk as he turned towards the child. 'Have you had enough, Peter?'

'*Ja* – yes, thank you.'

Crofton raised a dark eyebrow, but Maxine pretended she

hadn't noticed. She had to keep to the story she'd suggested to June and the others, but thankfully Crofton didn't press further. She realised her talk with Peter was becoming urgent.

'You haven't mentioned *your* job,' Maxine said, wanting to change the subject.

'Crofton Wells at your service.' He gave a mock bow with the top half of him.

Maxine smiled. 'A pilot?'

'Yes.'

She hesitated, longing to ask more but worried he might think she was prying and ought to know better.

As if he knew what she was thinking he said, 'Keeping watch on the Atlantic – air sea rescues – that sort of thing.'

'Do you fly planes as big as a Messerschmitt?' Peter asked, his eyes sparking with sudden interest.

Maxine cringed. The fewer people who knew about Peter's past, the better. But Crofton seemed to be taking it that the boy hoped Crofton's plane would be more than a match for a German one – at least she hoped that's what he thought.

'They can be different sizes.' Crofton winked at Maxine and grinned down at Peter. Maxine noticed Crofton's mouth lifted more at one corner in an endearing way.

'Can I see a picture of the one you fly?' Peter asked, his eyes shining with excitement.

'That's not possible, Peter,' Maxine cut in quickly. 'Everything is secret in the war.'

'Oh, please, Mr Wells—'

'That's enough, Peter.' Maxine rose to her feet and turned to Crofton. 'We must be going. They'll be expecting us back by now, but thank you very much for the coffee and cake. It was just what I needed.' She touched the boy lightly on the arm. 'What do you say, Peter?'

'Thank you, Sir,' Peter mumbled.

'That's all right, young man.' Crofton leapt up and stood in front of her. 'So you're running out on me again, are you?'

She'd forgotten how tall he was. Her heart began to beat too fast.

'No, of course not, but I'm supposed to be working today.'

'May I see you again?' Crofton said. They were only inches apart and she wanted to breathe in the masculine smell of him. 'And I won't take no for an answer . . . unless of course you say you can't stand the sight of me.' He grinned and a sudden tingle up her back made her almost overbalance. He put his hand on her arm. 'Maxine?'

She felt Peter's eyes on her and flushed. Crofton took his hand away.

'I-I've only just started working at Bingham Hall,' she stuttered, the impression of his fingers still warm on her arm, 'so I don't know what days off I'll have.'

'If you give me your telephone number, I'll ring you tomorrow.'

'I doubt I'll get any time off that soon.' Maxine didn't know whether to be relieved or disappointed.

'Try.' He took a pen from his inside pocket and a small notebook. 'Now, Bingham Hall's number.'

'I don't know it,' Maxine said truthfully. 'I have it written down, but it'll be in my room. I'm sorry.'

She was glad she didn't have the letter with Bingham Hall's telephone number. It was easier this way. No involvement, no getting close to someone and having your heart broken . . . no explaining about Teddy. To her horror, she felt her eyes swim with tears.

'Don't worry. I'll ask the operator.' He looked closely at her. 'Are you all right, Maxine?'

'Yes. But we really must go.' She held out her hand and

allowed her fingers to briefly touch his, then grabbing her shopping and a protesting Peter, she turned before Crofton could say another word, and they ran down the stairs and out of the shop.

'What about my shoes?' Peter said, stopping and crossing his arms. 'The ones I'm wearing are too small for me now, and they are my only ones.'

'Oh, Peter, I'm sorry. Next time someone goes into town I'll ask if they can pick them up now we know the size. But we've spent nearly all your clothing coupons today. I think we've done well, haven't we?'

Peter was silent. It was sad how little interest he'd taken in the shopping, Maxine thought, but he'd obviously come from a family who had plenty of money so buying things must be normal for him. But he surprised her with his next remark.

'I like Mr Wells.'

'Do you? Even if he isn't allowed to show you a photograph of the aeroplane he flies?'

Peter nodded. 'Yes, because he would like to show me if he was allowed.'

Maxine drew in a surprised breath. Peter was only eight, and until now he'd seemed suspicious of everyone. So why had he got such faith in Crofton Wells?

Chapter Twenty

'We're pretending the siren goes off sometime this afternoon,' June said to Maxine as she and Peter came into the Great Hall from their shopping. 'I've told everyone, but I won't say when I'll ring the bell so it's more of a surprise.'

'Do the children know?' Maxine asked, glancing at Peter.

'Oh, yes. We don't want to frighten them that it's a real bomb but they do need to know what to do if we hear a siren . . . which thankfully has only happened once since I've been here. We're lucky we're that little bit out of the direct line to the docks. But once we had a stray bomber who flew over us after a bombing raid on the docks and dropped his last two bombs, smashing one of the greenhouses and the gardener's cottage. That was awful. Our lovely gardener and his wife died.' She shook her head and Maxine wondered how they'd all coped. 'Anyway, I'll give our class bell three long rings so it will sound different from the normal dinner bell. The children know that's the signal for our practice.'

'I'll make sure we're ready.'

'I'm afraid I haven't shown you where the shelters are yet, which is very remiss of me, so you and Peter will have to follow the others,' June told her. 'They know where to go.'

Maxine glanced at Peter. She could tell by the narrowing of his eyes that he was listening intently.

All of a sudden he burst out, 'If our . . . the German pilots aren't dropping bombs, I shan't go to the shelter.'

'I'm afraid that isn't possible,' Maxine said quickly. 'You can't be left on your own, and if we ever have a proper raid, you won't know where to go or what to do and could be in danger.' She looked at June who nodded her approval.

'It's time for you to wash your hands, Peter,' June told him, signalling the conversation was over. 'Dinner is nearly ready. As it's Friday, it's fish.'

Peter pulled his mouth in tightly but went off, head down, hands deep in his pockets, scuffling his feet.

'He's not going to be easy, is he?' June said, watching him disappear. She turned to Maxine, eyeing the shopping bag. 'Why don't you come into my office a moment and show me what you've bought.'

'There wasn't much choice,' Maxine said, following June into her office and putting her shopping bag down.

'I know,' June grimaced. 'Some of the shops have completely empty windows. I don't know how the owners manage to make a living. Where did you go?'

'We went to Morrows,' Maxine said. 'I thought we might have better luck in a department store. But even they were woefully empty and there were very few customers around.'

She hoped June wouldn't notice her cheeks warming at the thought of bumping into Crofton Wells.

'Did you manage to get the things Peter needed?'

'Most of them, except there were no jumpers or pullovers, so I bought some wool. I'm going to attempt to knit him one. I forgot the needles though . . . oh, and a pattern.' She gave a rueful smile. 'I didn't do that well after all, did I?'

'I'm sure we've got needles and patterns here.' June smiled.

'I used to knit for my sister—' She stopped abruptly, and chewed her lip as though to stop herself from saying more – or bursting into tears.

Something had upset the young matron. It was when June had mentioned her sister. Maxine wondered if she should say anything but thought better of it. June would tell her in her own time if she wanted to. But she didn't like to think June was suffering. She wanted to say something – to tell June she was a good listener and it would go no further. To remember the old saying – a problem shared is a problem halved. She ignored the fact that she herself was keeping all her secrets tightly wrapped inside her chest. She could see tears gathering in June's eyes and quickly changed the subject of knitting.

'Oh, and he saw some shoes which he's already tried on and likes,' Maxine said, 'but we didn't have enough coupons, which was a pity because he says his are too small now and he doesn't have another pair. And he needs vests and under-pants, but there was no time after we'd had—' Maxine flushed again at the memory of Crofton sitting with them having coffee. It wouldn't do to let June, nice though she was, think she was about to indulge in any romance. Or waste time drinking coffee and eating buns, come to that.

'Some refreshments, I hope,' June finished, her expression calm again. 'I expect Peter was ready to sit down with a drink and a cake.'

'Yes, he was, and so was I,' Maxine admitted.

'I'll have a look in the cupboard and see if there are any shoes that one of the older children have grown out of.' She paused to make a note. 'By the way, have you had a chance to speak to him about his family yet?'

'No, but I plan to this afternoon after the drill.'

'I think that's a very good idea,' June said.

Maxine picked up the bags. 'I'll go and unpack these things and put them in Peter's locker before we have dinner. Then we're ready for the bell when it rings.'

A letter had been pushed under her bedroom door when Maxine opened it. She picked it up and was pleased to see Pearl's familiar flamboyant writing. There wasn't time to read it now as dinner was about to be served but she'd enjoy it after the drill, and when she'd spoken to Peter. It would be good to sit down with a cup of tea then and settle back to enjoy Pearl's letter.

The children made the drill into a game, even though Maxine, June and the other teachers tried to keep them in order.

June clapped her hands loudly. 'Go in pairs,' she said, her voice loud and clear as it echoed through the Great Hall. 'Don't look for your friends. Just hold the hand of the child nearest to you and keep moving. No talking. And no running.'

Children grabbed each other's hands and thundered through the hall and out of the front door, leaving Peter staring after them. Maxine immediately went to take his hand but as usual he shrugged her off.

'I can go by myself,' he said. 'Anyway, it's not real. There aren't any real bombs.'

'Peter, you will do what I say.' Maxine surprised herself with how sharp her words came out. 'It's for your own safety. The alarm's gone off and we should be in the shelter by now.' She grabbed his hand and held it tightly. 'Come on. I don't want to hear another word.'

'I'm staying here and you can't make me go!' Peter shouted, desperately trying to pull away.

She ignored him and gripped him more tightly. It didn't matter whether he liked her or not, she was determined he was not going to get the upper hand.

Peter was nowhere to be seen when everyone trooped back into the house after the drill. Somehow he'd managed to give Maxine the slip. She realised today was not the day to try to win his trust. He wouldn't be in the least receptive. She must think of something that would be nothing to do with orphanages, or being German. Only then would she be able to warn him of his vulnerable position at Bingham Hall where the children were concerned. If not, she could imagine him being bullied as soon as the first child discovered he was half German.

Maxine breathed a sigh of relief when she opened the door to her bedroom after dinner and saw it was empty. She reckoned she and Kathleen wouldn't see that much of each other as they worked different shifts, and although she liked Kathleen very much, she needed time to plan how she was going to approach the problem of Peter's background without upsetting the child any further. Her mind was spinning. She sat on her bed and removed her shoes and stockings, curling and uncurling her toes. There had been no opportunity to have a serious talk to him by the time she'd found him in the magnificent library on his own, his face only inches away from what looked like an atlas.

'There you are, Peter,' she'd said. 'We've been looking for you.'

He looked up and saw who it was, then dropped his eyes back to the book.

'What are you studying?' She came closer and looked over his shoulder. It was a map of Germany.

Peter turned and glanced up at her, his eyes filled with misery. 'Nothing.' He snapped the book shut and stood up to leave. 'Here.' He held it out to her. 'You can have it. I've finished with it.'

She felt a little unnerved by those blue eyes staring into hers. How was she ever going to win his trust? How would any of them?

'What class do you have next?' she asked.

'I don't know.'

'Then we need to ask one of the teachers, so come with me.'

Without a word he followed her to the Great Hall where the children had gathered ready to go to the various classes. The noise was deafening. The twin girls were shouting at one another on top of all the loud chatter and pushing each other until June appeared and clapped her hands.

'Quiet, children!' They stopped immediately. 'You all know where to go for your next class, except Peter. Is he here?'

'Yes, I have him with me,' Maxine said.

June looked at her notebook. 'Peter is with Miss Wright. History. Room four.' She looked round and called to a red-haired boy. His colouring reminded her of Edwin and Maxine swallowed hard. 'Ben, please show Peter where to go,' June went on. 'You're in his class, I believe.'

Ben had nodded and gestured for Peter to follow him. All Maxine could do was pray that nothing would come out about Germany or the Germans before she was able to speak to him. A history lesson could mean anything.

Now in her room she remembered Pearl's letter, and carefully opened the envelope, relishing the chatty news from her cousin, such a contrast to her mother's letters which were always full of how difficult it was for her to cope with

Dad and when was Maxine coming to see them, and how she was sure Dad needed her more than the children at Dr Barnardo's.

Maxine sighed and took the sheet of Basildon Bond notepaper from the envelope. How Pearl still managed to find decent stationery was a mystery to her.

Dear Max,

I rec'd your letter and am pleased you are settling in. It must be quite a shock being around all those kiddies, but at least there aren't any babies there to remind you.

Pearl had crossed out the last part of the sentence but the reference was enough to make Maxine's eyes smart. She hurriedly read on.

I have a much bigger part in a new show – another musical. Am not allowed to tell you anything about it now, but Liverpool will be the first to perform it before we tour the country. We're hoping it will get to the West End. We're just starting rehearsals and it will probably be announced by the beginning of next month. As soon as I can I'll send you a couple of tickets in case you've met a nice chap in the last fortnight and you can invite him! Or you can bring a girlfriend, but I don't think that would be half as much fun, do you? Ha ha.

In the meantime I'd love to come and see you – see where you work and say hello to the children. Maybe one afternoon when I get a few hours off?

All for now.

Much love,

Pearl XX.

Maxine was pleased her cousin sounded cheerful and had been chosen for a more prominent part in the next musical. It seemed like Pearl's dream was beginning to come true after a lot of hard work and determination. Her thoughts turned to Pearl's past. She hadn't had an easy time either. To have gone through something like that alone. If only Pearl had told her about the baby she would gladly have gone to look after her cousin. Maybe even persuaded her to keep it.

Tears sprang to her eyes. Pearl's experience was far worse than her own. Her cousin had lost her baby forever. Even if Maxine never saw him again, her darling Teddy was alive and loved – oh, please God let him have loving parents. That's all she wanted. All that was important.

She began to read the letter again, smiling now at Pearl's allusion to a possible new chap. Her cousin would love to know about Crofton Wells, immediately weaving a romance around the story, but Maxine was glad she hadn't mentioned him. After all, it was hardly likely she'd see him again. He'd only asked for the telephone number of Bingham Hall out of politeness, she was certain. But what if . . . Momentarily she closed her eyes and tried to dislodge the whisper of a dangerous question . . . What if his twinkling eyes . . . his crooked smile . . . were for her alone? Was she ready to take a chance with another man again?

Chapter Twenty-One

Maxine awoke with new determination. Whatever happened, she was going to have her talk with Peter. It couldn't be put off any longer. She'd see him this morning before his first class, and be blowed if he trusted her or not. It was her duty to help him settle in properly.

Happy that she'd made her decision, she flung the bedclothes aside, had a wash, thankful that tonight was her turn for a bath. She dressed quickly in her uniform, noticing a smudge on her apron. She gave a wry smile thinking of Sister who would have pulled her up immediately and made her change. But it would get a lot more scruffy by the end of the day.

She ran down the stairs to the floor below where the children slept. She'd got into the habit of helping Jenny, a girl from the village who came in every day to sleep in the girls' dormitory. It wasn't part of Maxine's nursing duties but she was glad to help in any way she could. At the moment there were only two children in the ward and there wasn't enough to do all day as far as nursing was concerned.

Entering the dormitory, she was surprised to find Jenny still asleep and little Betsy by her side shaking her arm. Jenny was always up early, a cheerful smile for the children as she got them dressed, calling out instructions as to what they were to wear that day and to be quiet when it became too noisy. Maxine stepped over to Jenny's bed and Betsy looked up, her brown eyes anxious.

'Miss Jenny won't wake up.'

'You go and get dressed, Betsy, and I'll have a look at Miss Jenny. I expect she's just tired.'

The child shot off.

'Jenny, can you hear me?'

The figure didn't stir.

Maxine pulled back the sheet. 'Jenny,' she said again, more urgently, grasping the girl's wrist. She didn't like the look of the young girl's pale waxy face, the dark hair lank on the pillow.

Oh, thank God. She could feel Jenny's pulse – rapid, but it was there.

'Is she dead, Nurse?' Lizzie was peering over Maxine's shoulder.

'No, of course not,' Maxine said a little sharply, not wanting the younger children to panic. 'Would you go down to the hospital ward and tell Nurse Kathleen that Miss Jenny isn't very well and would she come upstairs straightaway with the first-aid bag.'

'I heard Miss Jenny being sick in the night.'

'Yes, she's not well,' Maxine said, 'so we need to help her. Off you go now.'

Lizzie disappeared.

Jenny's eyes flickered, then opened.

'Jenny, it's me – Nurse Taylor. Lizzie said you weren't well in the night.'

'I was sick twice.' Jenny's voice was thin.

'How do you feel now?'

'Not very well.' Jenny tried to raise herself and Maxine put out a steadying hand.

'Just lie quietly for the moment, Jenny. Have you any pain anywhere?'

'My side hurts . . . and I've got the devil of a headache.'

'Which side?'

'The right. Just here.' Jenny pointed on top of the bedclothes to a spot which looked to be just below the girl's stomach.

Maxine gently pressed the area and Jenny gasped. Her abdomen was definitely swollen. Appendicitis. She was sure of it. And Jenny would need to get to a hospital fast if she was right. It could burst at any time, which would be highly dangerous as the poison could quickly spread through her body.

'Here I am.' Kathleen appeared and handed Maxine the first-aid bag. 'What's happened?'

'Could be a grumbling appendix,' Maxine said quietly. 'I'll take her temperature, but I suspect she'll have a fever.'

'Yes, she looks clammy,' Kathleen remarked.

The two nurses gazed down at Jenny who had closed her eyes but was muttering under her breath, then suddenly groaned and drew her knees up under the bedclothes.

'Arghh!' Tears streamed from the girl's eyes.

Maxine took her hand. 'We're here, Jenny, and we're going to call the doctor. You're going to be fine, don't worry.'

'Thank you,' Jenny whispered. 'Tell him to hurry. The pain's getting worse.'

'I'll go and ring him straightaway.' Kathleen dashed off.

Maxine tried to make Jenny comfortable, but by now all the children were awake and gathering round, trying to see what was the matter. Maxine was thankful that this was the girls' dormitory and there were fewer of them. And they were quieter than the boys.

'Pamela,' she said, 'as you're the oldest, can you make

sure all the girls are dressed properly and help any child who isn't. Then take them downstairs for their breakfast. We need to keep Jenny as quiet as possible until the doctor comes.'

Maxine was relieved when all the children were shepherded out of the door, Pamela at the rear making encouraging noises that they would be first in the queue for breakfast if they hurried, and would get the biggest helping.

'I've rung for the doctor,' Kathleen said breathlessly. 'Do you think we ought to move her to the ward?'

'No, she's safe here. We'll wait and see what the doctor says.'

'I'm afraid it's hospital for you, lass,' the doctor said when he'd finished examining Jenny. 'You've got appendicitis and we need to get you in quickly.' He turned to Maxine. 'The ambulance may be some time with so few available at the moment. Does anyone—'

'I'm sure Harold will be able to take her,' Maxine said. 'He's our chauffeur.'

'Oh, yes, I know him. Nice chap,' Dr Stevens said. 'But time is crucial.'

'Am I going to die?' Jenny struggled to sit up, her white face upturned to the doctor.

'No, of course not.' Dr Stevens smiled down at Jenny. 'Strong, fit, young girl like you . . . I should say not.'

'I'll get Harold,' Kathleen said. She shot off.

By eight o'clock, Jenny was on her way to the Royal Infirmary, Kathleen had gone back to the ward to finish the notes she'd taken on night duty ready for the handover, and Maxine was eating her porridge and listening to Betsy and Lily's somewhat exaggerated account of poor Jenny. She noticed Pamela was sitting quietly eating her toast and not saying a word. She was looking forward to getting to know Pamela better. She might be a great help with the younger children in another year or so when she was too old to be classed as one of the orphans. But Peter first.

June was quiet when she sat with Maxine later that morning in her office. 'You know, Maxine, we're awfully short on staff and now we've lost Jenny for probably several weeks. I originally came as Matron's assistant, so of course there were two of us running the home, and now there's only me. I've been thinking – you and Kathleen have to do long shifts and when you have a day off it falls to the other to do a twenty-four-hour shift, making it impossible if either of you become sick – heaven forbid – or go on holiday. Mr Clarke has advised me to hire another nurse to fill in. But the trouble is, we're on such a tight budget and we really need two new staff members.'

'Could someone do a dual role? Fill in for you when you have a day off, or a few days' holiday—'

'I've forgotten what they are' – June smiled – 'but that might be a good idea. One-and-a-half wages instead of two.'

'It makes sense, because although we're very quiet in the ward at the moment it could change at any time.' Suddenly a thought struck her. 'June, I'm thinking out loud as it's only just occurred to me – what would you say to *me* applying? I'd be able to keep up my nursing, but my other role would be to become more involved with the children's daily lives, which is what I'd dearly love. And you could then hire another full-time nurse and Kathleen would be relieved knowing I'd fill in the gaps.'

There was a silence. Maxine shifted in her seat. Had she gone too far? Been too presumptuous? Then a smile grew on June's face and her eyes twinkled with delight as she stood up and came round her desk, surprising Maxine by giving her a brief hug, bringing a lump to her throat as it reminded her so of Anna's affection.

'That's a perfect solution, Maxine. Why didn't I think of it? I'll put it to Mr Clarke right away.' She lowered her eyes, then looked up and gave a shy smile. 'I could then go on my honeymoon knowing you were here to take care of things.'

'I'd be honoured.' Maxine smiled back. 'But you haven't mentioned any wedding date yet.'

'We've not got anything definite, partly because Murray never knows when he's going to be allowed more than one day's leave, but mostly because I felt I couldn't just go off for even a short time with no one in charge. Miss Ayles, who was one of the teachers when I first came, had that unofficial role, but now she's retired there's no one else. Your idea will solve several problems at once, provided we can get a good nurse, which proved difficult last time until you came along.'

'Well, we shouldn't start making plans until we have Dr Barnardo's approval,' Maxine laughed. 'It all sounds logical to us, but they might have a very different opinion.'

'I think Mr Clarke trusts me where the staff are concerned,' June said, sitting down and making a few notes. 'But yes, I'll write to him outlining the idea.' She beamed at Maxine. 'You'll be able to keep a closer eye on Peter as well.'

'Is Jenny going to be all right?' Kathleen asked as soon as Maxine opened the door to the ward.

'I'm sure she is,' Maxine said. 'She's in safe hands now, but she'll have to have her appendix out.'

'Oh, dear. That's going to leave us short. We'll have to get one of the other girls in the village to come up. Jenny was so marvellous.'

'And will be again,' Maxine said. 'She'll be back before we know it.' She looked round the ward. 'Anything to report?'

'All very quiet. Harvey's dressed and ready to go back upstairs, so I'll take him with me, shall I, but Reggie's still not well. He must have caught it from Bobby, but his throat ought to have cleared up by now. I think we should get the doctor out to him.'

Reggie was one of the older boys and at thirteen looked almost a man with his thick dark hair brushed away from his face, his well-defined features and even a hint of a shadow on his jaw. Maxine wondered fleetingly how he came to be at the orphanage. She was impatient to know how all the children had arrived at Dr Barnardo's.

'I'll have a look at him, but you go now. Get some sleep.'

As soon as Kathleen and Harvey had disappeared, Maxine took Reggie's temperature and read the figure. Nearly a hundred and one. Still too high. This infection was going on much longer than Bobby's. She shook the thermometer and popped it in the bowl of Milton solution in the kitchen where she could still hear him coughing. She took a bottle of cough medicine from the shelf and a teaspoon.

'My throat's still sore, Nurse.'

'Open your mouth and say "Ahh".'

'Ahh.'

'Yes, it looks red, but I'm not surprised with all that coughing.' Maxine poured out a full teaspoon. 'Here, take this.' She put the spoon in his open mouth. 'You're the only patient I've got now, Reggie,' she said, 'so you need to get well soon.'

'If I do, you won't have a job.' Reggie gave her a cheeky wink.

She pretended to cuff him and made a note on his record sheet for Kathleen.

'Are you okay for a bit?' she asked him. 'Because I need to go upstairs for half an hour, so Hilda will come and stay with you.'

Reggie grinned. 'Is she babysitting me?'

'You don't need a babysitter, Reggie. Just someone to make sure you don't get into any mischief.'

'I don't mind getting into a spot of mischief with our Hilda.'

'You behave.' She wagged her finger at him, then tucked in the sheet which was dangling on the floor. 'Do you need anything before I go?'

'Orangeade, please, Nurse.'

Maxine made him his drink and left him reading. Sighing heavily with the thought of her next job, she rang upstairs to ask if Hilda would come down.

Hilda, for once, came in with a smile, but it did nothing to reassure Maxine that she was a capable girl who had the children's interests at heart. There was something about Hilda that worried her deeply.

'I'll only be a half an hour, Hilda,' she said. 'You can make yourself a cup of tea and there're biscuits in the tin by the caddy. Keep an eye on Reggie and make sure he has plenty to drink to get his temperature down.' She gave the girl a sharp look. 'Will you be all right?'

'Course I will. Why don't you just go?' Hilda's stare was challenging.

'Excuse me, Hilda, but that's not the way to address me, or any of your elders, in such a rude manner.'

I shall have a word later with that saucy young miss, Maxine thought crossly as she went up the stairs just in time to see Peter leaving the dining room after his tea break.

'Peter, I'd like to see you for a few minutes.'

He didn't answer but just stood silently watching her.

'We'll go to the turret room,' she said, 'where we can talk in private.'

The turret room was reached internally through a long corridor leading from the Great Hall. It had been converted into a small chapel, complete with beautiful stained-glass windows. Immediately as they entered, Maxine felt a kind of peace steal over her and she hoped the boy might feel it too, though when she glanced at him she saw the same stubborn set of his mouth that he constantly wore. It was a little cooler than the main house, but not too cold, she noticed, as she guided him towards a small table and chairs to the right-hand side of the entrance.

'How are you getting along here, Peter?' she asked.

'All right.' Peter's lips clamped together immediately he'd spoken the two words.

'I'm sure it still seems very strange to you,' Maxine said, 'and I know you must miss your mother and grandmother terribly. I'm so sorry you've lost them, but they'd want you to be happy – as we do.'

'I didn't lose them – they died.' Peter stared at her, the blue eyes unblinking.

Her heart turned over at his words. 'Do you feel ready to talk about them?' she asked. 'Anything you want to tell me is completely private between the two of us, and it might help to tell someone.'

He shrugged. 'I don't have anything to tell you about them.'

'Peter, you mustn't bottle things up or you'll never start to feel better. Even grown-ups talk to their friends or the vicar if they have a bad problem. And then they feel much better afterwards.'

He kept his lips tightly shut. She needed to change the subject quickly.

'What lessons do you like best?'

'I don't like any of them.'

'You must like one more than the others. What about English?'

Peter snorted. 'I already know English. I don't need lessons.'

'It's not just the language,' Maxine said, desperately wanting to pierce Peter's barrier. 'It's English literature as well as grammar.' She tried again. 'What book are you reading in class?'

'*Great Expectations.*'

'Ah, Charles Dickens. Are you enjoying it?'

'No.'

'Maybe you've not read enough yet to make a decision.' Maxine tried to smile but it was difficult when she looked at the stony-faced boy. 'Have you made any friends yet?'

'No.'

'That's a pity. It's always nice to have a friend.'

'I don't want to be friends with any of them. *My* friends are in Berlin.'

Maxine's shoulders sagged. How was she going to approach such a sensitive issue as warning the boy not to mention having lived in Germany when he gave her no proper response to her simple questions about school?

'Is that all you want me for?' Peter suddenly said, half rising from the table.

'Peter, please sit down. I have something important to discuss with you. I only hope you will understand what I want to say.'

Peter slumped back down on the chair.

'Peter, you're in England now, and you know there's a war between England and Germany, don't you?'

Peter nodded.

'It must be very difficult for you with an English mother and grandmother and a German father. It's putting you in an awkward position. But the good thing is that you speak excellent English, which I expect your mother taught you.'

Her heart went out to him as she saw his eyes brim with tears.

'I know you must miss her terribly, but we're trying to help you. While you're in England you must make friends here. English friends.' He sat watching her. 'Peter,' she went on, desperate to make him understand, 'before we came to Bingham Hall – you know I came here the same day as you – there was another German boy, also from Berlin, I believe, who came to England on the *Kindertransport*.' She caught his eye. 'Do you know what that is?'

Peter shook his head.

'It's the train to help Jewish children escape from Germany and Joachim's parents sent him to England on it. He went to live with foster parents like you, and eventually came here. But when the older children found out Joachim was German – apparently his English was not so good as yours – the children called him the enemy and made his life miserable. No one wanted to be friends with him.'

Peter shrugged.

'Matron had to explain to them that being a *Jew* in Germany was different. The Germans are treating the Jews badly because of their religion, and that's why the Jewish parents want their children to have a better and safer life in England. But coming on the train from Germany to England was very hard and upsetting for a little boy leaving his family behind.' She drew in a breath. 'It was only when the children realised that being a Jew made him a *good* German that they made a fuss of him and wanted to be his friend.'

She had no idea what the child was thinking.

'Do you understand what I'm saying?' she asked him, wishing he would say something.

Peter shook his head.

'I want you to keep it a secret from the other children that you used to live in Germany. Don't tell them about your friends or your father you left behind in Berlin. I want you to pretend you're as English as they are. Do you think you can do that?'

Peter's eyes never left her face. For a split second she felt he was wiser than her. That he knew things she couldn't possibly know. And then he shot up and rushed out of the chapel.

How could she have said things differently? However many times Maxine went over the scene with Peter, she never came up with an answer.

But we're doing it for his own good, she kept telling herself. His life at Bingham Hall wouldn't be worth living if the children found out his background. Children could be so cruel at times. And these children had worse problems than those who were part of a loving, stable family with two parents, and often took delight in being cruel to the others. Only yesterday she'd had to stop Arthur, an evacuee, from tormenting one of the little girls, an orphan, that she didn't have parents and he did. It was no wonder fights and arguments erupted almost daily.

'We only ever had a dozen or so evacuees,' June told her when Maxine mentioned Arthur's behaviour. 'Most evacuees have gone back to their parents now the worst is over – we hope. But some cases are just not straightforward and I don't think Arthur will be going just yet.'

Maxine kept a close watch on Peter. The boy was lonely

and scared. She'd seen it in the children's ward at the Infirmary often enough when they were ill and calling for their mothers and fathers who were not always able to see them regularly because of transport difficulties and the fathers often being away, what with the war on. The kiddies would play up, craving attention and love. Maxine and the other nurses would do their best, but it was naturally not the same as having their parents. Such was the case with Peter. He'd had to leave his father and his friends and everything he knew in Berlin, and just when he must have begun to get used to living in England, first his mother and then his grandmother had been snatched away from him. All his security and stability had gone.

It wasn't much, but she was glad that this afternoon the children would gather together for their first rehearsal. Their singing would cheer everyone up.

Chapter Twenty-Two

'I've had a letter from Mr Clarke,' June said, smiling broadly. 'He's quite happy for me to advertise for a full-time nurse if you'll do the dual role we discussed. And the best news is that he will pay you an extra ten shillings a week.'

'That will come in handy,' Maxine said, immediately thinking of Teddy. If only she was allowed to write to him – send him a gift on his birthday and Christmas. She knew his adoptive parents came from Scotland, but she wasn't permitted to know any other details. There was to be no contact at all. She swallowed hard.

'Is everything all right?' June asked, sounding concerned. 'You haven't changed your mind, have you?'

'No, not at all.' Maxine smiled, fighting back the telltale tears, and hoping June wouldn't probe further. She changed the subject. 'I'm looking forward to hearing the children sing this afternoon.'

Athena was sitting at the piano in the library flicking through some sheets of music and frowning.

'I can't really read music this complicated,' she owned up. 'I think I'll stick to playing by ear.'

'I'm sure the children won't notice.' Maxine grinned. 'Did you make a list of songs?'

'I jotted these down.' Athena handed a sheet of paper to Maxine who quickly glanced over it.

'They're a nice mix,' she said. 'Something for everyone. Nursery rhymes, English folk songs and even one or two American ones.'

'I thought I should include them,' Athena said, 'seeing as the Americans are helping our boys.'

The children filed in, the boys shoving and calling out to one another and working up the girls. There were some excited voices amongst them, although Maxine noticed Peter's face was devoid of expression. He was only there on sufferance, she suspected.

June clapped her hands. 'Children. Quieten down, please. This is the library and you know better. Now, if you're eight years or older stand to the right, all the younger ones to their left.'

There was more shuffling – Barbara making sure the younger children were in the right place. They all gazed expectantly at June.

'We told you we were all going to sing together this afternoon,' June began, 'and we hope you'll enjoy it so we can do this every week. The songs will be different from the hymns in the morning and if you know them, sing out, and if you don't, you'll soon learn. But all you children on the right, please let the young ones sing the nursery songs on their own. We'll start with them.'

Athena turned from the piano. 'Let's begin with "Teddy Bears' Picnic".'

Soon the library was filled with the sound of a dozen small children's voices. It was a happy sound and Maxine caught June's eye and smiled. If the older ones enjoyed this half as much, it should be a great success.

'Lovely,' Athena said when they'd finished 'Ring a Ring of

216

Roses'. 'Shall we let the older children sing one of their songs?'

'Yes,' chorused the little ones.

'No,' Lizzie shouted. 'I want to sing *all* the songs.'

June beamed. 'Just wait your turn, Lizzie, and listen to the grown-up songs. Then when you're a big girl you can sing them too.'

Lizzie pressed her little rosebud mouth tight.

'So,' Athena said, 'I'll start this one and see if any of you know it. It's an American song that the American children love, but we sing it here, too.'

She played a few notes, then began: '*She'll be coming round the mountain when she comes . . .*'

'*. . . when she comes,*' Arthur and Reggie threw in gustily.

'*She'll be coming round the mountain when she comes,*' Athena began the second line. '*She'll be coming round the mountain, coming round the mountain—*'

Maxine kept her eyes focused on Peter, willing him to know the song, to join in. There was nothing like singing for bringing people together, she thought. And it would be the same for children. The boy looked as though he was taking it all in even if he wasn't mouthing the words.

Then, to her horror, Peter violently broke from the line and rushed from the room, sobbing as though his heart would break.

Maxine stood for one shocked second and then she dashed after him.

'Crybaby,' she heard Bobby shout as she shot out of the door.

She caught him up as he was about to race up the stairs. 'Peter, what's the matter?'

'I don't want to be in any stupid concert.'

'Is it because you don't know the songs? I'll teach them to you. Then you'll be able to join in.'

He turned on her, his eyes flashing. 'I don't want to join in – *ever*.'

Chapter Twenty-Three

Maxine was just changing her apron in her room one Monday afternoon – little Daisy had been sick over it – when there was a strange scuffling and then a beating on her bedroom door. Frowning, she opened it to find Peter, red-faced and sobbing, and clutching his raincoat. He pushed the coat into her arms as he shot in. She closed the door after him, her heart hammering, wondering what on earth was the matter. Was someone hurt? It must be something awful as the children were under strict instructions never to go into any of the staff rooms, let alone their bedrooms, and Peter's habit was always to flee from her.

'What's wrong, Peter?' She dropped his coat on the bed and turned to him, and he flung himself into her, almost knocking her over. Alarmed, she held him close for a few moments, feeling his body tremble, then gently led him to her bed and sat next to him, her arm still around him.

'Take your time, love,' she said. 'But tell me what's happened?'

'H-Hil-Hilda took my raincoat,' he stuttered. 'She s-said the pocket inside was t-torn and she had to m-mend it.' He cried fresh tears.

'I don't understand,' Maxine said. 'Why is that so terrible?'

'She took it away and when she g-gave it back to m-me'

– he looked up at Maxine, tears streaming down his cheeks –
'it was g-gone.'

'What was gone? What are you talking about?'

'I put it underneath my raincoat . . . but it's gone. She took it.'

Maxine went to fetch him a handkerchief. Nothing he said made any sense. She waited until he blew his nose. Then he reached for his raincoat and held it out to her.

'Inside,' he said. 'Turn it the other way. Look inside. It's empty.'

She turned the raincoat inside out and saw the lining had been torn to pieces.

'I thought you said only the pocket was torn and Hilda said she would mend it,' Maxine said, still puzzled.

'Yes, she mended the p-pocket, but when she gave it back it was gone.'

'What was gone?'

'The photograph.'

'What photograph?'

'The one of my father.'

Oh, dear God. It dawned on her what had happened. He must have had a photograph of his father – by the sounds of it, his only one – and put it in the lining of his raincoat for safety so no one would discover it. But Hilda had found it and removed it. And when the girl had given the coat back to him, Peter must have felt for the photograph and torn the lining open in a frenzy trying to find it. But why would Hilda have taken it out? Or if she had, why hadn't she given it back to Peter when she'd mended the hole in the pocket?

'Peter, dry your tears. Hilda must have forgotten to return it to you, but I'll get it back, don't worry.'

'Do you promise?' He gave her such a beseeching look, her insides melted.

'I promise,' she replied. 'Has your father written to you since you've been in England?' she asked, dreading the answer but, knowing she needed to keep the conversation alive, she would press on, no matter how painful.

'When my mother was . . . alive, he wrote to her and to me. But nothing when I went to my grandmother's.' He sniffed hard.

Maxine swallowed. Could he have been sent to one of those dreadful camps?

'Did you write back to your father?'

'He doesn't receive my letters. They were all returned to my grandmother's address.' At that he burst into tears again.

'But he would have been notified about your mother's illness and your grandmother's accident,' Maxine said very gently, 'and told that you'd come here.'

'I don't know.' He brushed the tears away with the back of his jacket sleeve. 'He can't know I'm here or he'd write to me.' Peter's voice trembled. 'And now I've lost his picture,' he sobbed.

'I'm going to get it back. Remember, I promised. And I'll check to see if Dr Barnardo's has sent your father a letter to let him know this is where you're staying at the moment.'

Peter's head shot up at her last words. She took his hand.

'It won't be forever, you know. When the war is over, you'll be reunited with your father and be able to live in your country again. But until then we want you to be as happy as possible here at Bingham Hall.' *Please don't let his father be dead*, she thought, as she said this.

'I hate it here.'

'Peter, I understand how difficult it is at the moment, but everything will change once the others get used to you. And in the meantime I'm your friend. And it's not just children who have problems. Grown-ups do, as well.' She swallowed.

221

'I get lonely sometimes, too . . .' Maxine paused. She'd never admitted this to anyone, that after Anna and then Edwin . . . She stilled her thoughts. What was the point? The poor little chap had enough on his plate to tackle and certainly didn't need some unknown nurse moaning about her lot. Luckily he didn't seem to be taking much notice. She drew in a breath. 'I'm hoping you might be able to help by being my friend. You can talk to me about anything and I'll always try to help you. Will you trust me?'

Peter caught his lower lip with his top teeth, not taking his eyes off her. Maxine held her breath. If he said no or shook his head again, she knew she had failed with him.

'Peter?'

Very, very slowly, almost imperceptibly, he nodded.

'I think we'd better go,' she said, rising to her feet. 'Your class will soon start.' She held her hand out to him and pulled him gently upright. 'You're a brave boy and I'm proud of you. And while you're in class I'll go and speak to Hilda.'

But Hilda was nowhere to be seen.

Maxine gave a deep sigh as she sat at the table in the ward and made a few notes on her talk with Peter, added the date and signed her name. She'd have to talk to June again. This was a far bigger problem than any child of eight should have to cope with. Yet when she reread her notes she realised she knew a little bit more about him than she had before.

She stretched and glanced at her watch. Time for tea. She didn't really feel like joining the others so she put the electric kettle on.

Just as she was pouring the water over the tea leaves, she heard voices upstairs and laughter, and for a few seconds she wished she'd joined the others in the dining room. Yes, it was loud with children's chatter, but it would have been

222

company. Except for when she and Kathleen changed shifts and caught up for a half an hour on what had been happening both upstairs and in the ward, her job, she was slowly realising, was quite solitary. It would be good if June could find another nurse and Maxine would have more chance to be with the children.

There was a knock on the ward door. She went to open it and Hilda stood there unsmiling.

'Ah, Hilda, just the person I've been looking for. I wanted to ask you what you'd done with—'

'Matron says you're to come up straightaway. Someone's here to see you. A man.' Hilda's small eyes shone with importance that she could order her superior to do something.

Dad. She smiled delightedly at the thought and then her smile faded. Mum would never have let him come on his own. She'd have insisted on accompanying him out of curiosity. Her heart plummeted. The only other man who would possibly visit her was Mickey. *Oh, no, please not him.* He only came into her life when he wanted to borrow some money. There wasn't a brotherly bone in his body for her. But surely he was still in prison.

'Can you keep an eye until I come back?' she asked Hilda, annoyed that it must be her brother who'd chosen this moment to come and see her. He always brought trouble with him, not at all worried about causing a scene, which she must stop at all costs.

'I suppose so. I should've brought my magazine.' Hilda's lips turned down in a sulk.

Why was the girl always so difficult? It was as though she almost hated her. But Maxine hadn't seen much sign of Hilda's friendliness to anyone else so it was obviously her nature. At least she'd get a chance to ask her where the photograph was when she came back to the ward.

'I think Kathleen's got some in the kitchen. I shouldn't be too long.'

She was still scowling at the thought of her brother when she reached the Great Hall and saw a tall man in uniform, his arms full of bags. She blinked. It wasn't Mickey after all. The children were all giving him curious glances as they passed by on their way to class with their teacher – Judith Wright looking from the stranger to Maxine with raised eyebrow. Somehow that small gesture annoyed her. Why should she have to answer to Judith Wright's unwelcome curiosity? There was something about the woman she couldn't really take to. But the man was coming towards her. And her stomach was making funny little jumps.

'You look positively cross to see me, Maxine,' Crofton said, grinning. 'And that's before I've done or said anything.'

'I'm sorry.' Maxine attempted a smile. 'I thought you were someone else.' She didn't want to elaborate about her brother and why he would have been unwelcome, but Crofton gave her a questioning look.

'Do you mind my being here?'

How could she tell him how relieved she was that he wasn't Mickey, and that she was far from minding, though she'd been a bit deflated not to have heard a word from him after he'd made such a big fuss to have Bingham Hall's telephone number. Not wanting him to realise how very pleased she was, she used her professional voice.

'No, of course not, but it would have been better to have telephoned first, which you said you would do.'

'I know, but it's been all work lately and pretty grim, most of it.'

Immediately she felt ashamed. She knew he was understating what he and his pals were facing every day. Compared to them, she was having an easy time.

'I'm so sorry . . .'

'Don't worry.' He jerked his head to the parcels. 'Is there anywhere I can dump these bags? It's just a few treats for the children.'

'That's awfully kind of you.' She wished her heart wasn't beating so fiercely. 'Have you spoken to Matron?'

'Yes, he has.' June appeared from her office, a broad smile on her face. 'I told him he could put them in my office for the time being, but he seemed to want to clear it with you.'

'It's Matron who's in charge, not me,' Maxine told him.

'Why don't you both come into my office,' June said. 'I'm sure Mr . . .'

'Crofton Wells, Ma'am. At your service.'

'Well, I'm sure Mr Wells could do with a cup of tea,' June said. 'Why don't you two go on ahead and I'll get Bertie to make us a tray.' She hurried off to the kitchen.

Maxine told herself in no uncertain terms not to be so ridiculous as Crofton grinned and gestured with his arm for her to lead the way. Her pulse was racing alarmingly as she stepped into June's office.

'Is it all right if I put everything on Matron's desk?' Crofton asked.

'I'm sure it is.' She dared to look at him properly for the first time since he'd arrived. She hadn't forgotten those brown eyes with the amber flecks. Now, they were narrowing a little as he asked the question. Or was he trying to get the measure of her response at his sudden appearance? It was difficult to know.

He removed his cap and placed it on the corner of June's desk, then pushed back a lock of dark chestnut hair. Why did every movement he made fascinate her?

'Let me help,' she managed, as she unwrapped one of the parcels.

By the time June came back, the desk was piled with toys and books and crayons.

'How were you able to get us such a wonderful variety of things?' June said, picking up a teddy bear. 'We have to rely a lot on being given second-hand things from the people in the nearby villages and, of course, Liverpool. The children are going to be so excited, but whatever must all this have cost?'

'Don't worry about that,' Crofton said. 'We import a huge amount of stuff from America – it's what keeps us going. I happened to mention Dr Barnardo's to the Wing Commander and he said for me to put some things together for the children. Take whatever I wanted. So here I am.'

'Well, it's incredibly thoughtful of you and most kind of your boss,' June said, smiling. 'The toys are getting so bad now with wear, the children are going to be thrilled with these new ones. They're only used to having one or two toys of their own, and then a few more they play with which are kept in their playroom, so I'll probably dish these out slowly – maybe on their birthdays and special occasions. If they have everything at the same time they won't appreciate them nearly as much.'

'Long as they enjoy them,' Crofton said smiling and looking at Maxine.

'Am I allowed to ask how you know Nurse Taylor?' June addressed Crofton, and Maxine noticed her eyes sparkle with interest.

Crofton turned his head to Maxine. 'You mean you didn't tell Matron all about our first meeting? That evening meant so little to you?'

She was furious with herself for blushing. He was probably only teasing, but she didn't know him enough not to be

226

embarrassed. Quickly, before he could say anything more, she said, 'Actually, we met when I went to a musical in Liverpool which my cousin was in. He happened to sit next to me and we had a brief chat. And then when Peter and I went to buy him some clothes we bumped into him.'

'Ah,' June said, giving Crofton a warm smile.

For some reason, June's knowing 'Ah' grated on Maxine. As though that was all it needed to start a romance, or that's what it sounded like to her. But before things became any more personal, she was thankful to hear a knock on the door.

Crofton sprang up to open it, and there was Bertie, holding the tea tray but still managing to look him up and down, then giving a nod as though of approval.

'Bertie, this is Mr Wells,' June said as she made a space for Bertie to put down the tray. 'He's brought some toys for the children. And Mr Wells, this is our cook, Bertie.'

'Very nice to meet you,' Bertie said, wiping her hand on her apron before holding it out.

Crofton shook her hand and asked her, 'What's that wonderful smell?'

Maxine bit back a smile as she noticed his eyes stray to the plate of sliced cake.

'It's just out of the oven,' Bertie said. 'Dried fruit and apple. I hope you'll all enjoy it.'

The three of them talked of other things – the weather for the time of year, the number and ages of the children, how difficult some of them were because of their background – Maxine watched Crofton as closely as she could without his being aware, although once or twice he caught her looking and grinned, which made her cheeks go warm again.

When they'd finished their tea, Maxine and June gathered the toys together and stuffed them back in the bags.

'I'll put them in the playroom and lock them in one of the cupboards,' June said.

'I'll help you.' Maxine jumped to her feet, but June put out a restraining hand.

'No, you stay and keep Mr Wells company for a few minutes.'

'I don't like to leave Hilda too long,' Maxine said, feeling June was doing this on purpose.

'She'll be perfectly all right with her love magazines' – June smiled – 'but I'll pop down and see how she is.' She held out her hand to Crofton. 'It was very nice to meet you, Mr Wells.'

'Crofton, please,' he said, shaking her hand.

'Only if you call me June. And thanks again for those lovely presents for the children. You can definitely come and see us again soon.' June looked at him and laughed. 'Oh, dear, that sounded awfully rude. I meant you can come but only on condition that you're empty-handed next time.'

'I'll do my best to oblige,' Crofton said, chuckling.

Maxine remained quiet. They didn't need any comment from her, it seemed, but as soon as June left with the over-flowing bags, Crofton turned to her.

'She's nice, isn't she?'

'She's lovely,' Maxine agreed. 'Apparently the previous Matron was an absolute tyrant. June found out she was a supporter of Oswald Moseley, so Dr Barnardo's got rid of her *and* the handyman who had the same enthusiasm for that horrible man.'

'All the excitement happens here at Dr Barnardo's then.' Crofton gave her a cheeky grin. 'Bingham Hall harbouring British fascists. Whatever next?'

Maxine couldn't help smiling back. 'This was all before I came and it's settled down since June took over.'

'She seems very young to be a matron.'

'She started as an assistant to the matron I was telling you about, and when the woman was sacked, June was asked to take over. She's only been doing the job for a few months but the children love her, and she gets on well with the staff. It couldn't be better. I certainly didn't need any more—' She broke off but it was too late. Crofton immediately cut in.

'Didn't need any more what, Maxine? Excitement? Trouble? Problems? I'm afraid you can't escape them. Life's full of them, war or no war.'

'Yes, well I meant it would be awful working under someone who was a Nazi sympathiser. One of the teachers told me the matron gave June a rough time.'

'Well, she's gone now, so we can talk of other things.'

'I'm afraid I really must go.' Maxine rose for the second time.

Crofton looked up at her and caught her hand. Shock waves rippled up her arms. Their eyes held. 'Maxine, I don't want to let you go this time. Could we meet soon? Could you get the time off? It's likely I'll have the day after tomorrow off, though they can change their minds at any time. We have to take that chance.'

Maxine hesitated so long she realised it wouldn't sound genuine whatever she said now.

'I-I'm not sure.'

'Would you ask June? She must allow you out for a few hours. Unless you'd truly rather not see me again.'

How could she tell him her fears? How could she let him know she would dearly like to see him again but she was terrified she might fall in love with him and he would end up hurting her? She could never explain how Edwin had casually thrown her love aside when he'd told her he was married with children and would never put his family at

229

risk. He hadn't worried about their unborn child, she thought bitterly. Little Teddy. Her darling baby. She closed her eyes to ward off the pain. She couldn't go through such turmoil again. She could tell Crofton liked her. In fact, she was sure he was attracted to her – as she was to him. Then what?

They'd start seeing each other and he'd ask her personal questions about her husband – unconsciously, she glanced down at her wedding ring. If he mentioned children she knew she wouldn't be able to put on an act or tell a lie. Yet Teddy must be kept a secret at all costs. If Crofton discovered she'd had a baby, he would think her deplorable for giving him up for adoption. He'd think she was incapable of love or taking responsibility, and certainly he would assume she must have only been thinking of herself and her career. Even worse, he might think she was promiscuous and not fit to be a mother. Not at all the kind of woman he'd want for a wife.

And even if he was as genuine as she was sure he was, how would she be able to convince him she was none of those things? Even Johnny had hinted that she was selfish to want to keep working when her mother was blatantly in need of some help with nursing her father. He hadn't known her mother well enough to realise she loved bossing her husband around and fussing over him and enjoyed being a martyr.

Her eyes stung with unshed tears at the unfairness of it all. But it had been her decision. She could have chosen a different path. But it wouldn't have been the best path for Teddy, and that's what she'd focused on.

I made the decision for Teddy so he'd have a better life than I could give him.

She could only stare at Crofton, her lower lip quivering.

'Maxine.' He still had hold of her hand. He gripped it tighter. 'What's the matter? You can tell me. Please. I'm a very good listener.'

'Not here,' she said.

Not ever.

'Then tell me we can meet Wednesday.'

She could see by the set of his mouth that he wasn't going to leave before he had the answer he wanted. 'I'll have to ask June,' she said.

'Good.' He got up and adjusted his cap. 'I have every faith that June will let you go for an afternoon or an evening.'

At the front door, Crofton put his hand warmly and firmly on her arm. She looked up at him, saw his smile, felt the impression of his fingers on her arm even though he'd taken his hand away. Edwin had charmed her with his easy smile, his good looks, his air of authority. She'd trusted him and he'd betrayed her trust. She mustn't ever forget that. Mustn't forget in a moment of weakness. Crofton was probably the same as all men – charming and loving and kind until they got what they wanted. And then they had no compunction to tell you it was over. She was sure Edwin would have left a trail of broken hearts. Inwardly she stiffened.

As though he'd read the way her mind was working, Crofton broke into her thoughts. 'I'll telephone you tomorrow morning – unless there's any emergency,' he added.

She stood a long time at the open door watching his long easy strides towards the parked motorcars, not being able to put into words her feelings. Harold was giving a final polish to Bingham Hall's car, and both men acknowledged one another. Crofton opened his car door and folded himself behind the steering wheel. Several of the children ran out to watch him and she heard them call out to him.

'Mister!' Lizzie shouted. Crofton unrolled the window. 'What's in those parcels?'

'You'll have to ask Matron,' he said, starting the motor.

'Are they for us?' a skinny boy with very dark hair, whose name Maxine momentarily forgot, bellowed back.

'You'll have to speak to Matron.'

And he was gone up the drive, a cloud of smoke screening the last vision of him.

Maxine turned and stepped back into the Great Hall. How was she going to ask June if she could have some free time without being interrogated? However nice June was, Maxine was not going to give anything away. And that went for Crofton as well.

Chapter Twenty-Four

Crofton put his foot on the accelerator as soon as he was on the open road. He knew he had to leave as soon as he told Maxine he would telephone her. If he'd hung around she would have given him all sorts of excuses. Fine, if she wasn't interested, but he was certain she was by the way she'd glanced at him several times when they were in Matron's office and she thought he wasn't looking. The way she became a little flustered and her cheeks turned that delicate shade of pink when he touched her, however briefly. She knew he liked her – more than liked her, and he was sure she felt the same.

Her beautiful greeny-blue eyes fringed with the longest lashes he'd ever seen on a woman. And that thick hair like spun gold which she'd worn long and loose the two times he'd met her. Today she'd swept it up so it looked neat and professional for work and his fingers had itched to take the grips out of her cap, the hairpins from her hair, and let it fall to her shoulders. He'd wanted to bury his face in her hair, kiss her forehead, her eyelids, her nose, along her jaw to her neck, and finally those soft full lips – a mouth which seemed to him to be made for kissing.

He didn't know how he'd managed to hold back – not give any indication of how he was feeling. But Maxine was an enigma. There were depths in her eyes that he would probably never understand, but he wanted so badly to understand everything about her. She must have really loved her husband. How terrible to be a widow at such a young age. Just as well she hadn't had children. Yet there seemed to be something more besides pure grief. Someone had hurt her badly – knocked the wind out of her. Maybe it had been her husband. But he didn't think so or why hadn't she given an indication that she was well out of it when he'd died. No, it was someone else. Maybe someone she'd met after her husband's death who'd hurt her. The more he thought of that possibility the more he was sure of it. A ripple of anger made him want to punch the unknown swine's nose. Crofton gave a rueful grin and shrugged. He was getting carried away – probably reading something into nothing.

But when she smiled at him he felt on top of the world.

Face it, Wells, you're smitten – well and truly.

*   *   *

Maxine hurried down the stairs to the ward. She'd been gone much longer than she'd expected. Hilda would be getting annoyed by now, and she needed to speak to her right away. She felt guilty that she'd almost forgotten about the photograph in the surprise of seeing Crofton in the Great Hall, standing there with an armful of toys for the children.

'Hilda,' she called softly as she entered the ward. But there was no reply.

Where was the girl? She shouldn't have left her so long on her own. Dear God, what if something had happened?

'Sorry, Maxine, I didn't mean to give you a fright that we'd all gone and left the children.' June came in from the kitchen, beaming. 'I told Hilda to go – that I'd wait for you. I must say, I liked your Squadron Leader.'

'He's not *my* anything,' Maxine said a little shortly. 'I've only met him a couple of times. He's just an acquaintance.'

'He seems to regard you more seriously than I think he would one of his acquaintances.' June grinned. 'And he was very kind to bring those toys, but it was perfectly obvious it was a good excuse to see you again . . .' she broke off laughing, 'and now I've made you blush.'

'Only because it's hot in here,' Maxine said defensively. She caught June's eyes, merrily twinkling, and couldn't help bursting into laughter. 'You're making more of it than it is, you know.'

'Mmm. I don't think so, but we'll see.' She gave Maxine a searching look. 'Do you know, Maxine, you haven't laughed much since you've been here. Reminds me of when I first came; *I* didn't feel like laughing. But you look so much more relaxed. Maybe it's got something to do with Mr Crofton Wells.' She grinned at Maxine. 'Crofton. I rather like it. And it suits him. I think he's a little bit special.'

'How can you tell in such a short time?' Maxine demanded.

'Because he reminds me of Murray.' Maxine raised her eyebrows. 'Oh, not to look at,' June said, 'but his manner. And the way he looks at you.'

'What do you mean?' She couldn't breathe.

'Anyone can see he's in love with you.'

Heat rushed to Maxine's cheeks again. 'How can he be? I've told you, this is only the third time we've set eyes on each other.' She didn't mention that time in the tram.

'It didn't take me any longer when I first met Murray,' June said, her smile wide. 'Nor him me, apparently.'

'Do tell me how you met,' Maxine said. Anything to change the subject, which she didn't want to think about now. She'd ponder over June's words later when she was in her room.

'I will tell you, but it's a long story, not how we met, but how we finally got together. It was touch and go at one point. But I must get back to Freddie. He'll be wanting his supper.'

'Can I quickly tell you about what happened today with Peter?' She told June how he'd banged on her door earlier, and about the missing photograph.

'Oh, poor little chap,' June said, immediately serious. 'Maybe it had slipped through the slit into the bottom of the lining, and Hilda thought he'd worry that he'd lost it. She mended the tear, and intended to return it to him and forgot. I'm sure it's just a matter of reminding her.'

'I don't think it's that simple.' Maxine screwed her eyes up in thought. 'If you'd seen Peter an hour ago you'd have been quite worried . . . he was distraught. I've seen Hilda in action myself and often wonder why you keep her on . . . although it's probably none of my business,' she added hastily.

'Mr Clarke asked me to be patient with Hilda,' June said. 'I've never taken to her myself, so I completely understand how you feel. She lived with her mother, who's a bit odd herself and not a motherly sort of woman, so I understand. Hilda's not terribly bright, but at least Dr Barnardo's has given her a chance. Besides, so many of the young women have joined up. There are very few to choose from the longer this war goes on.' She paused. 'I really think you'll find it was a simple oversight on her part.'

As soon as June left, Maxine realised she hadn't asked her for permission to have a few hours off on Wednesday. Maybe it was just as well.

June obviously liked to see the best in people, Maxine mused as she handed over the notes she'd made for Kathleen who was on night duty. Kathleen was a dear and had done 'nights' since Maxine arrived, and Maxine was determined that next week she would give Kathleen a turn on the day shift.

Frustratingly, by the time she'd chatted to Kathleen it was eleven o'clock and too late to tackle Hilda. She'd have to find her first thing in the morning.

'I haven't got it,' Hilda said, a defiant expression on her face.

Maxine had tracked the girl down after breakfast and asked to see her. The art room was empty and she'd taken Hilda in, nodding for her to sit down at one of the tables.

Momentarily speechless, Maxine heard her own words to Peter playing in her mind. *I'll get it back. Remember, I promised.*

'Where is it if you don't have it?

'I'm not telling you.'

Maxine had to stop herself from pulling the girl to her feet and shaking her. She took in a jagged breath.

'Why can't you tell me, Hilda? You might as well, because I'll find out . . . believe me.'

Hilda's mouth drew in a determined line.

'Why didn't you return the photograph immediately to Peter?' Maxine demanded. Silence. 'Hilda, please answer me.'

'Because when I showed it to someone, they didn't give it back.'

'Who has the photo, Hilda?'

But Hilda remained tight-lipped, much to Maxine's annoyance.

She studied Hilda for some sign, but the girl's face was blank. 'For goodness' sake, Hilda, don't you have any idea what you've done? The child has lost his mother and his grandmother, and been torn away from his father, who's probably now in a concentration camp and he's unlikely to ever set eyes on him again. And you let his precious photograph leave your hands. It wasn't yours to let anyone *see*, let alone let them keep it. So why did you?'

Another silence.

'If you don't answer me now you could easily lose your job over this.'

Fear spread across Hilda's face. At least that was something, Maxine thought grimly.

'Hilda,' she said more gently. 'What is it about the photograph that you had to show it to someone else?'

'Peter's father is a German!' Hilda suddenly stood up and shouted. 'He's the enemy. And if he's Peter's father, then Peter Best is the enemy. And he shouldn't be allowed in Dr Barnardo's.'

'Sit down at once, Hilda,' Maxine ordered, taken aback by the girl's words and the vehemence with which she said them. 'We know nothing about Peter's father other than he made sure his son and wife escaped to England for safety. You can't blame him for that.'

Hilda sat down again and stared at her.

'Please tell me who has the photograph, Hilda.'

'I'm going to tell Matron about the little Nazi so she gets rid of him.' Hilda gave Maxine a challenging stare. 'We don't want anyone like him. You wait until the kids find out. They'll go mad.'

'Hush, Hilda, you don't know what you're saying. Matron and I already know about Peter. And if you dare say anything more to anyone, unless it's Matron or me, I will personally see that it will be *you* who leaves Bingham Hall . . . not Peter.'

'I'm not listening to you anymore,' Hilda said, jumping up.

Maxine grabbed her arm, but Hilda was a strapping girl

and managed to shake her off. Hilda stormed out, swearing under her breath. If she continued to refuse to say who had the photograph, then how was Maxine ever going to find out and return it to Peter? Even more troubling was Hilda's attitude towards an innocent child.

'Are you going to tell Peter Hilda won't say who has the photograph?' June asked when Maxine had finished telling her what had just transpired.

'I've already got to tell him I've broken my promise,' Maxine said.

'Well, you haven't broken your promise yet.' June gave Maxine a steady look. 'You just can't return it at this moment. But we'll find where it's gone, believe me. I'll speak to her and see if I can get her to see sense. If you'll stay here as well, Maxine.'

'Yes, of course,' Maxine said. 'Shall I go and fetch her in?'

'Please do.'

But June had no more luck than Maxine had had.

'Then I'm afraid I will have to report you to Mr Clarke,' June told a furious Hilda. 'And I don't have much faith in your chances to remain here.'

As she finished speaking, the telephone on her desk rang. Maxine's heart jumped. Crofton had said he would telephone her this morning. If it *was* him, he couldn't have picked a worse time, with Hilda glowering and June obviously in a quandary, wondering what to do for the best. It rang persistently and Maxine prayed June wouldn't answer it. Then June's arm stretched out to pick up the receiver.

'Bingham Hall. June Lavender speaking.'

'Ah, yes. I remember . . . She's here, as a matter of fact, sitting right in front of me . . .' She cupped her hand over the receiver and nodded for Hilda to leave. As the girl flounced out, June gave Maxine a mischievous wink. 'It's for you, Maxine. Your Squadron Leader.'

Blushing to the roots of her hair, Maxine took the receiver.

'I'm afraid it's not very convenient at the moment.' Maxine hated the sound of her voice, formal and not at all friendly, but she could hardly be otherwise with June's eyes twinkling at her. Then June smiled and left the office.

'Sorry, Crofton, there's a lot going on here, so you'll have to be brief.'

'I wondered if you had a chance to ask your young matron for a half-day,' Crofton's warm voice came over the wire.

'Um, well, no, I haven't. We've had a bit of a crisis here and it didn't seem appropriate to ask her.'

'Oh, I'm sorry to hear that. Anything I can do to help?'

'No, nothing,' she said. 'One of the children – Peter, actually.'

'Ah, the little chap I met in the store. Is he in some kind of trouble?'

'You might call it that.' Oh, why had she said so much? Crofton was bound to pick up on that and ask exactly what was the problem.

'Is it anything to do with him being German?'

So he *had* noticed Peter's small lapses.

'Yes, but I can't say more over the telephone.'

'Maxine, please ask June if you can at least have tomorrow afternoon off because we'll be leaving the day after. You sound awfully low and a problem shared is a problem halved.'

'I'm sorry but I wouldn't be allowed to discuss this outside the orphanage.'

There was a silence his end.

'Then I'll have to come *inside* the orphanage again,' he said, and she detected a chuckle in his voice.

'Crofton, I—'

'Sorry, Maxine, I'm being called.' The line went dead.

She clicked her tongue. She knew she'd been curt with him once again but it hadn't seemed to put him off. He was lucky that June had taken to him. Even so, the matron still might be annoyed if he arrived with no invitation. She gave a deep sigh. Everything had begun to spiral out of control.

Why did Hilda think that photograph was so important? Maxine wondered, as she went about her duties in the ward that afternoon. Maybe Peter's father had signed something on the back which would immediately identify him as a Jew if the wrong person got hold of it. She shivered, desperate to put it to the back of her mind. She wished she had more to do, but the ward was very quiet with only Jimmy, who had badly twisted his ankle and needed to rest it, and Thomas, who'd managed to break his wrist in a fight.

There was a light tap at the door and she opened it to see Judith Wright standing there looking a little sheepish.

'I'm probably here under false pretences,' Judith said. 'Might only be a cold.' She broke off coughing.

'Any other symptoms?' Maxine studied the teacher's face.

'My throat's sore and nose is running . . . that's why I think it's only a cold.'

'Your face is flushed so I'm going to take your temperature.'

She took a metal chair from a small pile by the wall and gestured Judith to sit down, then put a thermometer under the woman's tongue.

'I thought so,' Maxine said, reading off the figure. 'A hundred and one.' She looked up. 'Have you noticed any other changes? Tiredness, joints aching . . .'

'I have felt more tired than usual,' Judith admitted. 'My neck feels a bit swollen.'

241

'Let me have a look.'

Maxine gently pressed her fingers around Judith's neck, then noticed a rash round her ear.

'Right. Go upstairs, get your nightdress and toothbrush and anything else you need. I'm pretty sure you've got German measles and I don't want those two to catch it.' She nodded towards the two boys by the window. 'We'll have to call the doctor to verify it. Keep away from everyone. We don't want it to spread.'

'German measles? Are you sure?'

'No, I'm not absolutely sure – that's why we're going to have the doctor look at you.' She looked at Judith. 'Did you have it as a child?'

Judith shook her head. 'No. And because I didn't, I thought I'd got away with it – that it was a children's disease.'

'Not at all,' Maxine told her. 'Anyway, we'll soon find out for sure, but the doctor won't be in until tomorrow morning at the earliest, and meanwhile I'm keeping you in. Luckily, I can allow Jimmy to leave as his ankle has improved enough for him to use it a little, and Thomas can manage back upstairs too. I just don't want them to catch anything.'

Judith disappeared to pack her bag and Maxine rang through to June. 'I suspect Judith's got German measles.'

'Oh, no. That's the last thing we want – an epidemic.'

'The good thing is, it's not quite so contagious as ordinary measles, but we still need to keep the children and any staff who haven't had it away from the ward.'

'Have you had it, Maxine?'

'Yes, thank goodness, when I was a child. It's always worse when you're older. But I'm sure Judith will be all right.'

Judith came back to the ward with her overnight bag and Maxine directed her to the bed under the window. Then at least any child who was admitted would have a bed as far away from Judith as possible.

That evening Maxine didn't feel like being social with anyone. Judith wasn't an easy patient. She seemed to want to use Maxine as a recipient for all her grumbles and moans. She wasn't sure she wanted to stay at Bingham Hall because Dr Barnardo's wasn't all she thought it would be; the wages weren't good; the children were much more difficult than she was used to; she was a long way from her home in Cambridgeshire . . . It went on and on until Maxine's head buzzed.

It would be good to strip off her uniform and get out of her shoes, and put her feet up while Kathleen dealt with the woman for an hour or two. She'd write to Pearl. That would help to take her mind off things. She hadn't answered her last letter.

She unlocked her door and something on the floor caught her eye. A photograph. She picked it up. It was a picture of a man who looked to be about thirty. Dressed in an immaculate uniform, he stared back at her from under a peaked hat displaying an eagle and beneath . . . She peered at the image more closely and felt the blood rush through her veins. An unmistakeable symbol – the swastika. The same eagle and swastika was pinned on the right-hand side of his jacket. Slowly, she turned the photograph over. It simply read: *SS Sturmbannführer Carl Heinrich Best.*

Goosepimples crawled up Maxine's arms. Peter's father. So he wasn't the Jew they'd all assumed. He was a Nazi.

Bile formed in the back of her throat as she tried to take it in. Dear God, this was much worse than simple spite. Hilda was bright enough to know a swastika when she saw one, but not bright enough to understand the enormity of what she'd done by letting such a dangerous photograph out of her sight. Well, at least she'd had the sense to get it back from whomever she'd given it to and slide it under Maxine's bedroom door. Thank goodness Kathleen hadn't found it. The fewer people who knew this the better.

Maxine lay on the bed, her fingers laced at the back of her neck to support her head, trying to take it all in. After a while she raised herself up and took hold of the photograph again, staring at it for several long minutes. Peter's father was an extremely handsome man. Blond-haired with deep-set eyes that indicated no sign of cruelty but only appeared contemplative, and even concerned.

She shook herself. She mustn't form opinions of his characteristics which clearly didn't exist. She looked closer but couldn't get it out of her head that it was a good face, not that of a monster. He had a straight nose and well-shaped lips. Not brutal as his mouth ought to be, but sensitive-looking, somehow.

Stop this. You're making him into somebody nice. Someone he's not. He's a Nazi. And Hilda's right on one thing: he's the enemy.

Chapter Twenty-Five

Maxine left her room, the photograph in an envelope tucked into her bag, desperate to see June. This was serious and she wanted June's opinion on how to handle Peter now this bombshell had emerged. Unusually, the door to June's office was shut. She heard voices but decided it was too important to leave, so she knocked.

June poked her head round the door, saw it who it was and said, 'Oh, thank heavens it's you. Come on in.'

Someone turned round, immediately stood up and grinned. Crofton! She hadn't imagined he would actually show up this evening.

'Hello, Maxine.'

'Why are you here?' she blurted.

'I've come to ask June—' He broke off and Maxine threw June a look of apology on his behalf. 'Don't think I'm being too familiar,' Crofton said, 'but you were there when Matron invited me to call her "June".' June smiled her agreement. 'I stopped by to ask if I might see you for a couple of hours.'

'I've told him he's always welcome here,' June said, 'and that of course you can have tomorrow evening off.'

Crofton caught Maxine's eye and grinned. She pretended to ignore it.

'Sit down, both of you,' June said, 'and I'll order tea. You look as though you've got something on your mind, Maxine.'

'Something important has come to light where Peter is concerned,' Maxine said, 'but I believe it should be kept private.'

'Oh, I'm sorry, I didn't realise you needed a private conversation.' Crofton half rose, but June waved him back down again.

'Let me ask Bertie if she would make us all some tea.' As June opened her door to the hall, she said, 'Please stay, Crofton. We're very isolated here at the home and sometimes it's hard to know what's going on in the outside world. You might be able to throw some light on whatever Maxine's found out, or whatever questions come up, so chat about the weather until I come back.'

Crofton, Maxine knew, was trying hard to be friendly and make small talk, but the photograph of Peter's father with his swastika armband was weighing so heavily on her mind that she could barely mumble any reply. Thankfully, June appeared after a couple of minutes.

'Tea's coming,' she said. 'But we'll probably need something stronger if Maxine's serious face is anything to go by.' She turned to Maxine. 'So what have you found out?'

There was nothing for it but to show June the photograph in front of Crofton. And as June held out her hand for the photograph, Maxine understood what Peter had meant when he'd said he trusted Crofton. The man sitting next to her didn't crane his neck to see the picture she handed to June, didn't try to take over in any way, and his calm demeanour invited trust.

June studied the photograph for as long as Maxine had, then silently handed it to Crofton. He stared at it for a long minute, then turned it over.

'Well, it was never going to be a straightforward case, trying to blend him in with the other children,' he said, handing the photograph back to Maxine, who slid it back into the envelope.

'I admit there was nothing in the paperwork mentioning Judaism,' June ventured. 'I suppose I should have realised.'

'I find it so hard to believe that Peter's father is a Nazi,' Maxine said somberly. 'And of a high rank, going by all those medals. So how do I explain to Peter that his father is the enemy? It will seem like the end of the world for him. I don't think I can do it.'

Two pairs of eyes gazed at her.

Crofton spoke first. 'Poor little chap. I feel sorry for him. Especially with his mother and grandmother gone.'

'Do you suppose he knows?' Maxine said.

'I'm sure he does.' Crofton held her eye for some seconds, and for the first time, Maxine wished she was alone with him. 'He would have seen his father in uniform many times, and couldn't fail to recognise the swastika.'

'Although he was three years younger then,' Maxine said, her voice a little shaky from his gaze. 'He'd only be five. That's pretty young to understand what the swastika means.'

'I don't think so,' June said. 'The children here know what it stands for. Peter's bound to know and has been trying to keep it secret. What a burden for him.'

'How does he act with everyone here?' Crofton asked the two women. 'Not just the other kids but the staff as well.'

'He hardly joins in with the others,' June said. 'He feels very much an outsider, but whether he thinks everyone English is the enemy, I don't know. We're just not his family and the children aren't the friends he's left behind.'

'I agree with June,' Maxine said, 'but he seems to have given me his trust – grudgingly, I admit. It happened when

I promised I'd find his father's photograph and give it back to him. We seemed to turn a corner that afternoon.'

There was a knock at the door and Bertie came in with a tray, smiling at them.

'I've made some toast in case you haven't had any supper.'

'How kind of you,' Crofton smiled at her.

'It's imperative no one else finds out about Peter's father,' June said when Bertie disappeared, 'but Hilda refuses to tell us who she showed the photograph to.'

'Could be someone not even in the home,' Crofton suggested. 'The postman, milkman, coal boy . . .'

'You could be right.' June frowned as she stirred her tea. 'I often hear Hilda and the maids talking to the boys when they come to the tradesmen's entrance – they're usually giggling about the latest gossip or planning to go to the next dance.'

'Has Hilda got a boyfriend?' Crofton asked. 'If she has, she might be gossiping – feeling important that she knows something they don't.'

'She's a bit young at sixteen,' June said.

'That's not too young from what I see going on.' Crofton picked up his cup and gulped the contents.

'Whatever happens, the children mustn't find out,' June said firmly. 'Peter's English is practically flawless. We don't need to worry about the young ones, but if the older ones discover he's German they'll make his life a misery, not understanding that whatever his father is, it's not Peter's fault.' She paused. 'As far as I can see, we need to let the teachers and the rest of the staff go on thinking the boy is Jewish.'

'Do we know anything about Peter, other than he and his mother left Germany?' Maxine asked. 'It's not as though they weren't safe with the father working for Hitler.' She shuddered at the mention of the dictator's name.

'We know the boy's grandmother was recovering from major surgery, so I imagine the mother was given compassionate leave to see her.' June went over to the filing cabinet and removed a file. She sat at her desk again and flipped through it. 'Naturally she took Peter with her as his father wouldn't have had the wherewithal to look after him.' She looked up. 'I'm guessing that bit, of course.'

'But instead of Peter's grandmother dying, the boy's own mother died,' Maxine said.

'I wonder why his father didn't immediately send for Peter to return to Germany, but left him to live with his English grandmother – someone Peter barely knew – in a foreign country,' June contemplated.

'From what Peter told me, I don't think his father even knows his wife is dead,' Maxine said. 'He hasn't heard from him since he was sent to his grandmother's. He might not even be alive.'

'Where did Peter go after his grandmother died?' Crofton asked.

'To foster parents,' June answered. 'They had him for a while but they couldn't keep him.'

'Do we know why?'

June glanced at Crofton. 'From what I gather, he was a bit of a handful. They couldn't cope. And he would barely speak. The agency was desperate and asked us if we'd have him. Of course I said yes.'

'Is there anything else in the file that might help you to understand his background?' Crofton said.

'There's a bit in German I can't make out, though it's mostly family information, I think.' June looked at Maxine and smiled. 'How's your German?'

'Non-existent, I'm afraid.'

'I understand German,' Crofton said, 'but I'm far from fluent. Would you trust me to translate it?'

For some ridiculous reason, Maxine felt proud that Crofton knew German. She looked across the desk at June, hoping the young matron wouldn't feel he was going too far in his offer to help.

'I'd be most grateful.' June smiled as she handed him the file. She stood up and Maxine and Crofton followed suit. 'Why don't you both take it to the library and see what you make of it.'

'If you're sure it's all right for me to help,' Crofton said. 'I'm very aware of the confidentiality of the children's files.'

'It's either that or ask Peter,' June said seriously. 'If anyone had known German at Barnardo's Headquarters, they surely would have translated it. I'd feel a lot better knowing everything we can so we know how to talk to the boy.'

'I've been thinking about him a lot and how he'll cope,' Maxine said. 'Could your little Freddie help? He's such a happy dog. He might be just the ticket for helping Peter. Maybe Peter could take Freddie for a walk. Give the boy something to be responsible for who's no threat but who might become a friend.'

'Of course.' June beamed. 'Why on earth didn't we think of it before? We'll introduce them. Let's hope he likes dogs.'

In the library, Maxine led Crofton into a small room off the side. There was a round table and several chairs pushed under. Crofton pulled out two of them and when they were seated he opened Peter Best's file.

'Shall I read it out as I'm translating?'

She nodded, and Crofton cleared his throat.

'It's dated 20th August 1939.'

Maxine gasped. 'Goodness, only ten days before Germany invaded Poland. His wife and Peter only just made it.'

'Quite.' Crofton bent his head.

'Christine Susan Nichols born in England to English parents in 1907 in Liverpool, England. Married on 2nd October 1932 to Carl Heinrich Best in Berlin and resided there since that date.

'Peter Carl Best, born 10th August 1934 in Berlin to parents Carl Heinrich Best and Christine Susan Best.'

Crofton looked up. 'Either his father or Dr Barnardo's has pinned Peter's birth certificate to the report, so all self-explanatory so far.

'Carl Heinrich Best—' Crofton stopped reading aloud and Maxine watched as his eyes skimmed the rest of the page, nodding once to himself. When he looked up she noticed how his lips had tightened and a tiny muscle flicked back and forth under his left eye. She wondered how much sleep he'd managed to get lately.

'It's not what you'll want to hear, Maxine, but it's what we suspected. It says here that he joined the Wehrmacht in '36 and was promoted to Major in July '39 – hmm, just before he sent them to England. For obvious reasons it doesn't say anything about his actual position or his work in the German army. It goes on . . .

'Frau Best has been granted permission to travel to England on compassionate grounds as her mother has had a serious operation. Peter, her son, will be travelling with her.'

Frowning, Crofton raised his eyes to her. 'I'm slightly surprised she'd need permission as the war still hadn't actually started, even though they would have known the date by that time.' He looked at the sheet of paper again. 'There's very little else. Some bureaucratic instructions – not exactly sure what they are.' He gave Maxine a rueful smile. 'But I'm still puzzled about the whole set-up.' He shrugged. 'Well, there's nothing more we can do for the moment, so I'll just make a few translation notes – then June has it on file. It won't take long.'

The library clock ticked another ten minutes away until Crofton put the top on his pen and clipped it back into his tunic pocket, then tucked the translated report in the file.

'That's it.' He handed it to Maxine. 'So now that's done, can we please spend an evening together tomorrow? Your nice matron has agreed, so there's no excuse – unless you'd rather not, of course.'

Maxine hesitated. She wanted to see Crofton away from the orphanage more than anything in the world, but it seemed that every time she began to feel close to him she had to back further away so he had no possibility of finding out her past.

'You look so worried, Maxine, but it's just an outing. To have some fun. I've got tickets for a concert at the Philharmonic Hall. They're playing Chopin – one of his piano concertos. But if you say no, I promise I'll go and not bother you anymore. But I hope you won't.'

He was right. It *was* just an outing. So why was she getting so upset. She wasn't some naïve young girl. She could take care of herself. There was no need to worry about what he might ask her – how she should reply. They were simply going to listen to some beautiful music. Enjoy themselves. She drew in a breath.

'I'd like that very much,' she said. 'I've not been since they rebuilt it, though I've been meaning to. It's such a magnificent building. I always admire it when I walk by.'

Crofton got to his feet and put his cap on. 'We can have something to eat first.'

252

'That would be lovely,' she answered, as her heart did a little flip. 'Shall I catch the five o'clock bus and meet you outside the Philharmonic at half past? Would that be all right?'

'It would be perfect.'

His beaming smile banished all her worries – for the time being, anyway.

After returning the file to June, Maxine walked back to the library. June had said she'd send Peter in to see her so she could have her chat with him and return the photograph. There was a knock at the door and he appeared.

'Come in, Peter.' She took him into the recess where she and Crofton had sat just ten minutes before. 'Sit down.'

'Did you find my photograph?' Peter's intense blue eyes met hers accusingly.

'Yes, Peter, I have it. But first I must talk to you about it.' She hesitated. Did he know what his father represented?

'Why can't you give me my photograph?'

'I promise I will in a minute.' She hesitated. She must pick her next words with care. 'Peter, I've seen the photograph of your father and I understand why it's important to you, but we must be very careful with it. If the children find out your father is German they will do their best to make you miserable and angry. So you must always speak in English. We've talked about this before. But *if* they find out, you must pretend you're Jewish, just like Joachim, and then they'll accept you and be friends with you.'

She feared an outburst that he hated Jews and they should all be punished, but he sat quietly, his eyes not leaving her face.

The silence was unnerving. Then suddenly he shot up from his chair.

'I'm a Catholic, so I won't pretend,' Peter shouted, his face going bright red with anger.

'Peter,' Maxine said very gently, 'he's your father and I know you love him, but terrible things are happening in Germany and we want to keep you safe.'

'I want to go home. I want Papa.' Peter burst into sobs.

Maxine offered him a handkerchief. He snatched it and held it to his eyes, then crumpled it into a tight wet ball and handed it back to her, his bottom lip quivering.

All of a sudden he looked up with red-rimmed eyes and rounded on her.

'You don't know Papa,' he stormed, his eyes blazing, his voice choked with tears. 'You've never met him. He's the best father in the world. And the bravest.'

Oh, if only . . .

'I'm sorry, Peter, of course it's right that you should be loyal to him. But we must keep it a secret about your father being in the German army. You mustn't say anything to the other children. Your English is excellent, so don't even mention you were born and lived in Germany.' She put her hand on his arm, surprised that for once he didn't snatch it away. 'It will be hard, I know, but do you think you can do that?'

He didn't answer.

'Peter, I will help you keep your secret. But you must make that promise too.'

It wouldn't be fair to threaten the child. She handed over the envelope. He grabbed it as though she might change her mind, and half pulled the photograph out to reassure himself it was there, then slid it back.

'Peter – tell me you promise.'

'I promise.' He glared at her, his eyes so bright with tears she swallowed hard and had to force herself not to turn her head away.

254

'Would you like me to keep it in my room in a safe place where only you will know where it is? That way it won't get damaged or taken again and you can see it as often as you want.'

Peter shook his head vehemently. 'No, it's mine. I'll put it in the cupboard by my bed when no one is looking.'

She hesitated. If she insisted, he might become hysterical. She supposed he was old enough to take responsibility for it.

'All right,' she said reluctantly. 'Mind you keep it safe. Now run along and see your friends.'

'I don't have any friends,' he turned on her, blue eyes blazing. 'They all hate me.'

'Oh, no, of course they don't. You're imagining things. It takes a bit of time, that's all, when you're new.'

'I'm not imagining. Jack said yesterday he'll be glad when I go back home where I belong.'

What was that supposed to mean? Maxine wondered. 'And what did you say to Jack?' She mentally braced herself.

'Papa said I was not to say anything to anyone who was nasty to me. He said I must not fight. I must be a man and walk away.' He looked at Maxine with those bright blue eyes. 'I told you before – my father is the best father in the world.' He broke down in tears again.

How on earth would Peter ever come to terms when he knew the truth about his father? Should she say something now? Get it over with. But was it her place? He would hate her and she felt he was just beginning to trust her a little.

She tried to put her arm around his shoulder, but as usual he jerked away from her and jumped to his feet. She felt it was beyond her to ever explain to the boy that his father was an evil man – a Nazi. If only the war would end and Herr Best could send for his son. She gave an involuntary shudder.

'May I be excused, Miss?'

'Yes, Peter,' she sighed and looked at her watch. 'It's time for you to get ready for bed anyway.'

Chapter Twenty-Six

Every time Maxine thought of her date with Crofton her heart did a somersault. They'd never had a real date. Maybe they'd finally have a chance to get to know one another. And then her heart would plunge in fear. She longed to know all about him but she dreaded saying anything about her own past. And he'd be bound to ask questions.

The following day came quickly and with it a letter from Pearl.

18th October 1942
Dearest Max,

Can you believe what I've gone and done? Only broken my leg! I stepped backwards on the stage last Saturday and dropped into the orchestra. What a hullaballoo I've caused. Of course, the show came to a sudden halt. It must have been terrifying for everyone seeing me fly backwards through the air. I managed to break a valuable violin and slightly injured the musician. Everyone said I could have broken my neck, so thank goodness it's only this stupid leg.

I'm in the Royal Infirmary where you did your training, feeling more than a bit sorry for myself. Next week the show goes to the West End, but I shan't be with

*them. I could weep with sheer frustration that I had it
in my hands – my career, that is – and now it's in tatters.*

*The only bright spot on the horizon is my deliciously
good-looking surgeon. He's set my leg, which is now in
plaster, and comes to see me twice a day whether he needs
to or not, haha.*

*Anyway, Max, I'd so love to see a friendly familiar
face. If you get the chance, will you come and visit?
Visiting hours are from 2–4 every day. Please bring me
a magazine if possible, or a book to read. Am so bored.
Can't stop thinking of my stupidity. If you can't get away
soon I'll understand as the children must be keeping you
very busy, but please come when you can.*

Much love,

Pearl XX

Maxine read her cousin's letter with horror. Poor Pearl. It
wasn't fair after all her hard work to get where she had with
her singing and acting. She reread the letter, her heart sinking
at the mention of the Infirmary. The last thing she wanted
was to run into someone who knew her before . . . before
Teddy. She swallowed. She had to stop thinking that way or
she was doomed to skulk around forever, worrying that she'd
be recognised. She was bound to bump into someone who
knew her sooner or later. Well, she'd rather it be later.

She made up her mind to visit Pearl this very afternoon
– before her date with Crofton.

As Maxine entered the Royal Infirmary, the familiar anti-
septic smell, far stronger than in the ward at Bingham Hall,
assailed her nostrils. She stepped over to the reception desk
and asked for Miss Pearl Burton. The woman flipped through
her cards and looked up, smiling.

'Miss Burton is in the surgical ward,' she said. 'Through the double doors and up the stairs. Second corridor on the right.'

Maxine passed several doctors and nurses on her way to Pearl's ward, thankful that she didn't recognise anyone.

'May I help you?' A nurse came up to her immediately she set foot in the surgical ward.

'I'm visiting Miss Pearl Burton.'

'Ah, yes, Miss Burton. You'll find her at the far end by the window. She should still be awake as she only finished her meal a few minutes ago.'

Maxine thanked her and threaded her way through the beds until she spotted a figure at the end with her leg raised.

'Well, if it isn't my long-lost cousin.' Pearl beamed as soon as Maxine appeared. 'My letter has had an immediate effect – the very intention.'

'It was extremely powerful,' Maxine laughed, then glanced at the contraption where Pearl's leg was resting. 'You're going to be awhile with that leg strapped up.'

'I know. At least a month. Maybe six weeks. And it's making me crazy.'

Maxine sat down on the metal chair by the side of the bed and handed Pearl a couple of magazines she'd managed to spirit from the home.

'I'll have to take them back next time I come,' she told Pearl. 'Magazines are rather precious at the moment.'

'So I gather.' Pearl looked closely at her cousin. 'You're looking so much better than when I last saw you. In fact, you look absolutely lovely. That colour makes your eyes look positively turquoise.' She paused, her expression contrite. 'What a dippy thing to say. You were going through the worst possible time. Anyway,' she added quickly, 'does Barnardo's feel like home now?'

'It does in a way,' Maxine admitted, going a little pink at Pearl's compliment. She'd dressed extra carefully for her date with Crofton and worn her straight navy skirt and a new blouse she'd made from a silky material Barbara had offered her.

'Was it the right place to go to?' Pearl asked.

'Completely right. June is a darling. She's only my age but she's not afraid of hard work or responsibility, and we've become good friends in spite of—' She broke off.

'In spite of what?' Pearl jumped on to Maxine's hesitation.

'In spite of me keeping myself to myself where the others are concerned, though I like Kathleen – the other nurse – as she doesn't pry.'

'Don't close up,' Pearl said seriously. 'Give them a chance. You should all be part of a happy family – like we were in the show – still are, I expect, even though I'm missing.' Her bottom lip trembled.

'Poor Pearl. But you'll be back with them as soon as your leg's healed.'

'I hope you're right. It's what I'm clinging on to.' Pearl shifted a little but her leg remained static. 'Can you pass me the water, please?'

Pearl took a few gulps, then pulled a face and drew in a ragged breath.

'Are you in pain?' Maxine asked, full of concern for her cousin.

'Yes, a lot of the time. They do try to give me something when they can, but the pain pushes through everything.' She looked directly at Maxine. 'I meant what I said just now, Max, about the rest of the staff at the orphanage. Are they all women, by the way?'

'Except for Harold, the chauffeur, and Charlie, the handyman, yes they are.'

'Well, you don't want them to think you're snobbish by not letting them get to know you. It's very bad to bottle your emotions. Don't I know it.'

'You know how I feel more than anyone, Pearl. But I need to put it to rest or else I'll go mad.'

She gulped. Never would she be able to 'put it to rest' all the time Teddy was in her heart, but helping the children at the orphanage was proving to be a way of managing the ache.

'I understand.' Pearl's eyes glistened. Then she seemed to shake herself. 'What about the kids?'

'Most of them are grand, even the ones who've had a shocking start in life. But we have a new boy, Peter, who's half German – by the father. He came to England with his mother, but his mother died and he was sent to his grand-mother's. Then the house got a direct hit and killed his grandmother and took most of their possessions. He went to foster parents, but they couldn't handle him, he was so naughty. He's a bright child – fluent English, and all that – but he's shocked to the core with what's happened to his family.'

'I'm not surprised,' Pearl said. 'Poor little chap. Can you help him?'

'June wants me to try,' Maxine said, 'but it's not easy.'

They chatted on, about the show mostly.

Maxine glanced at her watch. It showed ten minutes to four.

'I don't know where the time's gone, and they'll soon boot me out, but it's been lovely catching up with you.' Maxine paused, wondering whether to ask the next question. She decided to risk it. 'Have your mum and dad been to see you?'

A shadow passed over Pearl's face. 'No. They don't know I'm in here.'

'I'd be happy to go and see them,' Maxine said. 'Explain what's happened. I'm sure they'd want to come and visit you.'

'No, don't do that. I—'

'And how's my special patient this afternoon?'

Maxine froze. Instinctively, she grabbed the arms of the cheap metal chair, her heart hammering loud in her ears. She had her back to the man, but she knew instantly who that voice belonged to. Oh, if only she'd said goodbye even two minutes ago she wouldn't have heard him. She wished the ground would swallow her up. She wished she was anywhere but sitting by Pearl in hospital. What should she do? Where could she go? She didn't want to turn around but she'd have to.

'Hello, doc,' Pearl said, her face suddenly pink and alive, her eyes shining.

Maxine reluctantly turned round and looked up at the tall handsome surgeon. It was gratifying to see the look of dismay on his face.

'My goodness. If it isn't Nurse Taylor.'

She hated the way his eyes glanced at her stomach. He knew she must have had the baby months ago, but it was as though he wanted to reassure himself it was no longer there. Her feeling of pure contempt for him deepened as, by the looks of Pearl, she realised this must be the 'deliciously good-looking surgeon' her cousin had described. Thank goodness with Pearl's condition, nothing much could happen – for now, at least. She gave an inward shudder.

'You two sound like you know each other,' Pearl said a little plaintively.

'We were at St Thomas' at the same time,' Edwin said smoothly, apparently ignoring any discomfort Maxine might be feeling.

She had to get out or she'd say something she'd regret. She brought her attention back to her cousin and bent to kiss Pearl's cheek. 'I'll come and see you again soon, Pearl.'

'Come as soon as you can. It's pretty lonely here. Except when the doc comes to visit me.' Pearl looked at Edwin from under her lashes.

'I will.'

She couldn't get out of the ward quick enough.

She'd almost made it to the corridor when a voice made her stop.

'Maxine. Can you give me five minutes?'

Ignore him. There's nothing he can say or do that would change anything.

'Please, Maxine.'

Against her will, she turned and faced him.

'My office is only just along the way.'

He took her by the elbow. She wanted to shake him off but his grip tightened and he guided her a few hundred feet, then opened a door marked 'Mr E. Blake' on a shiny brass plaque.

'Sit down,' he instructed her as he locked the door behind him and took his place behind the desk. He steepled his hands in front of him, reminding her of the first time she went into his office in St Thomas'. But this time it was different. Too much had passed between them. 'How are you, Maxine?'

'I'm all right,' she answered stiffly.

'Good. Very good.' He unsteepled his fingers, then keeping his palms together he made a silent clapping gesture as though wondering how to put something difficult to her. 'What happened to the baby?' he eventually said.

Her hackles rose. 'This is the first time in over a year you've enquired,' she said.

'Well, I'd like to know at least what happened to it.'

'I didn't get rid of *it*,' she emphasised, 'if that's what you mean, but thank you for so thoughtfully offering me the opportunity.' She couldn't help the sarcasm. She watched as he chewed the inside of his cheek and refused to meet her eye.

'I wish you had,' he said, 'for your own sake. Now you're saddled with a baby.'

'I would be honoured to be saddled, as you so charmingly put it,' Maxine snapped, not bothering to disguise her anger. 'And the "it", as you call the baby, happens to be a boy – *your* son as well as mine, who, in case you're interested, I've named Teddy.' She was gratified to see a slight flush appear on his cheeks. 'But you were right on one thing, Edwin. I didn't think it would be in Teddy's best interest to bring him up without a father, and some stranger looking after him through the day because I'd have to work, so I let . . .' she blinked back the tears, '. . . I let him go to be . . .' she swallowed hard, '. . . to be adopted.'

'It was the sensible thing,' Edwin said, leaning back in his chair, linking his hands behind the back of his head. 'You can now put it all behind you knowing he'll grow up with two loving parents.'

She shot to her feet. 'How dare you surmise that he'll be better with them than with me,' she slammed into him with her words.

'Steady on, girl.' Edwin rose from behind his desk, his flush deepening.

It flashed through her mind that he didn't look quite so attractive with his face all red against his auburn hair.

'And don't call me "girl".' She put both hands on the edge of his desk and leaned over so her face was close to his. Fury rose in her. 'And while we're at it – leave my cousin alone.'

He pulled back a fraction, his eyes narrowing. 'What the devil are you talking about?'

'You know perfectly well – Pearl Burton, who happens to be my cousin.'

'Pearl is your *cousin?*' He let out a bray of laughter. 'Well, I'll be damned.' Then a dark shadow crossed his face. 'What have you told her about me?' He cleared his throat and watched her face intently. Maxine waited, knowing what was coming. 'Have you told her I'm the father of your child?'

She wouldn't answer straightaway. Let him stew. Let him wonder. She was gratified to see sweat beading on his forehead as he waited for her reply. His Adam's apple moved up and down most unattractively. She'd never noticed it before, but then she'd never seen him quite this nervous – even when she'd first told him about the baby. She took in some calming breaths to slow her heartbeat, hoping to give him a few more moments of anxiety.

'I never told her your name. She doesn't know it's you.'

He blew out his cheeks, then took his handkerchief and wiped his forehead. 'That was sensible of you.' He paused, then said, 'Where do you work now?'

It would be an innocent question from anyone else, she thought, but from him it took on supreme importance. She almost lost her nerve. Almost.

'I'd rather not say.'

'Ah, I've got it.' Edwin lifted his chin and gave a triumphant smile. 'You're one of the nurses at Dr Barnardo's – Bingham Hall, I believe. Pearl happened to mention she had a cousin who worked there.'

He came from behind his desk and put his hands on her shoulders. Hands that saved lives but now felt as though they were trapping her. She backed away, thankful he let her

265

go, though she could still feel the imprint of his grasping fingers.

'I'm sure you're settled in and enjoying your job, aren't you, Maxine?'

The words were friendly but his tone had a distinct edge – almost menacing. Maxine shivered.

'I have nothing more to say to you.' She turned towards the door.

'Yes, you may go,' Edwin's voice was smooth, 'but be sure that if you mention anything of our relationship and the baby to Pearl, or anyone else for that matter, I will personally see that you lose your job.'

Her heart wouldn't stop hammering on the tram to the Philharmonic Hall. What a prize fool she'd been to ever have thought she was in love with such a despicable man. She felt sorry for his wife having to put up with such an arrogant philanderer who obviously had no sense of remorse what-soever. She'd certainly learned her lesson. It would be a very long time before she gave her heart to any man again.

She pushed away an image of Crofton and instead focused on Edwin. What a rotten coincidence that he'd transferred to the very same hospital where she'd begun her training and where Pearl had been taken. And by the way Pearl was eyeing him, she was already infatuated, if not head over heels in love with the man. She had to warn her cousin, but she wasn't sure she could face going back to the hospital. Should she write to Pearl instead?

Would he really stoop so low as to put the mother of his son out of work for the sake of having an undisturbed dalliance with Pearl? And then it struck her. Of course this wasn't about Pearl, it was his *wife*. That's what he was afraid of. That it would come to the ears of his wife.

266

He'd had to threaten Maxine with dismissal, hoping his seniority would be enough to intimidate her and keep her mouth shut. Because if she found out where his wife lived, which probably wouldn't take too much detective work, and told her a few home truths about her husband, then it would be the end of his marriage. But Maxine would have achieved two things: she'd have saved Pearl from any future heartache and at the same time saved her job at Bingham Hall, which she desperately needed to keep for her own sanity as well as her livelihood.

For the hundredth time, she wondered how Edwin could possibly have forsaken his own baby. To have offered her money to get rid of his child. The pain of his casual dismissal of Teddy was just as wounding now as it had been when she'd first told him she was pregnant. But in spite of the shock of seeing Edwin again, she realised one thing had definitely changed. She was no longer in love with Mr Edwin Blake. Even more surprising – she knew now, when it was all too late, that she never had been.

Chapter Twenty-Seven

Edwin weighed heavily on Maxine's mind as she hurried along Hope Street to the Philharmonic Hall, of which the people of Liverpool were so proud. She looked up at the building that had replaced the previous one, irreparably damaged by a fire. Her father had mentioned this new one was designed in the Streamline Moderne style, and she remembered the buzz of excitement when it had officially opened just before England was at war.

She was so engrossed in her thoughts, she didn't even see Crofton as he sprinted towards her, making her jump.

'Gosh, I don't usually have that effect on women,' Crofton said, kissing her cheek. 'I'm glad we're early so we can take our time. Relax. We could probably both do with a bit of that.'

She smiled at him as they walked along in perfect step. He grinned back and took her hand. He was so easy to be with. She wasn't on edge the way she'd been with Edwin – forever worrying that she wasn't good enough for his family, and not clever enough for Edwin himself.

'Penny for them,' Crofton winked as he steered her through the door of the restaurant.

'Oh, just nonsense really.' She felt her face grow a little warm and was glad he was behind her and couldn't tell.

'Good evening, Madam – Sir.' A waiter came up to them. 'Have you booked a table?'

'Yes. Name is Wells.'

The waiter nodded. 'Come this way, Sir.'

When they were settled and had menus, Maxine asked, 'Do you know the programme this evening?'

'I believe they're playing one of my favourites – Chopin's Piano Concerto No. One. And some shorter pieces – probably by other composers.' He regarded her steadily with his warm brown eyes and she felt herself melt. 'Does that sound all right?'

'It sounds wonderful.'

'There's not a great choice,' Crofton said, ruefully, as he scanned the menu.

'There is a war on, you know,' Maxine teased.

Crofton's eyes twinkled. 'Aren't I always reminded. That's why I was determined to be in civvies this evening. To forget about the war for a few precious hours and just enjoy your company.' He smiled at her.

She liked that he'd said the hours they were about to spend together were precious to him. Then she just as swiftly brushed the thought away. It was too dangerous. She wasn't ready . . . not brave enough to get involved . . .

They'd both chosen the fish and chips and peas, and Crofton ordered two glasses of wine. He'd wanted to order a bottle but she wouldn't let him.

'I can only drink one glass or I'll fall asleep.'

'And then I'd have to pick you up and carry you out of here,' he chuckled, 'though it might be awkward getting you into the seat at the concert.'

Their banter helped take her mind off Edwin and his threat, but once or twice she caught Crofton looking at her quizzically, and then he said, 'Maxine, is anything troubling you?'

'I'm not being the best company, am I?'

'It's not that at all. But if you've something on your mind you can tell me. It will never go any further. I have an older sister and even she comes to me sometimes for advice.'

'I didn't know you had a sister,' Maxine said, grateful the conversation had steered away from her. It was strange how he knew something was worrying her even though she was desperately trying to hide it. 'What is her name?'

'Natalie.'

'Is she married?'

'Oh, yes. Two children – Toby and Jemima. Five-year-old twins. Little rascals, but adorable.'

She could see the affection he had for all of them in his eyes.

'And you? Any siblings?' he asked.

She sighed. 'Mickey, my older brother. Always in trouble.' She wouldn't mention prison. 'He worries my parents to death. He doesn't seem at all like a brother. I hardly know him.'

'That's a shame.' Crofton finished his wine and smiled at her. 'Try not to worry about him too much. He can obviously look after himself.'

'Oh, it's not Mickey I'm worried about—' She stopped herself in time.

'Then who is it?'

She shook her head and her eyes grew moist. A lone tear slipped down her cheek, but before she could reach for her handkerchief, Crofton leaned forward and gently brushed it away with his finger.

'Don't get upset, Maxine,' he said softly. 'I wouldn't dream of pressing you. But if you ever want to talk about it, promise you'll think of me.'

'I will.' She gave him a watery smile.

*   *   *

270

In the concert hall, they found their seats – the last two on the aisle – reminding Maxine of the first time they met. It would be different this time. He was no longer a stranger but a rather dear familiar figure. Her heart beat a little louder and ridiculously she hoped he wouldn't hear it. As if he could.

'Are you all right?' he whispered as the lights went down and the orchestra struck up.

'Yes, I am now.'

'Good.' He reached for her hand, entwining his fingers through her own.

She sat back and closed her eyes, acutely aware of her hand, nestled safe and warm in Crofton's, and let Chopin's music weave its magic.

There was a silence for quite some seconds after the final notes faded away and Maxine stole a glance at Crofton. He caught her looking and smiled at her so tenderly it melted her insides. She smiled back as the audience gave the pianist and orchestra a thunderous applause.

'My hands are stinging with all that clapping,' she said as they made their way outside.

'Mine too. We obviously need to harden them up by going to lots more concerts.'

So he intended there to be more outings. Her heart lifted.

'What time is your last bus?' Crofton asked.

'Half past ten.'

'We have half an hour.' He looked directly at her. 'Shall we go and have a drink somewhere?'

'That'd be lovely.'

'Let's try The Cracke down Rice Street. It's small but cosy on a cold night.' He looked at her. 'Ever been there?'

She thought of the times before the war when Johnny

271

had taken her by the arm, saying he was dying for a beer. They'd often ended up at Ye Cracke. She was never crazy about pubs but she'd gone anyway. It was a chance to be with him, the same as when she was a child. They'd been happy in those days – she hadn't been faced with the dilemma of whether she should marry him or not when she'd only ever thought of him as her best friend. And there was no war on.

'A few times – with my late husband,' she gulped.

'Will you be all right?' Crofton sounded concerned as he took her hand firmly in his.

She nodded.

Ye Cracke was a charming old pub that had managed to escape any updating. Thankfully it wasn't as busy as it had often been with Johnny, but that was probably down to so many young men being away at war, though there was still plenty of chatter and laughter. Crofton found them a seat in a dimly lit corner of the room, showing no surprise when she asked him if she could just have a cup of tea.

She watched him as he walked towards her, carrying a tea tray and a half-pint of beer, giving her that special smile which lit up his face. She liked the way a lock of hair hung over his forehead. The strong nose. His mouth. For a crazy moment she wondered what it would be like to feel his lips on hers. Her pulse raced with the thought. But the clock was ticking. Quarter of an hour. And then he'd be gone. She'd be on the bus rumbling its way back to Bingham Hall and he would hitch a ride back to camp. Her tomorrow would likely be safe: his would be packed with risk and drama, his very life at stake. She swallowed hard.

'You've gone very solemn again, Maxine,' Crofton said, setting out her tea and taking the seat opposite.

'I was thinking . . .'

'About what?' He downed some of the beer.

'You,' she blurted.

'Me?' He pointed to himself in an exaggerated gesture, making her laugh. 'I love seeing you smile, Maxine, and even better to hear your laughter. I get the feeling you don't do this very often.'

'I didn't used to be serious,' Maxine said. 'But the older you get, you change, don't you? At least *I* do. You know all the bad things that can happen.'

'Don't dwell on the bad things . . . try to look for the good.' Crofton gazed at her. Their eyes held. Without warning, he leaned over the small table and lightly kissed her lips. The air crackled between them. 'I refuse to apologise,' Crofton said, 'because I've been wanting to do that for ages.'

'I've wanted you to kiss me for ages,' Maxine found herself admitting.

'Really?' Crofton's mouth twitched at the corners. 'Never thought of you as a brazen hussy.'

She grinned. 'Will this convince you?' And she bent towards him and pressed her lips firmly on his.

Immediately she felt the pressure of his response as his kiss lingered. She didn't know who drew away first.

'Phew!' Crofton raised both eyebrows and gazed at her unwaveringly. 'I'd like to try that again – in private.'

She smiled. She couldn't help it. All of a sudden she felt happy. Happier than she'd felt for a very long time. He seemed to catch her mood because he took her hand and winked at her. They talked about his parents who'd lived in their Shropshire house where he and their other three children had been born – Natalie and Ernest, who was in the Navy, and Lucy, only seventeen, who couldn't wait to join up. He told her how he'd been in his last year as an architect, hoping to open his own practice, before all his plans were altered. Before he knew it, he was in Coastal Command at Liverpool docklands, though he didn't elaborate any further.

'I should be able to pick up my studies again when it's over,' he said, his warm brown eyes gazing at her as though he never wanted to stop looking at her face, 'but war changes you. I might decide to do something different.'

She was intrigued. 'Like what?'

He held his gaze. 'I've always wanted to be a photographer – I'm pretty good with a camera.'

Maxine gave a start. 'That's quite a change.' She tucked the piece of information into the corner of her mind.

'I know. But my father wanted me to get what he considered "proper qualifications", so he well and truly nipped that idea.' He gave a rueful grin. 'But I'm a bit too old now for him to influence me the way he used to.' He glanced at his watch. 'Sorry to run on. You must be bored sick.'

She shook her head. She'd be happy for him to go on talking to her forever.

'Well, it's your turn next – promise?' He smiled. 'I want to hear all about your family. You mentioned a brother? Is he in the forces?'

Mickey. She swallowed. How could she possibly tell Crofton about him? The thieving, the black marketeering? How dreadfully upset she and her parents were that he'd gone to prison. A poster on the wall opposite caught her eye – a blonde, languishing on a chair surrounded by three men. 'Keep mum – she's not so dumb', and underneath was written: 'Careless talk costs lives'. She gave a sigh and saw Crofton's eyes swivel to the poster.

'The warning stuck on the wall in the mess is a bit more imaginative than that,' he said. 'Listen to this:

'Never in the bar or barbers
Talk of ships or crews or harbours
Idle words – things heard or seen
Help the lurking submarine.'

He looked at her and threw her a smile. 'Oh, dear, you're looking serious again.'

'It's just another reminder about how dangerous your job is.'

'You mustn't worry about me.' Crofton glanced at his watch. 'If you've finished, we should start walking to the bus stop. I'll come back with you.'

'You certainly will not,' Maxine said, jumping to her feet. 'I'll be perfectly all right.'

Crofton took her hand again. It felt beautifully, wonderfully natural as they walked to the bus stop where two other couples and two giggling girls were waiting.

'It'll be dark down that lane,' he said, as they took their place at the end of the queue.

'I have my torch. Look.' Maxine opened her handbag and showed it to him. 'And before you ask, I've got my piece of tissue paper to dim the beam so I don't get told off by a passing warden.'

'I still don't like to leave you.'

'Me neither, but not because I'm scared to go home alone.'

The words had slipped out. He put his hands on her shoulders and gazed at her intensely, his eyes darkening in the gloom. Then he took her in his arms and this time there was the deepest longing as she received his kiss. And just as the bus came round the corner, she knew she was falling in love.

It was only when she was in bed reliving Crofton's kisses that her cousin's plight took hold again. She had to do something to stop Pearl from going down the same path she'd gone, and the misery that man had brought her.

She sighed. Her mind was buzzing with Crofton. Her head filled with sensations she'd never dreamed she'd feel for any man again. She was sure he was beginning to care for her, but he'd only seen her best side. If he knew what she was hiding, he'd bow out of her life in an instant. The thought that one day she would lose him made her tremble. What had he said? *Don't dwell on the bad things . . . try to look for the good.* Somehow the idea comforted her a little. She would try to sort it out tomorrow. But now she needed sleep.

*   *   *

Crofton wanted to be quiet, to think. Even though it was late, he needed a coffee, so he decided to wander over to the officers' mess. There shouldn't be anyone about much at this time of the night.

Late though it was, there was the usual buzz, but thankfully he didn't see anyone he recognised as he sat down at one of the tables in the corner, where he hoped he wouldn't be disturbed, and asked the steward to bring him a cup of coffee. Aware that he should let it cool down a little, he took a gulp, burning his top lip on the edge of the porcelain cup as the hot liquid ran down his throat. The sudden sharp pain and the overpowering chicory taste made him pull a face. It was a poor substitute for coffee and he didn't know why he'd bothered.

But he'd needed time to think. He couldn't get Maxine's kisses out of his mind. She was a mystery. Sometimes he thought he knew her better than she knew herself and other times he felt he didn't know her at all. But he did know there was something troubling her deeply, stopping her from feeling happy, and all he wanted to do in the world was to be the one she would trust enough to confide in. To listen to her. Try to help her. Show her that he cared.

Show her that he truly loved her.

He brought himself up with a start. Was it true? Did he love her? How could anyone be sure? He'd thought it had happened once before and he'd been duped well and good.

He sighed and gulped the rest of the revolting liquid that had by now gone cold, and strode out of the mess hall, shutting the door behind him with a determined bang.

Chapter Twenty-Eight

Maxine awoke from a restless night. The sounds of explosions, though far away, had broken into her dreams and woken her so many times she'd not been able to have more than a couple of hours' sleep. They'd probably bombed the docks again.

She sighed. More destruction. When was this war ever coming to an end? Surely the German soldiers must be getting just as fed up as we are, she thought, as she dragged herself out of bed, eyes stinging with tiredness.

Judith Wright was sitting up in bed reading when Maxine took over from Kathleen after breakfast.

'Ah, the rash is coming out,' Maxine said, taking Judith's arm and inspecting it. 'How are you feeling?'

'Could be better. The doctor said it will take two to three weeks. The incubation period is apparently longer than plain old measles.'

There was a knock on the door and, without waiting for an answer, Hilda appeared, her face covered in light red spots.

'I've got German measles,' she announced, glaring at Maxine. 'It's not enough for them to bomb us – they're sending us their rotten diseases.'

'It's nothing to do with that at all,' Maxine couldn't help

snapping, annoyed that Hilda had barged in. 'You'd better get yourself undressed and into bed.'

'Nice to see you, Hilda,' came Judith's voice, 'though not under the best of circumstances.'

Maxine was surprised to see Hilda actually give what seemed a genuine smile. She couldn't name one person who showed they liked Hilda, and yet Judith sounded absolutely sincere. A sudden thought struck her. Could Judith be the person Hilda showed the photograph to? Should she say anything to Judith out of Hilda's hearing? She glanced over at the woman who was helping Hilda into her nightdress. Maybe it was best left alone. Peter had his photograph of his father and that was all that mattered.

It was just her luck. Two difficult patients. But at least it would take her mind off Edwin. Crofton was another matter entirely.

By evening, when Maxine was desperate to sit in the common room for a half an hour with a cup of tea, she still hadn't decided what to do for the best. Maybe this infatuation was all on Pearl's side. Maybe Edwin was simply being flirtatious and had no intention of pursuing Pearl. And then she remembered Edwin's threat and knew it was exactly what was in his mind.

She'd always been fond of her cousin, but after Pearl had so generously offered her a home for those months of anguish, and she'd taken Maxine into her confidence about losing her baby, Maxine had felt even closer. It would destroy Pearl if she ever went through something like that again. And Edwin, it seemed, had no scruples. She desperately needed someone to ask for advice.

There was only one person she felt she could trust who was discreet and wise – June. She wouldn't tell her about

Edwin's latest threat as her job was too precious to risk, but she could at least ask June's advice as a friend. She had to do something to warn Pearl – even if it meant disclosing her own secret.

The chance to speak to June came unexpectedly the following day when she made an announcement after breakfast.

'No classes today, children. We're going to pretend we're on holiday and have an autumn picnic outside, and if it gets too cold we'll go in the big barn. And you are all going to help to get everything ready to take over.' There was a sudden cheer from the older boys and squeals of delight from the girls and the younger ones. 'So help the teachers clear away the dishes and we'll meet in the Great Hall at five minutes to ten,' June instructed. 'We'll be going on a nice long walk while the sun's out and play any games you can think of.'

There was a more than usually enthusiastic rush from the children to pile up the dishes to take into the kitchen. They all talked at once to inform Bertie that they were going on a picnic.

'Never had anything like this before at Bingham Hall,' the cook said, smiling at Maxine. 'The Fierce One wouldn't dream of allowing the kids to have fun. But it will do them good.' Bertie turned to Ellen who was drying some dishes and banging the doors of the cupboards as she put the crockery away. 'Come on, Ellen, we need to get a move on. There'll be plenty of sandwiches to make.'

Barbara and Athena were in charge of the children's games, but soon most of the adults joined in, including Maxine and June. The teachers divided the children into two teams to pull a thick rope in a tug of war, but as the boys far outnumbered the girls, and the girls determinedly stuck together on one side, the boys pulled them over in a matter of moments. There were shouts of triumph mixed in with Daisy and Doris sobbing that they were too small against such big boys.

'Come on, you two,' June said, running over and grabbing their hands. 'You're in the egg-and-spoon race. I'm sure you can run as fast as the boys.'

She was right. Not only could they run as fast, their balance was better and they kept their eggs firmly on their spoons. Maxine smiled at their intent expressions, wishing she could have persuaded Peter to join in. He'd refused point blank, and instead had gone off with Freddie to the vegetable plots – to do some weeding, he'd said.

It was while they were having their picnic that Maxine grabbed the opportunity to catch June for a few minutes. The young matron was spreading out the tablecloths on the grass and Maxine and the two kitchen maids were opening the sandwiches wrapped in their greaseproof paper and setting out plates and cups.

'June, may I have a quiet word with you while the girls are sorting out the picnic?'

June looked surprised but all she said was, 'Of course.'

'I really wanted your advice,' Maxine began. 'It's about my cousin Pearl.'

'You sound serious.'

'It *is* serious. I'm really worried about her.'

'Go on.'

'It's hard to know where to start, though I suppose I'll have to explain where I fit in with all this.'

By this time June was looking at her curiously.

'After Johnny died,' Maxine began, 'I missed him more than I would ever have thought, even though we wouldn't have seen much of one another with the war on. But I missed

281

his letters. Knowing he was out there somewhere. I even missed worrying about him. But I wasn't alone. There were plenty of other women who had children and had lost their husbands. You have to get on with it. And when a new surgeon came on to the ward and began to take an interest in me – well, more than an interest – I was flattered. He's quite a few years older, very attractive, and highly respected. The other nurses were wild about him. Anyway, we became romantically involved—' She closed her eyes for a second to try to shut out the pain of the outcome. 'And he said he loved me. By this time I'd begun to think he was the one.

'Then one evening when things had become really serious, he told me he was married with two children. You can imagine how shocked I was. I wasn't going to get tied up with a married man, so we parted.' Absent-mindedly she took out some bottles of orangeade from the basket and set them under a tree, desperate not to see any judgemental expression on the young matron's face.

'Anyway,' Maxine went on, 'Pearl wrote to me that she'd broken her leg falling into the orchestra pit – she's an actress – and ended up in The Royal Infirmary, which is where I did my initial training. She finished the letter by saying her handsome surgeon was her only bright spot in the day, or words to that effect. I just smiled and thought nothing of it and went to visit her in hospital. But who should be her surgeon but my old boyfriend.'

June's eyes widened. 'Oh, my goodness. Did he speak to you?'

'Yes, afterwards. He told me how lovely Pearl was and that he hoped to take her out when he was no longer her doctor.'

'Does he know Pearl's your cousin?'

'Yes, I told him. He was a bit taken aback but still seems

intent on pursuing her.' She swallowed. 'Pearl is vulnerable at the moment. She recently had a very sad experience, and now this leg has put her out of the show which is awfully disappointing for her. I would hate her to be hurt all over again – so I think it's my duty to put a stop to this man. I was thinking of writing him a strong letter.'

'What would you say?' June sounded worried.

'Stop seeing Pearl and causing her misery or I'll report you to matron.'

'I don't think that's wise, Maxine. He doesn't seem like the sort who would appreciate being threatened. You say he's older than you – and very senior himself in the hospital. Do you really think matron, whoever she might be, would believe you over him?'

Maxine hesitated. Should she tell June the only other step she could think of?

'You're probably right,' she said finally. 'But there's something else . . . his wife . . . she must be here in Liverpool as well. Perhaps I should write to her instead.'

'She's probably used to his flirting and would find it amusing,' June said. 'I don't think it's enough for her to have a heart-to-heart with her husband.'

Maxine swallowed hard. Her chest was tight. Trying to release the tension, she breathed in deeply.

'But what if the wife found out there was a baby involved as a result of his philandering and that he'd offered to pay for an illegal operation?'

June looked puzzled. 'But he can't have done anything with Pearl whilst she's in hospital.'

'I'm not talking about Pearl.'

June's eyes widened in shock. 'Oh, Maxine. Is that what happened to *you*?'

'Yes.' Maxine's voice was almost a whisper.

'What happened to the . . .' June's hand flew to her mouth. 'Oh, Maxine, I mustn't ask these questions.'

'What happened to Teddy?' Maxine said in a shaking voice. 'I had to give him up for adoption. I wanted him to have two loving parents – give him the best start in life. He wouldn't have had that with only me, working all day and some stranger looking after him. My mother couldn't have coped, even if she'd offered – which she would never have done.' She swallowed the tears that gathered in her throat.

'Maxine, I'm so sorry.' June stepped through the grass to put her arm around Maxine's shoulder. 'Don't tell me anything more if it's too upsetting.'

'There's not much more to tell,' Maxine said, her eyes wet at the mention of Teddy's name. She scrambled to her feet. 'The children are coming over. I think they're hungry. But, June,' she looked at her new friend, 'thank you for listening. Just knowing you know everything makes me feel better.' She paused. 'June, if I'd told you I'd had an illegitimate baby would you still have taken me on?'

'It wouldn't have made a scrap of difference,' June said without a hint of hesitation. 'I knew you were right for Dr Barnardo's as soon as I set eyes on you. But you've asked me for my advice, so I'll tell you, for what it's worth. Don't let him intimidate you. Go back to the hospital this Friday when it's your day off. Tell your cousin right away – before it's too late.'

Maxine approached Pearl's hospital bed with trepidation. It had taken all her courage to step through the hospital entrance doors, knowing she might bump into Edwin at any moment. But June's words had given her the spur she needed, and she sent her cousin a warm smile. Pearl was sitting by her bed and a nurse was removing a thermometer from

Pearl's mouth; the nurse peered at it, then gave a nod of satisfaction.

'Normal, Miss Burton. And so was your blood pressure.'

'Oh, good.' Pearl spotted Maxine and beamed. 'Max, I'm so glad to see you. Pull up a chair. I want to hear all the gossip.'

The nurse shook the thermometer and smiled at the two women. 'I'll leave you alone then,' she said.

Maxine kissed her cousin's cheek and laid a couple of magazines on the bed.

'You look much better than last time,' Maxine said. She studied her cousin. It was true. Pearl's face was aglow with happiness. Her eyes were bright and sparkling and she looked like a woman in love. Maxine's heart dropped. How could she destroy the magic Pearl was feeling?

An elderly woman in the next bed suddenly cried out, 'I need a bedpan NOW!'

Maxine's immediate instinct was to jump up, but Pearl put a restraining hand on her arm.

'Nurse will go, Maxine. Stay and talk to me.'

They chatted for a while and Pearl told her about her parents visiting but Maxine realised this was not the right place to have a confidential talk.

'Have they said when you'll be out?' Maxine asked.

'Edwin . . . I mean Mr Blake, my surgeon – he says it shouldn't be more than a week and then I can go home.'

'That's marvellous, Pearl. But you'll need someone to help you manage.'

'Mam said she'll come and look after me. This accident seems to have brought us a bit closer together. When she came the first time to visit me she spoke to Sister, who told her I was really lucky – that I could easily have broken my neck and been a goner, or paralysed. Sister told me she went white.' Pearl gave a wry smile. 'I realise she's my mother . . . only one I've got, so I'll have to make the best of her. And she'll have to do the same.'

'I'm so glad.' Maxine patted Pearl's hand. 'That really is the best news. I know she loves you.'

Pearl nodded. 'How's Aunt Edna and Uncle Stan?'

'They're the same. Dad seems to be stable. Mum's always grumbling they don't see me enough. The usual. But to change the subject, have you heard when you'll be able to go back to the theatre?'

A shadow crossed Pearl's face. 'I don't know. The latest was that they'd found a replacement – supposed to be temporary – but I have a horrible feeling they'll keep her. Else why haven't they been in touch?'

'I expect they're leaving you in peace to get better and for you to let them know when you're ready to go back. Try not to worry.' She hesitated. 'Pearl, can we go somewhere private and have a chat?' Maxine tried to make her voice natural but it sounded strained to her ears. 'The patients' common room?'

Pearl sent her a sharp look. 'What's up, Max?'

'It's just that we can't talk freely in here.'

'You're right.' Pearl began to shift herself in the chair and Maxine rose to help her. 'Such a damned nuisance when I feel so well, but I need to have a walk round and we can gossip all we like.'

Maxine handed her the crutches and they made a painstaking walk to a gloomy, airless room off the corridor. It was sparsely furnished with a couple of tables and some upright chairs and a few shelves with books. Some empty cups had yet to be cleared, but to her relief the room was empty. She helped Pearl into one of the chairs and pulled one up for herself.

Pearl's face broke into a grin. 'I'm glad we're out of the ward, Max. Good idea of yours. I'm bursting to tell you, but you may have already guessed – Edwin and I are crazy about one another. I can't wait to get out of here. We obviously can't have a proper relationship while I'm in a hospital bed, except when he comes to examine me and draws the curtains round.' She giggled.

Dear God. This was worse than she'd thought. Maxine swallowed.

'Pearl, there's something—'

'What's the matter, Max? Don't you approve? I thought you'd be pleased I'd found someone at last, especially after what I told you about that other bastard. And Edwin's someone with a position. Someone I can be proud of. Think what Mam and Dad will say.' She grinned. 'That'll make them look up. Take notice of me.' She stopped as she saw Maxine's expression. 'Oh, I know what you're thinking, Max. He was a bit abrupt when you came to visit me, but he's not usually like that.'

'It's not that, Pearl. I do want you to find someone special. But I don't want it to be Edwin Blake.'

Pearl gave a start, her eyes anxious. 'Why do you say that?'

'Because I don't trust him.'

'You don't know him like I do. You've only seen him on the ward at St Thomas' and I doubt you'd have got to know him then, being a nurse.'

Maxine drew in a long breath and slowly let it out. 'No, Pearl. That's where you're wrong.'

Her cousin stared at her without blinking, then delved in her dressing gown pocket for her packet of cigarettes and pulled one out. Maxine noticed her hand shook slightly as she struck a match and lit it.

'Are you allowed to smoke in here?'

287

'I don't know and I don't care,' Pearl said fiercely. 'I need this. 'And . . .' she turned to Maxine, her eyes narrowing against the stream of smoke, 'I'm not sure I want to hear anymore.'

'You've already guessed what I'm going to say.' Maxine's eyes locked with Pearl's. She drew in a deep breath to steady her nerves. *It was now or never.* In a low voice she said, 'That he's the father of my child.'

There was a deathly quiet. Then Pearl stubbed her hardly touched cigarette so hard in the ashtray she practically bent it in two.

'I don't believe it.'

'You *must* believe it.' Maxine heard her voice rise. 'Remember I told you about Teddy's hair? A beautiful dark auburn. Well, it's the exact colour and shade of his father, the eminent surgeon, Mr Edwin Blake.'

Pearl's eyes were bright. 'My God,' she said, her voice coated with fury. 'The rotten stinking bastard. And from what I remember you telling me about him, he's married with two children.'

'That's right.'

'He had the nerve to tell me he was falling in love with me, but he can do nothing while I'm in hospital . . . though we do . . . *did* manage a kiss now and again when he pulled the curtains round us.' She caught Maxine's eye. 'Sorry, Max, but I didn't know – honestly.'

'Of course you didn't – how could you? So did he say he wants to see you when you're out of hospital?'

'Yes, he's talked about getting to know one another and seeing where it leads.' Pearl's mouth turned down unattractively. 'Not now, we won't. Not bloody likely.'

'What will you say?'

'I don't know. But it's not going to be pleasant.' She

looked at Maxine sharply and frowned as if remembering something. 'Did he follow you out when you left in such a hurry that time, because he rushed away from me almost as soon as you'd disappeared?'

'He asked me to go to his office.'

'Why?'

Maxine paused. Should she tell Pearl the details of that bitter conversation?

As though her cousin guessed what Maxine was thinking, Pearl said, 'You owe it to me to tell me everything, Max. I have to know.'

'He said if I told you he was the father of my child, or anyone else, he would make sure I lost my job at Dr Barnardo's.'

Pearl had the grace to flush pink. 'Oh, Max, I'm sorry I let it slip. You know when you first start liking someone and they want to know all about you. I was so proud of you being a nurse and all that, and helping the children, I never thought—'

'It doesn't matter,' Maxine cut in quickly. 'He showed me how low he could stoop. I seriously thought about telling his wife, but I'm not going to. He has two children and I wouldn't hurt them for the world – or his wife, for that matter. She's probably a really nice person.'

'I agree with you,' Pearl said, her hand to her face as she did when she was thinking. 'But he's not going to get away with this.' She gave Maxine a sly look. 'You don't have to do or say anything. Just leave it to me. I'll deal with him. This is nothing compared with what I've been through in the past. Mr Edwin Blake will wish he'd never set eyes on me.'

Chapter Twenty-Nine

'Murray and I have set the date,' June said one evening as she and Maxine were in the library chatting. Now, well into November, the nights were drawing in fast and Charlie had already pulled down all the blackout blinds and drawn the heavy curtains. He'd laid a fire and carefully set the heavy iron guard around it, telling June to call for him when it needed more logs.

'About time,' Maxine teased. 'And that's a most attractive blush, Junie.'

It was the first time she'd called her Junie. It had slipped out and she hoped June hadn't minded, though she'd noticed June give a start at the affectionate nickname. It was just that June was turning out to be so much more than simply Matron. She'd become a real friend. The first one since Anna. Maxine swallowed.

'So when is it to be?'

'Next month – Sunday the 6th of December.'

Maxine went over to June and gave her a hug. 'I'm so pleased for you,' she said. 'Murray sounds wonderful.'

'He is,' June laughed. 'I can't imagine being with anyone else.' She looked at Maxine. 'And I can't wait for you to meet him, but it probably won't be until the day, because he has so little time off.'

'If you love him, then I like him already,' Maxine said, smiling. 'What about your wedding dress? Have you thought about it?'

'I've thought and I've not come up with anything. I'm not a very good seamstress and material is rationed now. I can't help thinking I shouldn't be spending my coupons on anything as frivolous as a wedding dress.'

'It's your special day,' Maxine said, 'and it's only natural you want to look special.'

'Sometimes I wish I was in uniform and wouldn't have to worry. That's what a lot of girls in the forces do nowadays.'

'No, that wouldn't be right at all. With your colouring – that fair hair and gorgeous green eyes would be swallowed up in a dull uniform. You need something to enhance all that loveliness.' Maxine looked the young matron up and down. She suddenly knew what she could do. 'June, I made my own wedding dress as I'm pretty nifty with the needle and a sewing machine. I'm a bit taller than you and a size bigger but I'll cut it down to fit you – if you like it, that is. I'll get Mum to post it, as I'm not going home while we've still got German measles here.'

June's eyes went wide with delight. 'Maxine, how very kind you are. But you might go somewhere where the dress would be perfect and it won't fit you anymore.'

Maxine shook her head. 'I'd rather see you in it. It's a lovely memory of Johnny on the day we got married, but I'd feel strange wearing it again when he's no longer here.' She drew her brows together, picturing the McCall's pattern. 'It has a little matching jacket which will be trickier to adjust.' She thought for a moment. 'You'll need something warmer as it'll be a winter wedding, whereas mine was September. I'm going to find some velvet or some kind of furry fabric like imitation astrakhan – though that might be difficult to

291

come by – anyway I'll make you a new warm jacket so it will look like a completely different outfit. What do you think?'

June jumped from her chair and rushed over to kiss her. 'I can't thank you enough, Maxine.' She hesitated, then said, 'You called me Junie a few minutes ago.'

'I'm sorry. It came out. I felt it suited you. I won't anymore.'

June smiled. 'I liked it. Iris, the other nurse, used to call me Junie.' Maxine heard her take in a deep breath. 'And there was one other person. My sister, Clara. It reminds me of her, so please call me Junie.'

Maxine heard the wobble in June's voice. 'You always seem upset when you mention Clara.' She paused. 'I don't like to probe, but I feel there's something more.'

June nodded and pulled a chair closer. She smoothed the thick fair hair that she'd loosened from its pins and sighed, and Maxine could see it was difficult for her to start.

'Don't, if you don't want to,' Maxine said softly.

June lowered her eyes and shook her head. She cleared her throat. 'She was only eight.'

'Oh, June, did she die?'

'Yes.' It was barely a whisper.

Maxine touched her arm. 'What happened?'

She heard her friend swallow hard.

'It was Dad. He was coming after her to thrash her – he'd hit her for any little reason – and she lost her balance on top of the landing and fell down the stairs. She died almost instantly. And I can't . . . I just can't forgive him.' Tears rolled down her cheeks. 'He had the nerve to ask me to give up my job when I'd only been here a few months – and go and look after him. He pretended he'd had an accident on watch duty and was in a wheelchair. I was so furious when I saw he was perfectly all right I threw a vase at him. It hit him on the head and I really thought I'd killed him. Sometimes I wished I had.' She dissolved in tears.

Maxine put her arms round her. 'Junie,' she whispered. 'Don't cry. I'm here. You have a friend. And you know I understand what it is to lose someone precious.' She hugged June. 'Is that why you wanted to work with children? For Clara's sake?'

June nodded. 'I wanted to help vulnerable children. The job here was a dream come true.' She looked up with tear-stained eyes. 'And the strangest thing happened. On my first day, I met Lizzie curled up in a ball in Bertie's kitchen. I couldn't believe my eyes. Though she wasn't yet four she was the spitting image of Clara. Only difference was the eye colour. Lizzie's are brown and Clara's are . . .' she gulped and corrected herself, 'were green.'

'Like yours,' Maxine said, offering her a handkerchief.

June blew her nose and gave Maxine a weak smile. 'That's why Lizzie has always been so special to me.'

'She's a darling. You've done wonders.'

June shook her head. 'This home seems to have healing powers.'

'I think I understand what you mean.' Maxine was thoughtful. 'When I first came I was surprised it had such a good atmosphere. I wasn't sure how the children would be treated, how strict the teachers would be.'

'It was awful when I first arrived,' June said with feeling, 'because the matron was so horrible – not just to me and the other staff – but to the children, especially those she considered the troublemakers.'

'Yet they're the ones who need help the most,' Maxine said, 'and Bingham Hall is jolly lucky to have you as matron.'

She studied her friend closely. 'Are you feeling better now, Junie? About your father, I mean.'

June's face visibly relaxed. 'I only learned recently from my Aunt Ada that he's not my real father,' she said, to Maxine's surprise, 'and since the accident I decided I would never see him again.'

'Well, at least he can't pass on any of his rotten ways,' Maxine said mildly.

'No,' June agreed. 'I just wish I could have known my real father better. I only knew him as Uncle Thomas and I dearly loved him as an uncle but he died when I was still a child.'

'I'm sure he knew you loved him.' Dear June. And then it hit her. It would be the same for Teddy, not knowing his father. Maxine swallowed the tears which threatened to fill her throat. It wouldn't do for her to be caught weeping.

'You're going to start me off crying again,' June said, smiling. She sniffed and reached for the handkerchief. 'Not the way for a matron to behave.'

'Luckily there's no one here, then, to witness such a terrible spectacle.' Maxine grinned. 'So splash your face with some cold water and try to think where I can get some furry material for your new jacket.'

'Judith never stops complaining,' Kathleen said with a grimace, when Maxine went down to the ward the following afternoon. 'I'll be glad when she's over the measles and out of my sight. She's malingering, if you ask me, and totally unsuited for the job of teaching children.' She rinsed the sink and squeezed out the dishcloth, hanging it over the tap. 'Did you know she was a professor of modern languages at the Ladies' College in Cambridge?'

'No, I didn't, but it might answer the question of her not

really liking young children. She might feel resentful that this job is beneath her. I wonder why she left. Maybe something in her past is affecting her,' Maxine mused.

'Well, I can't warm to her,' Kathleen said. 'She smokes like a chimney. How she has the money to buy all those cigarettes, I don't know. She must have made friends with old Barney in the village shop because when I occasionally want to buy a packet he's always short. The place stinks since she's been here. The common room particularly.' She wrinkled her nose. 'I told her about it the other day. She just waved her fag in the air and said it was one of the mildest and it certainly wouldn't be her *du Maurier* that was causing the smell,' Kathleen finished.

Maxine laughed. 'Well, they are supposed to be the posh cigarettes.'

'Posh, my foot. She's no one special. But she thinks she's a cut above us.' Kathleen rinsed her cup.

There was a rap at the door and Hilda, as usual, stepped into the ward without knocking.

'I've come to take over so you can both go to Matron's meeting,' she said, 'even though I've not *completely* recovered from *German* measles'. She dumped her magazines on the desk and plonked down on the chair.

'I wouldn't have allowed you up if that had been the case,' Maxine said, trying hard to keep the irritation out of her voice. 'Anyway, I doubt we'll be long.'

June looked round the small group and smiled her welcome.

'We're planning to have a new member of staff joining us,' she said. 'Another nurse. It's so hard for Maxine and Kathleen to do twelve-hour shifts. So Maxine has agreed to do part-time nursing and helping me part-time with the children, so it should ease the nursing situation, and also my own.' There were murmurs of agreement. 'Unfortunately, we've only had a handful of replies because most nurses are in the forces. And out of them, only one has the right qualifications. So I've invited a Pat Baker along for an interview today.' She looked at her watch. 'In fact, she'll be along in an hour or so. Maxine and Kathleen' – she directed her gaze towards the two nurses – 'can you both make yourselves available when she comes. I'd like to have your opinion as you'll be working closer with her.'

'I just hope this Pat Baker is nice,' Kathleen said, as they shut June's door behind them after the short meeting. 'We don't need another Judith in the home.'

'I'm sure she will be. Probably relieved not to have to deal with the broken bodies of soldiers,' Maxine said fervently, remembering the terrible cases which seemed to have come unendingly to her ward in St Thomas'.

Kathleen sped off and as Maxine stepped into the Great Hall she noticed a thin young man seated by the blazing fire, his head down and rubbing his hands together. Even from a distance his hands looked blue with cold.

'Are you here to see someone?' Maxine asked.

He turned and stared at her with pale eyes. She noticed his sandy-coloured hair was already receding, and his neatly trimmed but meagre moustache had several gaps, showing his pale skin and giving him a vulnerable appearance. She felt a little sorry for him. He'd obviously failed his test to join up, though of course he could be in civvies. She'd never seen him before, but maybe the fish man or the postman or someone had been taken ill and he was filling in.

The young man immediately shot up and gave her a timid smile.

'I'm sorry, Nurse.' Ellen bustled up. 'I was looking for Matron.'

'May I help?' Maxine said. 'Perhaps I can tell Matron who it is who wants to see her.'

'Pat Baker,' the young man said. 'For the nursing position.'

'Oh.' Maxine gave a start. June had assumed Pat Baker was a female applicant by the way she'd referred to him as a 'she' throughout their recent meeting. She wondered what June would have to say about it. If she'd think it was appropriate for the children. On balance it was probably a good idea, as most of them had no dads and this might help in a very small way to bridge the gap. Besides, they'd had male nurses at St Thomas' and no one had thought anything of it. Maxine hid a smile. The others were in for a surprise.

'Very pleased to meet you,' she said. 'I'm Nurse Taylor.' She held out her hand and he took hers in his own thin cold one, giving a brisk shake, then let it fall back to his side again. 'I'll take you to Matron's office.' She'd fetch Kathleen when Mr Baker was settled with a cup of tea.

'Do sit down,' June said, as they stepped into her office, not showing any surprise, though to Maxine's amusement she caught her eye and gave an almost imperceptible wink. 'Did you bring your credentials, Mr Baker?'

'Oh, yes, they're here.' He opened a leather document folder and brought out some official papers.

June glanced at them and nodded and handed them over to Maxine.

She noticed he was an SRN, so would be her senior. Inwardly she shrugged. It didn't matter so long as he was a nice person who was good with children. He'd gained experience at two of the hospitals in Liverpool and had exceptional references. She studied the papers again and saw he was twenty-four. So why wasn't he in the forces? Just as she was thinking this, June said, 'Was there any reason why you've not joined up, Mr Baker?'

297

He lowered his head and stared at the floor.

'Mr Baker,' June repeated. 'It's important for me to know. If you have some sort of disability, we need to be aware of it. You'll be looking after children as well as adults.'

'Yes, I realise that,' the young man said, raising his eyes and glancing at both women. 'I want to do my bit to help people – use my nursing skills.'

'But aren't they desperately in need of people like you in the army?' June persisted.

He nodded.

'So why were you turned down?'

'I didn't apply to the army or any of the other branches. You see, I'm a CO.'

Maxine and June looked at one another.

'I'm sorry,' June said. 'I'm not sure what you mean.'

Mr Baker bowed his head for a moment, then looked up defiantly. 'I'm a conscientious objector.'

Maxine's eyes widened. She heard June give a sharp intake of breath. This was serious. She'd read that conscientious objectors were quite often sent to jail, or if they managed to avoid it, given the worst jobs possible. Called cowards and all sorts of awful names. But here was one looking perfectly normal and pleasant, though he was shifting in his seat, obviously embarrassed he'd had to explain to two women why he wasn't fighting for king and country.

'I'll have to refer the decision about something so serious to Mr Clarke at Dr Barnardo's headquarters, in that case,' June told him.

Pat Baker eagerly leaned forward. 'I'd be really grateful, Miss Lavender, if you'd put in a good word,' he said. 'I need this job. Need to prove to my family that I'm not a coward and I'm willing to work hard but I don't believe in murdering people – which is how I look at it. It's against my religion. I just want peace.'

'We all do,' June said, briskly. 'But if we don't put up a fight, we'll be overtaken by the Germans. Doing what they want us to do. Speaking their language.' She leaned forward and put her hands on the desk. 'Is that what you're prepared to let happen?'

Maxine was taken aback by June's outburst even though she heartily agreed. She was about to add her own piece but decided it wasn't her place. June was the matron. She would simply listen and speak if spoken to.

'I just don't want to kill anyone. There has to be another way.'

'I'm not sure what,' June said. Then her face relaxed. 'Well, we're not here to make moral judgements – we simply need another nurse.'

'Did anyone else apply for the position?' Pat Baker asked humbly.

'A few,' June admitted, 'but none of them were suitably qualified. That's why I asked you to come for an interview. Your credentials were exactly what we're looking for.'

'Then give me a chance, Miss Lavender,' he said, his eyes pleading. 'Please don't tell headquarters. They'll report me and I could end up in jail. It would be such a waste when there's a desperate shortage of nurses.'

June glanced at Maxine, who gave a tiny nod, then looked directly at the young man. 'I'll talk it over with Nurse Taylor,' she said, 'but I can't promise anything. I'll let you know our decision in a few days' time.'

Just as Pat Baker opened his mouth, there was the roar of a plane. His face turned grey. 'It doesn't sound like one of ours,' he said as he sprang for the door.

Maxine's heart pounded as she and June shot to their feet. For a split second her brain froze.

'Shelters!' June ordered as they rushed into the hall.

Seconds later children were pouring down the stairs, shouting and running to the front door.

'Go to the shelters!' Barbara shouted from the rear. 'Two-by-two. Hold hands. Quickly!'

Maxine ran after Pat Baker through the hall, grabbing Daisy and Doris. She saw him take hold of Betsy, then Beth who was screaming for her brother. Lenny caught up and grabbed his sister's hand and Maxine flew after them, gripping the twins. To her relief, she saw Charlie was unbolting the heavy door. A cold blast of air met her full on, as the children and staff pounded behind, Daisy and Doris clinging on either side of her like limpets.

'Mr Baker, this way!' Maxine called in the dusk, as she saw him heading in the opposite direction.

The plane was flying low – so close now she could just make out the ominous black crosses. Instinctively she pulled Daisy and Doris down with her, keeping an arm around each as she pressed their noses into the grass. She cricked her neck as the pilot jettisoned his bomb and roared upwards. The last thing she saw was Pat Baker and the three children being hurled to the ground as the bomb exploded, followed by a whooshing noise. Then smoke. And a terrible burning smell which instantly plunged her into the memory of the Nurses' Wing at St Thomas' when she'd been desperately searching for her friend. The horror when she'd discovered Anna had died in that inferno – the same way as Anna's own father, a London firemen. Maxine swallowed the bile that rose in her throat.

Dear God. Another explosion, further away. Silence – except for her heart thundering in her ears. Then sobbing. It was Daisy.

'It's all right, my love. You're safe with me. Don't cry. You'll start Doris off.' She tried to swallow, but now her

300

mouth was dry and tasted of metal. 'Come on – the nasty man has gone now. We'll go back into the house.'

She managed to pull herself up, trying to show she wasn't scared in front of the two little girls who were both shaking and crying as she gently brought them to their feet and covered their scarves over their noses.

'Are you all right, Maxine?'

Maxine turned to find Barbara, who had hold of a trembling Megan, both their faces white.

'Yes,' Maxine said, though it wasn't true. She felt sick with fear. 'Can you take the twins in? I need to see what's happened to the others.'

Barbara nodded and took the two little girls, still sobbing.

The smell of burning in her nostrils, Maxine ran towards the huddled group who lay in a dip the size of a crater, shrapnel and puffs of stinking smoke around them. One of the lime trees at the beginning of the drive had been uprooted and tossed in the air landing dangerously close to where Pat Baker had flung himself over Betsy. It was a wonder the tree hadn't killed them all, she thought, fear making her stumble down the slope the explosion had made. She knelt by the side of the young man and gently touched his shoulder.

'Mr Baker – Pat. It's over. Can you get up if I help you? You're squashing poor little Betsy.'

There was no sound. No movement. Fear rushed to her throat as she struggled to pull him off the child. Betsy's eyes were closed. So were Beth's and Lenny's as they lay side by side, their clothes and faces covered in blood and shards, the little girl's hand still clutching her brother's. The pit smelt of burnt flesh.

Please God, don't let them all— She thought she'd be sick with the smell but came to her senses and felt for Beth's pulse. Nothing. She screwed up her eyes against the dust and grit, and felt for Lenny's. It was too late. She was too late. Tears pouring down her face, she braced herself. Betsy. Not little Betsy as well. Betsy lay perfectly still, though Maxine could see no apparent wounds. But there was no flicker of life. Maxine put her fingers on the inside of the little girl's wrist. Was it her imagination? Or was there a faint beat?

'Betsy, it's Nurse Maxine,' she said urgently. 'Can you open your eyes?'

Hardly daring to breathe, she watched as Betsy's beautiful brown eyes opened, but now they were wide with terror.

'Oh, Betsy. Are you hurt?'

Betsy shook her head, and whimpered like a kitten. She stretched out her little arms and Maxine gathered her close.

'You're safe now, my love,' she said, fury rising at the German pilot for cutting down these innocent children's lives before they'd begun. She hugged Betsy and took in a deep breath, the stench almost making her vomit. 'Lie there quietly for a moment while I see to Mr Baker.'

She reached out to feel his pulse, then bit back a cry. His hand was missing. She laid her head on his chest but she couldn't hear any heartbeat. Gently, she lifted one of his eyelids. To her amazement there was a dim light in his pupil. He opened his mouth. Dear God, he was alive!

'I'm here, Mr Baker . . . Pat. It's Maxine, the nurse you met. Don't speak. You've been injured, but you're going to be all right. I'm getting help.'

'I'm so sorry,' he whispered. Blood trickled out of the corner of his mouth and she grabbed her handkerchief to dab it. He looked up at her, but she could tell his eyes weren't focusing.

'Pat—'

He opened his mouth, then gave a terrible gurgling noise, and as if in slow motion his head gently flopped to the side.

She swallowed her tears. She didn't know him. She and June had only spent half an hour with him at most. He'd bravely admitted he was a conscientious objector even though by telling them he was risking being denied the job at Dr Barnardo's. Maxine – and she knew June too – had been quite shocked. She'd once heard one of her mother's neighbours say that men who didn't go and fight for their country were cowards. 'Conchies,' the woman had called them, her lips tightening into a contemptuous line. She shivered as much with distaste at the memory as with the cold, which she was only just now aware of, seeping into every part of her body as she gently kissed the young man's cheek. It was only because he'd protected Betsy with his body that the little girl had been saved. Pat Baker wasn't a coward at all. He was a war hero. But the sad thing was that he'd never know it.

Chapter Thirty

Maxine sat on the cold, damp grass holding Betsy, who was sobbing and clinging to her. She had to get the child into the house before they both caught pneumonia, but she couldn't leave Beth and Lenny and Mr Baker out here. She looked around. All was silent. June and the teachers must have ushered the children into the shelters without realising there'd been such a disaster. She gulped. If only poor Mr Baker hadn't dashed off in the wrong direction he and Lenny and Beth would still be alive.

She heard the sound of bicycle tyres on the drive. Maxine pulled Betsy closer as she watched a man in a blue coat and white helmet jump off and lean the bike on one of the elm trees before he half ran towards her, the bag on his shoulder swinging.

'Are you all right, Miss?'

To her surprise and relief she saw it was Mr Jenner from the village post office.

'Yes, I'm all right. I didn't expect to see you though.' She peered closer at his armband and badge.

'It's my first week. Since Jerry dropped his bombs over here last year on his way back to Germany, the powers that be decided Bingham should have their own ARP warden in the post office to man the telephone for any alerts. So here I am.'

'Oh, thank goodness.' She could hardly speak for the lump in her throat, but it was such a relief that Mr Jenner stood in front of her; a man who'd fought in the last war yet always had a cheerful word with her when she posted her letters. He would understand more than most.

'Here, let me take the child.' He held out his arms, but Betsy let out a piercing scream and buried her nose in Maxine's neck.

'I'll take her in,' Maxine said. 'She's in shock. But I'd appreciate it if you could help with the others. They're all d-d-dead.' Her teeth rattled as she tried to get the word out, the tears gathering behind her eyelids.

'Don't you take on,' the warden said, bending down to extricate Beth's hand from her brother's. Maxine was grateful to see how gentle he was as he lifted up the child. 'You go on back to the house with that little one. I'll bring them in – poor kids,' he added, his eyes moist. 'Don't seem right – innocent children getting involved in men's affairs.' He nodded his head towards Mr Baker. 'Has he gone too, Miss?'

'Yes.'

'He one of the teachers?'

She swallowed. 'No. He was a nurse, just come for an interview to work here.' She looked up at him, no longer able to hold back the tears. 'He was very brave. He would have been a wonderful nurse.'

Mr Jenner had been marvellous. With the help of Charlie, the two men carried Mr Baker back to the house and placed him in the chapel on a mattress by the side of Beth and Lenny. Mr Jenner had linked the children's hands together again, and that small gesture made Maxine rush out of the chapel door to break down in tears once more.

'We're making hot drinks for everyone,' Bertie announced

305

as Maxine entered the kitchen. 'Why don't you get the children into the dining room and we'll bring out the trays.'

'Let me help,' Maxine said, needing to do something practical to take her mind off the horror she'd witnessed.

'No, hen. You're more help seeing to the children. I've got the maids and the laundry girls rallying.' She gave Maxine a stern look. 'You need to get those damp clothes off and into something warm or you'll go down with something yourself.'

When everyone had had a drink and biscuits, June stood up at the end of her table and banged a spoon against her glass for the chattering to stop.

'I have sad news to tell you that Lenny and Beth died from the bomb which dropped just now.'

'Have they gone to heaven, Miss?' Jack called out.

'Yes, Jack, they have.'

'Who was that man that came today?' Thomas asked.

'He was a nurse. He was coming here to work.'

'Oh.' He immediately dismissed the stranger and said, 'Where's Betsy. Is she dead?'

'No,' June said. 'The man, Mr Baker, saved her life. He was very brave. She's having a rest in the ward. Nurse Kathleen is looking after her.'

The children fired more questions and some of the younger ones started to cry. One little boy sobbed. 'I want me mam.'

'Your mam's in heaven, love. She sent you here to be safe with us,' Maxine said.

'But we're *not* safe,' Thomas shouted. 'Else Beth and Lenny wouldn't-a been killed.'

'Killed by a horrible German in his horrible aeroplane! Same as Peter here!' Hilda shot to her feet and pointed to him. 'His father is a Nazi who wants to kill us all!'

There was a deathly silence. All eyes turned to Peter, who was staring ahead, his mouth hard, not looking at anyone.

'You will come to my office immediately, Hilda.' June's voice was controlled, but Maxine sitting next to her could tell by the hissing breath she drew into her nostrils that she was furious. As June leapt to her feet, she said in an undertone, 'Please take over, Maxine.'

Hilda sulkily scraped back her chair and followed the matron out. Everyone had turned their attention from Peter to Maxine, and for a moment she didn't know quite what to say. Then she gathered her thoughts and stood up, but thirteen-year-old Alan beat her to it.

'He says "*Ja*" all the time. That's German, isn't it, so I wondered whether—'

'You will keep your thoughts to yourself, Alan,' Maxine snapped. Alan looked at her in surprise. 'Peter's father sent him and his English mother over here because Peter's grandmother was ill.' She stole a glance at Peter, whose blue eyes had turned on her as though beseeching her.

'His dad must've known we're being bombed all the time,' Bobby said. 'And now we know Peter's from a Nazi family he's as bad as—'

'Be quiet, Bobby,' Maxine cut in. 'No more of that talk here.'

Barbara got up and looked round at everyone. 'It's a difficult time,' she said, 'and today is a very sad one. We've lost two of our precious children. But we're going to try to think of nicer things.' She shot a look of apology at Maxine, who gave a smile of gratitude. 'We're going to start preparing for Christmas early. We've got lots of decorations to make, and Christmas cards for our friends, so I'd like to see as many of you as possible in the art room. We'll start in ten minutes.'

Maxine dismissed them and they went off muttering, completely ignoring Peter, but Barbara turned to him.

'Peter, I'd be pleased if you'd join us in the art room.'

He gave her a cold stare and then his face crumpled and he raced out of the Great Hall.

'Probably best if we leave him alone for a while,' Barbara said. 'This must be so difficult for him.' She looked at Maxine. 'Do you think there's any truth in what Hilda said?'

Maxine felt her neck grow warm. But she kept her voice neutral as she answered, 'I very much doubt it. Why would a Nazi send his child to England? They were bent on invading us not that long ago and might still be planning to, for all we know. And how could a Nazi justify such an action to his superiors?'

She desperately hoped she'd put Barbara off the trail. So far, only her and June knew. Oh, and Crofton, of course. Her heart beat fast at the thought. He would never tell a soul – she could stake her life on it.

Half an hour later a weeping Hilda roughly pushed past Maxine on the stairs as she was going up to her room, desperately in need of some quiet to take in the tragic events of the day.

'It's all your fault,' the girl choked as her rage hit Maxine with full force. 'We were doing all right till you came along and spoilt things.'

'I'm sorry you feel like that, Hilda.' This minute she didn't have the strength for any confrontation.

'Sorry? You're *sorry*?' The girl turned and spat at Maxine, who leaned back on the banister in surprise. 'Sorry you've lost me my job? Sorry you've cut me off from my family? Sorry—'

'That's quite enough, Hilda.' Maxine unhurriedly brought

out a handkerchief from her overall and pointedly wiped the saliva off her face. 'Yes, I'm sorry if you've lost your job, but I'm not the cause of it. We've put up with you and your uncalled-for comments far too long. And you've been extremely cruel to an innocent child.' Maxine swept up the stairs, seething at the girl's cheek.

'That German tike? Innocent?' Hilda's voice followed her up the stairs. 'He ought to be shot!'

If she'd had a shred of pity for Hilda, Maxine thought, the girl's last remark obliterated it. Wearily, she mounted the stairs, wishing she wasn't on night duty. But she mustn't moan. She was so lucky. She was warm, comfortable, well fed considering there was a war on, and she thought – hoped – that someone out there cared for her. Someone with a crooked smile to make her pulse race. Someone who she loved but could never let him know. Because if she did, she'd lose him forever.

The room was cold and she shivered but didn't bother to put on a warm cardigan. Instead, she sat on the bed and eagerly opened the latest letter from Pearl.

14th November 1942
Dear Max,

You'll be pleased to know I'm out of hospital and doing well. It's difficult to get around as I'm still on crutches, and the stairs take me an age to climb, but every day I feel stronger.

I know you must be very busy with all the kids at the orphanage. But come and see me again as soon as you can.

Mam and Dad actually came to visit me in the flat. They always said they would never step foot in this part of town. But when I was in hospital I think they realised they'd missed me more than they'd imagined. Seems the accident has had one positive outcome at least! They wanted me to go home with them so Mam could look after me, but I prefer to be independent. You know how I am!

Your cousin Pearl,

XX

Maxine smiled at Pearl's declaration. It was good to hear her mother and father had been to see her. Maybe that rift would now begin to heal. It was strange that Pearl hadn't mentioned Edwin. She wondered if her cousin had said anything to him, and hoped not, after all. It was a mistake to have told Pearl the whole episode and it would probably have died a natural death. When she'd thought about it, she realised Pearl was pretty cool-headed. She would have seen through Edwin sooner or later and finished with him. But through Maxine's own stupidity for blabbing, Edwin might well cause trouble, not only for her but for Pearl as well.

She'd go and see Pearl at the first opportunity.

Pearl beamed when she opened the door.

'Max, how wonderful. Come on in. I'll put the kettle on.'

Maxine kissed her and set her basket of vegetables and the little piece of stewing steak she'd managed to buy from the butcher's on the draining board. 'Let me make the tea. It must be awkward for you, still on crutches.'

'I'm used to them now.' Pearl grinned and waved her inside with one of the sticks.

'How are you managing with food and everything?' Maxine asked as she went inside, feeling strange all of a sudden that this used to be her home.

'The neighbours are really kind,' Pearl said. 'They do my

shopping and Mrs Burge downstairs cooks me a meal most days, and when she can't,' Pearl chuckled, 'I can always have fish and chips.'

'How long will you have to be on crutches?'

'At least another fortnight. But I'm managing with a walking stick most of the time.'

Maxine quickly busied herself in the kitchen and soon the two young women were drinking tea in Pearl's small living room.

'How are all the kids?' Pearl asked.

'A terrible thing happened last week.' Maxine gulped. 'A German pilot bombed us on his way back to Germany. We lost two little children, five and eight – brother and sister. Their funeral was yesterday in the chapel. It was so dreadfully sad, especially for some of the younger ones when it finally struck them that Lenny and Beth wouldn't be coming back. There were a lot of tears, but it was a beautiful service.'

Pearl's eyes filled. 'How awful. Oh, Max, I'm so sorry. This bloody war, excuse my French. But everyone else was all right?'

'Yes, except for poor Mr Baker – a young man who'd come for a job as a nurse. He rushed out, taking those two children with him . . . and little Betsy.' She briefly told her cousin how he'd saved Betsy.

'One minute you're all right, the next you're blown to kingdom come,' Pearl said soberly. 'Dear oh dear. I'm so sorry.'

'It was dreadful,' Maxine said, running her hand through her hair. 'The children are still not completely over it. It's the first time a child has died at the home since the war started.'

'Let's talk about something more cheerful,' Pearl said, taking several gulps of tea. 'And before you ask, I'd better put you out of your misery and tell you what happened.' She gave a sly smile.

Maxine braced herself. She knew her cousin wouldn't have minced her words. But she wasn't prepared for Pearl's account.

'I was nice as pie next time he came round,' Pearl said, 'just in case he'd spotted you last time and put two and two together. In fact, I let everything go on normally for the next few days. Then one day he came to my bed and swished the curtains round us. I was sitting up waiting for him. He bent over and kissed me and I kissed him back.' She threw an apologetic smile at Maxine. 'Awful to say it, Max, but he was a damned good kisser.'

It was true and Maxine's face flushed at the memory of his passion. He'd been exactly the same with Pearl. It was so humiliating. But if she'd saved her cousin from similar heartbreak she was glad.

'Anyway,' Pearl continued, 'he unbuttoned my pyjama top and put his hand on my breast and began to stroke it. This was nothing unusual but this time he had a terrible shock. I screamed blue murder. The look on his face was priceless. I wish I'd had a camera. He put his hand over my mouth, but it was too late. Sister came flying in like a bat out of hell and tore back the curtains. And there was my breast for all to see.

'"What's going on?" Sister demanded, glaring at Edwin, who was looking at me, and honestly, Max, if looks could kill I'd have shrivelled like a prune. "Mr Blake . . ." I started to cry – real tears.' Pearl looked at Maxine and grinned. 'After all, I *am* an actress. Sister gave me a sympathetic look. "Don't cry, Miss Burton. I'll be dealing with this." She rounded on Edwin. "Matron will send word to you, Mr Blake. I'm sure she will want to see you in her office immediately." She just

312

stood there, arms folded, waiting for him to leave. A bit later she stopped by and said, "You don't have to worry about Mr Blake anymore. He's no longer your surgeon. And in fact, he'll be lucky if he ever does another operation again."' Pearl grinned as she caught Maxine's eye and gulped down the rest of her tea. 'Are you proud of me?'

Maxine swallowed, hardly knowing how to answer. But she had to say something – her cousin was looking so delighted with herself. 'I think you're very brave,' she said. 'I just hope there aren't any repercussions. I still don't trust him.'

'I don't trust him as far as I could throw him, but I trust Matron. She was marvellous. She had me go to her room later that day and told me she was sending in her report and that he'd be struck off the register.'

Somehow it didn't make Maxine feel better. She was relieved that Pearl would now be safe from Edwin's despicable intentions, but it didn't alter the fact that he was one of the top surgeons in his field and now his skills would be wasted. A disgraced member of the medical profession he may be, yet he was still the father of her child. But she wouldn't remind Pearl of that. She made herself smile and got up to hug her cousin.

'You were wonderful, Pearl. Now all you have to do is get that leg completely healed and get back on that stage!'

Chapter Thirty-One

'Parcel for you,' June said, holding out a large brown package.

'It's actually for you.' Maxine grinned at June's puzzled expression. 'Your wedding dress to be.'

June's face lit up. 'Oh, lovely. Can I see it?'

'Not yet. It's a surprise. I've already measured you so I want to cut it down and tack it together first. Then we'll do a fitting.'

The problem with finding another nurse hadn't been resolved, but June had decided to leave it until after Christmas.

'That's when people sometimes look for a fresh start,' she said. 'I want to concentrate on the children. Peter seems to have settled better since Hilda's been gone, don't you think?'

Maxine was sure Peter hadn't settled in as well as June seemed to think. He'd become extremely introverted and rarely joined in with games. She tried hard to talk to him, especially about his family, sure that by bottling up his feelings he would feel worse, but he usually shrugged her off by saying none of the children liked him but it didn't matter because he didn't like them either, though he'd taken to Freddie as a playmate. The little dog seemed to understand the boy's struggles and always wagged his tail when he spotted him, knowing he'd be going for an extra walk if Lizzie wasn't around. But try as Maxine and June might, they couldn't force the children to make friends with Peter. Hilda's outburst had destroyed any burgeoning friendships he'd begun with Alan and Bobby. After classes in the afternoon he appeared at his most content, curled up in the library with a book, often on the subject of historic warfare. Had his father instilled this fascination? Maxine's skin prickled at the thought.

'Can we do a fitting this evening?' Maxine popped her head in June's office. Her eyes stung now with straining too long sewing under the dim light in the ward so she didn't disturb the sleeping patients. But she was pleased with the way the dress was taking shape, her needle flying as she'd tacked the last seam on what was her last night shift for a week.

'How exciting.' June looked up and gave Maxine her wonderful beaming smile. 'Do you want to come over to the cottage after supper this evening?'

Maxine was about to answer when Ellen interrupted.

'Please, Matron, there's someone here to see you.'

June frowned. 'Oh, Ellen, I'm rushed off my feet this morning. Can you find out what she wants?'

'I did try to ask, but she said it was an urgent matter which she couldn't discuss with anyone. But she's carrying what looks like one of them portable safes.'

June gave Maxine an apologetic smile. 'It sounds as though I'll have to see her. Do you want to hear what she has to say that's so urgent?'

'Yes, if you'd like me to.'

June nodded. 'Then show her in, Ellen.'

'Right you are.'

The maid was back in a few moments. 'Mrs Brown, Matron,' Ellen announced with a bob of her head.

The middle-aged woman looked about her as she heaved a large basket onto June's desk, then shook out her umbrella.

'Good Morning, Mrs Brown.' June rose from behind her desk. 'Let me take your umbrella. Ellen should have put it in the stand by the front door.'

'I like to keep me eye on me things,' the woman said.

Maxine and June exchanged glances as Mrs Brown pulled off her knitted glove and they all shook hands. Her thin fingers felt almost dead to Maxine's touch. Poor woman – she looked exhausted and terribly underweight.

'Do sit down,' June said, gesturing to one of the visitor's chairs. 'I'm sorry but I'll only be able to give you a few minutes. We're really busy today.'

'It won't take up much of your time,' Mrs Brown said, sitting on the edge of the chair as though she was ready to spring up at any moment. She looked washed out. 'It's a long way up the drive from the bus stop. I'm soaked.'

'Oh, dear, it is quite a walk when you're not used to it. Why don't you take your hat and coat off? You'll be far more comfortable.'

'No, I'm all right as I am. It's not that warm in here. Not that I'm grumbling, mind, what with the war on an' all.'

June smiled. 'Yes, we're lucky here with food for the children, but we're short on coal and coke, as everyone is. But let me arrange for a cup of tea for you.'

'That would be right welcome, Miss Lavender. That would warm me up nicely. And perhaps a biscuit or two to go with it.'

Maxine hid a smile. What a strange woman. 'I'll ask Bertie to bring us all one, shall I, Matron?'

June nodded and Maxine hurried along to the kitchen.

'I'll see to it, hen,' Bertie said. 'You go back and see what she's up to. Ellen will be there in two shakes of a lamb's tail.'

When Maxine took her seat again in June's office, she was amused to see a look of relief in her friend's eyes as she caught her own. Then June directed her gaze on the woman, who was shifting nervously in her seat and grabbing up folds of her shabby brown coat which had the top button missing.

'What were you saying, Mrs Brown?' June asked encouragingly.

'That I think you'll be interested in what I've brought with me. That box' – Mrs Brown nodded her head towards June's desk – 'when the house took a hit – you know what boys are like—' A sudden moan escaped her lips and her face drained of blood.

Immediately Maxine sprang to her feet but was too late to catch Mrs Brown as her chair slid backwards and tipped her onto the floor.

'Oh, goodness, is she all right?' June rushed to her other side.

'She's just fainted,' Maxine said. 'Can you help me get her back onto the chair?'

Even though the woman was so scrawny, Maxine and June had a struggle to lift her, but finally they got her slumped into a seating position. After a few seconds, she opened her eyes.

'Wh-where am I?'

'You're at Bingham Hall, the Dr Barnardo's home,' Maxine answered.

'Am I hurt?'

'No, Mrs Brown, I don't think so,' Maxine said. 'Unless you feel any pain.'

Mrs Brown shook her head very slowly, but Maxine could tell she was dazed by the way her eyes stared blankly back at her.

'Why am I here?'

'You brought in a metal box to show us,' June prompted.

'I need my smelling salts. In my bag.'

Maxine opened the cheap black handbag and felt around until her fingers closed over a tiny glass bottle. She opened it and put it under Mrs Brown's nose, who promptly coughed and spluttered. June handed her a handkerchief and Mrs Brown dabbed at her eyes, when there was a knock at the door. Ellen appeared with the tea tray.

'Thank you, Ellen,' June said, taking the tray from her. Pushing the basket containing the metal box to one side, she set it on her desk.

'Can I help you with anything, Ma'am?' Ellen asked, curiosity making her eyes almost pop from her head as she glanced towards the slumped figure in the chair who by now was sneezing into June's handkerchief.

'Nothing, thank you, Ellen. She'll be fine with a cup of tea and biscuits inside her.'

Ellen quietly closed the door behind her.

'I don't know what came over me,' the woman spoke, her words slurring a little. She put the bottle of smelling salts to her nose again, and Maxine felt her own nostrils clear with the sudden release of the ammonia.

'Don't worry at all,' Maxine said. 'Would you like to lie down for a while after you've had your tea?'

'No, no, I have to get back. But I've come to give you this box.'

The two women waited.

'It's quite a story,' Mrs Brown said, seeming to gather her wits. 'And it was a good job I was home at the time.'

318

Maxine drew in an impatient breath. At this rate they'd be here all morning.

'Go on,' June said, nodding.

'The box was my neighbour's – Mrs Goodfellow's. But it weren't hers really – no, it belonged to her daughter.'

Maxine and June exchanged glances. Mrs Brown was obviously still confused.

June frowned. 'I'm not sure I'm following you, Mrs Brown. Who is Mrs Goodfellow?'

'My neighbour. Mrs Best's mother,' Mrs Brown said with a tinge of impatience.

Maxine gave a start. 'Do you mean Peter Best's grandmother?'

'Yes, that's who I mean. Grandmother to the *German* boy.'

Maxine cringed. Would people ever stop labelling Peter in such a condemning way, as though he had anything to do with the war?

'Well, I said I'd do the favour cos I liked the old girl, and she *trusts* me. You can't trust everyone these days. You have to be careful who you talk to. But she's *English,* or was, God rest her soul. Though if her daughter hadn't been one of us as well I wouldn't have dreamed of getting involved. It wouldn't've been my business. I was just sorry for her having a daughter who was married to a Nazi.' Mrs Brown lifted the cup to her lips, but not before Maxine had seen the disapproval hardening them. She gave a deep slurp, then took a biscuit, crunching it while her eyes darted from June's to Maxine's faces.

'We try not to use that word, Mrs Brown,' June said firmly. 'It's bad for the children to hear such names, and we do sometimes get German Jewish children staying with us – and we treat them all exactly the same. Dr Barnardo himself would not tolerate hatred or discrimination of any kind.

319

The children have enough difficulties trying to come to terms with the loss of their parents, whatever their circumstances.'

'I didn't mean no harm, Miss.' Mrs Brown's bony hand stretched out for another biscuit.

'I'm rather confused,' June said. 'Did you know Mrs Best, Peter's mother?'

'Oh, yes. She came to see her mother two or three times, bringing the boy. Until she got ill, that is. Luckily she gave the box to her mother – that's Mrs Goodfellow – the last time she visited.'

'Why did Mrs Goodfellow give you her daughter's box?'

'She didn't. I saw it once after her daughter died and Peter went to live with her. She showed me where she hid it – at the back of her wardrobe. She told me if anything happened to her . . .' Mrs Brown lowered her voice, '. . . she got cancer, you see. Here.' She pointed to her own left breast. 'That's when her daughter came over from Germany. Mrs Goodfellow got over the op, but then a year or so later her daughter died of TB. She were broken-hearted. What mother wouldn't be? So Peter was sent to her to live.' Mrs Brown gave herself a little shake. 'What was I saying? Oh, yes – if anything happened to her and Peter was taken away, I was to give the box to him. Important papers in it, she said. She would never-a known she'd be killed by a bomb and the house would be practically sliced in two. She was always worried it would be the cancer to get her, leaving Peter with no one.' She looked at the two women as though to make sure they were taking it all in,

'Do go on, Mrs Brown,' June said, tapping her fingers on the desk.

'Well, some boys found it in the rubble. You know what little devils they can be, messing around on the bomb sites.' She pursed her mouth. 'I was in a state meself, I can tell you. Shaking like a leaf, I was. Luckily, I remembered the box and came out and saw them with it. Threatened I'd go to the police if they didn't hand it over.' She paused for breath, and blew her nose, then continued. 'I thought I'd better take it to the council and let them deal with it, and then I thought, no, Mrs Goodfellow said not to let it out of my sight until I gave it to her grandson. Took a while before I found out he were at Bingham Hall, so here I am.' She looked up triumphantly.

'You did exactly the right thing, Mrs Brown,' June said. 'Would you like more tea . . . and another biscuit?'

'They're very nice,' Mrs Brown said, helping herself to two more. June topped up her cup and Mrs Brown took a deep gulp. 'Shall I open it for you?'

'Before you do, Mrs Brown, have you already looked inside?'

'Oh, no.' Mrs Brown's eyes gleamed and Maxine was sure she wasn't telling the truth. 'Well, I may have had a peep, but it ain't my business to poke my nose into someone's personal stuff. Especially not them letters.'

June gave an imperceptible shrug, and Maxine rolled her eyes.

'We'd be grateful if you'd open the box,' June said. 'Was there a key with it?'

'Oh, yes. It's locked, all right.' Mrs Brown delved into her bag and brought out a purse, then drew out a small key. It made a little click as she turned it. She opened the lid, twirled it round, and pushed it towards June. 'Here, Miss Lavender. You see what you can make of it.'

Chapter Thirty-Two

Maxine watched as June pulled out a black velvet bag from the metal box Mrs Brown had unlocked and gently shook out a string of pearls. They gleamed up at the two women under the electric bulb over June's head that she'd had to switch on during these dark winter mornings. June put her hand inside the bag again.

'There's more,' she said, pulling out a pearl bracelet and matching drop earrings.

'It's beautiful – a beautiful set,' Maxine said, picking up the necklace and turning it over. She swallowed, imagining Herr Best fastening the necklace around the soft white throat of his English wife. How could she accept such presents from a Nazi? But he was her husband and presumably she loved him. Or did she? Had she been disgusted to see her husband in the Nazi regime? Was she simply using her sick mother as an excuse to take her child out of a country which wasn't hers – which she no longer wanted to live in? Or be part of? What a dilemma the poor woman must have been in.

There were a few sepia-tinted photographs which June looked at before handing them to Maxine. She studied them closely. One was of a couple on their wedding day, dressed in Edwardian fashion. They must have been Peter's grandparents on his mother's side as they looked so English. Yes, the boy looked a lot like his grandfather – same nose and mouth, but his eyes were exactly the same shape, depth and expression as his German father's. And then a black-and-white photograph of a young smiling woman, her hair curling softly underneath, and her mouth slicked with lipstick. She could easily have been a film star, Maxine thought, but she was certain she was looking at Peter's mother.

June laid a bundle of letters tied up with a blue-ribboned bow on the desk.

'Here, Maxine.' June gently pushed the pile over to her. 'Why don't you have a look? They might throw light on things . . . not sure what. I'll get Peter's file out.'

Maxine untied the bow and picked up one of the envelopes. She peered at the postmark but the print had blurred. Lifting her head, she saw June looking curiously at her.

'Don't you think we should open it?' June asked.

Maxine shook her head. 'I'm not sure. It's private property . . . though maybe we should just check to see what language they're written in.'

June nodded and handed her the letter opener. Maxine immediately slit it open, conscious of Mrs Brown leaning towards her, trying to peer over her shoulder. She caught a whiff of a stale odour on the woman and, trying hard to ignore it, pulled out two single handwritten sheets. She read: *Mein liebling Chrissie,* then skimmed her eyes to the bottom of the page, not understanding a word, written as it was in German. Disappointed, she turned to the second page and wasn't surprised to read that it was signed: *Your Carl.*

The proximity of Mrs Brown was making Maxine feel quite uncomfortable. But at least the envelopes didn't appear to have been tampered with in any way. She would have thought Mrs Brown wouldn't have been able to stop herself from ripping them open. Maybe she'd been worried she would have been in trouble from the authorities. She glanced at the writing again and spoke to June. 'This is from Herr Best to his wife.'

'Love letters, by the looks of all them kisses at the end,' Mrs Brown put in, her lips pursed as though with disapproval that a man should be so sentimental about his wife.

To Maxine's relief June was obviously thinking along the same lines as herself.

'Well, we're very grateful to you, Mrs Brown for the safe-keeping of this box,' June said crisply, taking out a file and closing the cabinet. 'It will be perfectly safe here at Bingham Hall and I will report it to Dr Barnardo's headquarters that you kindly brought it in. I'm sure they will write to thank you.'

'So that's all, is it?' Mrs Brown said in a cross tone, snatching off her glasses and putting them in her handbag. She snapped it closed. 'I've kept it under difficult circumstances and that's all you have to say? Am I not to know the contents of them letters?'

'They're not for the general public, no,' June said swiftly. 'They're private, and Herr Best is still alive, we presume. We will try to find him and return them to him. But in the meantime, will you just write your name and address down?' She put a piece of paper and pencil in front of Mrs Brown, who looked at them dubiously.

'Is anything the matter?' Maxine asked.

Mrs Brown swung her head round, her face red with annoyance. 'I never did no reading nor writing,' she said. 'If I had, you can be sure I'd have opened them letters.'

Maxine hid a smile. 'Well, you'd need to be pretty good at German,' she said, 'because *I* can't understand a word.' She picked up the pencil and sheet of paper. 'Just tell me your address, Mrs Brown, and then we have it if we need to contact you again.'

It was in one of the poorer parts of Liverpool, Maxine noted.

Mrs Brown sniffed the air like a dog. 'Something smells nice coming from the kitchen,' she said.

Oh, no, Maxine thought. *She's hinting she wants to stay for dinner.*

'Yes, Bertie is a very good cook,' June said, rising to her feet. 'I need to speak to her about something. Maxine, would you ring for Ellen to ask Harold if he'd take Mrs Brown home? We can't send her off in this weather.' She nodded towards her window where the rain was bucketing down and disappeared.

Maxine rang the bell and gave Ellen the message. Mrs Brown sat in silence, unnerving Maxine again. What was it about the woman that she found quite obnoxious? Was it the way her sharp eyes seemed to miss nothing? As though she were weighing up the place. It was more than mere interest, or even curiosity. Thankfully, June was back in a trice, holding a package wrapped in greaseproof paper.

'For your trouble, Mrs Brown,' June said, handing it to her. 'It's one of Cook's best pies. And a slice of cake to go with it.'

'That's most thoughtful,' Mrs Brown said, taking it from her and putting it in her basket. 'But I think I deserve something more for me trouble.' She gave June an unblinking stare.

'I'm not sure what you mean,' June said in a deliberately neutral tone, though Maxine was certain June knew exactly.

'It's very hard to manage these days,' Mrs Brown said, 'with the war on. And my Hilda not working here no more.'

Maxine gave a start. So that's who she was. Hilda's mother. And June was just as surprised, if she wasn't very much mistaken.

'Ah, Mrs Brown. I should have connected,' June said

quietly. 'Of course Hilda came here long before I did so I knew very little about her. I'm afraid she stirred the children up by making an example out of an innocent child, just because he happened to be from Germany. And it wasn't the first time. She was warned then but took no notice.'

'He's not even a Jew-boy,' Mrs Brown said, her eyes glinting with hate. 'My Hilda was right to speak up. When she told me his name – Peter Best – I had to keep me promise. But the boy is worse than a Jew, if anything. His father is a Nazi. I might not know me letters, but I know a swastika when I see one.'

Maxine gave a quick intake of breath. So Hilda had shown the photograph to her mother. June looked steadily across her desk.

'As I said before – we don't use that language. It's what cost your daughter her job.'

Mrs Brown opened her mouth to argue, but before she could speak there was a knock at the door.

'Is the lady ready, Matron?' Harold turned his hat over in his hands.

'Yes, I believe she is,' June said, nodding to Mrs Brown. 'This is Harold, our chauffeur. He will take you to your door, but he needs to go now as he has several errands to do later. So we must take advantage of him.' She hesitated, then put her hand out, but Mrs Brown ignored her and rose to follow Harold, who had been swept up in the children's rush for dinner.

'So Hilda gave Peter's father's photograph to her mother,' June said, shaking her head when Mrs Brown had vanished.

'Yes, and now she's after money,' Maxine said when she sat down again.

'I know,' June answered wearily. 'And I think there's a

threat behind those innocent words – she's obviously bitter about her daughter no longer working here.' She paused, doodling with her pencil underneath Mrs Brown's address. 'I'll have to have a word with Dr Barnardo's. See how they want me to handle this.' She looked up. 'Do you have a clue as to what's in those letters?'

'I only know that *"liebling"* means *"darling".'* Maxine dropped her eyes to the letter again. 'But it might hold clues as to where the boy's father is and we could send word to him that his son is here.' She looked up. 'I think you told me headquarters haven't had any reply to their letter telling him Peter is safe with us.'

'Yes, that's right,' June answered. 'It's a worry because it means we don't even know if he's aware that both his wife and his mother-in-law are dead . . . which means we'll have to read a letter or two. It's a real nuisance he's written in German.'

Maxine didn't mention that the only two people who would be able to translate the letters were Peter himself, which wouldn't be at all appropriate, and Crofton.

As though June read her mind, she said, 'Crofton? Would he, do you think?

'I'm not sure,' Maxine said, flushing at the mention of his name. 'I haven't seen him for several weeks . . .' her voice trailed off.

June gave her a sharp look. 'You don't look as though you're sleeping very well. You've got dark circles under your eyes.'

'I'm not,' Maxine admitted.

'It's awfully hard for the men to keep in regular contact. I'm sure he's fine.'

Maxine swallowed hard. 'I hope you're right.'

'I think we'll have to look at the last two letters or so, or else we'll never know what the situation is. She must have wanted Peter to read the letters for himself one day when he was older, or why did she keep them, and hand them over to her mother?'

'I expect she thought they'd be in safe hands,' Maxine said soberly.

'But reading a couple of letters will give us more of an insight than that brief report I had from headquarters,' June persisted. 'I really think we should ask Crofton if he would be kind enough to translate them. I can trust him not to let this go any further, and after all, he's been there right from the beginning . . . when you and Peter bumped into him in Morrows.' She threw Maxine a knowing smile.

Maxine sighed. 'All right,' she said. 'I'll try to telephone him.'

The last thing she wanted was for Crofton to think she was making an excuse to see him again. Her cheeks warmed at the thought.

'You don't sound convinced,' June said, her voice sounding concerned. 'Would you prefer me to ask?'

'It might be better coming from you,' Maxine said. 'More professional.'

'You don't want him to think you're chasing him,' June smiled sympathetically. It was strange how June was beginning to know her so well, Maxine thought. 'He won't,' June added. 'He's not that type at all.' She stared directly into Maxine's eyes. 'Are you sure you want me to ring him?'

'No, I'll do it,' Maxine said.

'Maxine!' Crofton's deep warm tones came over the crackling line. 'You must have wondered where on earth I've been these last weeks.' There was a pause. 'This line's none too clear. Can you hear me?'

'Yes.' She felt miserable. He should have been the one to

ring her and now he'd be trying desperately to think of some excuse as to why he hadn't been in touch.

'It's wonderful to hear your voice. We've had a bit of a rough time of it lately.'

Dear God, what had happened to him? If only he was allowed to tell her where he was exactly – what he did – she'd feel closer to him somehow. She was thankful he couldn't see her dismay.

'Are you all right?' She felt her voice shake.

'Yes, don't worry about me. I was going to ring you this evening. Plan our next outing.'

Her heart lifted. So he did want to see her again. Just because she'd not heard from him didn't mean he was losing interest. He was fighting a war, for goodness' sake. Of course he wasn't always going to be able to keep in touch with her.

'Are you still there, Maxine?'

'Yes, I'm here.'

'Did you need me for anything?'

'Yes,' Maxine said, resisting the impulse to tell him she needed him more than anything in the world. 'We've come across some letters written by Peter's father to his wife when she took the boy to England. They're all in German. June wondered if you'd be kind enough to interpret them.'

'Of course I would,' Crofton said immediately. 'How did you come by them?'

'We'll tell you when we see you,' Maxine said. 'Will you have some time soon?'

'After what the boys have been through I've given most of them some time off,' Crofton said, 'but I could get away the day after tomorrow for an hour or two. Say, eleven o'clock. Would that do?'

'It would do very well,' Maxine said, her heart lifting. 'I'll have the kettle on.'

Chapter Thirty-Three

Try as she might, Maxine could not stop her heart from fluttering out of control. Crofton would be here in a few more hours. She hopped out of bed and went over to the window. A fine sheet of ice clung to the pane on her side, but for once she didn't feel cold. She couldn't help smiling. Crofton had sounded pleased to hear from her, though she'd noticed his voice was tired.

She had a shock when she saw him waiting for her in the Great Hall. His face looked gaunt and he had bags under his eyes. He'd obviously not been sleeping much. Even his uniform hung a little loose. But he leapt to his feet and his beaming smile was the same. Just as he gave her a quick peck on the cheek, she saw Alan and Bobby out of the corner of her eye and quickly stepped back, but too late – they threw loud wolf whistles at her as they smirked their way to the dining room for elevenses.

'Little monkeys,' she said, trying to cover her embarrassment, but Crofton merely chuckled.

'Shall we go to the library?' he said.

'It's the most private,' Maxine said. 'Oh, June said to tell you she's sorry but she's had to go into town today and couldn't lose the chance of a lift with Harold. But she sent her regards and hopes you'll have success with the letters.'

'I hope so, too.' Crofton smiled. 'Shall we get started?'

Ellen brought a tray of coffee as soon as they'd sat at the round table in the small room off the main library.

'Don't know how your cook gets hold of this real coffee,' Crofton said, appreciatively licking his lips after the first gulp. 'It's a darned sight better than *we* get.'

'She only brings it out on special occasions,' Maxine admitted, then could have bitten her tongue out.

'I'm glad she recognises this is one of those occasions,' Crofton laughed, pressing her hand.

She quivered at the sudden tingle and managed an embarrassed smile.

'This is a box Peter's grandmother's neighbour brought in the day before yesterday,' she said, trying to keep her voice steady as she opened the lid. 'Besides some jewellery there was a bundle of letters and a few photographs.'

She laid out the photographs and Crofton picked them up, one by one, and studied them, as Maxine explained who the people probably were.

'June thought if you could just translate the last couple of letters or so, we might get an idea of the situation – if Herr Best knew his wife was ill – anything, so that after the war we'll know what to do with Peter.' Crofton raised an eyebrow. 'Oh, that sounds awful,' she added quickly, 'but I know he desperately misses his father now he's lost his mother and grandmother. It must be terrible for him, and if he could go back to Germany after it's over and be with his father, that would be the best thing for him, I'm sure.'

'When the war ends there will be a lot of questions the Nazis will have to answer,' Crofton said grimly. 'I wouldn't be at all surprised if they're tried, and if found guilty, executed.'

Maxine shuddered. How could the child go through what might prove to be the worst horror of all?

'Let's don't think of it for now,' she said, handing him an envelope – not the one she'd glanced at already – but the second from the top of the pile. 'Is your German good enough to translate it as you go along?'

'Depends,' Crofton said, taking out the sheet of paper. 'Let me have a look.' His eyes roved swiftly over the page and to the second sheet, much as Maxine had done, though without understanding a word of the letter she'd picked; she was sure Crofton wouldn't have the same problem.

'It's dated 21st November 1941.' He looked up and shook his head slowly. 'That's a year ago.' He cleared his throat. '*My darling Chrissie, I hope you are much improved from the last time you wrote, which seems a long time ago. I'm worried about that cough you mentioned. Try not to smoke too much. Also, of course, how is your mother? If only I could be with you I would take care of you both, mein Schatz.*' Crofton looked up. 'That means "my treasure".' He grinned. 'Seems Herr Best is not your typical cold-hearted Nazi. Anyway, he goes on, *How is our son? I miss you both so much. Sometimes I find it difficult to get through the days. You know I cannot say what I am in the middle of, but be sure of one thing – you can both rest with a peaceful heart. You remember our special song, dearest . . .*' Crofton frowned. 'Oh, yes, I see,' he muttered. 'This next bit's in English.'

Maxine waited. So far it had all been words of love. Not what you'd expect from a Nazi, but the words of a husband or a lover – she went pink at the idea as she caught Crofton's eye. She always felt he knew what she was thinking.

'Sorry.' Crofton sent Maxine an apologetic smile. 'Where was I? Oh, yes, the song.' He bent his head again.

'*You remember our song, "She'll be coming round the mountain when she comes"?*'

What an odd song for a husband and wife to love, Maxine thought, frowning. As far as she knew, it was an old American folk song. It wasn't a scrap romantic, in complete contrast to Herr Best's lovey-dovey manner towards his wife in the rest of the letter.

Crofton looked up. 'I don't know what you make of it, Maxine, but I think there's some kind of special meaning there.' His lips moved silently as he formed the words of the song again. 'I need to think some more about that.'

'It does sound a strange thing to write in a love letter,' Maxine said, then wished she could swallow back the words as she uttered the forbidden word.

Crofton didn't appear to notice and instead turned to the next page. 'He's gone back into German now. *You are always in my thoughts and dreams and heart, mein liebling . . .* my darling . . .' Crofton looked directly at her, and she wasn't sure whether he was deliberately translating those last two words, or Carl had gone into English. She held her breath. She couldn't tear her eyes away. It was as though an invisible thread bound them together. He, too, seemed reluctant to drop his eyes, but finally he bent his head and cleared his throat again. '. . . *until I hold you safely in my arms once more and press you to me so our hearts beat as one, I will say goodnight. Give our dear child a kiss for me. Tell him I love him. You already know how I feel about you. But to remind you, I love you with all my soul.*' Crofton's voice held a slight tremor. '*Be strong. Your Carl,* followed by a row of kisses.' He set the letter aside. 'What's your first thought, Maxine?'

Without hesitation, she said, 'He doesn't sound one bit like I would've expected.'

'Well, even Hitler loves his dog,' Crofton commented

dryly. 'But I agree, that's my impression as well. And that song that's supposed to be special for both of them – it's not your usual wartime love song or anything you'd expect between a husband and wife who seem to adore one another.'

'Unless it's a private joke between them,' Maxine offered.

'Hmm. It's possible, I suppose. But Germans don't usually joke in that way. They're not normally playful with words the way the British are.'

'Maybe he's caught his wife's sense of humour,' Maxine said.

'I can't see it myself.' Crofton picked up the letter and studied it again. '"She'll be coming round the mountain when she comes". I'm wondering . . .' Maxine thought she might melt under his gaze. 'Could it possibly be a coded message?'

Maxine's eyes flew wide. 'Do you mean what I think you mean?'

'I'm not sure what you mean?'

'We seem to be speaking in code ourselves,' Maxine laughed nervously. 'I mean, could it be something *he's* about to do – something he's planning, and that's where the line, "She *will* be coming round the mountain" fits in, and he will let her know when he's arrived . . . "when she comes"?'

'It's a bit far-fetched—'

'Yes, I suppose it is,' Maxine interrupted, feeling a little foolish.

'. . . but I think you're right. You'd make a good code-breaker, you know.' He gave her a look of approval, and Maxine felt her cheeks flush. 'The Germans would never understand that one,' he said. 'And I'll go even further . . . I'd even question whether he's a Nazi!'

There was a stunned silence as they held one another's gaze. Maxine broke it.

'If that's true, it would be the best piece of news possible for Peter.'

'It certainly would.' Crofton leafed through the dozen or so envelopes. 'I'll just have a look at the last one he sent. Are they in date order?' She nodded. 'Okay, let's see if he's made any progress on his plans, whatever they might be. We could be completely wrong about him, so we shouldn't get our hopes up.'

He pulled out the only sheet of paper, his lips moving as he quickly read through it. She was fascinated. His mouth was such a beautiful shape. Lips that turned up a little at the corners as though he could easily break into smiles and laughter.

'I think we're definitely on to something,' he said looking up, catching her staring at him. She looked quickly away. 'This is written a fortnight later. I'll cut out the romantic stuff . . .' he gave her a wink, 'and read you this bit. *I am pleased to tell you that she's come round that mountain.*'

'That definitely sounds like a code,' Maxine said excitedly, 'else why would he change the words?'

'Exactly. Something he's planned has happened. We just need to find out what.'

And then it struck her with such force she almost reeled. 'Crofton! We're right!'

'What is it, love?'

He looked at her and Maxine felt a flame leap between them. He'd called her 'love', though it was probably the excitement of the moment. She'd think about it when she was alone in her room.

Feeling her cheeks flush a little, desperate to concentrate, she said, 'We all sang that song shortly after Peter came here. Athena, by coincidence, chose it along with some others. She started it off and two or three of the older children knew it and chimed in. Peter was in the row behind, but I could see his face. It kind of crumpled and then he suddenly rushed out. I didn't put two and two together until now. I'd just thought he hated being with a group of children who always ignored him.'

'He clearly knows that song very well,' Crofton said. 'Are you going to speak to him?'

'Oh, yes.' Maxine glanced at her watch. 'June shouldn't be too long. We'll tell her what you've translated and what we think.'

'Would June mind if I stayed here and listened to what Peter has to say?'

'I don't think she'd mind at all.' Maxine collected the coffee cups and plates together and put them neatly on the tray, wishing her heart would stop thumping so loudly. At this rate he'd be able to hear it. 'I'll just take this to the kitchen and go and find him.'

Minutes later she was back with a sulky-looking Peter, but his face lit up when he saw who was in the library.

'Hello, Sir,' he said, thrusting out his hand.

Crofton took it in his own large one. 'The same to you, young sir,' he said. 'And thank you for coming to talk to us.'

'That's all right, Sir.'

He gave Crofton a rare smile and Maxine's heart soared at the trust between the two of them, until she remembered why they were all here.

'Peter,' she began, after he was seated, 'we need to ask you something and you're probably the only person who would know the answer.'

Peter's smile quickly faded. He silently stared at her.

'Do you know the song "She'll be coming round the mountain when she comes"?'

Maxine watched him closely. Was that a tightening round Peter's mouth, a glint of alarm in his eyes, or was it just her imagination?

'No, Miss.'

'Are you absolutely certain?' Crofton gently questioned the boy. 'You know Nurse Taylor and I can be completely trusted not to get you in any sort of trouble.'

'I know, Sir.' Peter looked in Maxine's direction but kept his head lowered. 'May I go now, Miss?' He shuffled his feet as though he couldn't get away fast enough.

'Peter,' Crofton said softly, giving Maxine a very gentle nudge under the table, 'may I talk to you in private – just the two of us?'

Peter nodded.

Crofton caught her eye and Maxine immediately rose to her feet, leaving the two of them together. She only hoped June would not be annoyed with her for leaving Peter alone with Crofton to deal with such a confidential and sensitive subject.

She didn't know what to do with herself. All she could think of was Crofton, trying to talk man-to-man with Peter. But she knew one thing. She trusted Crofton completely that he would say and do the right thing. But for now she'd have to wait patiently. She'd pop down to the ward and see how her charges were getting on.

She gave Crofton a quarter of an hour, and then went back up the steps and towards the library. Carefully opening the library door, she was in time to hear Crofton say, 'Your secret is safe with me, but I need your permission to tell it to the right people so we can try to locate your father.'

Maxine hesitated, then stepped into the open doorway where Crofton and Peter sat close together, his hand on the boy's shoulder.

'Ah, there you are,' Crofton said, standing up.

'Is everything all right?' She glanced at him.

Crofton nodded.

She tried not to linger on Peter's tear-stained face but said brightly, 'The children are just going in for dinner so why don't you follow them in?'

Peter scrambled up, then sought Crofton's eye. 'I don't mind if you tell Nurse Taylor about Papa,' he said.

'Thank you, Peter.' Crofton smiled at him. 'Now run along and join the others.'

'My goodness,' Maxine said, taking Peter's seat. 'What happened?'

'He spilt the beans.' Crofton sat down again. 'It's quite a story, but the quick version is that before Peter and his mum came to England, Herr Best had a private talk to Peter. He told him he must be good and take care of his mother. That whatever anyone said, Peter must always believe his father is a good man and a good German, and after the war people would find out not all Germans were bad people. He promised Peter he'd come to England one day for him and his mother, even if it took a long time. But until then Peter had to remember the song, but never sing it unless he was completely by himself. Even if he only sang it in his head, he would know his mother and father were near him and thinking of him. Oh, and he must never, ever tell a living soul.' As though without thinking, Crofton took her hand. 'Quite a burden for a five-year-old, as he was then, I should think.'

'Poor little chap.' Maxine genuinely felt for him but she couldn't stop the fierce beating of her heart when her hand was so firmly and warmly in Crofton's. 'Do you still think it could be a code for planning something?'

'I've no doubt about it,' Crofton answered unhesitatingly.

'Promising to come to England . . . not mentioning that he'd come when the war is over . . . To me, it sounds as though he's in some kind of resistance movement and his letter smacks of escaping from Germany.'

Goosepimples flashed up her arms and across her scalp.

'If only we knew for certain that he's still alive,' she said softly.

'We won't know that unless he manages to step foot in England,' Crofton said. 'And if he does, he'll be interned immediately.'

'Until the end of the war?'

'Probably. Any information he has, Baker Street will be most interested.' He stroked her hand in an absent-minded fashion. 'We have to hope for the best and expect the worst – that even if Herr Best has left Germany, I'm afraid it's doubtful there'll be a happy ending.'

By the time June returned, Crofton had left. Maxine swiftly told her all Crofton had translated and what they suspected had happened.

June's mouth fell open. 'It brings the war even closer somehow,' she said. 'A German who sounds like a good German trying to leave his country and what would be considered his duty to Hitler, to find his wife and son. And that his escape might have been successful.'

'Crofton says we mustn't put too much hope into that,' Maxine said. 'It would be a dangerous undertaking – especially as Peter hasn't heard from his father for a year or so. I just pray we don't have to tell him more bad news. I don't think he could bear it.'

The following morning June asked Maxine if she could pop into her office for a few minutes. She took one look at June's face, her eyes anxious, and knew she'd had some unpleasant news. Bracing herself, she sat down.

'Oh, Maxine, I've had a letter from Mrs Brown. She's threatened to report me for taking something which isn't mine – the metal box.'

'That's ridiculous. We all know it belongs to Peter and we're keeping it safe until it's the right time to give it to him. And we can prove it's his. But anyway, Mrs Brown said she couldn't write.'

'I expect she got someone to do it for her,' June said. 'Maybe Hilda. Anyway, she's asking for ten pounds.'

'Don't let her do this,' Maxine said crossly. 'We'll be depriving the children. And you'd have to clear it with Mr Clarke. I don't think he'd be too happy.'

'But she's not going to let it rest,' June said. 'I've a good mind to report her to the police.'

'Maybe as a last resort,' Maxine said. 'In the meantime why don't we sent her a pound note inside a card to wish her and Hilda Merry Christmas? Then it can't be looked upon as you succumbing to blackmail.'

'Good idea,' June said, then looked at Maxine and hesitated.

'You look serious.' Maxine's heart turned over. June obviously wanted to say something more difficult than Mrs Brown's pathetic attempt at blackmail. 'Is there something else?'

'Don't take this the wrong way, Maxine,' June said, her green eyes anxious, 'but Mr Clarke telephoned the other day and wanted to know how you were getting on with your studies, and if you'd applied to take your finals. He reminded me that it was the one condition of hiring you.'

'I haven't forgotten, Junie.' Maxine breathed out a sigh, glad it was nothing more ominous. 'I've applied, but I might have to go back to St Thomas' to take them. I had hoped I could do it at one of the hospitals here, and I'm still looking into it. It seems a long way to go just to take an exam.'

'I'll let him know,' June said. 'Anyway, I can't afford to let you go off to London before we hire the new nurse.'

'Is there any news on that?'

'We have someone coming to see us next week,' June said. 'A Miss Dolores Honeywell.'

'Sweet name,' Maxine chuckled. 'Let's hope she lives up to it.'

Chapter Thirty-Four

December 1942

Maxine carried the dress over her arm as carefully as she did on the day of her own wedding. What a lot had happened since then. She had a job she loved, looking after the children, and everything she did for them she hoped Teddy's adoptive parents would be doing the same. For fleeting moments she could no longer conjure up his dear little face, his neat ears covered by a thick growth of auburn hair. The pain of her guilt was sometimes unbearable. She shook herself. She mustn't keep thinking about Teddy – she had to let him go – for now, anyway. Perhaps one day when he'd grown into a young man . . . Until then he had loving parents who were looking after him. She prayed with all her heart that he meant the world to his new mummy and daddy.

Now, glancing down at the dress, she hoped it would bring her friend better luck. Maxine had known as she'd walked down the aisle that she shouldn't be marrying her best friend, Johnny – she should be feeling passion, not simply affection – but she'd been too much of a coward to say anything. She only hoped June was going into her marriage with those green eyes of hers wide open.

Taking a deep breath and watching it stream out in the

cold air, she knocked on June's cottage door and walked in as June had invited her to. Immediately, Freddie came hurtling down the stairs wagging his tail and trying to jump up.

Brrrr! It was cold this morning and the cottage wasn't very warm. She quickly shut the door behind her.

'Not today, Freddie, while your mistress needs to get ready.' She patted his silky head, enjoying the feel of him; his smiling mouth and his enthusiasm. 'Junie! It's me.'

She heard light footsteps tripping down the stairs and June appeared in her dressing gown, a little flushed now her big day was here.

'Thanks for getting here early,' June said, smiling. 'Freddie, behave! Sorry, Maxine. I'm all at sixes and sevens. My hair won't go right.'

'Don't worry. I'll do it for you before you put your dress on. Are you nearly ready?'

'Yes, I've had my full five inches of bathwater,' June laughed.

Upstairs, Maxine sat her down at her dressing table and within a few minutes June's thick fair hair was brushed through and swept up at either side with silver combs.

'They were a present from Murray,' June told her, turning her head each way, a delighted smile on her lips. 'You've done it beautifully, Maxine. I could never have got it quite that perfect.'

'Are you wearing a veil?' she asked.

'No, nothing that fancy.' June grinned. 'Murray will probably have difficulty recognising me in my beautiful dress as it is. He's never seen me looking so glamorous.'

'He'll be thrilled. I can't wait to meet him.' Maxine opened her handbag and brought out a compact. 'Here,' she said. 'Use this. I've washed the puff, so you can dab your cheeks and nose.'

'You're so thoughtful, Maxine,' June said, looking up at her in the mirror after she'd powdered her nose. 'And cutting down your dress just for me was such a lovely thing to do.'

'Don't be silly . . . it's what friends are for.' Maxine scrutinised the young matron. 'All you need now is lipstick and a dash of scent. Not too much. You don't want to drive him wild straightaway.'

June laughed and then her expression turned serious. 'I've been meaning to ask you something, Maxine, as I don't have my mother, and I don't think I could have asked her anyway – I'd be too embarrassed.'

'I know exactly what you're going to ask, Junie.' June caught Maxine's eye in the mirror. 'And it does.'

A frown stole over June's forehead.

'You're talking about the wedding night, I presume. And yes, it hurts. But you get used to it. And then you might even like it.'

June's face was pink. 'I keep worrying about it.'

'Do you love him?'

'More than anyone in the world.'

'And he loves you?'

'He says the same.'

Maxine fought down a twinge of envy. 'Then he'll be gentle and loving and thoughtful. And you'll be absolutely fine, though it *is* a bit painful the first time. The next is better and you'll probably end up a brazen hussy asking him to make love to you at all times of the day and night.'

They laughed together like young carefree women. It was good to feel like this, Maxine thought, even though it wasn't real for her. But June's friendship *was* real and she was truly grateful.

She slipped the wedding dress over June's head and

344

fastened it, then arranged the imitation fur cape she'd made on June's slender shoulders.

'Walk across the room,' she said. 'You need to get used to the feel of the train.'

'I've never worn anything so lovely and such a perfect fit in my life.' June turned to Maxine, her eyes brimming.

'You look absolutely beautiful,' Maxine said, swallowing hard. 'So if you don't need your personal maid any longer I think I'd better go and change and make sure Lizzie is washed and in her bridesmaid's dress. Athena said she'd help her, so I'll go and check she's ready.' She looked at June. 'By the way, when are you going to tell Lizzie the news?'

'I think when we're back from our honeymoon,' June said, 'which will be in exactly two days' time.' She gave a rueful grin.

'Not long for a honeymoon,' Maxine said. 'But then Johnny and I only had three.'

'Oh, Maxine, I'm being selfish talking about me when this must bring back sad memories for you.'

'You, selfish?' Maxine chuckled. 'You're the least selfish person I know. And your wedding day is not in the least painful to me. I'm thrilled for you and can't wait to meet the man of your dreams.'

'You're a dear.'

'Nonsense.' She brushed June's cheek with a soft kiss. 'Freddie will see me out, so you just sit down with a cup of tea as it's still early. There's no need to rush because today is *your* day.'

'Do I look pretty?' Lizzie screeched, immediately she spotted Maxine in the Great Hall. She was wearing a pink wool dress with a large pink bow in her hair and white socks and shoes.

'Where's the little furry cape I made you?' Maxine asked.

'I've got it here.' Lizzie ran to the chair by the telephone table and grabbed it. She flung it around her small narrow shoulders.

'My word, you do look grown up.'

Lizzie's smile shone. 'Is it time yet to go to the church?' She hopped up and down.

'We're not going to the church,' Maxine said. 'We're staying here and going to the chapel.'

'That's what I meant . . . the chapel, the chapel,' she sang out.

It was impossible to think of Lizzie not speaking for all those weeks when June had first arrived. Maxine smiled. There was nothing wrong with Lizzie's lungs now. She took the little girl's hand.

'We have to wait and let everyone else go into the chapel, Lizzie, so we'll stay here in the hall. As soon as we see June come in, you and I will walk behind her and make sure she doesn't trip over her train.'

'Oh, I hope Miss Junie comes in soon,' Lizzie said. 'I want to see her pretty dress.'

The chapel was bursting by the time the teachers and nurses and maids took their places and the children had squashed onto the benches, elbowing one another and talking until Barbara told them in a very firm voice to be quiet and settle down.

There was no organ in the chapel, but Athena had offered to play 'Here Comes The Bride' on the piano, which had been especially moved from the library with great difficulty by the male staff. She sat on the stool, her hands poised over the keys, and when Harold, standing at the back, sent her a nod she began to play.

June appeared to float down the aisle, her arm through

Mr Clarke's. He wouldn't exactly be most young women's first choice to give them away, Maxine thought, but he was obviously taking it all very seriously by the way he was holding himself as straight as one of the fluted columns, turning to June every few steps as though to reassure her. Perhaps she'd chosen him because he'd given her a proper chance in life.

Maxine held Lizzie's hand as they followed, Lizzie practically skipping. June looked perfectly poised as she got nearer to the man she'd given her heart to. Not like herself on her own wedding day when she'd got cold feet as she was walking up the aisle. It was only Johnny who'd looked so happy as he'd turned round and watched her. How full of plans for their future, he'd been, and all so tragically snatched away.

She was relieved when June and Murray had said their vows and signed the register and they'd all moved to the dining room for the magnificent spread Bertie had put on, buffet style. Once again she was amazed that the cook found such ingredients with the rationing and only thanked her lucky stars that the government ordained that hospitals and children's homes were top of the list where food was concerned.

Maxine picked up a small plate and helped herself to one ham sandwich triangle and a sausage roll and strolled over to a nearby table, where she joined Kathleen and the teachers who were already tucking in. June had whispered that Lizzie could eat at the top table and the little girl had shrieked with delight. Maxine looked around curiously. This was the first time she'd seen Murray properly. June had already warned her that Murray had been shot down in his plane and almost lost his eye and had badly injured his leg. He had not yet sat down but was chatting to his best man, who had taken a worse hit than Murray by the looks of his poor face, terribly scarred with serious burns.

Murray himself seemed all that June had described. He was still an attractive man, Maxine thought, and although one of his eyes didn't quite focus, the colour was the same bright blue as the other. June had mentioned he didn't have much sight in it. They were a striking couple, she mused, as she turned to glance at them again, sure they were made for one another, though it made her feel even more alone. She was selfish, she knew, but she couldn't bear to lose June's warm friendship. Everything was bound to change now June had a husband.

Maxine watched Lizzie straining her neck to keep her eye on June and Murray, her expression rapt. The little girl was going to be mad with excitement when June and Murray told her they were going to be her new mummy and daddy, though Maxine hoped they would have their own baby as well one day. They deserved to. She closed her eyes and little Teddy's image floated in front of her. Tears formed under her lashes. If only she knew if he was being looked after and loved, she would feel more at peace. But she was powerless. *Please keep him safe*, she whispered to herself. *Please God, look after him.* She gave a deep sigh, not at all sure there was a God after all. The war had made her cynical.

'What was that big sigh for?' Someone slid into the seat next to her.

Her eyes flew wide. She knew that voice.

'Crofton. I didn't know you were—'

'June told me not to say anything as I wasn't sure I'd get away.' He looked at her. 'I didn't have time to change. Do you mind?'

'Mind if you're in uniform,' she said smiling, joy stealing into her heart, 'or mind that you're here? Well, if you must know, I don't mind either.' She felt the telltale warmth steal into her cheeks as Crofton deliberately took one of her hands and kissed it.

'I know I keep turning up, but I'm desperate to talk to you alone. This isn't the time, but it was nice of June to invite me and it gave me a wonderful excuse to see you again.'

'So you need an excuse,' Maxine retorted, chuckling.

'Not really,' he laughed as he looked towards the table where June and Murray sat.

June sent a warm smile, then immediately got up and came over. 'Crofton, it's lovely to see you,' she said, extending her hand, but he kissed her cheek instead.

'I know you're not supposed to congratulate the bride,' he said, 'but warmest congratulations anyway.'

'Thank you, Crofton. You must come and meet Murray after we've all had something to eat.' She smiled at him. 'I'm so glad you managed to get here.'

So am I, Maxine thought, as Crofton nodded to June, then turned to her with a beaming smile. *So am I.*

Murray was every bit as nice as June had described, and Maxine completely understood why June had fallen for him. What made it even nicer was the way the two men got on so well. While they were talking, Maxine would sometimes give a surreptitious glance at Crofton. He was taller than Murray and a little broader. She couldn't help thinking how handsome he looked in his uniform. Once or twice he caught her glance and grinned. And once he even winked and she blushed, hoping June hadn't witnessed it. But June had seen it and sent the wink on, chuckling as she did so.

Why was she being so coy? It was plain to anyone that Crofton more than liked her. Why couldn't she just relax and enjoy his company?

Because she couldn't bear to carry such a secret she could never reveal. If she did it would destroy Crofton's trust. She resolved to bury it even deeper.

'Will you have dinner with me this evening?' Crofton asked her as he was saying his goodbyes to June and Murray.

'I'd like that,' she heard herself saying. She'd been dreading the time when he would turn to her to say goodbye. But now, it seemed, the day wasn't over. She was going out with him. They'd finally spend some hours in one another's company. Her heart beat a little unsteadily.

'Shall we go right away?' Crofton slipped his arm lightly round her shoulders.

Maxine quivered at his touch. 'I'll have to get my coat,' she said.

He was a good driver. It was an old car but he handled it as gracefully as if it was new. He chatted, but she only answered yes or no, and listened. She liked the sound of his voice, but the further away they were going, the more nervous she became.

'Are you all right, Maxine?' he asked more than once.

'Yes, thank you,' she answered perfunctorily.

'You're not,' he said, turning to look at her. 'Something's on your mind. You know you can tell me anything, don't you?'

'Maybe,' she said, immediately wanting to clam up.

'I mean it.'

Without warning she began to cry.

'Maxine. What is it?' He pulled over and stopped the engine. Turning to her, he tried to hold her, but they were both in an awkward position, thought she could feel the solid muscles of his arms. She wanted to lay her head upon his shoulder – tell him everything. She was tired, so tired of trying to hide her heartache.

'Maxine, my darling,' he whispered. 'Tell me what's wrong. I won't be upset or judge you. I only want to help you. Don't you know how dear you are to me?'

He put his hand under her jaw and turned her head. She looked directly into his eyes – eyes that had darkened with tenderness.

'You wouldn't l-like me as much if you knew,' she stuttered.

'I'd like you even more for trusting me,' he said gently. 'Is this about someone else?'

'Someone I thought I loved,' she answered miserably. 'I met him at St Thomas' hospital in London. He was a surgeon – one of the top ones – and I was just a lowly nurse. He kept singling me out. Giving me more attention than anyone else. I didn't even like him at first – but he wore me down.' She gave him a wan smile, wondering what on earth he was thinking. 'He wined and dined me. He knew I'd been married and was a widow. It probably made him even more keen. Told me he loved me and I – well, I thought I was in love with him. I was happier than I'd been since Johnny died. I thought we'd get married. The natural thing for two people who loved one another. Then he confessed he was married with two sons. He didn't want our "love affair", as he called it, to upset his family.' She glanced at Crofton and saw his eyes were watching her intently. She plunged on. 'We had a terrible row and I brought it to an end.'

'You poor darling.' Crofton brushed away the tears falling down her cheeks. 'What a swine. So you left St Thomas'?' She nodded. 'Is that when you came back to Liverpool?'

'Yes.' Her lips clamped together. She waited for some kind of relief to settle inside her, but there was nothing. She felt even worse knowing she wouldn't tell him the rest of the story. The crucial part. Oh, why had she started all this when she'd only just told herself she must never tell anyone what had happened?

Her thoughts tumbled around her mind until she thought her head would burst.

He hugged her. 'Damned seats. I can't get close enough to you.'

'Crofton . . .?'

She had to know and the sooner the better. 'Are you married?'

A shadow passed across his face. 'I was. I no longer am.'

'Oh, Crofton, did she die?'

'No. Nothing like that. In some ways it wouldn't have been so bad if she had.' Maxine gasped. 'Yes, that sounds terrible but, you see, I have my secrets too. And they're not very pretty.'

Maxine sat in silence while Crofton told her about his wife.

'I thought I was very much in love with her, though we only knew each other for six weeks when I asked her to marry me. She said yes straightaway. In the hotel on the night of our wedding, she said, "I've got something to tell you." I knew at once it was something serious, but I never expected her next words. "You're not going to like it," she said, "but I'm expecting . . . a baby."'

Crofton paused and Maxine saw a bitter smile hover over his lips. Why could that be so bad? This war made everyone act differently. They'd made love before they were married, which was not anything so terrible these days, though she couldn't stop the stab of envy that Crofton had had a wife he'd been very much in love with. She shook the thought away. His new bride probably ought to have told him before the wedding so it wasn't such a shock for him, but it wasn't her place to comment. She waited quietly.

'My wife of a few hours finished her story by telling me it was another man's child! And I knew it was true because I didn't want to make love to her until we were married. Didn't want to spoil her reputation. What a fool I was.'

Maxine sat stunned, trying to imagine something so terrible. So deceitful. She found herself feeling angry towards this unknown woman. How could she have treated such a lovely man with such total disdain? But wasn't she behaving nearly as bad? Almost as deceitful? She was treating Crofton in a similar fashion by not telling him the rest of her own story. Feeling sick at the thought, she wondered what had happened to the baby.

'After the shock settled in I was prepared to bring up the child as my own, and told her so. But she decided she didn't want to be burdened with a baby, is how she put it, and conveniently had a miscarriage.' He raised his eyes to look at her and Maxine felt he could see right into her thoughts. 'I'm not sure why it happened or even how,' he added wearily. 'I only know our marriage lasted exactly eight weeks. I filed for divorce, which took nearly two years and I've never seen her again. Don't want to.'

'When did all this happen?'

'Just as war broke out. But it's put me off getting close to another woman – until I met you.'

She looked at him, so close to her, his face anxious. Almost without thinking, she put a hand up to his face.

'Oh, Crofton, it's such a sad story. I've never heard anything like it.'

He took her hand and kissed the palm.

'I was almost glad the war had started and I could join the RAF – do something useful. Trying to spot U-boats bent on destroying our convoy really makes you concentrate on the job in hand.'

'It sounds awfully dangerous to me. I couldn't bear it if anything were to happen to you.'

'Couldn't you really, Maxine?' He leaned even closer.

She didn't answer. It was impossible. He had already covered her lips with his mouth. She put her arms around his neck, hungry for his kiss. They drew a little apart and gazed at one another. With a moan she pulled his head towards her again and kissed him back with a passion that surprised her.

Breathless, they separated.

Crofton chuckled softly. 'My goodness. I didn't expect quite that response.'

Immediately the warmth rushed to her cheeks.

'Did you mind?'

'Mind?' He grinned. 'There's not a man on this earth who'd mind such kisses.' He hugged her to him. 'Maxine, I—'

'Don't say anything more,' she whispered.

'Why not?'

'Because you might regret this in the morning.'

Her heart practically came to a standstill as she waited for his reply.

'I'll never regret it, my darling. But next time, we're going to be in better surroundings than squashed together in this damned car.' He turned the key and pressed the starter button, then turned to her and smiled. 'After all those confessions I think it's time we had something to eat, don't you?'

Chapter Thirty-Five

So many times she'd nearly confessed to Crofton that she had a child, little Teddy, and had had to go through the torture of having him adopted, but she just couldn't bring herself to say the words. It would be the end of their relationship, especially when he'd gone through something similar on his own wedding night. She couldn't face having her heart broken all over again. She'd never get over giving Teddy away, but at least her heart had mended from Edwin's betrayal. But this was different. Crofton was different. She loved him and she was certain he loved her in return. She couldn't begin to think of the look of horror in his eyes when she told him about Teddy – so she didn't. But she couldn't relax and be comfortable with him either, as she ought to be, knowing she held a secret inside which would split them apart if ever he found out.

It was Pearl who made her see sense.

'There's a war on,' Pearl said when Maxine next went to visit her to hear all about Pearl's new show where she'd landed the part of the leading lady. 'You fell for the wrong man and paid a terrible price. He turned out to be a complete waster. A no-good, pathetic coward. Crofton isn't like that, from what you've told me. He won't be judgemental. He'll have seen more than enough misery in the military. Tell him, Maxine. You won't have a prayer for a life together if you can't see that this has to be cleared up between you. Just tell him—'

'He's never mentioned he wants a life with me,' Maxine interjected. 'He's never even said he loves me.'

'He's probably waiting for you to say something,' Pearl said. 'Just to reassure him he's in the running, let alone that you're crazy about him. I bet he already senses that you're still holding back on something.'

'Do you really think so?'

'I really think so. So do it now, before it's too late.'

December was galloping along and the children were planning the Christmas decorations.

'We'll let the girls decorate the tree this year,' June announced after supper one evening to an outcry from the boys, but the young matron remained firm.

Several girls shouted 'Hurray' and jumped up and down in their chairs.

'The boys are too rough and dominating,' June explained later to Maxine when they were in the common room. 'The older ones can help Charlie chop logs and they can choose a tree with him – have a say in where we put it.' She glanced round the room. 'Though it does work well here. I remember last year we sang carols and Joachim, the little Jewish boy, sang "Silent Night" in German. It sounded wonderful. I never realised the German language could be so beautiful.'

'I'd love to have heard him,' Maxine said wistfully. 'Last Christmas was awful. I was with my parents and had to keep my pregnancy a secret. The only good thing was that Dad seemed in quite good form.'

'It must have been very difficult,' June said. She hesitated

356

and looked at Maxine. 'Maybe I shouldn't ask, but have you told Crofton about Teddy?'

'Not yet.' Her stomach churned as it always did at the thought.

'You love him and he loves you.'

'He hasn't said.'

'He doesn't have to. It's as plain as the nose on his face.'

Did he love her? Sometimes she dared to think it might be possible and then she'd take herself in hand – it could never be.

'So don't have secrets from him,' June went on. 'It doesn't make for a healthy relationship.'

Not only Pearl, but now June seemed to think she ought to confess. Nausea caught in her throat and she looked miserably at her friend.

'I expect you're right. Pearl said the same.'

'When are you seeing him again?' June asked.

'I don't know. He rang yesterday but hasn't been given any definite time off. I was hoping to see him sometime over the Christmas holiday.'

'I know we're both working over Christmas,' June said, 'and I doubt I'll see Murray, but you'll want to see your mum and dad, won't you?'

'Yes, I told them so long as you have enough cover I'll go as soon as I can after Boxing Day.'

But two hours later, Maxine's plans fell apart. The telegram boy cycled up and delivered a telegram. Rose brought it into the ward while she was changing the beds.

Thankfully all was quiet. The only patients were Timmy and Gordon who both had broken ankles and cuts and bruises from falling out of trees, and they were now sleeping as innocently as angels.

Stealing herself, Maxine opened the envelope. *Don't let it be Crofton. Please, God.* She couldn't bear it. With racing heart she unfolded the paper.

DAD VERY BAD STOP COME RIGHT AWAY STOP MUM

Oh, poor Dad. She'd pack immediately. But try as she might, she couldn't push the thought away that God, or whoever it was, had answered her prayer. Crofton was safe – at least for the time being.

Liverpool looked in a sorry state when she arrived at the bus station. If there'd been a taxi at the station she would have taken it, but the rank was empty. The wind gusted around her and flapped her coat, wanting to whip off her hat as she began the twenty-minute walk to her parents' house. She couldn't think of it being her home any longer. Bingham Hall had taken the place, even though she didn't even have her own room. How things had changed, she thought, as she picked her way along debris and masonry from what must have been a recent hit. She tried not to think about who'd been injured, or killed, but concentrated on getting to her father.

Her mother opened the door, white-faced. 'So the children have finally managed to spare you for a bit of time to spend with your poor old dad,' were her words of greeting. 'Just as well you're not too late.'

Maxine bit her tongue to stop a retort. 'How is he?' she asked instead.

'Not good at all,' her mother said. 'You'd better go upstairs and see him. He's asking for you. The doctor's just left. I'll put the kettle on.'

Maxine left her mother to it and moments later put her head in the doorway of her parents' bedroom, dreading how she would find him.

'Dad,' she said, her voice not quite steady. 'Are you asleep?'

'Come in, love,' her father croaked.

She ran to his bed and knelt so her face was only inches from his own. All her nursing experience told her he was near the end by the grey pallor of his skin, the dull eyes, and the effort of every breath.

'Dad, I'm so sorry.'

'What for, love?'

She gently pressed his hand, feeling the guilt wash over her. Any longer delay and she would have been too late. 'For not being here when you needed me,' she said. 'And me, a nurse. I should have been looking after you. I feel so ashamed.'

'You shouldn't be. Those children need you more than me. I've had my life. And your mother's been good. Don't be too hard on her. She does love you, you know, though she has a strange way of showing it sometimes. And don't you worry about me. It's *you* I'm concerned about.'

'Me? Why?'

'I wanted to see you settled with a good man again before I go,' he said, his voice fading on the last words.

'Dad . . .'

'Yes, love.'

'I *have* met someone. Someone I know you'd approve of.'

'What does he do?' Suddenly her father's voice was brighter.

'He's a Squadron Leader in Coastal Command.'

'Ah.' An approving smile hovered over his lips. 'The Cinderella Service.'

'What do you mean?'

'Coastal Command has never been given the same backing as Fighter Command – or Bomber Command, come to that. They have to fly very low to keep those damned U-boats underwater so they're forced to go more slowly. That gives the convoy a fighting chance to get across the Atlantic safely to bring back our supplies from America and Canada – we'd starve if it weren't for the Merchant Navy in particular, and Coastal Command plays a vital part in making sure they succeed.' He turned his head towards her. 'You can take it from me – your young man is extremely brave.'

It was the most she'd heard about Crofton's job and it made her stomach churn. What must it be like for Crofton and his crew? Trying to sink a U-boat with the Germans trying to shoot back. Feeling overjoyed to get one so it wouldn't give them any more trouble, yet feeling terrible he and the others had brought about premature deaths to dozens, perhaps hundreds, of young men who probably didn't want to fight any more than the British. What a dreadful position to be in. She shuddered.

'It sounds terribly dangerous.'

'Most jobs at the moment are dangerous. It's dangerous to be a nurse in London,' her father added pointedly.

Immediately her thoughts flew to Anna. She swallowed.

'How do you know all this about Coastal Command?'

'Same thing happened in the last war. The navy went across the Atlantic in convoys to bring food back to Britain. Goes without saying it's happening again. But this time you've got the RAF involved.' Her father's voice had become weaker.

'I'm sorry, Dad, I'm tiring you.'

'I think I will have a nap. But first I want to know something from *you*.' He turned his head and caught her eye. 'Does he love you?'

Maxine's heart lost a beat. 'I think so.'

'Do you love him?' He gave her hand a light squeeze, almost as though he was encouraging her to speak the truth.

'Yes.'

'Then that's all that matters.' Her father gave a deep sigh and managed to turn his head and smile.

It was still her father. Even though he lay there breathing harshly, the love in his eyes was just as tender as ever. Her heart went out to him. He'd stuck up for her in his quiet way many a time when her mother had been unreasonable. He'd been proud of her and encouraged her. He'd tried to be a good father and was only stopped by the steel hand of his wife, who constantly complained that he spoilt her. But Maxine loved him as she never had, never would, her mother.

She heard her mother's footsteps and sprang up to open the door, then stepped back, startled. It wasn't her mother at all. Standing there was Mickey, wearing what looked like a smug grin.

'Hello, Sis.' He bounded in and planted a wet kiss on her cheek. She immediately wiped it away with her fingers, swallowing the feeling of revulsion. His grinning expression dropped for a second or two before it appeared again, broader than ever. 'Surprised to see me, eh?'

'You didn't tell us you were out,' Maxine retorted. 'It's been so long, I hardly recognised you.'

'Whereas you haven't changed one bit, Sis,' he smirked. 'Still the same old sarcasm.'

She ignored the flicker of anger threatening to rise, and instead asked, 'When did they let you out?'

'I expect you're just being polite.' Mickey lit a cigarette and drew in deeply. 'I'm sure you're not really interested, but I got out a couple of months ago.' His gaze alighted on the bed in the corner. 'How's the old man, then?'

'The old man hasn't gone yet, if that's what you think,' came a thin yet firm voice.

'Just joking, Dad.' Mickey brushed Maxine aside to reach his father's bed. He pulled up a chair.

'I'll leave you two together,' Maxine said coolly. 'We haven't seen sight of you for I don't know how long, so you'll have a lot of catching up to do. But first, Mickey, will you put that cigarette out? It's bad for Dad.'

She threw him a glare – she couldn't help it. Her brother made her flesh creep. Not surprising that he'd only turned up when Mum had managed to get hold of him to let him know his father was so ill. The way he treated Maxine and their father had always been abysmal. Dad as though he was an old man who'd lost his wits, and herself as though she was a silly, empty-headed girl who ought to be looking for a husband to keep her firmly in hand and have babies, which was all women were good for, he'd said more times than she could count. Their mother was a different matter. He always turned on the charm with her, getting his own way, ever since he'd been a nasty little boy. She shuddered at the memories and closed the door quietly behind her, feeling sorry for her father who had to face such a remnant of a son.

'Isn't it wonderful Mickey's home?' her mother said as soon as she walked downstairs.

It wasn't a word she would use to describe how she felt, but Maxine knew it was pointless to say so. Her mother adored Mickey and always had an excuse for him whatever he did and however long he stayed away, in prison or not.

'I'm glad you're pleased,' was all Maxine said in a tight voice.

Her mother gave her a sharp look but Maxine pretended not to notice. 'I've made Mickey a cup of tea,' her mother went on, 'but he's bound to be hungry. If I'd known he was coming, I'd have made him his favourite meat pie. As it is, I don't know what I'm going to give him.' She stirred three teaspoons of sugar in Mickey's cup, saying defensively, 'I'll forgo my sugar today to give my son a treat.' Without meeting her daughter's eye, she said, 'You have your tea, dear, while I pop out and see if there's anything left at the butcher's.'

Maxine knew this was her cue to offer to go but she was so annoyed with Mickey that she kept her lips pressed tightly together. There'd been no mention of how her mother would obtain the extra meat ration but she was obviously more worried about Mickey's demands than she was her husband's health. Maxine was turning over these thoughts when there was a knock on the front door.

'That'll probably be the postman, Maxine,' her mother called as she was taking Mickey's tea upstairs. 'Can you get it?'

Maxine opened the door and her jaw dropped in astonishment for the second time in ten minutes.

'Hello, Maxine.'

'Crofton! What are you doing here?'

'I wanted to see you.' He gave an apologetic smile. 'I hope I'm not intruding.'

'How did you know where I was?' Her heart was pounding in her ears.

'I had to pry it out of your nice matron.' He hesitated. 'I've only got the rest of the day and tomorrow . . . well, you know I can't say any details, but I won't be around. When I explained the situation to June, I think she decided to take the risk and tell me your address. Would I be allowed in?'

'Oh, of course.' She felt her face warm as she opened the door wider, her emotions running wild. It was wonderful to see him but now there was no escaping him finding out about her brother.

He walked in, dwarfing the narrow hall.

'Come on through,' she said, her brain racing.

Her father was upstairs dying, her wayward brother had made his first appearance in years and her mother was fussing

363

over him as though he were the prodigal son . . . and now Crofton was here. It had been a long week since June's wedding and it was heaven to feast her eyes on him but she almost wished June hadn't told him where she'd gone. There wouldn't be any privacy to talk.

'June mentioned your father is very ill,' Crofton said, removing his cap. 'I'm so sorry.'

'Well, at least he's awake and still speaking. Mickey, my brother, arrived just now and is upstairs with him.'

'I'm glad you've got some support at such a difficult time.'
If only . . .

She couldn't bring herself to agree, and merely showed him into the front room. She noticed the aspidistra on the windowsill was dying. Probably because her mother hardly ever allowed visitors in, she thought grimly. She made herself smile. 'Let me take your coat.'

He unbuttoned it and handed it to her and she draped it over one of the leatherette armchairs, inhaling the scent of him.

'Please do sit down.'

'I realise I've come at the wrong time but—'

'It's all right – though everything's a bit fraught at the moment.' She swallowed.

He caught her hand and held her gaze. 'Can I help with anything?'

'Not really.' She drew in a breath. 'It took me by surprise, that's all, seeing you standing there on the doorstep. But I'm glad—'

'Who are you talking to, dear?' Her mother appeared at the door and took a step back as though in alarm at seeing a strange man. Maxine dropped his hand as Crofton sprang to his feet.

'It's all right, Mum. It's a friend of mine.' Her mother

bustled into the room. 'Mum, this is Crofton Wells, Crofton, my mother, Edna Grey.'

After a short hesitation, Mrs Grey held out her hand. 'I'm sorry,' she murmured. 'Maxine's never mentioned you.' She threw her daughter an accusing look.

'Very pleased to meet you, Mrs Grey.' Crofton smiled and stepped forward to shake her hand.

'How long have you known my daughter?' her mother said, making the question sound like a demand, and withdrawing her hand after the briefest acknowledgement.

Oh, no. Surely she wasn't going to interrogate him.

'Several months, Mum,' Maxine said quickly before Crofton could answer.

Crofton caught her eye and gave the faintest wink. 'If it's all right with you, Mrs Grey, I've come to take Maxine for a spot of lunch. I've only got the chance of a few hours before I'm sent away. But of course I quite understand if she doesn't feel she can leave her father.'

Mrs Grey hesitated. Her eyes narrowed and Maxine knew she was trying to weigh up the situation. Who exactly was this man? Was her daughter keen on him?

'I suppose it will be all right,' she said eventually. 'I would normally ask her father, but he's too ill, so I shall have to take the responsibility.'

For goodness' sake, Mum, we're not living in Jane Austen's day, Maxine thought irritably. She was about to make a snappy retort when Crofton broke in.

'I'll take good care of her,' he said. 'I promise to bring her back by . . .' he studied his watch, 'three o'clock.' He tilted his head towards her.

'It will have to do,' Mrs Grey said, 'though if anything happens to her father, I don't know what I'll do in the meantime.'

'Mickey's here, Mum,' Maxine reminded her. 'And I'll be back before you know it.'

'Oh, yes, of course. But Mickey doesn't have the medical knowledge you have, dear, so don't be too long.' She gave Maxine a sly glance. 'Would you bring a bit of brisket back for our tea as *we* won't have eaten.'

Why did her mother always manage to make her feel guilty?

'We'll do our best,' Crofton put in quickly.

'I'll get the coupons then.' Maxine's mother disappeared to the kitchen.

'Is that all right with you, Maxine?' Crofton enquired. 'I'll honestly understand if you want to stay here.'

'I think Dad'll be safe for a couple of hours. I'll go and fetch my coat and hat.'

She was back in a flash, not wanting to stay a moment longer. The house felt as if it was closing in on her now that Mickey had come home.

'Here you are,' Mrs Grey said, handing Maxine the ration book. 'Get what you can if Mr Jackson hasn't any brisket.' She glanced at her daughter. 'I'll be in the kitchen if anyone needs me.'

Maxine put the ration book in her handbag, but just as they were leaving Mickey thundered down the stairs.

'Maxine. You'd better go up. Dad wants to speak to you . . . *alone.*' Mickey's voice was coated with annoyance. He caught sight of Crofton. 'Oh, who are you, then?'

'Crofton, this is my brother, Mickey.'

Please, Mickey, for once in your life, try to act like a normal brother.

'I'm surprised my dear sis has actually acknowledged she *has* a brother,' Mickey scowled.

Maxine stiffened. 'Mickey . . .' She tried to catch his eye but he was focused on Crofton.

366

'Crofton Wells.' Crofton put his hand out but Mickey ignored it. Crofton shrugged and let his hand fall back.

'Yep, I'm the brother. But it don't count when our dear dad's got *Daddy's girl* here. No time for me, as usual.' He glared at Maxine. 'Go on, Sis. *Daddy* will be impatiently waiting for his favourite.'

Flushing at his remark, Maxine glanced at Crofton.

'Take no notice of my brother.' She paused. 'I won't be long.'

'Take as long as you need. I'll still be here.' Crofton gave her one of his special smiles, immediately lifting her mood, but not before she saw Mickey roll his eyes.

Reluctantly she left Crofton with her embarrassment of a brother.

'Dad?' she said as she entered her parents' bedroom.

'Maxine.' Her father took hold of her hand. 'Who's that downstairs? I heard a man's voice.'

'It's Crofton Wells. The man I told you about. He's asked if he can take me into town for some lunch.'

'You go with him, love.'

'Will you be all right for an hour or two? He's being sent away tomorrow.'

'Course I will. You enjoy yourself. No one knows what's going to happen these days. Anything could change from minute to minute. I only wish I was fit and young enough to do my bit.'

'You did your bit in the last war, Dad.'

He stroked her face with his hand. 'You're a dear girl,' he said. 'I just want you to be happy. I'd like to meet your young man.'

'Maybe when we're back and you've had a rest,' Maxine said.

'I hope so.' He paused and then took in a rasping breath

367

that turned into a cough. Maxine held a glass of water to his mouth and gently tipped it. He swallowed.

'Don't worry, love. I'll still be here when you get back – much to your brother's disappointment.'

'Has he upset you?'

'No more than usual. He asked if my will was up to date. Cheeky devil.' He winked at her. 'I never answered him. Just looked vague. He thinks I've gone doo-lally. It *is* up to date as a matter of fact, but I'm not having him prying into my affairs. He never bothers to come and see us unless he thinks there's something in it for him. I'm not giving him the satisfaction.'

She couldn't answer him. She knew he was right. Bending her head to kiss his paper-thin cheek, she heard him sigh. This time when he spoke his voice was weaker.

'Even your mother doesn't know where I keep it,' he grunted. 'Anyway, you go down and see that young man of yours.'

His eyes flickered and closed. She'd tired him. He needed to rest. She watched him for a minute or two, his chest rising with each irregular painful breath. Then in front of her eyes it became more shallow – quieter. Had he simply fallen asleep? In her panic she couldn't discern his breathing at all. Her heart in her mouth, she desperately reached for his hand but his pulse was still there, quite strong. He opened his eyes.

'I'm all right, love. Just having a nap. Don't you worry. Come and see me when you're back from lunch and bring your young man . . . Christopher, was it?'

'Crofton.' She planted a kiss on his forehead and shut his bedroom door softly behind her.

She went downstairs, but just as she was heading for the front room she heard Mickey speaking in his usual brash tones.

'I behaved myself and they finally let me out.' He laughed.

Oh, no. Why did he have to tell people in that swaggering tone as though he was proud of it?

'That's a relief, I'm sure.' Crofton's voice was quieter and non-committal.

'Yeah, well . . . it weren't that long. And no regrets making a good living out of it – one deal leads to another – know what I mean?'

Maxine could almost see the wink and cringed.

'But now I'm out I want to spend time with the old folk – and my dear sister, of course.' There was a pause. 'So what d'ya think of this war between us and Germany which should never have been?'

'I beg your pardon?'

'Britain doesn't have any axe to grind with Germany. It's a Jew war. Everyone knows that. They're taking over – fingers in too many pies. Some people say they've got to be stopped – no matter what it takes.'

Maxine stood transfixed. Her brother. *My God.* He sounded as though he was a *fascist*. No wonder he'd somehow escaped conscription. He wasn't going to risk his neck for something he didn't believe in. She felt the bile come up in the back of her throat with shame as she clutched the doorknob, her forehead beading with perspiration. She strained her ears for Crofton's reply.

'I doubt my views are in accord with yours so it's probably best not to comment,' she heard him say in an icy tone.

'What branch of the RAF are you?'

'I really can't discuss it.'

'Come on – I'm only asking if it's Fighter Command or Bomber Command. Surely you can tell me that.'

'I'm sorry.'

'Careless talk costs lives, eh?' She heard her brother's

contemptuous chuckle. 'Well, well, it must be secret stuff you're doing if you can't even tell me what sector you joined up with.'

She'd heard enough. Maxine stepped into the doorway and immediately Crofton leapt to his feet.

'Dad said he'd be fine for a couple of hours, so if you're ready, Crofton . . .' She deliberately made her voice crisp, trying to get the message across to him that she wanted to leave right now.

Mickey was sitting with one leg crossed over the thigh of his other. Languidly rising, his eyes never leaving Crofton's face, he leaned on the mantelpiece, a mocking smile hovering over his lips. He was beginning to make Maxine uneasy.

'I'm ready,' Crofton said, looking visibly relieved to be going. He faced Mickey. 'Well, nice to meet you.'

'Likewise.' This time Mickey shook Crofton's outstretched hand, then turned his attention to Maxine. 'Oh, Sis, before you vanish with your *boyfriend*, who by the way can't or won't even disclose what branch of the RAF he's in . . . strange, don't you think?' He looked directly at her and smiled. 'And also strange why you didn't let me know you've made me an uncle. You know how much I love children.'

Maxine stared in the direction of her brother's voice but the room dipped. She couldn't move. Couldn't think. She felt the blood leave her head. She was going to pass out. Instinctively, she wrapped her arms around her stomach, trying to anchor herself, but her legs no longer supported her and she overbalanced, grabbing the back of the nearest armchair and shook her head. The sound of her heartbeat crashed in her ears and her chest felt it would burst with pain. She wanted to be anywhere but in this room. Like a trapped animal, she locked her gaze with

Crofton but immediately turned away when she saw his dazed expression.

Mickey looked from one to the other, then threw her a look of triumph. 'Well, Sis, what do you say?'

Dear God, her parents. They mustn't find out. Not after keeping Teddy a secret all this time.

Without daring to glance at Crofton again, her breath ragged, she said, 'What on earth are you talking about?' It came out a croak, but she forced a laugh, hoping to mask the turmoil inside her. Teddy. Just the thought of his blue eyes staring up at her tore her heart out. How dare Mickey . . .? Her feet felt as though they were glued to the floor. Out of the corner of her eye she could see Crofton watching her closely.

'That kid of yours,' Mickey persisted. 'The one you had *long* after your dear husband died. Good old Johnny. Never knew he had it in him. Fancy him able to make a baby from the grave.'

Dear God. How could she have such a snake for a brother?

'You must be mixing me up with someone else,' Maxine's voice cracked, desperately calling on her professionalism as a nurse not to show her fear. She managed to force a smile. 'I don't have any children. If I did, don't you think you'd know about it?'

'Oh, but I *do* know about it. You had a baby at the Maternity Hospital right here in Liverpool. Named him Edward Taylor . . . poor old Johnny's surname, even though the brat isn't his. I'm surprised you still wear your wedding ring now you've got your new boyfriend.' He cocked a glance at Crofton.

'Mickey . . . please . . . you don't know what you're talking about so—'

Mickey snorted. 'Unfortunately for you, darling sis, I know

371

all about it, though I don't know where you've hidden him. You'll want to know how I found out. Well, it was the tea lady in your ward – Doreen Moon. Remember her? She happens to be the sister of my cellmate, Eric Moon. She used to comfort you, so I understand. The grieving widow. Pat your hand and bring you a cup of tea, she did.' He turned to Crofton. 'Maxine's always turned her nose up at me, being sent to prison, an' all – but *she's* no angel either. You did *know* about little Edward, didn't you, Crofton?' He paused. 'Crofton,' he repeated and frowned. 'Odd name, that.' He swivelled to look at Maxine. 'And then of course there's Mum and Dad. Do *they* know, Sis, that they're grandparents to a sweet little baby boy?'

His time in prison would seem almost mild compared with the shame she would bring to them.

'I'm going before I say anything I shouldn't,' Maxine said, her voice shaking with fear and anger. *How could he? Oh, how could he?*

She grabbed Crofton's arm and led him outside, all the while wondering what she could possibly say to him to make him understand that Teddy was too precious to casually mention. That he held a secret place in her heart that nothing or no one could ever replace. How could Crofton ever forgive her? She'd seen how hurt he'd looked when he'd told her about his ex-wife. She bit her lip so hard she tasted blood. How could she ever tell him she would love to start a family when she couldn't even look after the one she'd already borne? There was no future for them. Her dreams were in ashes.

'Is it true?' Crofton looked at her, but all Maxine could see reflected in his eyes was disbelief and shock.

'Yes,' she whispered.

'This isn't the place to talk, or the time, especially with

your so father ill.' She opened her mouth to interrupt but he stopped her with his hand. 'Not now, Maxine. Your father needs you, so I'm going to leave you in peace.'

He kissed her cheek briefly and she watched him in stupefied misery as he walked out of the door – and no doubt out of her life.

Chapter Thirty-Six

Maxine stepped back through the front door of her parents' home sick at heart. The only saving grace was that her mother hadn't witnessed such a terrible conversation. But now she heard in her mother's voice a lilt she didn't hear very often, and knew it was because Mickey was home.

'Oh, has your young man gone already, dear?' she said as soon as she saw her daughter come in. 'I would like to have got to know him a bit more.'

'Yes, he thought it better not to go out to lunch with Dad so poorly and I agreed,' Maxine said, her eyes downcast.

Her mother looked at her with sharper eyes than usual. 'What's wrong? You look as though you've lost sixpence and found a penny.'

'Shall I tell her, dear sis?' Mickey's expression was bland as his cool grey eyes, reminding her of Edwin's, fixed on his sister.

'Please, Mickey . . .'

'Please tell Mother, or please don't,' Mickey said, his mouth twisting into a grin.

'I'll tell Mum, but in private. She has enough to worry about with Dad.'

'Tell me what?' Mrs Grey demanded, glancing at the two of them.

'All right, I'll let you tell Mum,' Mickey said. 'After all, you were left holding the baby, so to speak, so you'll be able to give her all the gory details.'

Maxine looked steadily at her brother so that in the end he dropped his eyes. What satisfaction could he possibly get from being so cruel? But then what kind of child would grab birds' eggs out of their nests and smash them, tear wings off butterflies and throw stones at kittens for fun?

She drew in a deep breath as she prepared to say she'd talk to their mother in private, but it seemed Mrs Grey must have thought Mickey was simply making a figure of speech as she merely said, 'You can tell me later, dear, but it's your father who needs the attention now. I'll run upstairs and see if he wants another cup of tea.'

One minute later they heard their mother scream.

'Maxine! Mickey! Come upstairs at once!'

Mickey was a step ahead of his sister.

'What's the matter, Mother?' He stormed into the room and was stopped by their mother.

'Oh, Mickey, my darling boy, your father's dead!' She flung herself in her son's arms sobbing. 'He died as I was trying to puff up his pillows to raise him up. He suddenly slipped from my hands. I thought he'd just fallen asleep but . . . he'd stopped breathing.' She pulled away and looked up into Mickey's face as though he would provide the answer. 'Oh, what shall I do without him?' She burst into fresh tears.

'Mum . . .' Maxine tried to put an arm round her mother but she practically shook her off. She couldn't have made it clearer whose support she wanted. Maxine swallowed. Couldn't her mother see through him? It was what he'd been waiting for – counting on. Now he'd inherit some money to pay off his debts that her parents had worked so hard for. Any left over he would surely gamble away.

* * *

Everything happened in a blur. Maxine hung on to the fact that she'd had some time with her father on her own – that he was relieved and happy she'd met someone she cared for – but then her eyes would fill with tears as she thought of Crofton waiting downstairs. If only she'd gone to fetch him up – introduce him to her father before Mickey had time to spread his poison. Crofton would never want her now.

He must have thought she didn't trust him enough to tell him about Teddy. But it wasn't like that. So many times she'd wanted to confide in him, ease the burden of carrying such a secret, but it never seemed the right time. And now he'd heard it from her despicable brother, who was a jailbird. He wouldn't want anything more to do with her or her family. And she couldn't blame him.

Maxine threw herself into all the preparations for the funeral, thankful June had given her some time off, assuring her all was well in the home. Someone had to take charge as her mother had gone to pieces and Mickey had unsurprisingly disappeared.

'Let me know when you find the will,' was his last remark. 'Being the son, I don't hold much hope out for you, Sis.' He tore a piece of paper from a small page in his diary and scrawled his name and an address she'd never heard of. She put it behind the clock on the mantelpiece, praying he would go.

She thought she would scream every time her mother mentioned Mickey and how wonderful it had been to see him again, and thank goodness he was now out of prison and they'd be sure to see more of him, and that he'd promised to attend the funeral, to support her, he'd said. Her mother had run on and on.

'I've never believed my son was involved in anything like

the black market,' she said to Maxine on more than one occasion and Maxine had to button her lip to stop herself from the scorn which threatened to burst from her.

Every night she cried herself to sleep.

She'd heard nothing from Crofton. His last words replayed over and over in her mind. 'I'm going to leave you in peace.' *In peace.* In her bedroom that was hers as a child, she closed her eyes and mouthed the words, wondering if she would ever find peace again.

She had to take herself in hand. She owed it to her father.

The day of the funeral, only ten days before Christmas, could not have been more gloomy. It was dark and pouring with rain, the wind flinging it in all directions. By the time Maxine and her mother arrived at the church they were soaked through. Maxine's feet squelched in shoes that were not sturdy enough for such stormy weather as they made their way to the front of the church. She sat down, shivering inside her raincoat, even though she wore a vest underneath her twinset and a thick skirt. She decided to remove her raincoat, even though the church was icy cold, so she had a chance to dry out, and folded it over, wondering where to put it for the best. Her mother wordlessly took it from her and put it in the space on the pew next to her. Maxine's hair, which she'd tied back that morning, was slick to her scalp, and when she took her hat off the raindrops fell down her face like tears.

Angrily she brushed them away. She didn't want anyone to think she'd already started to cry. There'd be time for tears in private – not now.

Her mother clutched her hand throughout the service, squeezing it so tightly it dug into Maxine's ring. When all the words were said and all the songs were sung and it was finally over they joined the back of the queue to stand at the graveside. This was the part Maxine dreaded more than anything. Her beloved father packed tightly in a wooden box and lowered into the waiting pit. She felt sick and faint at the same time. Her mother glanced at her through her veiled hat, actually looking concerned, even attempting a wan smile. This wasn't the time, but she knew there'd be no cuddles from her even when they were back at home. Her mother's love was always reserved for Mickey.

The vicar's voice droned on and Maxine thought it would never come to an end. Her feet felt leaden and her fingers inside her gloves were numb. She said the Amens automatically, hardly hearing the words. Her mother threw a clod of earth on the grave, mumbling something, and when Maxine thought she couldn't stand it a second longer, the vicar brought it to an end. People began to drift away from the graveside and make their way to the local pub, where Maxine had ordered tea and sandwiches for those dozen or so invited.

'Well, that's that,' her mother said, taking her arm. 'I never thought he'd leave me to cope on my own.'

'It was best this way round,' Maxine said sincerely, as they walked along the church path. 'You'll cope because you're practical, but Dad wouldn't have been able to look after himself, even if he hadn't had a bad heart. You never taught him to cook or buy food or wash his clothes.'

'Of course I didn't.' Her mother's voice was shocked. 'I was his wife. That's what wives are for. To look after their husbands. They must come first, even before the children. I hope you remember that the next time you marry, Maxine.'

'I doubt there'll be a next time,' Maxine answered with growing conviction.

'What about the young man who came to see you when Mickey was here? I forget his name.'

'Crofton . . . Crofton Wells.' The words felt awkward as she said them.

'Oh, yes, that's right. It's unusual.' She stopped so abruptly, Maxine almost overbalanced. 'He seemed quite taken with you.'

'He's a friend, that's all,' Maxine muttered, looking away. She prayed her mother would stop questioning her, but it seemed her mother hadn't finished.

'Did you invite him to the funeral?'

'No,' Maxine said in a sharper tone than she'd meant.

'Why did he disappear so suddenly?' Mrs Grey persisted. 'The last I heard was that he was taking you out for something to eat.'

'Mum,' Maxine's voice was despairing, 'I don't want to talk about it.'

They walked along the road in silence. And then her mother said the words Maxine had been dreading.

'What was Mickey on about when I came to make your dad a cup of tea? Something about being left holding the baby. Don't know what on earth he meant by that. But you said you'd tell me later.' Mrs Grey blinked. 'It escaped me at the time because I was so excited to see Mickey and worried about your father that I meant to ask you that evening. But then . . . I found Dad . . . oh, it's so horrible, I can't bear it.' She burst into tears and fiddled in her handbag for a handkerchief.

'Come on, Mum. Don't get upset. You don't want people to see you all tear-stained. We'll be there in a couple of minutes.'

Maxine prayed her mother would forget what Mickey had said, but she knew it was futile. Her mother wasn't going to let that go.

The small reception at the Rose & Crown thankfully only lasted an hour. Maxine couldn't get away quick enough, though strangely her mother seemed reluctant to leave. But finally they were home, sitting in the two armchairs that would normally have been occupied by her mother and father.

'Thank goodness that's over,' Mrs Grey said, stirring yet another cup of tea. She took a few gulps, then gazed directly at Maxine. 'You're keeping something secret and I'm your mother. I have a right to know what's ailing my daughter.'

Maxine swallowed. 'If you must know, Mum, I fell in love with a married man when I was at St Thomas' hospital.'

Mrs Grey's jaw dropped. 'Oh, my dear—' Grabbing her handbag, she reached inside for her smelling salts. 'What a terrible thing to happen,' she muttered as she unscrewed the top. 'Thank goodness it happened in London and not here in Liverpool. Think of the scandal.' She sniffed over the contents of the tiny bottle and began to cough. 'Silly me,' she said, her words catching in the next bout of coughing. 'I always do that.'

'It's the ammonia, Mum. I'm not sure it's good for you to use it as often as you do.'

'Don't be ridiculous.' She threw a glare at Maxine. 'Now, what were you saying? Oh, yes – the married man.' She emphasised 'married'. 'What was he – a doctor?'

'A distinguished surgeon.'

'Then he should have known better dallying with an innocent young girl.'

'Hardly innocent, Mum. I *was* married.'

Her mother drew in a sharp breath. 'Don't tell me you went to bed with this man, Maxine – distinguished surgeon or not. I couldn't bear it if you did.' Maxine felt the heat rush from her neck to her cheeks. She couldn't answer. Her mother caught her eye. 'Don't say another word,' she warned her daughter sharply. 'I can see in your face that you did.' She shook her head. 'I find it almost impossible to believe. We didn't bring you up like that.' Suddenly she burst into tears and sank her head into her hands.

A spurt of anger rose in Maxine's chest. Why couldn't her mother be human, just for once, and show some motherly love? All she thought about was a scandal which would bring shame to the family. As if Mickey hadn't already brought plenty himself.

'Maybe now you can see why I didn't want to discuss it,' Maxine said bitterly. 'But as far as scandal, no one at the hospital suspected. And I was completely taken in. I thought we were going to be married. When I found out he already had a wife, I came back to Liverpool.'

She would go to her grave before she told her mother anything more – about Teddy. It was simply too painful to discuss, and goodness knew what it would do to her mother in the state she was in at the moment with the idea her daughter had gone to bed with a married man, let alone had an illegitimate baby.

'Well, you're best out of it.' Mrs Grey sat up, then leaned back on her chair and closed her eyes. 'Wipe the slate clean and make sure you learn your lesson from it. This Mr Wells, from the little I saw of him, appears genuine.' Her eyes flew open as though she'd suddenly thought of something important. 'But for heaven's sake don't spill all that out to him. No man likes to think the woman he's chosen for a bride is tainted.'

Tainted. Not for the first time Maxine thought how old-fashioned her mother was. How much she clung to the old rules.

'Luckily I won't have to face that problem,' Maxine muttered under her breath.

'Will you make a fresh pot of tea, Maxine?' her mother said. 'Mr Ramsbotham gave me a copy of your father's will. I'll read it out, but be prepared, dear. I'm sure your father will have left you a little something. I often thought you were his favourite, but our Mickey is the firstborn and his son – so he will be the one to have the lion's share, of course. I still don't understand why he *promised* he'd be at the funeral and didn't turn up.' She looked at Maxine with anxious eyes. 'I hope he's all right – not ill, or anything. He should be here when we read the will. *I* shan't be expecting anything, though your father should have heeded me when he won the pools that time. I wanted him to use it for a down payment on a house of our own. No, he wouldn't listen and we had to rent because your father wasn't ambitious – that's why I wanted the best for you . . .'

Maxine thought she would scream if her mother didn't stop. She rose to make the tea.

'Your father never thought to mention to me, his *wife*, where he put his will,' Mrs Grey carried on as soon as Maxine returned with the tea tray, 'but luckily he left a copy with our solicitor.' She slit open the envelope with a paperknife and unfolded the document. She adjusted her glasses and began to read. The minutes ticked by. Finally, she looked up and gazed at Maxine with an odd expression. 'There must be some mistake.'

'What kind of mistake?'

Her mother looked at the will again with a deepening frown. 'I'd better read it to you.'

Something was patently wrong. A feeling that she was not in the room – that her feet were not solidly on the floor – stole over Maxine.

'*I leave my wife, Edna, five hundred pounds and the rest of my savings amounting to just over two thousand pounds at the time of writing this will to my beloved daughter, Maxine, and any chattels my wife does not want. I particularly want Maxine to have my camera collection as I believe it has some value.*' Mrs Grey paused and seemed to find it difficult to read out the next sentence. She cleared her throat. '*To my son, Michael George, I leave twenty-five pounds only.*'

Maxine drew a sudden intake of breath. *Could* there be some mistake? Her mother looked up from the document and stared at her daughter, shaking her head in bewilderment. Maxine swallowed. Mickey was going to be furious. Her heart missed a beat at the mood he would take when he found out. Well, she wasn't going to be the one to give him such news. Her mother would have to do it. As they held one another's gaze, Maxine saw fear in her mother's eyes.

'We could never agree on how to spend his winnings,' she said finally, stopping to wipe a tear from her eye. 'And to leave our Mickey only twenty-five pounds and *you* two *thousand* . . .' There was almost wonder in her voice. 'Whatever will the lad say when he finds out? If anybody needs it, he does.' An anxious expression crept over her large features. 'But it seems, dear, I was right – you *were* your dad's favourite, after all.'

Chapter Thirty-Seven

Exactly one week later Maxine was back at Bingham Hall. From the moment Charlie helped her with her luggage, taking it to her room, she felt a weight lift from her shoulders. She didn't have to listen to her mother complaining or going over and over why her husband hadn't left their son more. Maxine hadn't even tried to explain that Mickey was trouble. That he would have gambled any monies away without a thought of the hard graft his father had gone through to achieve it. And that maybe Dad had thought along the same lines and had decided he wasn't going to encourage his son.

Two thousand pounds was a vast sum of money though, and it needed careful thought. Maybe she could help Crofton become a photographer. Start his own business. He might be able to use the cameras her father had left her. Then she scolded herself. Any dreams she'd had to spend the rest of her life with him were shattered. She hadn't heard from him since that ghastly day and didn't think she ever would. Her life was here now with the children. She'd put some money away for Teddy's future . . . She daren't think any further.

She looked round the room she shared with Kathleen. Something was different. Where were Kathleen's bits and pieces, usually spread out over the chest of drawers, her book by her bed? There was no sign of the young nurse.

She ran downstairs and tapped on June's office door and immediately June closed a file she was reading and came from behind her desk and hugged her.

'I'm so glad to see you,' she said, her wide smile practically splitting her face in two. 'What did you think about having the room to yourself? I found a separate room for Kathleen on the top floor – my old room when I was first here. Don't know why I didn't think of it before – probably because it was rather grim when I had it, but Charlie's given it a lick of paint and I ran up some new curtains – well, out of some old material – but it's much brighter now.'

'It's lovely to have a room to myself,' Maxine admitted, sitting on the visitor's chair, 'though Kathleen was no bother and I hardly saw her with doing separate shifts.'

June nodded. 'Your face looks a bit thinner,' she said. 'All the upset, I expect. I'm so sorry about your father.'

'I was so lucky to have him,' Maxine said, feeling the sudden prick of tears. 'He was a wonderful father – just wasn't a match for Mum. But I'm glad it's over – he had a lot of pain.' She smiled. 'Don't let's talk about it. I'm just so happy to be back.'

'Has it taken you long to get here?' June asked.

'The buses are still erratic, but it wasn't too bad. I think the drivers are getting used to all the diversions.'

'Let's have tea and you can tell me anything you want to. You know it won't go further.'

After Bertie had left the tea tray, Maxine poured out all that had happened – Mickey turning up unexpectedly, then Crofton, Mickey telling Crofton about the baby . . . June gasped but didn't interrupt.

'Then Mickey asked me in front of Mum if I'd told her about the baby, but it was only a few minutes later that Dad died,' Maxine said shuddering, 'so Mum didn't really take it in at that moment. But after the funeral and she'd calmed down she remembered what Mickey had said. I hoped she'd thought it was just a figure of speech but she kept questioning me. I managed not to say anything, but it was awful. She thinks I've brought enough shame on the family by having an affair with a married man – even though I kept repeating that I never dreamed he was married.'

'Gosh, you poor thing,' June said. 'One shock after the next.'

'Not the only shock.' Maxine bit her lip. 'Dad left me practically all his savings – two thousand pounds, and Mickey just twenty-five pounds.'

'Good gracious.' June's jaw dropped. 'Whatever will you do with so much money? It's more than enough to buy a house.'

Maxine's eyes widened. 'I hadn't even thought of that. I'll put it in savings, first of all. Take my time to think. But keep some back for a few treats for the children with Christmas round the corner.'

'That would be wonderful.' June smiled. 'How kind and generous you are.' Maxine was silent. June touched her hand. 'What about Crofton? You haven't told me his reaction to Mickey's outburst.'

Tears filled Maxine's eyes. 'He asked if it was true and I said it was. He said now wasn't the right time to talk and he would leave me in peace. But I haven't had any peace since he left, thinking I didn't trust him enough or care for him enough to tell him about little Teddy.'

She broke down in sobs, and June immediately jumped up and closed the door. Maxine felt her friend's arm slip round her shoulder.

'What are you going to do about him?' June's voice was gentle.

'What can I do?' She looked up, her face running with tears. 'He couldn't have made it plainer that he wants nothing more to do with me.'

'I don't believe it,' June said firmly. 'I've seen the way he looks at you. You don't just turn the tap off like that. He needs time to take it in – it's a shock for him, too, but I'm sure he'll come round.'

'I don't want him to come round,' Maxine snapped, then caught June's hurt look. 'I'm sorry, Junie. I didn't mean to take it out on you when you're only trying to help. But I'm so het up.'

'Of course you are with what you've been through. But work will help – I know it's true. When I thought Murray had been killed, it stopped me from losing my mind. Besides' – she smiled – 'the children keep asking when Nurse Maxine is coming back.'

Maxine couldn't help smiling back. 'That's the best news I've had in quite a while,' she said.

Maxine went over and over her last disastrous meeting with Crofton. Whatever must he have thought of her? She found herself changing a bed in the ward which she'd only just changed an hour before – even though there'd been no occupier, her eyes brimming over with tears. She couldn't carry on like this or she'd start making serious mistakes and June would be forced to give her the sack.

Come on, Maxine, pull yourself together. You love this job and the children. You'll never get another opportunity like this with such a lovely person as June in charge.

But it didn't stop her from feeling sick with apprehension – would Crofton ever take the trouble to ask her to explain?

* * *

387

Christmas came and went. She didn't know how she got through it and it was only the children who unwittingly saved her from breaking down. She gave Peter as much attention as she could without causing the other children to be jealous, sad that they still weren't including him much in their games outside the classroom.

But when the New Year slipped in and still there was nothing and she thought she must face the fact she'd lost Crofton, June handed her a letter one cold, dark morning.

'Is it from him?' June asked pointedly.

'Maybe.' She was certain by the way her pulse was racing that it must surely be from him.

'I daren't open it,' she said, her eyes glinting with tears. 'It must be bad news. If he'd forgiven me he would telephone.'

'Not necessarily,' June said. 'Do you want me to sit with you while you read it?'

'That's kind of you but I'll go up to my room for a few minutes, if that's all right.'

'Take as much time as you need,' June said. 'You're not on duty for another hour.'

Maxine sat on the edge of her bed and tore open the envelope with her fingers. With shaking hand she pulled out the two sheets. Her heart leapt at the first words:

My dearest Maxine,

I'm so terribly sorry not to have been able to get in touch with you. There was an emergency at sea. It's a long story and I'm not able to speak about it except to say I'm safe and not injured badly – unlike some of the men. As soon as the doc fixed me up I was given compassionate leave as my mother was suddenly rushed to

388

hospital with a stroke. I stayed with her for over two weeks as she couldn't speak at all and hardly moved, but am glad to say she's slowly but surely on the mend.

But this letter isn't about me. It's you I'm concerned about. You must have thought I was so shocked or angry (or both) with your brother's disgraceful outburst that I didn't want to see you again. It's the very opposite.

Darling Maxine, you must have gone through such a terrible time feeling you could tell no one about your baby. But I want you to know you can tell me <u>anything</u> and I would never think less of you – not for a minute. I imagine you have had him adopted and you must hang on to the fact that the parents love and cherish him, just as I know you do.

I love you and always will. If you can find it in your heart to forgive me for rushing off as I did, I promise I will never leave you in such a way ever again. You can rely on that.

Please write back what is in your heart.
Your Crofton

Maxine read the letter again, tears streaming down her face, but this time they were tears of joy. He loved her and still wanted her in spite of everything. She couldn't wait to tell him all that was in her heart. In fact, she couldn't wait to write a letter. She'd ask June if she could telephone him that very evening.

'Maxine! I'm so happy you've phoned. Did you get my letter?'

Maxine swallowed. He only had to say her name and she was all of a flutter.

'I – um – yes, I received the letter a few hours ago.'

'Are you all right?' His tone was urgent.

'Yes, I'm all right. I'm more than all right. I wanted to hear your voice – to make sure *you* were all right.'

'I am now I've heard from you, my darling.' There was a long pause.

'Crofton?'

'I'm here. I just need to know something.' He paused. 'Have you forgiven me?'

'Me forgive *you*?' Maxine felt a pricking behind her eyes. 'It's the other way round.'

'It wasn't like me to leave you like that. But if I hadn't left that minute I would have landed a punch on that brother of yours. I could see immediately what his game was. How could he treat you so cruelly?'

'He's always been horrible to me, ever since we were children. He's brighter than me in many ways but he was lazy and wouldn't study, whereas I always had to work hard at school and he'd taunt me. "Goody Two-Shoes", he used to call me.' She blinked back the threatening tears. Her brother had actually set out to ruin her life. 'Would you really have gone for him?'

'I was angry enough to.' Crofton's voice was serious. 'His announcement brought back some painful memories for me, as you can imagine. Then your father was so ill that I didn't want to load anything more on you. And when I felt we might both be calmer and could discuss things, I had some difficulties at work – one after the other.'

'It doesn't matter now. I understand.'

'Do you really?'

'Crofton, listen to me. I love you. I love you more than anything in the world.'

You and Teddy, her heart whispered. She took a deep breath. 'But I thought I'd lost you when you left so suddenly.'

There was another pause – this time so long she wondered if the line had gone dead.

'Crofton – are you still there?'

'Oh, darling,' his voice was warm with relief, 'if you knew how happy you've made me. This telephone is coming between us. How can I propose to you along a wire?'

Maxine couldn't help smiling. 'It's probably been done before,' she said. 'And the reply has probably been said before as well. If not, I'll start off a new fashion.' She took a deep breath. 'Yes, please, Crofton.'

'I haven't actually asked you yet,' he teased, and she could picture his grin.

'I know, but in case you do, you have my answer.'

'Good.' He gave his deep infectious laugh. 'That means when I *do* ask you – which I prefer to do in person – I know I shan't have to face rejection.'

Chapter Thirty-Eight

On the very day Maxine arranged to see Crofton, June went down with a heavy cold. Swallowing her disappointment, Maxine said, 'The best place for you is in the hospital ward where we can look after you.'

'Honestly, it's nothing,' June said, sneezing four times in quick succession. 'Just the usual winter cold.'

'Maybe, but we don't want it to develop into influenza,' Maxine said firmly. 'And I'm not keen on running back and forth to your cottage in this rotten weather.'

'Oh, I'm sorry, Maxine.' June looked contrite. 'I didn't think of that. But what about your arrangement with Crofton this afternoon?'

'It doesn't matter,' Maxine said untruthfully. 'We can make another time.'

'Don't alter it,' June said frowning. 'It's too important. Tell him to come here in my office. It's more private if you shut the door. You'll be in here today anyway, as my stand-in.'

'And *you'll* be under the watchful eye of Kathleen and the stricter eye of our new nurse, Dolores,' Maxine chuckled, her spirits lifting that she might still see Crofton today after all.

'All right, Nurse Taylor. You win. I'll go and put a few

bits into a bag ready to stay a couple of nights then.' June removed her raincoat from the hook behind her office door.

'You'll be at least three days in the ward,' Maxine called after her. 'So mind you bring enough with you to last.'

At precisely two o'clock Ellen brought Crofton to June's office where Maxine was waiting for him, filling in the time by going over a new file for Nora Johnson, another orphan who would be arriving in a week's time.

'Squadron Leader Wells, Nurse,' Ellen said, giving a bob. 'May I take your coat, Sir?'

'Yes, please.' He handed over the damp greatcoat.

'Thank you, Ellen.' Maxine got up from behind June's desk.

The maid shut the door behind her, but not before Maxine heard her giggle with Rose. Ignoring them, she turned to Crofton who stood there smiling at her and holding out his arms.

She walked straight into them and he held her close.

'I need to tell you,' she said, pulling away a little. 'Before you say anything else, I need to tell you about my baby. I named him Edward, though I always called him Teddy.' She gulped and Crofton gripped her arms and looked into her eyes. 'You were right. I let him be adopted. My mother and father are very old-fashioned. My dad's had a bad heart for a long time. He might have understood, but it would have killed my mother if I'd told her I was having a baby out of wedlock. I didn't know what to do – who to turn to. I had very little money of my own as most of my wages went to Mum. As it was, my cousin Pearl helped me. I stayed with her and that's when I first met you – on my one and only outing, besides check-ups at the hospital. I liked you immediately, but if you'd known I was expecting and wasn't married you would've run a mile.'

'You didn't give me a chance.'

'You were a stranger,' Maxine persisted. 'You can't go around telling strangers who you're attracted to that you're having another man's child – someone who doesn't love you after all. Then later you told me you'd already gone through that with your new wife, so I had even more reason not to say anything.'

'That was completely different,' Crofton said. 'She'd been seeing another man at the same time as preparing to marry me. You thought you'd met someone you loved and would marry when you were at St Thomas'.' He kissed her forehead. 'Besides, you never seemed like a stranger. I felt I'd known you all my life that first evening. I wish you'd said something then.'

'I couldn't. And by the time I got to know you and care for you, and hope you did me, it was too late. You were too precious and I couldn't bear the thought of losing you. Which I thought had happened when you walked out of the door at Mum's.'

A shadow crossed his face. 'I'll never be able to tell you how sorry I am,' he said. 'It was a shock, I can't deny, to hear you'd had a child. But now I know his name – Teddy – he feels more real to me.' He indicated the two visitors' chairs. 'Shall we sit down?'

He turned his chair towards her and moved it closer, then took her hand in his.

'Do you know anything about Teddy's adoptive parents?'

'Very little.' Maxine looked down at their linked hands, and he gave hers a little squeeze of encouragement. 'They live in Scotland and lost their baby girl a year ago. The nurse told me they were so thrilled to be given Teddy and promised they would always love him and look after him as though he were their own. And one day they hoped to adopt a little girl so he had a sister.' She swallowed hard.

'I love you,' Crofton said. 'And when we have children we'll tell them about their older brother, Teddy.' He tipped her face to his. 'Teddy will always be our firstborn – never forget that. One day the law might change to make it possible for a natural mother to meet her child. We'll never give up hope.' He kissed her lips. 'So darling Maxine, will you marry me?'

She kissed him back. 'I thought you'd never ask.'

After . . .

Four months later
May Day 1943

The day before the May Day celebration Barbara persuaded Harold to remove the long pole he'd stuck in the ground, already draped with coloured ribbons she'd supplied for the maypole, so the children could give him the ring of bright artificial flowers they'd wired together in the art room to go on the top. With his usual good nature, he fixed the flowers and finally had the pole firmly back in position again, to the cheers and claps of the children.

The afternoon was not going to be any brighter than yesterday, Maxine thought, as she looked up at the dull grey sky, but it hadn't affected the children's pleasure at all, by the look of them. She stood on the lawn with Kathleen and Dolores watching the children show off to the staff and any children not dancing, their spindly arms and legs joyfully moving more or less in time to the tunes Mr Reynolds from the village was playing on the accordion. Their shrieks of laughter as they became entangled, then realised they needed to dance in the opposite direction to free themselves, seemed like a miracle to Maxine. They were behaving much more like normal children, forgetting their sorrows and enjoying the moment. Four of the boys were huddled together round the pole itself, their arms around their knees, saying to anyone within earshot they were too old for this kids' game, yet not wanting to miss anything. Peter, Maxine noticed with a pang, was nowhere in sight.

June, who was visiting for the day, sat with the little ones on the grass, her arms round the twins, Doris and Daisy, who were recovering from severe colds and had been in tears because Dolores hadn't allowed them to take part. *Dolores is stricter than Kathleen or me*, Maxine thought, but she was sensible, and under her gruff manner she loved them and was keeping a sharp eye on the dancing children in case one of them should fall. It was more than you could say for Judith who had little sympathy for them and was only there, it seemed, out of sufferance.

Out of the corner of her eye, she saw June say something to Daisy and Doris and scramble up. Maxine gulped, her eyes lingering on the gentle swell of June's stomach under her dress as she strolled over. Maxine couldn't be more happy for her – June looked so completely comfortable in her pregnancy and she'd make a wonderful mother. It would come naturally to her.

Maxine fought back the tears. If she'd had any kind of backbone she'd have kept her baby. Teddy was almost a year old now. She would have seen him every day. Been there with his first smile. Soon he would say his first words, take his first steps. She thought of his new parents – she'd rather think of them as new than adoptive, for some unknown reason. They'd lost their baby. That was so much worse. At least Teddy was alive and well and happy and would grow up not knowing any difference. That was what she had to remind herself – as often as needed. And maybe one day, far in the future, when he was old enough to understand . . .

An image of Crofton floated in front of her eyes. His dear face. His twinkling eyes. His total understanding. As far as he was concerned, Teddy belonged to them both. She glanced at the diamond sparkling on her engagement finger as she did a hundred times a day. They hadn't set the date, though Crofton was determined they weren't going to wait for the war to end. There was no telling how long it would go on for, he said. And yet there was something in the air – something in the speeches Churchill was broadcasting to the nation. A turning point in November when Montgomery won the battle against Rommel at El Alamein. Maybe this time next year it would be over. She had to believe it.

'Are you all right, Max?'

There was concern in June's voice and Maxine brought herself up sharply.

'Couldn't be better.'

'Are you sure?'

'I'm sure,' Maxine answered. 'I was just thinking how much I'm going to miss you.' It was true. Bingham Hall didn't seem the same without Junie, and she'd only been gone a month, although it was wonderful that Mr Clarke had offered Maxine her cottage.

'You're going to make a wonderful matron,' June said fervently. 'And I'll come and visit often.'

'You'd better. I want to get to know that baby of yours.' Maxine swallowed hard, thinking of Teddy.

June pressed her hand and Maxine knew her friend understood.

'It's a pity Murray and Crofton couldn't make it,' June said a little wistfully. 'That would have made the day perfect.' She looked at Maxine, then grinned. 'We could have had another celebration of your Florence Nightingale Badge to let the world know you're now a *proper* nurse.' The green eyes twinkled mischievously.

Maxine chuckled. 'I enjoyed that sneaky glass of wine after they'd all gone to bed, but it was a celebration I didn't want to spread around.' She directed her attention to the maypole, her laughter fading. 'I just wish Peter would join in with the other boys. *That* would make my day perfect.'

The two women looked over where Peter was weeding the vegetable plot, happier there than dancing round the maypole. Lizzie was with him, using her little trowel, and he was issuing instructions to her and Freddie who was leaping around them with his usual enthusiasm.

'At least the children seem to accept him a little better now,' June commented.

'I'd love to hear him laugh – see him have some fun,' Maxine said, 'but he never does. Oh, well, at least he's become really interested in gardening. The gardeners say he's a real help to them.'

June watched him for a few moments. 'I see he still likes being in the vegetable garden, but I think it's the flowers he really loves.'

'They're something beautiful in his sad little life, I suppose,' Maxine said soberly. 'But although he's a long way from being healed, he's a different child from when he first arrived.'

'Thank goodness,' June said fervently. 'And it's down to you,' she said smiling. 'You've made a real friend of him.'

'Crofton more than me,' Maxine said truthfully. 'He trusts him implicitly. And Freddie, of course.'

June grinned. 'I told you Freddie works miracles.' She paused. 'By the way . . . did you ever hear anymore from Hilda's mother – Mrs Brown?'

'Not a dicky bird,' Maxine said. 'I think that pound note did the trick.'

The purr of an engine interrupted their laughter. The two women swung round in the direction of the drive, though the car was not yet in view.

'I wonder if it's Murray,' June said, her face lighting up. 'He said he'd try to come for an hour or two if he could before we make our way home.'

'I know it won't be Crofton,' Maxine said with a grimace. 'He's away until next week. And his car sounds much more cranky than this one.'

'Let's go and see who it is then.'

They wandered towards a sleek black motorcar that the driver had parked some distance from the house. Maxine noticed a tall figure sitting beside him. Two men were in the back of the car and they both climbed out. One was older, and although short and stocky, had an air of someone who was used to taking charge. The two men came towards them.

'Good afternoon, gentlemen. I'm Mrs Taylor, the matron,' Maxine said, stepping forward, her hand outstretched. She turned to June. 'And this is Mrs Andrews who used to be the matron until recently.'

'How do you do?' the older man said. 'Detective Inspector Mason and my assistant, Sergeant Carroll.' He flashed his identity card in front of her.

Maxine's heart turned over. Had they come about Mickey? She and her mother had heard nothing from him since he'd been told about his father's will.

'May I ask the nature of your call?' she said.

'Certainly, madam,' answered Detective Inspector Mason. 'We believe you might be of some assistance though it's a rather delicate matter. Is there somewhere we could go in private?'

'We'll go into my office,' Maxine said, glancing at June and nodding for her to attend as well.

'I'll bring him in then, shall I, Sir?'

The detective turned to his assistant. 'Go easy on him, Sergeant. Remember, this is a two-way street. We have to keep our side of the bargain so he keeps his, but there's no need for any heavy nonsense.'

'Of course, Sir.' Sergeant Carroll looked mildly disappointed before he turned and headed back to the car.

Maxine caught June's eye. *What are they talking about? Who is this man?*

June frowned and shook her head. 'I'll go and get extra chairs,' she said to Maxine, and disappeared.

Maxine stayed outside with Detective Inspector Mason, ready to take the men to her office. She watched as a very tall man, hatless, his broad shoulders held back stiffly in position, walked towards the house, the sergeant glancing at him every so often and saying something. The sun had just shown itself and it glinted on the man's blond head which he held high. He turned his neck once to look towards the children who were dancing around the maypole. Everything about him – his height, his bearing, his stride – told her instinctively that this was someone of importance who didn't enjoy being in the company of the two policemen. She couldn't see his face from where she stood, but there was something about him . . .

After a few moments the two men joined the detective, and the three of them followed Maxine into the house. She took them to her office, where June was setting out the chairs, then put her head in the kitchen door and asked Bertie if she would make tea for five.

'Who are they, hen?' the cook asked curiously as she put a casserole dish in the oven. She stretched up and blew out her cheeks. 'I caught sight of them when they came in after you. They looked like coppers to me – well, two of them anyway. Not sure about that third one without a hat.'

'I must go and see to them,' Maxine said, scurrying out before Bertie fired any further questions.

Maxine sat at her desk, June by her side, preparing herself for whatever the three men had to say. She noticed they had placed the hatless man in the centre. He'd had his head bent a little when she'd walked in, but now he lifted it and looked at her directly with deep-set clear blue eyes – it was as though he was appealing to her. She grasped the edge of the chair in disbelief. Although his face was thinner than she recalled on the photograph, he was still an extremely good-looking man.

'This is Herr Best,' said Detective Inspector Mason, his plump face serious as he threw a glance at the two women. 'Peter Best's father,' he added unnecessarily.

'I recognise you from the photograph Peter showed us,' Maxine said, determined to keep her voice steady though her mind was in turmoil. Herr Best raised his eyebrows. 'It's his most precious possession,' she went on hurriedly.

'Is it truly?' Herr Best's accent was strong but the words came easily as he leaned forward.

'Truly,' Maxine said. She wanted to smile at him, assure him they were not here to judge him, but her face remained neutrally serious. 'He'll be overjoyed to see you. We didn't even know if you were alive.'

Herr Best was silent, his eyes unblinking.

'As you can imagine, Peter's going through a very difficult time,' Maxine continued, 'especially as we couldn't tell him any details – we didn't know ourselves – if you were in prison, or if you were a—' She stopped herself in time, but not before she saw Herr Best flinch, 'if you'd been injured

– shot by one of ours, or . . .' She trailed off, embarrassed by the direction she was taking the conversation.

'You can tell the ladies briefly your story, Mr Best, but no details, please.' It was Sergeant Carroll speaking for the first time at the meeting.

'Please, we'd like to hear it,' June said, as Rose knocked on the door and appeared with a tea tray, Ellen following with a second one of scones and biscuits.

The men were silent as June poured tea and Maxine handed round the cups, still reeling from the reality of sitting opposite Peter's father.

'I knew from Hitler's ridiculous ambitions we would soon be at war,' Herr Best began. 'That is when I sent Christine and Peter to the safety of England in the August of 1939. The excuse was for her to be there for her mother's operation. And it was better they knew very little. Only Chrissie knew the true nature of my work. I told her I would come to England as soon as possible to join her and Peter.'

He paused and took a gulp of tea, looking up apologetically at Maxine and June. 'You may not believe, but not every German is happy about the Führer, but they feel helpless.' He gave a grim smile and raked his hand through his closely cropped hair.' Maxine opened her mouth, but before she could speak he gently stopped her with the palm of his hand. 'The British knew I was working against the Party and they arranged for my escape to England. They took me straight to London where they questioned me but I said I will not answer until I see my wife and son. I find out my wife died long ago.' His eyes became moist. 'I knew it in my heart. She was ill with a very bad cough and had not written for some time. And they tell me my son went to his *Oma*. And then they tell me her house was hit by the Luftwaffe and my son is alone. *Gott sei dank* he wasn't in the house at the time. They tell me he has been sent to an orphanage. But he is not an orphan. His Papa is here.'

No one spoke. Herr Best closed his eyes and let out a deep sigh. All the while he'd been speaking, Maxine had barely moved in case she disturbed his train of thought. Her heart soared. It was the most wonderful news possible. Not only was Peter's father alive and actually in Britain, but it appeared he'd been working *against* Hitler. She remembered how Crofton had made a remark that he wouldn't be surprised if Herr Best was not a Nazi after all. She remembered her immediate reaction when she'd first laid eyes on Peter's photograph of him. He hadn't had the hard features she'd expected for a Nazi, even though he was wearing the uniform. How she hoped London would believe him. And that he had some information they would find useful so he wouldn't be imprisoned.

'What a story,' June breathed. 'I wish you could tell us more, but for now, shall I go and fetch Peter?'

'*Nein.* No, no, please not.' Herr Best sprang to his feet but the two men waved him down again. 'I must see him on my own. It is all I ask.'

He fell silent.

'Detective Inspector Mason,' Maxine said, 'I believe we are able to arrange it. Peter is in the vegetable garden. It's one of the things he enjoys most. May we allow Herr Best to see his son alone?' She looked him in the eye. 'It's only a hundred yards away from the house.'

The detective hesitated, and Maxine held her breath. Then he broke into a smile for the first time since he'd arrived. 'I don't see why not,' he said, 'but I request that you ladies take Herr Best to the vegetable garden and keep an eye to make sure everything goes well.'

'We will make sure,' Maxine said firmly, rising to her feet. 'We have a responsibility towards every one of our children.'

'But I am not one of those children,' Herr Best reminded her. His words were strong, but Maxine saw his eyes gleam.

Outside, Maxine and June led Herr Best over to the greenhouses and pointed to the various vegetable plots. Peter was on his knees, his face in profile, red with exertion, trying to pull out a particularly stubborn-looking weed. Lizzie had already given up and gone to hold one of the maypole ribbons, but Freddie had remained by the boy's side.

Maxine stole a sideways glance at Herr Best. His face was aglow. Ignoring the two women, Herr Best started to walk slowly towards the boy. As he got closer, he stopped and whistled a tune. Peter's body froze. Then his head shot up and he turned round. From where she stood, Maxine saw the boy's startled expression, his mouth forming an O. Seconds later his lips curved into a smile of pure joy. Maxine held her breath as Peter scrambled to his feet and began to sing in a piping voice:

'*She'll be coming round the mountain when she comes . . .*'

'Peter! *Kommst du.*' Herr Best held his arms wide.

'Papa!' The boy raced the few yards between them and hurled himself into his father's open arms.

Maxine and June watched as Herr Best folded his son to his chest as though he would never let him go – ever again.

The two women beamed at one another, tears running down their cheeks. They stood for a minute or two, lost in the scene. Maxine knew instinctively June was thinking the same as her. That Herr Best was no Nazi monster but had been working as a resistor, and that his only concern now was for his son.

'Come on, Junie,' Maxine said, finally dragging her gaze away. 'They'll be fine without us gawping.' She turned towards the two policemen who were standing in the doorway, their attention firmly fixed on Herr Best and Peter.

The sergeant caught her looking in his direction. He made an exaggerated play of examining his watch, then nodded to her, and she knew he was demanding that the German and his son should return to the house immediately. She nodded back, and strolled over to Herr Best and Peter, trying to make her steps take up as much time as possible to give them a few more precious moments.

'Herr Best,' Maxine said quietly.

'*Ja* – yes. You have come to part me from my son. They want me back.' He gave her a direct look.

'Yes, I'm afraid they do. But you can bring Peter.'

'No. Peter should not hear these things. He is better to keep in the garden.' Herr Best bent and gathered his son close again, whispering to him.

Peter nodded, his eyes full of tears. Giving his father a last hug, he ran the short distance to the vegetable plot, Freddie rushing ahead and barking.

'It's very sad . . .' Maxine began.

'*Ja*.' Herr Best shrugged. 'But I told my boy I will come to see him when I can, and explained I am helping the people in England. I said one day, when this terrible war is over, I will come to fetch him and we will make a new home together.'

'Did he understand?' Maxine couldn't keep the anxiety from her voice.

Herr Best suddenly smiled. 'He is my son. He understands everything I tell him. He is very happy to see me. And I am even more happy to see him.'

'I'm so glad you've finally found one another.'

They walked to where June was waiting, a big smile on her face. The two policemen hadn't moved from the doorway. Leaving Herr Best with them, Maxine took June's arm.

'I'll begin and you come in on the next round.' She smiled

at June as she took in a deep breath. '*She'll be coming round the mountain when she comes . . .*'

'. . . *when she comes . . .*' June sang out, '*she'll be coming round the mountain when she comes . . .*'

'. . . *when she comes . . .*' Maxine put in, laughing. 'All together!' She linked arms with June and they opened their mouths wide. '*She'll be coming round the mountain, coming round the mountain, coming round the mountain when she comes.*'

The two women entered the Great Hall, arms still linked and singing lustily, '*She'll be driving six white horses when she comes . . .*' And by the time they stepped into Maxine's office with Freddie now at their heels, barking with excitement, their final rendition of '*driving six white horses*' was practically swallowed up in their gales of laughter, much to the bewilderment of Detective Inspector Mason and Sergeant Carroll following behind with Herr Best. The two policemen simply looked at one another and shook their heads.

Read on for an exclusive extract from
the next Molly Green novel . . .

An Orphan's Wish

Coming November 2018

Before . . .

Lana read Dickie's letter for the umpteenth time. It was dated 23rd August 1941.

My darling dearest girl,

I hated leaving you for yet another tour but I'll be home before you know it. I can't wait to see your lovely face again, bury myself in that wonderful hair of yours, but all I have at the moment is your photograph. I'm gazing at it now as I write this.

I miss you so much, Lana. When I get my next shore leave we'll go on long walks, hand in hand.

Keep safe for me, darling. I long to hold you in my arms again. I love knowing my grandmother's ring is nestling between your breasts, but it's hidden, and I want to put it on your finger to let the whole world know we're engaged to be married – the sooner the better. I know you prefer to wait so we can tell your parents together, but it's so frustrating with this damned war.

Give my love to them, and if you get time, I know mine would love you to call in at number 10. You're always welcome – you know that. If you let them know

411

ahead of time, Mum will make your favourite liver &
bacon dish.

Will close now and try to get a couple of hours' kip
before the next shift. Will write again soon.

I love you so much.

Dickie xxx

Lana blinked back the tears. Her dearest love. He'd worked in their special code – created by them because of the severe censoring of all letters between members of the armed forces and their parents, wives and girlfriends. She loathed liver, but it meant he'd be docking at Liverpool, and his parents' address at number 10 meant he'd be home in the tenth month – October. She couldn't help smiling as his parents' number had changed more than once to suit his homecoming date. Her hand automatically touched the ring – Dickie's ring that she'd put on a thin gold chain and worn around her neck ever since his proposal on her birthday, 6th August.

Though his letter was dated 23rd August, she had only received it today. It was 4th October; the month he said he'd be home. As usual, the letter had taken several weeks to arrive. But the year was now 1942. And the diamond and ruby ring was still around her neck.

Chapter One

February 1943

'Is there something wrong, dear?' her mother said, her voice anxious.

'They won't accept me for driving,' Lana said dully, as she slid the sheet of paper back into the envelope.

Her mother's eyes widened. 'Why not? An intelligent young woman – healthy—'

'Seems I'm not.'

'What—?'

'They say I've got flat feet. I'd never be able to march. They might be able to find me a job in an office as a *civilian* – well, they can forget that.' She rounded on her mother, the gold in her hazel eyes flashing. 'The woman who interviewed me more or less said they'd welcome me with open arms as an experienced driver. Some welcome.'

'Well, at least you haven't got anything serious,' her mother said calmly. 'You had me worried for a moment.'

'You don't understand, Mum. Joining up was going to change my life. Pay back those bloody Germans for killing Dickie.'

'Don't swear, dear,' her mother said mildly. 'I know how you must feel but if I may say so . . . and don't get cross

413

with me, but that isn't quite the right spirit. You want revenge for Dickie's death but that's going to keep you bitter. Not all Germans are Nazis. I'm sure many of them don't want to fight any more than our boys. I *do* understand your feelings but—'

'I'm sorry, Mum, but you don't understand at all,' Lana said, her voice rising as she sprang to her feet. 'I'll never forgive them – never!'

Knowing she was behaving badly but not being able to stop herself, she rushed from the room.

'You shouldn't take it personally, Lana,' her father said when she'd calmed down a little and stepped into her parents' grocery shop a quarter of an hour later. 'They haven't rejected *you* – it's just one of those things.'

It was pointless to argue with her father. She knew he was right anyway. But it didn't make it any less hurtful.

'Your mother and I have been talking. The last thing we want is to keep you at home now Mum's getting better. Working in the shop is not for you – it would be a waste of all your training. Now Marjorie has left to join up, I've put an advertisement in the paper for a part-time assistant.' He glanced at her, and she saw the love and concern reflected in his eyes. 'You have to decide now what you want to do. Personally, I think you should go back to teaching. Your mum says the same.'

'You sound like Dickie,' Lana said, more than a little annoyed.

'I'm not surprised. Dickie was right. We all know how the children loved you. I think they thought you were a little eccentric – different from any of their other teachers – and that was why they adored you.' His eyes twinkled with humour and she couldn't help giving him a small smile. 'I think that's where you're needed. Not fighting Jerry.'

She couldn't think of a reply so she busied herself with undoing a box of tinned sardines that had just been delivered.

'Any eggs this week?' she asked, more for something to say, as there wasn't much hope of any.

'We're expecting our allowance tomorrow,' her father said.

'Well, at least that will stop Mrs Mason from her perpetual moaning.'

Her parents' words tumbled over in her mind the rest of the morning. Maybe they were right. Maybe her strength lay in teaching. And if she was honest, she'd missed it terribly these last few months when she'd come home to look after her mother, when a severe case of influenza had turned into pneumonia. Lana closed her eyes for a moment. It had been touch and go. At one stage she'd thought she was going to lose her mother as well as her fiancé. Now her mother was finally regaining her strength, Lana had some thinking to do. She was uncertain as to whether the headmaster would give her back her old job, even though they knew her slightly unconventional ways worked, and couldn't deny how much the children responded to her.

She remembered standing in the headmaster's office when she'd asked him if he could hold her position by having a temporary teacher for the time it took her mother to recover. He couldn't guarantee it, he'd said. It depended upon who came in her place. What their situation might be. At that moment in his office, under his stern gaze, she'd made up her mind never to go back to that school, whatever the circumstances.

'Even if he offered it to me it would be going backwards,' she said aloud as she checked the list of items they were waiting for delivery. She'd always taken pride in starting something new if things didn't turn out as expected or if she was unhappy. Begging for her old job would be akin to admitting failure.

When Marjorie Drake had suddenly announced to Lana's father that she was joining the WAAFs and would be leaving in a week's time, Lana had felt a spurt of envy. She'd decided then and there to join the ATS. To fight Jerry. For Dickie's sake. But she had come up against a brick wall.

'The library was shut early today,' Lana grumbled to her father after supper a few days later, when her mother had retired early. 'Staff shortage, I suppose. It's so annoying. I've finished my book and I've got nothing else to read.'

'Try these.' Her father put down his newspaper and tossed a couple of magazines over to her. 'Mrs Randall-Smith dropped them in this afternoon when she came to see your mother. You might find something of interest.'

They were sitting in opposite easy chairs in the parlour, which they used more these days since her mother had been ill. Lana had lit a fire but the room was still chilly even though the ugly blackout curtains were disguised by a second thick pair of richly flowered ones. Lana shivered. All the curtains did was give the impression the room was cosier than it felt.

Lana flipped through one of *The Lady* magazines her mother's friend had left, then looked up. 'No response yet for an assistant?'

'Not yet. Everyone seems to have joined up.' He looked suddenly contrite. 'I'm sorry, love. That was a bit tactless of me.'

Lana gave a rueful smile. 'Don't worry, Dad. I'm all growed up now.'

Her father's face broke into a grin. 'You certainly are,

Topsy. I'm hoping it won't be long before we have some replies – then you'll be free to continue your own life.'

It was her father's old nickname for her when she was still a child. Impulsively, she sprang to her feet and kissed her father's cheek. 'You're the best father in the world,' she said, 'but you're encouraging me to be the most selfish daughter.'

'Not at all,' he said, giving her an affectionate kiss back. 'You haven't had an easy time with this war and—'

'No different from thousands of others,' Lana interrupted, her expression grim. 'I so badly want to get back at the Germans for what they took away from me, Dad, but Mum thinks I'll end up a bitter and twisted old maid.'

'Did she actually say that?' Her father looked at her in surprise. 'Doesn't sound like your mother.'

'Not in those words exactly, but that's what she meant.' Lana grimaced. She went back to her chair and picked up the magazine again, but she couldn't concentrate. She sat thinking while her father quietly read his paper, until he folded it and yawned.

'I think I'll turn in,' he announced.

He'd been a handsome man, she thought, as she watched him struggle to his feet, but the strain of another war – the first one where he'd lost a brother, and now two sons away at sea – had begun to tell on his features. His mouth had lost some of its fullness and his cheeks were a little sunken, but his eyes still held their teasing sparkle. A lump came to her throat.

'G'night, love.' He dropped a kiss on top of her head.

'Night, Dad. Sleep tight.'

'And don't let the bed bugs bite,' he finished, smiling.

It was how they'd always finished saying goodnight when she was a little girl.

She grinned back.

In bed, she opened the magazine and read a couple of articles, wrinkling her nose at the 'Let's Make Do & Mend' article. If this war went on much longer she'd need to improve what little sewing skills she had. Idly, she turned to the Situations Vacant pages and her eye roved down the columns. Her attention was caught by one, enclosed in a box.

Urgently seeking temporary headmistress for village school in Bingham, nr Liverpool. Must be an experienced teacher and willing to supervise small team while headmaster is abroad fighting. Pls reply to Mr G. Shepherd, Box 3032 at The Lady.

Lana's heart turned over. Dickie's home port had been Liverpool. She'd been there once to see him off and had been horrified at the devastation in the city. It had looked every bit as bad as London, having only just suffered its own blitz. Beautiful buildings turned into heaps of rubble and debris, people picking their way through it, children playing games amongst it, and the animals that had once been people's pets looking dazed by the way their world had changed in an instant, ribs sticking through their unkempt coats, foraging for scraps. Lana shuddered, remembering how every bombed building, every church destroyed, every ship struck had all brought it home to her – the danger Dickie faced every day. She'd caught the train home on the same day, not only sad at parting from Dickie but frightened on his behalf, and thoroughly depressed with the ruined areas of the city that he and his friends seemed almost to accept as part of war.

Safe in what had been her old bed at home, she pulled

the blanket up further so she could tuck the ends around her shoulders. The room was so cold it was difficult to think straight, but she knew that was true for most of the nation. She wondered how far Bingham was from Liverpool, and for the children's sake she hoped this place was miles out in the sticks. She shook herself. Why did it matter how far the village was from the city? She wouldn't dream of applying. A headmistress was different altogether from a teacher. It would be far too big a leap and she wasn't going to put herself through more humiliation by being rejected – this time for not being experienced enough. A pity, really. If they'd been advertising for a teacher she might well have been tempted to apply.

Acknowledgements

Heartfelt thanks to my dear agent, Heather Holden-Brown of HHB Agency, with her wisdom and kindness, together with her delightful assistant, Cara Armstrong. You make a great team!

Thank you to Rachel Faulkner-Willcocks, senior commissioning editor at Avon HarperCollins. Not only are you gorgeous but you are so talented and always understanding. Then there's Katie, Sabah, Phoebe, Molly, Elke, Zoë, and a whole team at Avon who are so enthusiastic about my Dr Barnardo's series and determined to get the books in front of as many readers as possible. I'm so grateful to you all.

Thank you to Megan Parker at Dr Barnardo's headquarters in London for gathering much of the information I needed to create an authentic setting for the orphanage. You provided fascinating details such as the wide variety of country houses, some of which were commandeered, all transformed into Dr Barnardo's homes during the Second World War; the various duties of the staff, and some touching photographs of the children themselves during that terrible period. I've kept several of those faces in mind when they appear in the story.

This leads me to the founder of Dr Barnardo's – Thomas John Barnardo (1845–1905), an Irish philanthropist. At first, he took in all boys because he was a bachelor, but upon his marriage to Sara Louise who worked side by side with him, they were allowed to take in girls as well. A staggering 60,000 children have passed through Dr Barnardo's homes.

I must now mention my fantastic writing friends. I belong to a small (and select!) group, all published – we call ourselves the Diamonds. The four of us, Terri Fleming, Sue Mackender, and Joanne Walsh (and me!), with April Hardy as an honorary member who occasionally turns up from Dubai, meet every month in one or other of our homes for a whole day. We critique each other's work amid valuable brainstorming, encouragement and laughter. We come away totally inspired to get on with that elusive next chapter.

There is another small group of writerly friends who have generously opened their homes (and holiday cottages) to me regularly for writing retreats. Although we're only able to meet occasionally, when we do it's like yesterday. Again, we are four: Carol McGrath, Suzanne Goldring, Gail Aldwin and me! Looking forward to meeting in Port Isaac and Greece this year, girls, for our next writing get-togethers!

And then there's Alison Morton – superb thriller writer, and the best critique writing partner one could ever hope to find. She reads all my manuscripts in both early stages and later, using her brutal red pen which makes my heart plummet when I get the pile of pages back. She's annoyingly right 94.23% of the time. Happily, I get my own revenge when *her* manuscript comes through for me to read! Somehow we've remained great friends!

I mustn't forget the Romantic Novelists' Association – a unique organisation for making writerly friends who support one another through good and bad, and are never more than a tweet away.

Writing books can be isolating, and not everyone is lucky

enough to have a beautiful white cat with amber eyes who keeps me company in my writing cabin, padding his way over my keyboard and coming up with amazing plot ideas. Yes, Dougie, I'm talking about you!

I need to thank the following people for helping me with the research for this book:

A larger-than-life porter kindly took me down into the cavernous basement of St Thomas' Hospital. We seemed to walk forever along dimly-lit corridors and miles of old exposed pipework. I tried to imagine the staff during the war running the entire hospital down here with the bombs falling. I'd asked him to show me the famous 'White Rabbits'. I won't say more – just go and see them for yourself!

I was once acquainted with a lovely man who was a sub-officer in the fire department, and went through the London Blitz. When I found out his first name was Crofton I pounced on it. I'd never heard the name before but immediately knew it would be the name of my next hero. I wish he was still around so I could tell him, as I think he would be amused.

My sister, Carole, introduced me to a lady in her knitting group called Nina Foord. She and her brother spent many of their childhood years in a Dr Barnardo's home although they weren't orphans as their father was in the military. Nina gave me some lovely descriptions of the naughty things she and some of the other children got up to, and I've enjoyed incorporating several of these into this series.

One of the joys of writing historical novels is the research. I went to Liverpool with a list of buildings and places I needed to see. My first and most important was Western Approaches, the building where the whole of the Battle of the Atlantic was plotted and organised. I couldn't believe it when I read a scrappy notice on the door saying it was closed for refurbishment. Almost in tears I walked back to the docks where three tourist buses were lined up, huge maps painted on the sides. I asked the drivers where they went. One of them, a bear of a man, pointed to his bus. 'We stop here to see Gerry and the Pacemakers, then we go on to the Beatles' place where they first sang, then we go to this fabulous shopping centre—' 'Stop!' I cried. 'I want Second World War stuff.' 'Oh, you want to go to Western Approaches.' When I told them it was closed and how upset I was, the bear of a man said, 'Come here, pet.' He gave me a huge hug. The other two started laughing when I said I felt better already. 'Go over to the Maritime Museum,' the bear advised. 'They're sure to have all the information you need.' He was right!

My husband, Edward Stanton, self-made historian, particularly of the two world wars, checks the manuscript before the final proofread. He is great at spotting those wily anachronisms and advises on military matters, being an ex-RAF chap, but always warns that any errors in the final version are mine!